PRAISE FOR SHOLES AND MOORE'S AWARD-WINNING COTTEN STONE MYSTERY SERIES

The Grail Conspiracy

ForeWord Magazine's 2005 Book of the Year for Best Mystery

"Gripping!"—*Mystery Scene*

"Spellbinding!"—Book Sense

"A thriller ... the *Da Vinci Code* meets *Jurassic Park*."—*ForeWord*

"This page-turner is bound to show up ... at public libraries across the country."—*Library Journal*

"Religion and science battle through a spectacular hold-your-breath conclusion when the Holy Grail supplies the blood of Christ to the forces of evil."—M. Diane Vogt, author of *Six Bills* and other Willa Carson novels

"From a dig in the deserts of Iraq to the inner sanctum of the Knights Templar, this multi-layered tale is a gripping blend of modern science, ancient ritual, and page-turning suspense."—Christine Kling, author of *Surface Tension* and *Cross Current*

The Last Secret

"Fascinating and breathless. Sholes and Moore are true storytellers with unerring eyes and the souls of artists. You'll love this one!"—Gayle Lynds, *New York Times* bestselling author of *The Last Spymaster*

"A great book makes you think when you're done. I'll be thinking about *The Last Secret* for years to come."—Nelson Erlick, author of *The Xeno Solution* and *GermLine*

"Demonic possession, strange suicides, and Biblical prophecy collide in Sholes and Moore's *The Last Secret*, an intelligent religious thriller with bite."—James Rollins, *New York Times* bestselling author of *Black Order*

The Hades Project

"An exceptional novel, a dark labyrinth of suspense, international intrigue, and apocalyptic horror."—Douglas Preston, *New York Times* bestselling author of *The Codex*

"Fans of religious-themed thrillers like *The Da Vinci Code* will enjoy."—*Library Journal*

"A riveting blend of early Christian lore and high tech. Don't plan on putting this one down."—Gregg Loomis, author of *Gates of Hades*

The 731 Legacy

"Far superior to *Angels and Demons*, [*The 731 Legacy*] has a bit of everything found in popular thrillers: destruction of civilization, ancient religious lore, modern science, and non-stop action."—*Mystery Scene Magazine*

"An outrageous and terrifying read. I can't get enough of Cotten Stone!"—Lincoln Child, *New York Times* bestselling author of *Relic*

"Moore and Sholes are the new Preston and Child. From the very first chapter, *The 731 Legacy* wraps a rope around your neck, pulls it tight, and never lets go. This is what masterful storytelling is all about!"—Brad Thor, #1 *New York Times* bestselling author of *The Last Patriot*

THE PHOENIX APOSTLES

ALSO BY LYNN SHOLES AND JOE MOORE

The Grail Conspiracy

The Last Secret

The Hades Project

The 731 Legacy

THE

PHOENIX

A SENECA HUNT MYSTERY

APOSTLES

INTERNATIONAL BESTSELLING AUTHORS

LYNN SHOLES & JOE MOORE

First Edition
First Printing, 2011

Book design by Donna Burch
Cover design by Kevin R. Brown
Cover illustration © Gary Hanna

Midnight Ink, an imprint of Llewellyn Worldwide Ltd.

Library of Congress Cataloging-in-Publication Data

Sholes, Lynn, 1945–
The Phoenix apostles : a Seneca Hunt mystery / by Lynn Sholes & Joe Moore. — 1st ed.
p. cm.
ISBN 978-0-7387-2666-3
1. Women journalists—Fiction. 2. Aztecs—Antiquities—Fiction. 3. Archaeological thefts—Fiction. 4. Mass murderers—History—Fiction. 5. Cults—Fiction. 6. Mexico City (Mexico)—Fiction. I. Moore, Joe, 1948– II. Title.
PS3619.H646P56 2011
813'.6—dc22 2011002581

Midnight Ink
Llewellyn Worldwide Ltd.
2143 Wooddale Drive
Woodbury, MN 55125-2989
www.midnightinkbooks.com

Printed in the United States of America

DEDICATED TO

Jayne Ellen

ACKNOWLEDGMENTS

The authors wish to thank the following for their assistance in adding a sense of realism to this work of fiction.

Dr. Ken Muneoka, PhD
Department of Cell & Molecular Biology
Tulane University

Dr. John Gore, PhD
Director of Imaging Science
Vanderbilt Kennedy Center
Vanderbilt University

Special thanks to Chris Fineout

“Wherever the corpse is,
there the vultures will gather.”
—MATTHEW 24:28

“The evil that men do lives after them;
The good is oft interred with their bones.”
—WILLIAM SHAKESPEARE, *JULIUS CAESAR*

AUTHORS' NOTE
THE DOOMSDAY PROPHECY

ALMOST EVERY CULTURE AND religion throughout history has had a *doomsday* prophecy. Probably the most well-known predictor of such an apocalypse is the ancient Mayan calendar. Archaeology has revealed that most Mayan locations had astronomical observatories that enabled them to predict events based on equinoxes and Venus cycles. They possessed such advanced knowledge of time and space that their calendar was more precise than any in use today.

The Mayan calendar is three calendars in one: a solar calendar based on 365 days which is ten-thousandths of a day more accurate than the currently accepted Gregorian calendar; a ceremonial calendar based on 260 days, the same as human gestation; and the combination of the two where the number of days and months only repeat every fifty-two years. The ancient Maya and other Mesoamericans used this same fifty-two-year pattern, or a cycle called the Calendar Round.

The Maya also had what they called the Long Count that began measuring time elapsed since their beginning—August 13, 3114 BC—and ending 5,121 years later. December 21, 2012. The Aztec calendar had a date very close to the Mayan. The same date can also be calculated using the ancient classic Chinese text, *I Ching*. And there have been other similar prophecies and predictions of doomsday from the Hopi, Nostradamus, Mother Shipton, and Cumaean Sibyl, along with many interpretations of various legends, scriptures, and numerological constructions.

So what might occur on the predicted doomsday? A rare cosmic alignment that happens every 26,000 years when, on the winter solstice, the sun lines up with the center of the Milky Way. At the same time, the Earth completes a wobble on its axis and a pole-shift takes place—the North and South Poles reverse. The resulting cataclysmic effect on life as we know it could be beyond imagination.

The next time this galactic phenomenon will come together is exactly on the date predicted by the ancients.

December 21, 2012.

RESURRECTION
1876, NORTHERN SONORA, MEXICO

Billy Groves didn't know if he was dead or alive. His lungs were starving. He attempted to draw in a breath like it was the first in a long time, but the dirt choked him.

He clawed at his face and suddenly realized what was wrong.

He was buried.

Panicked, he scuffed away clods of soil and debris, fighting to breathe, to take a single life-saving breath.

Which way was up? Was he digging in the wrong direction?

Scratching and plowing, he pushed with his legs, trying to squirm free of the blackness. The panic grew and his body convulsed. He would have cried out but there was no air to power his lungs.

Finally, his fist broke through. He pushed at the heavy layer of gravel and earth until he saw light. The heat from the sun struck his skin as he opened his mouth and gulped in the air.

Spitting grit, he crawled out of his would-be grave and collapsed beside it. Groves brushed the dirt from his eyes and looked around. He saw what was left of the valley floor and suddenly started to remember everything—the cave, the gold, the Apaches, the earthquake.

And the arrow.

Groves forced his gaze to his torso. The arrow was there, it had run him through nearly to the fletching, entering his chest at an angle and exiting from his side. He twisted and looked at it in fearful anticipation of what he would find at the end of the shaft. But there was no arrowhead. It had broken off.

Gripping the arrow protruding from his chest, he grimaced and yanked. The shaft tore free of his flesh.

The arrow should have killed him. He inspected the hole in his chest. It was there but it wasn't bleeding—

What the hell is going on?

The wound seemed to be already healing as he watched.

Some kinda miracle?

He'd been shot with an arrow and buried by an earthquake.

And he just rose from the dead.

THE RELIQUARY
2012, MEXICO CITY

"What doesn't make sense?" Seneca Hunt stood under the protective tent covering the archaeological dig site and watched the images appear on the video monitor.

Daniel Bernal, the dig master, who was also Seneca's fiancé, wrapped his arm around her waist as he called to the video tech, "*Mueva la cámara a la izquierda.*"

"*Sí.*" The tech adjusted the joystick, panning the probe to the left. Mounted on a flexible neck, the tiny camera was fed down a hole drilled through the stone floor. The LED collar on the camera bathed the sealed tomb below their feet with light.

Seneca leaned into Daniel. "What do you see?"

He pointed to the monitor. "There's the altar where the remains should be. But there's no funerary jar."

A few other members of the Mexican dig team crowded around for a better look.

"Grave robbers?" Seneca raked her russet hair away from her face, missing one highlighted coppery strand that fell across her cheek. She pulled away and stepped back, immediately missing the feel of him next to her. "Let me get a couple of shots." Raising the Nikon D3 hanging around her neck, she snapped off several pictures, trying to capture the look of concentration on Daniel's face.

Seneca was a staff writer working on assignment for *Planet Discovery Magazine* and making double use of her time in Mexico. Tomorrow morning she and Daniel would fly to Playa del Carmen to marry and spend their honeymoon on the white sands at The Tides Riviera Maya. Soon, she would be Mrs. Daniel Bernal, wife of the noted archaeologist and professor of Mesoamerican Studies at the University of Miami.

"No," Daniel said. "Pot hunters wouldn't take the ashes and leave behind all those valuable grave goods. It would have been the other way around. Just look at all the artifacts and jewelry, the gold, the jade ..."

His slightly accented words, which Seneca found quite sexy, died off to a whisper as his finger tapped the monitor.

She moved behind him to frame the video screen over his shoulder and purred next to his ear. "I adore the way you roll your Rs."

"You're shameless." He spoke low enough that only she could hear.

Seneca steadied the camera on his shoulder. She had written articles on other archaeological digs, and like always, she felt the flutter of excitement in anticipation of what was about to take place—a glimpse into an ancient world and all its grandeur.

"The tomb appears dry and undisturbed. If the Aztecs built this city in the middle of a lake, why isn't it flooded?" She paused from taking pictures.

"The burial chamber was never under water. At one time it was level with the base of the temple, but like everything else, the Spanish built over it." Daniel motioned to the monitor. "Now that's interesting. See that small chest resting on what appears to be a wooden table to the right of the altar? The silver one about the size of a cigar box?"

Seneca strained to see, then nodded.

"Definitely not Aztec. I would guess European—very ornate surface design. Maybe a reliquary."

"A container used to hold religious relics, correct?"

He nodded.

"How would a European reliquary get inside the tomb?" She started snapping pictures again.

"Most likely a gift from the Spanish, and something the emperor wanted to take with him into the afterlife." He turned to the video technician and instructed him to zoom in on the object.

The man manipulated the remote controls.

As the object grew larger on the screen, Daniel said, "There's an inscription. It's in Latin."

"Can you read it?"

He concentrated on the image. "I can make out the word *sudarium* which means sweat-cloth. And the word *facies* which is face. The lighting is just too weak to read the rest."

"Do you think Cortés might have given it to the emperor?"

With a shrug, Daniel said, "Maybe. Obviously, it was something Montezuma treasured enough to want it in his tomb. Compared to the condition of the other objects, it's aged especially well. I'd have expected much more tarnishing. It looks as if it were placed there in more recent times."

"Is that possible?"

"Doubtful. The tomb was probably sealed right after the burial. Judging from the video so far, it hasn't been touched in five hundred years."

Daniel leaned back and stretched, dropping into what she called his classroom voice. "These people lived surrounded in opulence beyond what most of the world had ever seen before. And then, within a blink of time, the Spaniards destroyed it all. Except for a chance discovery like this—one that appears to be in such pristine condition—all we ever see is the rubble of crumbling ruins. It's a shame how so much has been obliterated throughout history because of what I think of as the double-G factor—gold and God."

Seneca continued snapping pictures as she listened to Daniel express his fascination with what he and his team had discovered. He was so passionate about his work. When he talked about it, she loved how his face seemed to grow even more handsome. His dark eyes became sparkling black diamonds surrounded by thick black lashes. His tan skin glowed. It was all so magical to him. It brought out the boy-child, a part of him that always charmed her.

The previous afternoon she had conducted her formal interview with Daniel on the history and culture of the Aztecs, and particularly the significance of his discovery. But today was the money shot—the actual look inside the tomb, even if it was only by video. This was the first finding of an Aztec leader's burial site, but not just any Aztec leader's tomb. Daniel had discovered the resting place of the infamous Montezuma II, the man whom some historical records accused of killing more than eighty thousand people in the span of four days.

Whenever Seneca made a proposal to the editor at *Planet Discovery*, often his response was, "That's not enough for a story, yet. Keep digging." This was going to surpass even his expectations.

To her excitement, not only was she going to get an intriguing story, but there appeared to be a bonus—an additional mystery unfolding.

"So, what do you think happened?" she asked Daniel. "Where are Montezuma's ashes?"

"My guess is that maybe there is no funerary jar because there was no cremation."

"But I thought you said it was their custom."

"Yes." He stared back at the monitor. "Wait! See that?" He turned to the video tech sitting nearby. "*Pare ahora mismo. ¡Mira!*"

The technician froze the image.

"That's very strange." Daniel tapped the screen.

Seneca lowered her Nikon.

Flattening his hands together as if to pray, Daniel touched his forefingers to his lips. "*Mi dios, no puedo creer lo que veo.*" He kept staring at the monitor, a pallor chalking his face.

Seneca's flesh prickled. "What is it?" She only caught the Spanish *Mi dios*—My God.

"Sorry, sorry. I can't believe what I see. Look." He used his fingertip to zero in on an object on the screen. "There's the funeral shroud."

Seneca saw what appeared to be a large piece of material lying on the floor. "What does it mean?"

“The Aztecs bundled their dead in a burial shroud before cremation. But look at this one. It’s untied and crumpled on the ground. Like he shed it as if there was no need.”

Seneca leaned in closer. “Almost as if Montezuma got up and walked away.”

TREASURE TROVE
1876, NORTHERN SONORA, MEXICO

On shaky legs, Billy Groves stood beside the hole that should have been his grave, unsure of why he was even alive. He heard the distant sound of water rushing over rocks and followed it until he found a nearby creek. He knelt and washed his face. As the spring water cooled his skin, the memory of what had happened continued to play out in his head.

It had all started the previous day while he was on the run, coming up from Santa Ana after killing a man in a cantina fight. He figured he had lost the Mexican banditos tracking him and decided to bed down for the night on a high ridge overlooking a mountainous ravine called Renegade Pass. He remembered being jarred awake by the sound of hooves on the rocky floor of the wash below. Drawing his pistol, he crawled to the edge of the rock ledge and peered over.

Expecting to see his pursuers in the pale light of daybreak, instead he spotted a dozen Mexican Federales riding into the pass, followed by at least twenty pack burros. Canvas tarpaulins covered the backs of the animals, and judging by the way they moved over the uneven terrain, he figured their loads were heavy.

Soon the entire column had entered the narrow pass. As he watched the slow-moving procession snake through the ravine, the air sprang alive with the whoosh of arrows. The hair on his neck bristled.

Apaches!

Fierce yelps of the Apache warriors echoed off the rock walls drowning out the screams of the trapped Mexicans.

Indians streamed into the pass from each end, attacking until every soldier lay dead or dying.

He watched the Apaches dismount and move from body to body. Placing a knee between the shoulder blades of the victim, they sliced a long arc in the front of the soldier's scalp. Even as the survivors begged for mercy, the Apaches pulled back the hair and ripped the scalp from the skull.

Sickened, he turned and crept away from the ledge. Covering his ears, he waited until the shrieks finally faded. Warily, he crawled back for another look.

One of the Apaches, a barrel-chested brave wearing a blue Union Army jacket that hung down to his knees, gave an order. Another moved to a burro and lifted the tarpaulin exposing leather saddlebags. He untied one and reached inside, pulling out a canvas sack, heavy enough that he seemed to need both hands to lift it. He slit a small hole in the bottom with his knife. A stream of gold dust spilled onto the blood-stained earth. The leader held out his hand and let the gold flow through his fingers, then made a bold gesture with his arm, and his fellow braves whooped.

Before the blood of the Federales dried, the Apaches had the burro train moving. Soon the last pack animal disappeared around a turn in the pass.

Mesmerized by the gold and the notion that he might be able to get his hands on some of it, Groves decided to follow the Indians. Watchfully, he led his mare down the side of the ravine into the wash, past the dead soldiers whose bodies were strewn about like broken dolls.

Keeping his distance, he tracked the Apaches throughout the morning and into the afternoon, going from deep ravines to dense forest and finally into the rugged Sierra Madre Occidental Mountains.

After a full day of shadowing the war party, he crested a hill and gazed down into a narrow valley with sheer rock walls on both sides and a small rapid-flowing river running through the middle. The Apaches had halted and were unloading the bags from the burros.

He tied up his mare and proceeded on foot, working his way along a ridge protected by a line of Douglas firs until he cut the distance by half. Concealed in the shadows of the forest, he lay flat on the ground and watched the braves carry the saddlebags into a thick stand of trees at the base of a cliff. When they finished, the Indians remounted and started up the pack train again, passing out of the valley and into the mountains beyond.

He waited for over an hour before retrieving his mare and riding down into the valley to where the Indians had unloaded the gold dust. He tied up his horse and explored the trees, finding a narrow path that led to a small opening in the rock, just wide enough for a man to pass through. Cautious, he drew his gun and listened. Drawn by the lure of the gold, he followed the zigzag passage until coming to the mouth of a cave. It was late afternoon and the sun had already dipped below the tops of the mountains. The inside of the cave appeared as dark as the coming night.

Crouching to slip beneath the low ceiling, he moved forward, bumping his foot in the process. He reached down to discover a torch, still warm. Striking a match, he lit the tightly packed reeds, throwing orange light across the walls. Centuries of the Apaches and their ancestors' footfalls had packed the sandy floor hard, and the ceiling was black from their torches.

A few paces farther, his light fell on a large chamber, the contents causing him to gasp.

What he saw was gold piled upon gold. And what appeared to be an equal amount of silver.

Like cordwood waiting for the fire, bars of bullion were stacked four and five feet high. Chests of coins marked with names he recognized like Carson City Mint, US Army, Confederate States of America, and others lined the walls, sometimes two and three deep. Many bore the crests of Spain and what had to be those of various Spanish families. There was Aztec turquoise and Mexican silver jewelry. His eyes found the forty or so bags of gold dust from the pack train. What had appeared like such a great amount now paled in the vastness of the treasure trove.

It must have taken the Apaches a hundred years to amass such a fortune, he thought. Slowly he moved from pile to box to crate to bag, feeling, smelling, even tasting the precious metal. Unable to resist, he dropped a handful of gold coins into his pocket.

Scattered among the treasure were swords, muskets, rifles, shields, many decorated with the signs of a Spanish army long gone from the Mexican countryside.

He opened a small silver chest but was disappointed to discover it contained only a folded swatch of cloth about the size of a bandana. Propping the torch nearby, he lifted the cloth and examined it, wondering why it deserved to be among such an immense amount of treasure. In the flickering light, he saw that it bore the face of a man with long hair, mustache, and short-cropped beard, wearing what resembled a crown with a plume of feathers. The image was faint, almost as if it was part of the threads rather than painted on.

A creaking noise jolted him. He froze—his heart feeling like it had come to an abrupt halt, too afraid to beat. Then he realized it was only the trees groaning in the wind outside the cave. Nevertheless, the fleeting scare made him break a sweat—the interruption shook him back to reality. If he was going to get any of the treasure, he'd better hurry. The Apaches would not leave this place unguarded.

He wiped the perspiration from his face with the cloth before dropping it back in the chest. He had to make a quick decision on what to take. The gold dust would be the easiest to convert into cash, and he figured the Indians would never notice one or two bags missing. Plus he had already pocketed a few coins.

He grabbed a bag and headed out of the cave. If the torch lasted long enough he'd go back for a second, but only one more. He didn't want greed to get him killed. As he emerged from the cave, a voice startled him.

"Ah, Señor Groves, we were beginning to think you would never come out of the mountain."

He stared into the big .44 gun barrels of the three banditos from the Santa Ana cantina. Perhaps he should have been looking over his shoulder as he tracked the Apaches.

"What have you got there, amigo?" one of them asked, his gaze falling on the bag. "Have you brought us a—"

A sudden series of thuds in quick succession caused the bandits' bodies to go rigid, then limp. They drooped over their horses before dropping to the ground, arrow shafts protruding from their backs.

A small band of Apaches emerged from the trees. They glared at their next victim with cold indifference.

A searing pain in Groves's chest caused him to look down. Shocked, he reeled backward. Buried in his chest was the stub of an arrow—its eagle feather fletching sticking out a few inches. His knees buckled and he collapsed, coming to rest on his back.

As he lay staring at the Apaches, feeling his warm blood pool beneath him, a low rumble filled his ears. Distant at first, it built to a roar.

Was this the sound of death?

The earth moaned and the cliff wall leaned out as if breathing. The ground vibrated, then rippled and formed waves passing like ocean swells.

The Indians' horses struggled as if standing on the swaying deck of a ship.

Now, as he knelt by the stream splashing water on this face, he remembered it all—the wrenching sound racing across the floor of the valley, the fissure slithering over the ground like a snake, swallowing everything in its path.

First the Apaches, then him.

WALL OF SKULLS
2012, MEXICO CITY

Seneca left the protective tent covering the excavation to stand in the sunlight. She focused her camera at Zócalo Plaza and the gigantic Mexican flag flying in the center. Daniel came to join her.

She clicked off two shots before turning to him. Hand in hand, they took a stroll. "It's incredible to look around and realize we're only a few hundred feet from the Metropolitan Cathedral. Like we're standing between two worlds in the middle of a time warp."

Daniel squeezed her hand, then pointed to the remains of Templo Mayor behind them. "Over there is what's left of the Wall of Skulls—a wall literally made of human skulls and covered in stucco. That tells you how much blood was spilled down the steps of that temple. I have to keep in mind that it was just a different culture—a culture *ruled* by its religious beliefs."

"You don't think what Montezuma did was wrong?"

"I didn't say that. Only that we need to try to understand the *why* as well as the *what* and the *how.* We have to understand the customs and belief system of any civilization."

They paused as he studied the ruins. "Sometimes I feel like I'm almost able to step through some fine filament of time and space and be right in the middle of their world. I've even touched artifacts that *speak* to me. Sounds weird, I know."

"Not at all." Seneca always marveled at his enthusiasm. His excitement was contagious and stirred her soul. "How do you put up with me? I'm such a boring purist at heart. It's my nature to rely on the facts—the data. Sometimes I've wished I were less analytical."

"Ah, but that makes for a good journalist."

She rested her palm on his cheek and tilted her head to the side. "God, I love you, Daniel Bernal."

He covered her hand with his. "So, before I indulged myself by climbing up on my soapbox, you were asking what could have happened to Montezuma's remains."

"What do you think?"

He shrugged. "It was a chaotic time. The Spanish might have forbidden them from cremating the emperor. After all, cremation and the Church don't mix well. Right now, it's a five-hundred-year-old mystery. We'll probably never know. I wish I could run the missing funerary jar discovery by my old mentor, Professor Flores."

"Why don't you? Isn't he still here in Mexico City at the university?"

"He's retired and moved off to some jungle island somewhere."

"Can't you talk the government into letting you dig up the temple and do a complete excavation? There's no telling what else you might find."

Daniel shook his head. "The Spaniards built right on top of Tenochtitlan. They covered up the entire Aztec city with their own. The historical value of the Spanish buildings prohibits destroying them, which is what we would have to do. We're lucky we've been allowed to do this much."

"What's next?" Carlos, the technical assistant came to join them.

Daniel rubbed his lips with his index finger. "I'd like to make some notes before we continue exploring the tomb with the camera probe."

Carlos and the video tech were on loan to the Mexican dig team from TV *Mexicali,* and unlike most of the others, Carlos spoke fluent English. He seemed to Seneca to be anxious and a bit nervous.

"Dr. Bernal told me that you might be a descendent of Montezuma?" Seneca said to Carlos.

"Yes. My family still carries the last name."

"Montezuma?"

"Moctezuma." He emphasized the slight difference in pronunciation. "Here." He handed her his TV *Mexicali* card. "See how Moctezuma is spelled."

Seneca looked at the name, then pronounced it slowly. "Easy to understand how it morphed to Montezuma."

"The Spanish wrote what they believed they heard," Daniel said.

"I've thought about taking a different first name—a *Nahuatl* one, but everybody knows me as Carlos."

"Then you must have a special interest in this site," Seneca said as she slipped his card into her pocket.

"More than you know."

Daniel said, "Why don't we stop for lunch. I think everybody needs a break. We'll gather back here in an hour and continue the video documentation."

"We could go as a group." Seneca nodded to Carlos. "I read in my guidebook that there's a famous cantina a short walk from here called *Bar La Opera.* Pancho Villa supposedly rode in on his horse and demanded service by firing his pistol into the ceiling. It said that the bullet hole is still there."

"It's for tourists," Carlos said.

"I think I'll stay behind," Daniel said. "I need to spend more time on my notes. I'll grab a bite with the rest of the team."

The video tech came out of the tent and gestured as if to ask what to do next.

"They want to stop," Carlos said.

"Is it safe for me to leave my gear?" Seneca held up her camera.

"All of *Mexicali's* gear is here." Carlos motioned to the handful of soldiers stationed just beyond the roped-off perimeter of the excavation. "And there are the security guards."

The Mexican authorities had provided them to keep the curious at a distance from the dig site.

"Come on and go with us, Daniel." She pulled at his hand. "It'll be fun."

"I need this time to finish up my work. And the sooner we finish, the sooner we can be on our way to the Yucatan."

"Want me to stay with you?"

"No, you go on."

"Then go have fun with your notes. But promise you'll eat something." To Carlos, she said, "Let me put my camera away and grab my purse. Don't leave without me." Hooking her arm in Daniel's, they headed back to the tent.

A few moments later she reemerged and glanced around.

The video tech waved as he stood near the Wall of Skulls.

Seneca joined him. "Where's Carlos?"

He shrugged. "*Él no está aquí.*"

"He left? Well, that's strange. We had talked about going to—"

The shockwave from the explosion slammed into her with enough force to lift her into the air and toss her twenty feet across the ancient stone pavement. Crumpled and dazed, Seneca lay motionless. Finally able to open her eyes, she found herself sprawled at the base of Templo Mayor, staring at billowing black smoke that blotted out the sky.

Her eyes drifted to the body of the video technician several feet away, his head at a peculiar angle like it had relocated from the center of his spinal column and twisted atop his shoulder. His glare was frozen and fixed in her direction.

The sound of sirens and shouts of panic filled the air. As the heaviness in her lids forced her eyes to narrow slits before finally closing, the smoke cleared long enough for her to gaze upon the Wall of Skulls.

DEAD SILENCE

2012, MEXICO CITY

SENECA'S EYES FLUTTERED OPEN. How long had she lain there? A few moments, she guessed—maybe only a second or two as no help had yet arrived and the sky was still black with smoke. Every muscle, every joint, every bone felt aflame with pain. She struggled to sit up, coughing from the stench of smoke. Blood trickled into her eye and she wiped it away. Her fingers probed to find the source. A gash on her scalp, wet and sticky. Everything hurt. Her body shook, her lungs fought for air, her hip burned where she had slammed into the ground, her eyes refused to stay open, and her ears rang with a high-pitched squeal that matched the screaming sirens and calls for help.

"Daniel!" She tried to shout, but what came from her throat was a weak and garbled wail.

Her first attempt to get to her feet failed. She plummeted back to the ground.

"Please, someone help me! Daniel. Where are you?"

Straining and grunting, Seneca drew herself up to stand, then staggered toward where the tent had once stood.

Scorched debris swirled about in small eddies and cascaded over the stone pavement. The distance she struggled to walk seemed measured in miles. Bits of paper drifted down from the dirty sky like black confetti.

"Daniel!" This time her cry had some volume. She felt as if time had been reduced to a reluctant slothful beat, and everything around her was out of focus. In that sluggish Seneca-time she trudged on searching for Daniel, but seeming not to make any progress getting there. The distinct odor of seared flesh and singed hair permeated the air, dominating even the smell of the smoke. "Daniel!" The sound of her voice was warbled and distorted.

Slivers and chunks of metal, cardboard, wood, stone, and other unidentifiable rubble littered the ground. Then to her right she spotted what appeared to be a human form. She stumbled closer. Her stomach retched as she recognized it was a torso, dangling fibers and threads of tissue the only vestiges of what was once a person. Wisps of smoke drifted up from burnt cloth and skin.

Then just ahead, she saw what might be another victim. She fell to her knees beside the mangled body. "Daniel." As she took his head and shoulders into her lap, he made a thin, tinny whistling noise, and a wet sucking sound accompanied his shallow breaths.

"Hold on. Help is coming." Her words were stuttered with sobs. "Stay with me, babe. Hang on."

Oh, dear God, his shirt is soaked with blood.

She tore open the buttons to find a gaping chest wound that bubbled up with frothy foam, the source of the whistling and sucking noises. She smelled the coppery scent of his blood as she placed the heel of her hand firmly over the wound trying to stop the bleeding, but blood oozed between her fingers and drizzled down in tiny crimson rivers.

There was so much blood.

And beneath her palm she felt his faint, thready, almost airy, heartbeat racing but no stronger than the flutter of a hummingbird's wings.

"Sen?" His voice sounded thick as blood choked his words.

"Shh, don't talk." She heard the sirens. What was taking so long?

She cradled Daniel closer, rocking him, feeling him shivering from shock, and cursing her inability to warm him.

A police car screeched to a halt nearby.

"Over here!" Seneca screamed and waved. "Over here! Help! Please help!"

And then she noticed the silence. The dead silence. The absence of the terrible sounds coming from Daniel's body. The cessation of the flutter of the hummingbird. The heaviness of his body.

"No, no, no. Please, Daniel. Please, don't leave me."

More emergency vehicles arrived.

But it was too late.

Seneca leaned back her head and stared up at the sky. "Why? Why?" She dropped her gaze to the man she loved and gently stroked his face before pressing her lips to his forehead. Her tears mixed with his blood as she looked back into the smoke-filled sky. "Why?"

BLOODY MARY

2012, LONDON

"THIS PLACE GIVES ME the creeps." The disciple whispered into the tiny mic extending from his earpiece to just beside his mouth. His night-vision goggles created an eerie green glow over the narrow passageway three levels below the main nave of Westminster Abbey. Over three thousand bodies were buried beneath the ancient London landmark, and he moved cautiously past the rows of crypts.

He and his partner were dressed in military black. The first disciple aimed a stock-mounted automatic machine pistol at the tunnel ahead while the second disciple gripped the handle of a duffel bag in one hand and an ultra-sensitive underground GPS unit in the other—its signal utilizing four miniature directional antennae secretly prepositioned around the church. As the two men moved through the pitch-black subterranean labyrinth, the second disciple whispered their location every thirty seconds. "Almost there.

St. Paul's Chapel is directly overhead. Henry's Lady Chapel just ahead, slightly to the right."

The first disciple spotted a set of steps and stopped at their base. "This it?"

The second disciple checked the GPS display. "We're just past it. Go up the steps."

The first disciple glanced around before proceeding. His friend waited until the first disciple was a dozen steps above him before following.

A few moments later, they stood in the basement level just below the Lady Chapel. The second disciple again studied the GPS. "Follow the passage west until you come to a wall."

As they moved along the tunnel, the first disciple read off the names on the marble to his right until he saw the last. "It's a duplicate of the inscription on the main tomb above." Aloud, he spoke the Latin, "*Regno Consortes Et Urna Hic Obdor Mimus Elizabetha Et Maria Sorores In Spe Resurrectionis.*"

The second disciple translated. "Partners both in throne and grave, here rest we two sisters, Elizabeth and Mary, in the hope of one resurrection."

The first disciple turned to his friend. "For someone who had three hundred people burned at the stake, Mary was quite optimistic she'd be coming back."

"Probably never thought it would be this soon."

Javier Scarrow stood in the study of the Dorchester's roof-level Harlequin Suite, overlooking Hyde Park. Darkness had enveloped London. It was the last day of his U.K. Phoenix Ministry, and even though the service had ended hours ago, thousands of faithful were still making their way out of the park. In the distance, Scarrow could see the top of the sprawling metal and glass pyramid structure that took up the majority of the northeast corner facing Marble Arch. Tomorrow morning, hundreds of workers would descend upon the Phoenix pavilion, disassemble it, and get it ready for its journey to the next destination.

Scarrow had removed his elaborate red and black ceremonial garb and was now dressed in a floor-length robe of simple white linen. He sipped Roederer Cristal as he watched the reflection in the window of the dignitaries and VIPs filling the hotel suite behind him. He recognized members of Parliament and the National Trust, London city officials, ultra-rich socialites, even a sprinkling of religious leaders, all having expressed support and dedication to his growing worldwide Ministry.

He turned away from the reflection to see a young man standing next to him. The nametag said he was the public relations director of the British Museum.

"So where is your next stop?" asked the PR director.

"São Paulo." Scarrow smiled seeing that like so many others who were drawn to his message, this man's eyes sparkled with wonder and fascination at meeting what many were calling a modern-day prophet, a twenty-first-century messiah. Placing his hand on the man's shoulder, he said, "Thank you for coming."

"It's an honor." The director held up his glass in a toast, then took a sip of his champagne. "And from São Paulo?"

"On to Moscow and Paris with a final stop in Mexico City."

"Where you'll prove that your message is the only hope left for the salvation of mankind?"

Scarrow nodded. "Exactly."

"I've also read about your amazing crusades in so many countries—Germany, China, Saudi Arabia, Uzbekistan."

"We didn't refer to it as a crusade during our visit in Saudi Arabia. There, we simply paid a cordial visit to the Saudi monarchy in the name of helping to preserve the earth for future generations. But even they agreed with us that there are millions of souls needing guidance in every corner of the world. We are all members of a universal family that goes beyond religion and politics."

"Truly amazing. But having heard your message of hope for the future, I can see why so many are in search of your guidance."

Scarrow noticed a man in a tuxedo approaching—one he so anxiously awaited.

"Good evening." The first disciple made his way through the crowded hotel suite to where Scarrow and the young man stood. "I'm sorry to be so late."

"I trust you bring good news?"

"Yes, very good news, but first, can I offer to have your drinks refilled, gentlemen?" He nodded to Scarrow's empty glass, then waved to one of the catering staff.

"What would you like?" Scarrow turned to the man from the British Museum.

"More of the same, if you don't mind." He raised his crystal flute.

"And you, sir?" the first disciple asked Scarrow. "The same?"

"No, I want to try something different. Do you think they can make me a Bloody Mary?"

The disciple smiled. "Consider it already done."

The warden moved silently through the subbasement of Westminster Abbey on his morning rounds. There had been reports of a small outbreak of rodents, and he used the beam of his flashlight to inspect the corners and crevices along the passageways. He had started at the lowest level and worked his way up until he was now in the basement crypts just below the Lady Chapel. Moving down the row of tombs, he noticed patches of debris in his path and small particles that reflected his light. He walked slowly, swinging the beam like a blind man's cane, the heavy odor of earth and stone invading his nostrils. His concern grew with each sweep of the light. Was there some sort of shift in the foundation of the ancient church that caused bits of the ceiling to shower down? Perhaps it was an outbreak of mold or fungus. He'd recently read about something like that affecting the catacombs in Rome and hoped if that were the source of the particles, perhaps he had caught it before it could spread.

He approached the end of the passage, his head down, his eyes focused on the floor. Suddenly, the passageway became covered with dust and small chunks of marble. He came to a halt and slowly lifted his gaze.

"Sweet Jesus and Mary!"

Before him was a gaping hole in the side of the wall exposing the crypt of Queen Elizabeth I and her sister, Queen Mary. Shining the light into the darkness, he saw the skeletal remains of Elizabeth. But Bloody Mary was gone.

FOG LAMPS
2012, MIAMI

After passing through Customs, Seneca stared blankly at the luggage carousel on the arrivals level of Terminal E. She was emotionally drained and physically beaten up.

She had spent two days in the hospital after the bombing recovering from a concussion, multiple lacerations to the scalp and arms, along with contusions that left widespread bruising to her hips and legs. She'd stayed on another few days for Daniel's family to fly in from Guadalajara and make arrangements. Daniel had confided in her many times that if something were to ever happen to him, he didn't want a funeral. He believed the cost of funerals was outrageous and that funeral directors preyed on grieving family members. All he wanted was to be cremated and his ashes sprinkled over his Mexican homeland.

She still hadn't been able to stop asking why God had let this happen? Why was she spared and Daniel taken along with the others at the dig site? But as many times as she asked those questions, no answers came. The pain of losing Daniel was incredible, sometimes so numbing that she had no emotion at all. The mind's way of dealing with it, she thought. She and Daniel's mother had clung to each other, sobbing as they watched Dan's father release the ashes in the Mexican wind. Daniel had become her life—such a gentle and kind man with a great depth of understanding for all people, past and present. He didn't deserve dying like that—no one did. He was just doing a job that he loved. It was so unfair. Survivor guilt was a terrible feeling, especially when there was no way to help find justice.

After Daniel's family left, she grieved alone. No one should have to grieve alone. How she so needed to call her mother and be comforted by her like Seneca had been when she was a child. But her mother wouldn't understand. Not now.

While Seneca was in the hospital, the Mexican police questioned her. She hadn't been able to provide them with any helpful information.

The incident made front-page news across Mexico and was the lead story on all their television networks. No group had yet claimed responsibility for the bombing, but the authorities felt certain it was one of a handful of violent political groups vying for attention in the media or perhaps drug-gang related. The drug wars were escalating with each passing day. This was not the first time something like this had happened, the investigators told her.

She wanted to wake up and find it all a hideous nightmare. The irony was that even when she did sleep, her real dreams were nightmares reliving the bombing and Daniel shivering in her arms as his life drifted away. She had never really considered what death was until that moment. Now she had witnessed up close what it was like to die, and the recurring images and haunting sensory detail tortured her—the bloody torso with its trails of tissue, the smell of singed flesh and hair, Daniel's blood-saturated shirt, the metallic odor of his blood so sharp in her nose that she could even taste it, the wheezing as his body desperately attempted to breathe. The whole process of dying was grisly and horrifying.

As the luggage started to appear in the baggage claim area, Seneca reached inside her handbag and withdrew a plastic bag with the meds prescribed for her by the Mexican doctors. She opened one amber plastic bottle, tumbled a small five-sided pill into her palm, popped it in the back of her throat and swallowed. It was hard to get it down with her dry mouth and no water. The Ativan would take the edge off. When she got home she'd take a sleeping pill. That should numb her for the night... or at least most of it until she woke up in a sweat, or crying, or screaming, or all of the above.

How was she going to live without him? She couldn't even remember what life had been like before Daniel. He was her first true love—the ones before him were never this deep, this real. She'd had a serious relationship with one guy while studying journalism at the University of South Florida in St. Petersburg. It was her junior year, his senior. When he graduated, he moved to Washington to work on his masters, and the long distance along with his cheating on her with an exchange student from China, quickly killed their love affair. It was a totally different story with Daniel.

Seneca had fallen for Dan as soon as she set eyes on the man. She'd been freelancing a piece on Little Salt Spring, a sinkhole on the west coast of Florida that yielded remains of animals and humans more than ten thousand years old. Because the sinkhole was similar to the *cenotes* of the Yucatan, Daniel had paid the site a visit which happened to be at the same time Seneca was there. Both had been delighted to find out they were practically neighbors back in Miami. She was a rare Florida native. He had lived there for the past nine years, teaching at the University of Miami after getting his doctorate in archaeology in Mexico. Daniel proposed a lunch date when they returned from Little Salt Spring, and Seneca had accepted eagerly. That was the beginning of the magic.

It was meant to be, the two often said. Back then, coming back home had meant something to look forward to. But not this time.

Seneca watched the snake of suitcases slither along—the drone of her fellow passengers' voices and constant whine and clatter of the conveyer spawned a fatigue in her like some kind of hypnotherapy. Her eyes tried focusing on the carousel as if it were a silver pendulum dangling before her by the hand of an invisible magician.

The luggage thinned as the passengers collected their bags and wandered off. An unclaimed suitcase and a tattered knapsack were all that remained on the carousel. She likened the reappearance of the two pieces to recurring blips on a radar screen.

Where were her bags? The anti-anxiety drug hadn't had time to kick in and the stress inside was intensifying. Seneca paced from one end of the carousel to the other, ending where the bags emerged from the chute. Finally, the conveyor ground to a stop. She leaned over and looked through the rubber-flap ribbons in case her bags were somehow jammed behind them.

The explosion had destroyed her camera gear, photo disks, audiotapes, laptop, and notes from the second day of the interview. Losing those *and* all her other personal items and clothing seemed to be a final, cruel blow. What else could she lose—could be yanked away from her?

Her head hurt, and she thought about taking a painkiller, but decided that might be unwise. She tried some slow, easy breathing.

The last of the passengers disappeared into the humid South Florida night leaving Seneca standing alone. Soon, a baggage handler came to remove the two unclaimed pieces from the carousel.

"Hey!" She scurried over to the man. "Any more back there? My bags never came out."

"That's it, lady." He hefted up the two orphaned pieces and started to walk away. "You can follow me to lost baggage and make a report."

Seneca looked at her watch. It was nearly one in the morning; she was dead on her feet. The passing thought with the word *dead* in it made a rush of sudden dizziness sweep through her followed by a wave of nausea.

"You okay, lady?"

"Just tired from my flight." She followed him to lost luggage.

After leaving the airport's long-term parking lot, Seneca made her way to the Dolphin Expressway and finally onto 27th Avenue. She was thankful for the sparse, middle-of-the-night traffic as she drove her ice-white Volvo south. She considered putting the convertible top down but decided she didn't need the noise right now. The whoosh of the wind with the top down was something she loved. So did Daniel. Tonight she wanted quiet.

Her thoughts were filled with images of Daniel, his infectious smile, his boyish giggle, and the life they had planned. After their dream wedding, they would move into a spacious new apartment overlooking Biscayne Bay. Dan would continue teaching at the University of Miami while she advanced her career as a journalist. Getting the exclusive on Montezuma's tomb because of Daniel was an omen of how right they were for each other. But all that had come to a devastating end. Daniel was gone, and so befitting, the Mexican government declared the dig site off limits and ordered the small hole used by the camera probe sealed. If Montezuma's tomb still remained intact below the cobblestones of Zócalo Plaza, it would be as much an unsolved mystery as the emperor's missing ashes. The excavation ended in a flash of death at a place with such a violent past—the Wall of Skulls.

She was heartsick at the possible loss of her luggage. Not so much for her personal belongings, but her bag contained the last pictures she had of Dan preserved on her photo disks. There were also her notes of the interview with him and the recording of his voice—all had been stuffed in her luggage. Not only would she lose those wonderful images of his smiling face and sweet voice, but the items needed to write her story would be gone.

The Mexican police felt the bombing was to gain notoriety—perhaps to instill fear or destabilize the tourist trade, disrupt the economy. They recited a dozen reasons. And she was sure the police were right. What a waste of innocent lives. These people, these terrorists, had no soul, no conscience. They were totally self-absorbed bastards. They didn't even have the balls to declare responsibility. She felt her hands clenching the steering wheel and her teeth grinding, her brows furrowing deep into her forehead so much it was making her squint.

"Stop it!" *You're going to drive yourself nuts. Let it go, for God's sake.*

Something drew her attention to the traffic in her rearview mirror. It was a set of double headlights—lights with orange fog lamps below them—lights that had been behind her since leaving MIA. While other cars passed or turned onto side streets, the one with the orange fog lamps stayed steady in her wake about a half block back. Even with the light traffic, it would be highly unusual for the same car to keep pace with her for so many miles unless it was intentional.

She changed lanes and watched the trailing vehicle duplicate the move. Out of nervousness, Seneca turned off the radio—one less distraction. The singing of the tires on the pavement and the hum of the motor replaced the music as she steered her C70 south. She fixed her eyes on the reflection of the car's headlights in the mirror. Only ten minutes to her Coconut Grove apartment. Watching the now-familiar headlights follow, a peculiar notion hurtled into Seneca's head.

"Let's have a test," she said to the reflection. When she got to the intersection at South Dixie Highway, rather than going straight into the Grove, she would turn and head north. If the car in her mirror kept on going, she could attribute it up to nothing more than a creepy feeling from an overburdened and fatigued mind.

Without flipping on her blinker, she whipped north onto Dixie.

QUESTIONS
1876, SOUTHERN ARIZONA TERRITORY

"WHERE'D YOU GET THESE?" Charlie Pykes examined the coins Groves had just placed on the scale in the front room of the Calabazas Land and Mining Company office. Pykes was the local assayer.

"Found 'em." Groves touched his chest through his shirt and rubbed the place where the arrow had entered. It was still sensitive and sore, but there was little of what should have been a wound. It didn't make sense, almost as if it never happened—nothing more than a bad dream. He had acquired enough cuts, scrapes, and bruises over his thirty-seven years to know how long things take to heal. This was crazy.

"Where 'bouts you find 'em?"

Already too many questions. "What difference does it make? I just want the money to buy me a wagon. Any crime in that?"

"No crime, Mr. Groves. We just don't get too many old Spanish coins in here. Any more where these came from?"

"Beats me." Groves glanced around the empty office. A couple of cowboys rode by on the dirt street outside the front window. The town was quiet in the early morning. That didn't stop him from sweating at the thought that someone would discover his secret.

"You okay, Mr. Groves? Look a bit jumpy."

"Just tired awaitin' for you to give me my money so I can be on my way. If we could get on with our business, I'd be much obliged."

"Where'd you say you're from?"

"Over near Tombstone," he lied.

"No foolin'? Now what in heaven's name would a bunch of Spanish coins be doing over there?"

"Maybe somebody lost 'em. I don't know."

"And you gonna use the money to buy some diggin' gear?"

"I said I need a wagon and a couple of mules. That's all. Do I get my money or do I have to go up to Tucson?"

"No, you don't have to do any of that. Just wonderin' how you came across such a nice collection of gold." Pykes took the coins off the scale and started counting out a stack of paper money. "Looks like at twenty dollars an ounce minus my exchange fee, you're gonna get more than enough for a fine wagon and some strong mules. I'd say you should be all set to head back to Tombstone and look for more of them coins."

"Don't want none of that paper money." Groves pointed to the bills. "And where I go ain't your concern."

"No problem." Pykes opened his safe, took out a handful of $20 gold pieces and handed them to Groves. "Roy over at the livery should be able to fix you right up. Mention my name."

Groves took the money and turned to leave. It occurred to him that if the word got out he'd found a stash of Spanish treasure, everybody would be wanting a share. "Actually, I'm thinking about headin' west to Gila Bend. Probably leave tomorrow."

"Gila Bend, is it? Well, good luck finding more of them coins."

Groves stood on the wooden boardwalk outside the assayer's office and glanced in both directions along the main street of the frontier town. An uneasy feeling came over him. If word spread about the coins, then getting out of town with a wagon full of digging gear and some dynamite was going to be harder than he figured. "The livery's in that direction."

Groves spun around to see Pykes standing behind him pointing.

"Thanks." He stepped off the boardwalk and headed along the dusty street.

"Come back and see me if you find any more gold."

Groves didn't look back, but he knew if he could get his hands on the Apache treasure, it probably wouldn't be the last time he saw Charlie Pykes.

THE PRAYER

2012, SÃO PAULO, BRAZIL

JAVIER SCARROW LAY IN the all-white satin bedding of his suite in the *Hotel Emiliano*. As his life's mission came closer to fruition he sometimes found it hard to sleep. His body seemed to pump out adrenaline by the gallon. And his mind whirred with checklists and visions of the future, and sometimes after ingesting the ancient god's mushroom, *teonanácatl*, chased with a drink of chocolate prepared in the old way, he experienced apparitions and hallucinations that led to prophecy.

Tonight he stared at the ceiling, trying to calm himself enough to at least doze. Scarrow reflected back on the day so many years ago when the gods had finally answered his prayers. It was 1960 and he worked as a research analyst for the Smithsonian Institute. The name Javier Scarrow was the latest he had taken to hide his true identity—there had been many others. He remembered the night as if it were yesterday when he had opened the window of his third-story, two-bedroom Bethesda, Maryland, apartment to let the pungent smoke escape.

A small stone altar called a *tezcatlipoca* sat in the middle of the bedroom. Atop the altar a single-stem marigold lay beside a one-inch, carved jade figure of a jaguar head he had secretly pocketed while cataloging a private collection donated to the Institute. Scarrow knelt before the altar, then sat back on his heels.

In the center of the stone slab was a sculpture he had carved of *Quetzalcoatl*, the deity he invoked that night. There was also a clay basin in which splinters of wood burned. This was not the Eternal Flame; he had no right to light *that* fire. Not yet. But he prayed the day would come soon. Most of the smoke rose up from the incense burner, another bowl filled partway with sand on which rested a burning charcoal tablet topped with copal, an aromatic resin.

Deftly, he drew his obsidian *tecpatl* blade over the inside of his forearm, a blade sharper than a surgeon's scalpel. Tiny beads of deep red blood percolated to the brim of the paper-cut-thin slice in his flesh. He lifted his head, eyes closed. He had consecrated this room making everything in it sacred. It was a sanctuary, a make-shift temple, dedicated to worship.

"I come again, yet another day, to beg for your forgiveness." His eyes had flickered open, and he wished it were the stars in the night sky he saw rather than the plaster ceiling. "Hear my pleas, *Quetzalcoatl*, oh mighty one. I give you my reverence and honor, and am grateful for your eternal presence and the constant bounty you have given me. I praise your infinite wisdom, power, and beauty." He lowered his head, eyes cast down. "I am wretched and unworthy."

Scarrow had reached for a small earthenware bowl and held his forearm over it at an angle so that a few drops of blood trickled into the hollow of the vessel. "I give to you that which is right—my blood."

As happened each time he brought himself to this altar, his eyes stung with tears, and his throat painfully constricted as he wept. "It was I who offended you by allowing the downfall of our people. I was the one who misread the prophecy. It was I who mistook the arrival of the barbarian, thinking it was your glorious and foretold return."

The sobs came unrestrained, and he found himself stuttering. "I understand that this curse of immortality, this blessing of agelessness you have given me, is my atonement. I beg of you to give me guidance as to what I must do. Every day I see the universe convulsing with your wrath. Fires, earthquakes, floods, famines, disease—all because of me. If I am to right it, then I need your blessed intervention. Let me once again walk in the light so that I might see."

He drew the knife across his other forearm, crisscrossing a net of fine, thread-like scars. Holding both bleeding arms above his head, he said, "I give to you what is right." He dropped his arms and bent over his thighs with deep, bellowing sobs.

Scarrow knew that the universal balance was askew and would lead to disaster. If he could just find a way to return the harmony. He understood that was his task and that it called for suffering, and he wanted the gods to know that he accepted that responsibility. He had a purpose and needed the help of the gods. The doomsday predicted by so many ancient calendars and legends was coming, the day Einstein suggested would come, the day science theorized that the magnetic poles of the earth would shift and the dire effects would destroy the world as we know it. It had happened before, 200 times over the last 178 million years. And it was going to happen again.

Unless he could stop it.

Scarrow sat up, drew the fingers of each hand across his bloodied arms and used them to paint scarlet lines down his chest as he whispered the ancient prayers.

When the ritual was complete and his body spent, he shivered—the deep meditation had expended much of his core heat. He extinguished the incense with the sand, and smothered the bowl of glowing wood embers with a clay lid. Exhausted, he left the room, locking it behind him.

Scarrow trudged to the apartment's kitchen to make some hot tea. He glanced at the newspaper he had tossed on the table earlier and caught a glimpse of a picture that made him more than curious—a face he was sure he recognized. He picked up the paper and skimmed the obituary of the deceased in the photograph.

Bracing himself against the table, he uttered a prayer. "Oh, most giving and resourceful *Quetzalcoatl*, I offer my gratitude and service."

Scarrow opened his eyes as he lay in the Brazilian hotel room. Those memories from so many years before were as clear as if they had just happened. It had been a day that changed his life. For after seeing the face in the paper, he knew the gods had finally answered his prayers.

THE MESSAGE
2012, MIAMI

Seneca sped up as she headed north on Dixie with the mystery car steadily stalking a block or so behind. As a series of bright streetlights temporarily illuminated the car behind her, she caught a quick glimpse of the three-pointed star in the circle on the front grill, that and the high profile of the vehicle told her it was an older model Mercedes SUV with orange fog lamps.

"Ready for another test?" She watched the reflection. There was little traffic for her to be concerned with, so as she kept an eye on the fog lamps in the mirror, she took her foot off the accelerator and let her car start to coast. It seemed like it took a few seconds for the mystery car's driver to realize what was happening. The Mercedes closed the gap quickly but then slowed as well.

"Okay, asshole." She slammed on her brakes and came to a halt in the outside lane of Dixie Highway. The Mercedes immediately veered right onto a side street and disappeared. As soon as it was out of sight, she stomped on the accelerator and sped off, moving into the center lane and taking the first left onto 17th Avenue. At Coral Way, she doubled back and headed south into Coconut Grove, monitoring her rearview mirror the whole way. This time there were no orange fog lamps staring back.

Seneca pulled the Volvo into the parking garage on the ground floor of her South Bayshore Drive apartment building. Daniel had moved in with her six months earlier. It wasn't the most deluxe apartment, but it was comfortable and all they had needed. The lease was up at the end of the month, and as a wedding gift to each other, she and Daniel had put a deposit on a place in a more upscale section of Bayshore Drive. It wasn't something she could have afforded alone, even though she had a staff position with one of the premier magazines, *Planet Discovery*. Nor could Dan have made the payments on his own. Together it was more than doable.

Inside her second-story apartment, Seneca spotted the mail stacked on the coffee table. A retired neighbor watched out for the place whenever they were both away. He collected the mail and made sure to feed their two clown fish, a mutual Valentine's Day gift she and Dan had purchased. They bought the salt water aquarium and fish together. As she passed the small aquarium, she switched on its hood light.

Seneca wandered into the kitchen, dropped her purse beside the sink, and took a glass from the cabinet shelf. She filled the tumbler with water, then dug in her purse and withdrew the plastic bag, dumping three amber vials onto the countertop. She lined them up neatly against the backsplash, stared at each for a moment considering which she would take. She chose the sleeping pills since she was planning on going straight to bed and just sleeping—just being oblivious to the world—just finding a black hole to slip into for some peace and relief from the physical and mental pain. She took one tablet in her hand, then washed it down with a gulp of water.

Refilling the glass, she returned to the living room and sprawled on the couch, not ready to face the bed, yet.

Their bed.

Seneca stared at the aquarium as the fish swam serenely and silently working their tranquility on her. But tired as she had been earlier, the ride home from the airport with the suspicious car had given her a second wind. After awhile she began to doubt the medication's potency.

Leaning back on the couch cushion, she set the glass of water on the coffee table and rolled her head to the side. The sudden shooting pain brought her hands to the wound in her scalp. The blinking light on the answer machine caught her attention. She'd considered giving up her landline at one point, but it was difficult to part with tradition.

Seneca inched toward the end of the sofa to see the answering machine better. One message. She pushed the button. After hearing the first several words her body stiffened as if flash frozen. When the message finished, she sat up, doubled over her knees, and put her head in her hands.

She remained in that position, breathing in and out in her palms, rocking, thoughts rising up from the shadows of her heart. Finally, she went to her bedroom closet and looked up at a small box. It was a little larger than a shoebox and made out of some light wood that her mother had decoupaged back in the early seventies.

Seneca pulled the box from the shelf and placed it on the bed. She opened it and studied the collection of envelopes, all addressed to her. Letters, birthday cards, photographs, postcards. She probably should have thrown them out long ago.

Over the years he had only written.

Now he was calling.

TEN-EIGHTY

2012, SÃO PAULO, BRAZIL

The director of the São Paulo Institute of Forensic Medicine sipped his coffee as he read the morning edition of *A Tribuna*. Always first to arrive at work, he took advantage of the quiet time to mentally prepare for his day while he caught up on the news.

A front-page story on the recent Phoenix Ministry's *Great Awakening* event intrigued him. Held at Morumbi Stadium, the event had ended the previous day. Tens of thousands came to hear the words of one man.

Someone named Javier Scarrow was responsible—a man the media described as a charismatic spiritual prophet and believed by many to be the new messiah. His devout followers spanned the social, economic, and political spectrum—even embracing those of all faiths. His crusades drew huge crowds around the world as did his online and television ministries. And all he preached was to be in balance with the universe.

Rather simplistic, the director thought. Why would so many people want to hear something as basic as that? But then, getting back to basics might be just what this world needed. Or was it too late—too far beyond basics with all the threats society faced daily? It made him think of the cliché: you can never go home again.

He took the next twenty minutes to finish his coffee and the paper before checking his calendar. His first appointment was with his granddaughter. She had graduated with a journalism degree and managed to get a job with a medical journal doing research on cutting-edge forensic procedures. He would be one of her first interviews.

"Doctor," his granddaughter remained formal and businesslike, "my last question is about something called brain fingerprinting. Can you tell me what it means, is it accurate, and is it admissible as evidence in court?" She typed her question into her notebook resting on her lap as she smiled across the desk at her grandfather.

He returned her expression of affection but also remained on a professional level. "The basic difference between someone who is guilty of a crime and someone who is innocent is that the guilty party has a record of the crime stored in his or her brain. The innocent person doesn't. Until brain fingerprinting was developed, there was no real scientific method of detecting this fundamental difference."

"Does brain fingerprinting determine guilt or innocence?"

"No. That task always resides with the judge and jury. What brain fingerprinting does do is give the courts compelling evidence based on science to help them arrive at a verdict."

"Will you explain exactly what it is?"

"It's a scientific technique to determine whether or not specific information is stored in an individual's memory. The procedure measures brainwave responses to words, phrases, sounds, and pictures. While conducting the interview, we use details that the subject would have encountered in the course of committing a crime, but that an innocent person wouldn't know. We can tell by the brain wave response if the subject recognizes the stimulus or not. If the suspect recognizes the details of the crime, this indicates that he has a record of the crime stored in his brain."

"How accurate is it, and does it obstruct our rights to mental sovereignty and cognitive liberty?"

"In cases where a determination of information present or information absent was made, one hundred percent of—"

The director looked up at his office door. "Yes, what is it?"

"Sorry, Doctor," his assistant said, "but can I see you a moment."

"I'm right in the middle of an interview. Can it wait?"

The woman grimaced. "I'm afraid we've had a break-in." She stood unmoving in the doorway.

The director came to his feet. "When?"

"Apparently over the weekend. The blue safe was broken into."

He came around his desk, eyebrows arched in disbelief. "And the contents?"

"Ten-eighty is gone."

"My God!"

"Is everything all right, grandfather?" The girl closed her computer.

"Wait here."

"May I go with you?"

His mind was focused on the break-in, and it took him a moment to respond. "Stay by my side."

The three marched down a long hall lined with glass panes—offices on one side and a series of medical examination rooms on the other.

Arriving at a heavily fortified set of double doors, the director swiped his ID card before entering. Continuing along another corridor, this one lined with doors but no windows, they finally entered a large room marked *Evidence* at the end of the hall.

Endless shelving held thousands of legal-size boxes. At the back of the room, the director and his assistant stopped where a handful of other lab technicians dressed in white medical coats had already gathered.

Sitting on the floor against the wall was a blue safe about the size of a kitchen dishwasher—its door agape. It contained only one shelf, which was empty.

The director glared at the safe while he pulled nervously at his mustache. "It *would* have to be ten-eighty."

"What is it?" His granddaughter touched his arm. "What was stolen?"

The assistant turned to her. "The human remains of ten-eighty."

"Was ten-eighty someone famous?"

The director hesitated, then stared into the eyes of his granddaughter. "Infamous."

AMBUSH
1876, NEAR THE ARIZONA TERRITORY-MEXICAN BORDER

Groves climbed to the top of a rocky outcrop and cupped his hands around his eyes. The glare from the morning sun blazing over the mountain peaks made it painful to keep them open. He had left Calabazas before dawn with his newly purchased wagon, mules, and supplies. Ten miles from town, as he entered the foothills of the mountains, he pulled up in a ravine and climbed to the top of the outcrop. Squinting, he saw a faint trace of rising dust on the horizon, dancing in the morning light. Two riders.

He knew it would be slow going, and he couldn't outrun them. The wagon could only follow passable trails and roads. He could wait here and make a stand. But they wouldn't try anything until they were sure he had led them to the source of the Spanish gold. Instead, he would let them follow him deep into the mountains, perhaps even to the lost valley. He needed to get them to a place where their bodies would never be found.

After three days, Groves entered a mountain pass that he remembered was a few miles north of the lost valley. Mercifully, he had seen no sign of the Apaches. Back in Calabazas he'd heard that troops from the Sixth Cavalry out of nearby Fort Huachuca had captured or killed a large war party. He hoped it was what was left of the Indians who had ambushed the Federales. Only a handful of them had returned to the cave that day and died in the earthquake. If the Apaches were out of the way, things could be a lot easier and safer. But Groves was sure that if any of the Indians were still around, the last thing they would do would be abandon their treasure.

Then again, it occurred to him that they may not want the treasure for its value as much as to simply steal it from the white man, depriving their enemy of having it. If the Indians meant to trade or sell any of it, they would have done so long ago. And who would they sell to? Still, he planned to keep a sharp eye out for any signs of those murdering savages.

As for the two riders, they kept their distance, lagging back until they became no more than shadowy forms among the mountain trails and forests.

Groves backed his wagon into a well-concealed gap between two rock walls. He unhitched his mules and removed the tools and supplies. Strapping the equipment onto the backs of the two animals, he filled his backpack with enough food for three or four days. He had his Colt Schofield .45 and had bought a Sharps "Big

Fifty" buffalo rifle with a scope from the blacksmith in Calabazas—a guaranteed kill at one-thousand yards. With everything ready, he and his mules began the hike up the winding trail over the last few miles to the lost valley and the Apache gold.

Groves entered the valley mid-morning. It was as he remembered. He saw the thick stand of trees at the base of the cliff hiding the narrow gap and entrance to the cave. Many of the trees were leaning at odd angles or toppled over. Debris from the earthquake cluttered the valley floor. The river had reestablished its course and seemed to be flowing unhindered.

Groves led his pack mules into the trees and tied them up. Even from a distance, he smelled the stench of decomposing flesh—the banditos and Apaches along with their horses. By the time he worked his way to the clearing at the base of the cliff, he found the source of the stench. Although wild animals and buzzards had feasted on the bodies, there were still plenty of remains left to cause bile to rise in his throat. It was all he could do to keep from puking.

He slipped past the corpses to the base of the cliff. A portion of the rock wall had collapsed in the tremors, and the narrow gap in the cliff leading to the cave entrance was partially blocked. He climbed to the top of the rock pile and looked down at the passage—it was clear. In the shadows beyond was the entrance to the treasure cave. As long as the cave had not collapsed, all he needed was to blast away the obstructions at the base of the cliff and get on with his task.

Groves had already decided to start with the gold dust—something that was untraceable and easy to exchange for money. Once he had enough he would buy up a parcel of land near Calabazas and build a house with some sort of fortified structure to store the other treasure. And from there, he could expand into ranching, cattle, maybe even mining. Pykes could help him with that.

Judging from his memory of the treasure, he felt it could possibly take as many as a dozen trips. But that long a stretch might be too dangerous. He reconciled himself to the fact that he'd just get as much out as quickly as he could. With a smile of satisfaction, he climbed down and moved back into the trees, retrieved his two mules, and continued south out of the lost valley. By this time tomorrow, he would be ready to deal with the two riders.

Groves lay on the same ledge overlooking Renegade Pass from where he had witnessed the massacre of the Mexican soldiers. It was late afternoon and the shadows grew long and dark. His neckerchief, wrapped around his nose and mouth, filtered the nauseating stench of the rotting corpses below. Tired from the long trip, he was about to doze off when he heard the clatter of hooves. The sound preceded the rider long before he appeared around a bend in the canyon. Only one man.

Groves wondered if this was one of the two men trailing him or someone else. Had the pair decided to let one go into the pass first to see what would happen? What if they had found his tracks leading into the trees back at the lost valley?

Maybe he was about to be ambushed.

He slipped the .50 caliber shell into the single-shot Sharps and used the scope to bring the rider into the crosshairs. Groves pictured the stacks of gold in his mind, held his breath, and squeezed the trigger.

In the confines of the canyon walls, the Big Fifty sounded like a cannon, its echo seeming to go on forever before finally mingling with the echo of the galloping horse's hooves on the stone. The riderless animal ran south and finally disappeared around a bend. Through the scope, Groves saw the crumpled body of the rider on the ground. Even at a distance, it was obvious that the big gun had blown off most of the man's head.

"Sorry, mister," Groves whispered. "Them's the breaks."

He waited motionless, listening for sounds of the other rider. All he heard was the whistle of the wind through the pass. He wondered if he should go after the dead man's horse, but decided against it. If he showed up back in town with the man's mount, there would be too many questions. He'd have to be satisfied with his two mules for now. Soon, he could afford as many mules and horses as he wanted.

Groves stood and slung the Big Fifty over his shoulder. He was about to make his way back along the ridge to where the mules waited behind a thick grouping of trees when he heard the crunch of boots on loose rock.

"Murderin' bastard!" A man stepped from the trees.

Groves dragged in a breath at the sight of the Colt in the man's hand. "Listen, mister—"

"Where's the gold?" The cowboy's eyes burned with malice.

"What gold?"

"Don't play dumb with me." He took a step forward.

"Don't do nothin' foolish." Groves raised his hands. "We can make a deal."

The stranger took another step forward. As he did, one of the mules wandered out of the trees—it had come untied. The cowboy turned at the sound.

Groves pulled his pistol and fired, hitting the man square in the chest, a cloud of smoke belching from the barrel of his Schofield .45. He watched the cowboy collapse to his knees, eyes now filled with fear. Groves raised his gun to fire again. But as the man fell forward, he squeezed off a single shot.

Billy Groves felt the impact of the bullet slam into his gut like a white-hot sledgehammer. In disbelief, he dropped onto the rocky ledge.

THE STRANGER

2012, MIAMI

SENECA AWOKE AT MID-MORNING instead of her usual 6:30. She'd gotten to bed late, but still it was unusual for her to sleep in. The medications must have done their job. She lay in bed staring blankly with a jumble of thoughts. Daniel, the whole scene in Mexico, the SUV with the orange fog lights, lost luggage, and that message on the machine.

Groaning, she rolled away from the window and the light that sliced through the blinds. She tried to go back to sleep, but her internal clock was set to 6:30 and she'd already blown past that. Still, she didn't want to get up. The day was just going to be shitty anyway, so why bother.

Thirty minutes later she finally lugged herself out of bed.

The shower helped wash away the uncontrolled crying, but not the heartbreak of knowing that when she got out, she would still be alone. Her mother would have ordered her to get up, go outside, and blow the stink off. Brenda Hunt had a way of going straight to the core.

As Seneca dressed, she started forming a mental checklist of the day's tasks. She had already spoken with her editor a number of times from her hospital room in Mexico. Even though she wanted to go back to work right away, he had insisted on her recuperating at home, then slowly getting back into her routine when she was mentally and physically ready. She promised him that a story would come out of all this, but his response was to let it go, "You don't have enough for a story," he told her—always his favorite line to push her harder for more material. So her first order of business was to call and check on her luggage. If the bags were found, at least she would have some of her data to use for the article.

Five minutes later, after getting the bad news, Seneca dropped the receiver in the cradle. She was usually good with hunches, and her best intuition was that her bags weren't delayed, they were lost for good. Was this the way the rest of the day would go?

She felt as if she were slightly hung over, sluggish, depressed, and she anticipated the onset of a bad headache. Maybe taking a combo of the medications had been bad judgment. In the bathroom, she cupped her hand under the faucet and took a drink. After an English muffin washed down with Diet Coke, she dressed, donning a baseball cap to hide the scalp wound, and headed out. Might as well get the most painful task of the day over with first.

"How's my mother doing?" Seneca spoke to the short, pudgy nurse whom she had come to know since her mother's admission to the facility six months prior.

"Some days are better than others."

"And today?"

The nurse shrugged.

Seneca gave her an "I understand" nod and continued down the hall of the Park View Nursing Home to her mother's room. God, she hated these kinds of places and had detested having to put her mother in one. But inevitably it came to the point that for her mother's safety and well-being, it had to be done.

Brenda sat in a chair by the window, staring out, a stuffed toy dog in her lap, clear tubing just under her nostrils delivering oxygen. She was frail, and her skin papery, blotched with deep purple bruises; a result of the prednisone medication. A tray sat on the stand beside the bed, food untouched. The room smelled of stale perspiration.

"Mom?" Her mother turned, and Seneca's heart sank. She could read the disconnect in her mother's eyes. Residing in those gray eyes that had once been a sky blue was a haze that probably mimicked the fog in her head.

"Belle, did you bring the cards?" Her voice sounded hoarse and weaker than normal.

Seneca's body responded with a demand for a large intake of breath. She took the breath and spoke on the outflow. "Mom, it's me, Seneca." She drew close and stooped beside her mother.

Brenda tilted her head. "The cards? We can't play without the cards."

Seneca had often listened to her mother reminisce of Belle, another free spirit in a passel of Brenda's college friends who had, among many other adventures like sit-ins and protest marches, headed to Woodstock back in 1969 for three days of peace, love, music—and of course drugs. Breakfast in bed for 400,000, her mother liked to say. That was a quote from somebody, but she could never remember who said it at the festival. The other favorite cliché was that if you remembered the sixties, you weren't really there.

It was hard to look at her mother now—hair completely gray and unkempt, arthritic knobs on her finger joints, sagging flesh along the jaw line, the raspy voice of an ex-smoker, and those vacant eyes. Her lips were dry and cracking. Long gone was any trace of the vibrant, passionate woman's activist with a taste for the wild side.

"No, Mom, it's me." She gently held her mother's chin with her hand to keep her attention. "It's Seneca. Your daughter. Why aren't you eating? We talked about this last time I was here. Remember?"

She knew her mother was somewhat of a drama queen and not eating might be a ploy for attention. For an instant a mix of anger and frustration flared inside. "You know the emphysema isn't going to kill you, you're going to let yourself get so damn weak—"

Seneca hadn't come to fuss with or chide her mother. It just made her so angry that she was losing the only person left on the planet who loved her or gave a shit about her—at least Brenda *had* at one time when her mind...

Her mother stared blankly, and Seneca couldn't help but ask, "How did you stay so tough all your life? What is it that kept you so confident and independent? Until you got sick I never saw a flicker of doubt in yourself, or a moment of indecision. Always so damn strong. Why didn't I get those genes? Sometimes I think I'm going to cave in." She turned away from Brenda. "Shit, who am I kidding? I'm a train wreck." She stifled her tears. "Mom, Daniel—"

"I think Belle cheats. But I let her win. It's important to her that she wins." Just those few words left Brenda sounding winded.

After several more seconds Seneca released her mother's chin and took her boney hand. "Are they taking care of you, Momma? Are you having a good day?"

"Yes, but I was hoping to play cards."

Seneca moved to the edge of the bed and sat. "I hope you're having a good day." She patted her mother's hand. "I think you'd be proud of me. I had one helluva couple of weeks, but I'm still vertical." That was a dumb saying, she thought, but true.

It was so odd trying to engage Brenda in conversation when the woman didn't even recognize her. Her mother had become a stranger. There were days she had unpredicted moments of clarity. At first there had been stretches of lucidity, but those dwindled over the years to what were now infrequent sparks that the disease quickly extinguished.

Seneca had no idea how to hook a tiny part of her mother's mind and pull it into reality. After a brief pause, she started again. "I just got back from Mexico. Do you remember I told you Dan and I were going to get married down there? Do you remember that?"

"Did you order the ear candles?"

Seneca scored her bottom lip. Before the diagnosis of Alzheimer's, her mother had owned a New Age and alternative medicine shop. Ear candles were a part of the inventory.

"Yes. They've been shipped." *A white lie.* The shop was sold over a year ago. It had never been lucrative, but it paid the bills. She looked at her mother and felt that now-familiar uneasy churning inside. "But I'll double-check on it to be sure. Wouldn't want to be without ear candles."

Seneca stood, bent, and kissed the top of her mother's head. "I love you, Momma," she whispered. "And miss you."

"And don't forget the Echinacea. Flu season is coming."

"Right." Seneca paused. "I'll take care of everything."

"I'm so thirsty."

Seneca reached for the plastic water pitcher on the nightstand. It was empty. Not only empty, but desert dry. When was the last time it had been filled? She lifted the plastic cup and found it in the same condition. "Son-of-a bitch."

She grabbed both the pitcher and cup. "I'll go get you some water."

Brenda Hunt smiled at someone, but Seneca knew it wasn't at her.

Down the hall, Seneca parked herself in front of the nurses' station. "Excuse me." She glared at a young nurse who was on her cell phone, head coyly cocked to the side and giggling. "Excuse me." This time in a louder tone.

The nurse flipped her phone closed.

"My mother doesn't have any water." Her voice was low and calculated sounding.

"Someone will be around shortly."

"No." Her pitch and volume rose. "Not shortly. She hasn't had any water since God knows when, and she's very thirsty."

"We make our rounds. You realize she's not the only patient here. We do the best we can."

Seneca slammed the pitcher and cup on the station desk. "The goddamn pitcher hasn't had water in it for hours, maybe days for all I know. What else does she do without? She doesn't eat. Doesn't anybody care? I can't stay here all day, every day, to ensure she gets the care she needs—that's what I pay you for."

"Ms. Hunt, just calm down."

Seneca spun around to find that the voice came from the older nurse she'd encountered when she'd arrived.

"All I want is some peace of mind. I want to know that when I leave here someone takes care of my mother. Someone has some kind of compassion for her. Did she eat today? Did you change her diaper?"

"We all—"

Seneca made her voice slide down into a calmer zone. "Just get her a pitcher of water, all right? If that's not too much trouble?"

"I'll see to it right now." The nurse took the cup and pitcher from her.

Seneca turned and marched down the hall. Before she headed out to her car she entered the Park View accounting office and wrote a check for the fee to keep her mother's crappy care going another month. In the parking lot, she put the key in the ignition, but didn't turn it. Instead, she braced her arms on the steering wheel and rested her forehead on them. She needed to get her mother into a better facility. But that was going to be expensive. Although her salary at the magazine was good, it wasn't great. The lease was up on her apartment; she couldn't afford the new place that she and Dan were to share, and didn't think she could get the deposit back. And what if she couldn't renew her lease?

One thing for sure, sitting here mulling over every little thing wasn't helping. "Blow the stink off, Seneca." She sat upright and turned the key. "Take the world head on, one task at a time, one day at a time."

The things she still had on her checklist to deal with that morning were finding out about the apartment lease, and making a decision on what to do about that message on her answer phone.

Ten minutes later, Seneca turned her C70 into the parking garage of her apartment complex. Suddenly, she jammed on the brakes.

"I don't believe it!" Backed into her parking spot was a dark-colored Mercedes SUV with orange fog lamps.

LUCKY MAN
1876, NORTHERN SONORA, MEXICO

GROVES OPENED HIS EYES. The full moon was directly overhead. Something had awakened him. But he couldn't remember—

Growling! The sound came from close by. Two, maybe three animals.

He sat up. In the gunmetal-gray light of the moon, a pair of coyotes stood over the corpse of the cowboy he had shot, their eyes catching the light, bared canines glistening.

He moved his hand to his .45. Gripping it firmly, he was about to aim at the animals when a fierce cry broke the midnight air. The coyotes lifted their heads and sniffed—their threatening postures melting. It was a mountain lion, and it was close.

A second shriek, this time only yards away. The coyotes bolted for the trail leading down from the ridge to the wash below.

Groves got to his feet, ready to fire if the big cat approached. He knew it had come for the body of the—

"What the hell!" He looked down and grabbed his abdomen. Dried blood caked his shirt. The cowboy had shot him, he remembered. The pain had been enormous, the impact sending him to the ground. There was no way he could have survived his guts being ripped apart. And yet...

He probed the bullet hole in his shirt, confirming that he had definitely been shot. He lifted the shirt and ran his fingers over his belly. Tender to the touch and still sore, but the wound was almost healed!

Out of the corner of his eye, Groves caught the cat on the move. It leapt silently from the ledge, landing a short distance from the dead man. The animal crouched low, poised, one front paw barely off the ground. Groves stood still, holding his breath. Then the cat slinked toward the cowboy's body. And toward Groves.

Keeping his eyes on the cat, Groves slid his hand down his side until he grasped the grip of the .45.

BOOM!

He fired the Schofield. The blast thundered across Renegade Pass and echoed off the rock walls causing the mountain lion to retreat toward the higher ledges, disappearing into the darkness. The bullet had missed, but at least the animal was gone.

Trying to gather his thoughts, Groves slung the Big Fifty over his shoulder. He moved into the clump of trees searching for his mules. No luck. In the moonlight he made his way down the narrow path to the floor of the wash. One of his mules lay dead—probably panicked and tumbled off the cliff trying to escape the initial shootout. The other was nowhere around. It was vital that he not only find it, but now he needed another animal as well—the wagon required two to pull it. Maybe one of the cowboys' mounts was still nearby.

As Groves headed south along the rocky wash, he rubbed his stomach, trying to figure out why there was dried blood but hardly a trace of the wound. How could he still be alive? One miracle was incredible, but two …

Maybe he was dead and didn't even know it.

At sunrise, Groves located his mule in a box canyon south of Renegade Pass. Soon afterward, he saw one of the two riders' horses. He would have to do some explaining back in town about how he came across the horse. Could say it was a stroke of luck that after his mule was snake bit and died, he found the horse wandering in a ravine.

He mounted up, and with the mule in tow, headed back north through the pass. As he slowly made his way along the wash and what was left of the dead Federales, he glanced up in the direction of the high ridge. The flutter of black wings told him vultures were already feasting on the cowboy he had shot. A short distance later, he came across the body of the first cowboy—the head wound from the Big Fifty was even more destructive than Groves had thought. After all, it could bring down buffalo with one shot. The vultures that gathered around the corpse angrily moved out of the way long enough for Groves to pass. Looking over his shoulder, he saw them flapping and hopping back to continue their feast.

Groves waited at the edge of the trees and glanced in both directions along the lost valley. The call of a single crow, the distant ripple of the creek, and the whisper of the wind were the sounds he heard. Nothing moved in either direction.

He turned and walked through the trees to the clearing at the foot of the cliff. A few moments earlier he had placed the dynamite sticks at the base of the rock pile covering the passage leading to the cave. Now he bent, struck a match on the rocks, and lit the fuse. He stood watching it burn for a few seconds before trotting back through the trees to a brush field a hundred yards away.

"Get ready, boys." He called out as he ran to where his mule and the horse were tethered to a stump. If his other mule had bolted at gunfire, no telling what these two might do with an explosion.

Thirty seconds later, a muffled boom sounded from the direction of the trees, the ground vibrated, and a cloud of dust swirled up over the treetops before the breeze swept it away.

"Let's go see our handiwork." He untied the two animals, gathered their reins, and led them toward the trees. A few moments later, he stood staring at the pile of rubble blown out by the charge. The opening to the narrow passage was almost totally free of obstructions. More good fortune.

Groves tied up the animals and headed along the narrow gap in the rocks until he came to the cave entrance. He found the torch, lit it, and entered the Apache treasure trove. Soon he stood gazing in wonder at the piles of gold, the treasure chests, and the hundreds of priceless items collected by the Indians.

As the light of the torch glittered off the precious metal surfaces, Groves took in a deep breath. He felt the hole in his shirt where the bullet had pierced the material.

"I'm one lucky man," he said as he headed toward the bags of gold dust.

AZTECA

2012, BAHAMAS

SCARROW WATCHED ANDROS ISLAND appear out of the gray clouds as rain streaked across the window of the Learjet. The small, six-passenger plane dropped out of the storm and banked hard on its final approach into Andros Town International Airport. Painted on the nose of the aircraft was the gleaming red phoenix bird rising from a flaming inferno.

He glanced over at the opposite seat. The white box, about the size of a microwave oven, sat secured with seatbelts. He could see *São Paulo Institute of Forensic Medicine, specimen 1080* written across the top.

Within minutes, Scarrow stood in the light rain and watched his men place the specimen box into the trunk of the Bentley Continental GT. Keeping Scarrow dry by holding an umbrella over his head was his chief of staff, Coyotl. Closing the trunk, Coyotl protected Scarrow from the rain while he got into the driver's side. Then he went around and slipped into the passenger's seat. Scarrow shifted the Bentley into drive and shot across the tarmac to the two-lane highway heading north.

Coyotl was on his cell phone discussing dinner arrangements with the kitchen staff. Scarrow glanced over at the handsome young Mexican who had been with the Ministry for more than five years. He oversaw Scarrow's personal affairs while handling any special projects that arose, including the recent event in Mexico City. Scarrow recruited Coyotl from a list of native Aztecs and chose him based upon several reasons, one of which was his graduate degree in Latin American history and his textbook knowledge of the ancient Aztec empire. His loyalty had proven invaluable on many occasions.

It didn't take more than ten minutes before the black step-pyramid-shaped building appeared out of the rainy mist. During the 1970s, the industrial giant, Groves Lumber, had deforested much of the indigenous pine forests that grew on North Andros. Now replanted pines covered the landscape like rows of dark green soldiers. And in the distance, built deep in the pine forest was Azteca, his home—a six-story monument that reached to the heavens like the great Aztec pyramids of his native Mexico. Soon he saw the high wall surrounding Azteca with its intricately carved ancient pictographs and glyphs. He turned into the entrance gate as it swung open—his armed security guards saluting.

Coyotl finished his call while the Bentley glided along the mile-long, palm-lined entrance road. "Imported Beijing duck with your favorite hot and spicy soup from Singapore. And Tiger beer."

"A wonderful homecoming meal." Scarrow reached to push a button on the console, causing one of the dozen garage doors to open along the ground floor of Azteca. He pulled the Bentley inside and shut off the 550hp engine. The garage fell silent. "How is William doing?"

"Restless and short tempered." He turned to face Scarrow. "But at least he's taking his meds."

"And our newest guest?"

"Mary is like a child on Christmas morning. Everything is one amazing discovery after another. Her eyes are filled with excitement."

"What about the rest of the apostles?"

"Growing more confident every day in their new roles."

Scarrow's voice changed and had an intimidating edge to it. "And the status of the survivor in Mexico City?"

Coyotl nodded apologetically. "I hope to have that matter cleaned up soon. It was a miscalculation on my part."

"Find her and take care of the problem." He turned the conversation. "Have the men remove the box from the trunk and secure it in the lab. Schedule a meeting with the reconstructive surgeons first thing tomorrow morning. There's much still left to do."

Scarrow opened the door to the anteroom of the penthouse suite on the top floor of Azteca. The movement of the door automatically set off the fans blowing out the intruding air that came in with Scarrow. A sanitizing chemical sprayed through misting nozzles creating a haze. Scarrow put on a pair of disposable green booties from a pop-up dispensary. He slit open a shrink-wrapped package with the accompanying small blade and extracted a green paper gown he slipped on over his clothes. Ready, he opened the stainless door and entered the suite. The heavy door closed behind him with a whoosh of compressed air.

Scarrow waited until his eyes adjusted to the dimly lit living room—the air conditioning was set so low, he could almost see his breath. Thick blackout drapes covered the wide expanse of plate-glass windows across the far wall.

The air smelled antiseptic, not unlike a hospital. It mixed with the scent of Indian incense, strong and pungent. The smoke from the incense slightly fogged the room, almost like standing amidst clouds. A sound machine somewhere in a far corner created the constant drones of an Australian didgeridoo and bullroarer.

Scarrow moved through the rooms until he came to the bedroom, its door ajar. He pushed on it enough to enter. In the center of the room was a canopy bed with fine netting hanging down from the support frame to cover all sides. The scent of the incense caused him to cough. Hundreds of candles burned around the room on stands and tables. Their light made the room ethereal.

Scarrow walked to the side of the bed and waited.

"They're not boiling my water long enough for my tea." The voice came from behind the netting.

"They use distilled water." Scarrow heard a grunt of disapproval. "And they boil it for thirty minutes before brewing."

As his eyes grew accustomed to the low light, he saw the man sit up and maneuver toward the edge of the bed. A skeleton-like hand parted the seam in the diaphanous netting and a moment later, he stood a few feet away from Scarrow.

Billy Groves was tall and frail, clad in a white long-sleeved shirt and boxer shorts, his bare legs stuffed into cowboy boots. A week's growth of beard made his face look pasty white. Tired eyes gazed out from under bushy brows as he moved to a chair and sat.

"How are you feeling, William?"

"Someone is trying to poison me."

"Why do you say that?"

"Have you tasted the food?"

"It's the same food we've been serving you since we moved here. No one is trying to poison you."

"I think it's the fucking Apaches. They want to punish me."

"There are no Apaches, at least not in the Bahamas."

"Has anyone been around asking about the gold?"

"No."

"We can't let them know about it."

"The gold is long gone, William." He walked over to Groves, reached out and felt his pulse.

"I don't like it here. I want to move back to my ranch in Arizona. Even that place in Greece or the island in Thailand was better than this."

"The ranch was sold thirty years ago." Scarrow released Groves's wrist. "Are you taking all your medications?"

"I don't like them."

"They keep you calm and level-headed. Lowers your anxiety. You need to take them. You know how depressed you can get."

"What happened to the gold?"

"You know exactly what happened to it."

"Where's the veil? It's not in the vault. What have you done with it?"

"It's somewhere safe. Nothing for you to worry about."

"Why is it so hot in here?"

"It's freezing, William. I need to wear a parka when I come in here."

He stared with compassion at William "Billy" Groves who had allowed his 170 years to intrude on his sanity. Yet he himself had managed for nearly 500 years without such consequences. But Scarrow understood the difference. Unlike Groves's, his immortality came with purpose. And at last, it was coming to completion.

"They're not boiling my water long enough." Groves glanced around nervously as if expecting others to appear out of the shadows. Then he looked directly at Scarrow. "I want to know where the veil is. And what are you doing with those people?"

"What people?"

"The ones you're digging up?"

TOO LATE
2012, MIAMI

SENECA'S BREATH DAMMED UP for a moment before she composed herself. It was probably just a coincidence, and she scolded herself for entertaining the idea that this Mercedes was the same one that followed her last night. She pulled into a nearby visitor's spot and waited, unable to tell if there was anyone inside the car or not because of the dark-tinted windows. *Weren't windows that dark against the law?* After several minutes she seized her courage, got out, and approached the SUV. It sure looked like the same car that had spooked her the previous night. But there were plenty of Mercedes SUVs on the roads in South Florida.

Standing beside the driver's door she tapped on the window. Getting no response, she put her hand to the glass and peered inside. The car was empty. Nothing appeared out of the ordinary.

Shaking off the twinge of worry, Seneca returned to her car and collected her things. She entered the building and climbed the steps to her apartment, keys jangling at her side. At her door, she inserted the key in the deadbolt, but found it already unlocked, causing her to back away. Maybe she wasn't paranoid. Should she call 911? What if she simply forgot to lock the deadbolt? She couldn't remember if she had or not. If she called the police wouldn't she look stupid if she just hadn't locked the door? Seneca reached for the knob and turned it, then thrust the door open.

A man sat on her couch, and she was sure she recognized the face from pictures—the face that belonged to the voice on her answer machine. She took what felt like a scalding gulp of air.

The man stood. He was well over six feet and beneath his starched shirt and pleated trousers appeared to be a trim body in good shape—especially for his age. Silver salted his close-cropped dark hair, particularly heavy at the temples. Few lines creased the olive skin of his face.

"Hello, Seneca. I hope I didn't startle you. I'm your—"

Seneca clenched her teeth, then blew a puff of breath. "I know exactly who you are. What do you want?"

"I anticipated this would be awkward, but I was hoping for the best. I understand why you feel the way you do, but I *am* your father."

Seneca tossed her keys and purse on a table by the door. "No, to me that word implies parenting."

Alberto Palermo rolled his eyes. "You prefer your mother's terms? Sperm donor? Gamete giver?"

"I don't prefer anything. I never had a father."

Al's eyes closed and opened in a slow, painful-looking blink. "No, I suppose you think not. That was your mother's choice. You know that you were never off my mind. How many letters, how many cards did I send? Did I ever forget a birthday? I was never even sure your mother passed those things along to you as I asked her to. I hoped she would."

A tiny pang of guilt plunged through Seneca, but it only lasted a second. Her mother had passed his communications along, and Seneca kept every one of his letters, now stored away in the box in her closet. But he'd never called. Many of his last letters had asked to see her, but he had left that option up to her. She declined by not responding.

"How's your mother doing?"

"Why don't you pay her a visit? Mom's here in town, only a few minutes away. I'll give you her address and you can pull a surprise visit just like this one." She felt the heat rise in her face.

Al held up both hands, palms toward her. "Can you dump the hostility for a minute?"

She gave out a snide laugh. "Just like that? You've never been a part of my life—ever—then out of the blue I get a message that you are coming to see me, and you didn't even have the decency to wait for my reply or invitation. You break into my apartment and then have the audacity to ask me to drop the hostility?" Seneca flipped her hair back with a toss of her head. "Big brass ones, that's what you've got."

"Seneca, I've tried and tried to talk to you for years. But your mother preferred that I didn't. I know I'm going against her wishes, but I'm not getting any younger. I knew you wouldn't invite me in if I knocked on your door. You've made that clear by never answering my letters. I was willing to take the risk, knowing you'd be angry. So I—"

"Broke in. Since you obviously know how I feel, why don't you just leave before I call the police and have you arrested for breaking and entering?"

"Don't you want to know why I'm here?"

"Oh, I know exactly why. You feel guilt for abandoning me. Now, after so many years, you want to, what, hang out together? Do some father-daughter stuff? That should make up for everything. Am I close?"

"I do want to make things right with us. That much is correct. But I know what you've just been through. I thought you might need a little help—a friend. Not only that, but I want to make sure your mother is properly cared for before she—"

"Dies? My mother died a year ago when she finally got to the point that she couldn't remember who I was. On that day, I became an orphan." Seneca felt as if a kink had knotted in her throat. But she'd be damned if she'd choke up or cry in front of this man.

Al glanced down before returning his gaze to her. "I just want to help."

"I don't need your help."

"A lot has happened since I last saw your mother. But I've thought of her—and of you—every day. Seneca, there's a great deal you don't know." He paused a moment, looking at her before continuing. "I remember the day you were born. I was there. Did she tell you that?"

She didn't answer. Her mother had never mentioned one way or the other.

"You are right about one thing. I want to try to start over, to be your father, to get to know my daughter. I can never get those years back, only the days to come."

"Are you dying or something? Need one of my kidneys?"

Al laughed. "God, you're just like Brenda. Quick on the uptake and cynical. No, I'm not dying, and I don't need you to donate an organ. I've always wanted to be a part of your life, it's just that—"

"Then you should have been. And if you haven't heard the saying, cynics are only wounded romantics."

"Like I said, that was always your mother's choice."

Knowing Brenda, Seneca didn't doubt him. The only revelations her mother had shared about Al Palermo were that the two had met at Woodstock in 1969, had a hell of a weekend together and the sex was fantastic. Why her mother would want to share the part about the sex, she couldn't understand. But that was the way her mother was—brash and bold, and open, holding nothing back. Then her mother and Al had met again at the Democratic National Convention seven years later. They had a serious affair that lasted for over a year and left Brenda pregnant with Seneca. After that, the stories her mother told of Al disappeared from Brenda's shared memories as if he ceased to exist. The only thing she would say was that Al had betrayed her. No other details.

"If you had really wanted to stay in my life, you could have found a way. You could've done better than letters, photos, and birthday cards. Did you think I was supposed to treasure them? They were from someone I didn't even know, someone I'd never met. They didn't mean jack shit. Just paper. There were lots of avenues you could have pursued. There weren't any legal issues to stop you that I know of."

"No." He shook his head. "None. Just your mother's wishes. She was so independent. Bra-burning Brenda, I used to tease her. She didn't need me—or any man."

Seneca bit back the emotions that came surging up. She *had* treasured all his letters, and that's what gave her so much pain. Through those letters he became real to her, someone she could miss, even long for. But he didn't deserve knowing that. No way was she going to let this man into her life. Not after this long. She had done just fine without him up until now, and didn't dare allow herself to be hurt. If her father swooped into her life now and tomorrow suddenly disappeared… No, she wasn't going to allow herself to be vulnerable.

"You say I should have tried other avenues. That's what I'm doing showing up here."

"It's too late. Just get out."

"You're wrong. You don't know the whole story."

THE FIRST DEAL
1881, NOGALES, ARIZONA TERRITORY

"Gentlemen, this is Charlie Pykes, my partner and general manager of Calabazas Land and Mining Company."

Groves stood under a vibrant yellow-blooming Palo Verde tree inside the fortified walls that surrounded his ranch house. The structure was a ten-room adobe with twenty-five-inch-thick walls. It sat on a hill commanding panoramic views in all directions. Located near the junction of Potrero Creek and the Santa Cruz River, it presented an imposing form to anyone who ventured near. And if they did, they were usually met by one of Groves's fifty *vaqueros*—men known to be as good with a gun as with a lariat. His *vaqueros* were responsible for protecting Groves and his five thousand head of cattle from rustlers and random skirmishes with the Apaches. Unknown to the *vaqueros*, they also protected the ranch house's large basement that was filled with the treasures from the Apache cave. With the help of Charlie Pykes, the assayer Groves first met when he cashed in the original Spanish gold coins, he had exchanged much of the gold and silver taken from the mountain trove and deposited funds in bank accounts in San Francisco, St. Louis, and Chicago. With a portion, he bought up hundreds of thousands of acres throughout the southern Arizona territory. On more than one occasion, Pykes had declared that Billy Groves was a natural at investments.

Groves watched as Pykes stepped forward and shook the hands of LeLand Simpson and Matthew Hopkins.

"Pleased to meet you." Pykes gave each man a courteous nod.

Simpson and Hopkins were entrepreneurs helping to finance the Southern Pacific Railroad. Simpson was the railroad's general manager and Hopkins served as legal counsel for Southern Pacific.

As they sat in wooden chairs beneath the yellow tree a Mexican servant brought them lemonade. While he watched each man take a glass, a moment of insecurity flickered through Groves. These two men were some of the richest in the region, bankrolling the railroad as it made its way across Arizona. He was about to make them a crazy offer that could bring him a great deal of money over the long term. And as each day came and went, and he stared in the mirror, Groves had a nagging feeling that he would need long-term investments.

"Your proposition is a bit out of the ordinary, Mr. Groves." Simpson took a sip of his lemonade.

"I think my offer will save your railroad a great deal of money and still bring in a nice little profit for me and my homestead."

"A *little* profit is exactly what it will be," Hopkins said. "First, you want to lease us the easement through your land at half the cost of what your fellow ranchers are asking. And you're only asking us to pay ten cents for every railroad car that passes over your land?"

"Mr. Groves is not a greedy man," Pykes said. "You should take advantage of it."

"Some folks would say we're robbing you, Mr. Groves." Simpson drained his glass. "Seems to me you'd have to live another fifty years or more to see a sizeable return."

Groves smiled. "The only stipulation is that I don't want no time limit on our deal. What did you call it, Charlie?"

"A perpetual royalty, Mr. Groves."

"That's it. A royalty that won't never end. That way my children and their children will have something to count on."

"Well, sir," Simpson said, "if that's what you want, then we're prepared to sign the papers right here and now. Mr. Hopkins has been kind enough to draw them up in advance. Would you care to have your legal counsel review them?"

"Are you an honest man, Mr. Simpson?" Groves looked him in the eye.

"I like to think so."

Hopkins pulled the documents from his inside coat pocket.

"Then there's no need to bring in a lawyer." Groves took the papers and reached out to Pykes, who handed him a fountain pen. "You understand gentlemen that I'm just learning to read and write. So right now, my mark will have to suffice. My partner will witness."

"That's good enough for me." Simpson grinned broadly.

Groves placed an X on the dotted line. "Then it's a deal."

THE PROCEDURE

2012, BAHAMAS

SCARROW WATCHED THE FEED from the genetics lab appearing on the large plasma monitor. The image was of Dr. Raymond Blakely and his team as they stood in ghostly white sterile lab suits opening the box containing specimen 1080. Even with their faces hidden behind hoods and surgical masks, he knew each one. Three years ago Scarrow had supervised their recruitment from top universities and research centers, giving each expert a chance to perform controversial experiments considered illegal in their home countries. Blakely was the former director of stem cell research at the Freeman Institute in La Jolla. Beside him stood experts in plastic and reconstructive surgery, genetics, accelerated tissue regeneration, and molecular biology. There was also the former CEO of the electronics firm that invented *Engage*, the first brain-implanted wireless processor programmed to allow the patient to think in his native language and instantly speak in another. The implanted electrode recorded pulses from the surrounding speech-generating neurons and instantly translated the thoughts into English. And it acted as a gateway interpreter, translating incoming speech into the patient's native tongue.

Each one of the specialists retired or took a leave of absence to come and live inside the Azteca compound. They were given luxurious apartments and state-of-the-art-equipped laboratories. Their bank accounts were filled with more money than they could earn in multiple lifetimes, all secretly funded by the Phoenix Ministry.

Once the doctors and scientists completed their tasks, they would return to their countries, bringing with them the knowledge acquired while working without constraints at Azteca. Scarrow assured them that they would undoubtedly be the future recipients of enormous grants and positions of prestige in the science and medical communities, possibly even considered for the Nobel Prizes in Medicine, Physiology, and Chemistry. Their task was to perfect methods to restore the bodies and give life to the remains of twelve specific specimens. Whatever resources were needed, he supplied his team without question.

The completed project result would be the creation of his twelve Phoenix apostles, the recipients of new lives, new bodies, even new faces. Once trained, the chosen twelve would be sent to their original homelands to perform the human sacrifices needed in bringing the universe back into alignment. And when the day of reckoning passed and his gods were appeased, he would grant his twelve the ultimate reward.

Scarrow sat in a large leather chair in his private observation theater. Sitting beside him, Coyotl spoke quietly on his cell phone with the senior managing director of the Phoenix Ministry in Moscow. He closed the phone.

"There are a few hang-ups securing the final permits to hold the Ministry in Red Square. It will cost us roughly ten percent more than the estimated budget. They have come up with yet another list of city officials who need to be paid off."

"The cost of doing business."

"And for some good news. Your Ministry in Brazil has generated over twenty-five million dollars just since you flew back. They certainly loved you in São Paulo."

"They loved the message."

"And the messenger."

Scarrow never took his eyes off the plasma monitor as the skull of specimen 1080—Josef Mengele, the infamous Nazi concentration camp doctor known as the Angel of Death—was removed from the box. He felt a shudder of excitement when the empty, black sockets seemed for an instant to stare right at him. He wondered what the doctors' reaction would be if they knew whose remains they were handling; a number of the scientists were Jews. He watched as each bone was removed from the box and laid out on a large stainless-steel table under intense surgical lights—every step documented by multiple high-definition cameras and digital recorders.

Scarrow heard the conversation between the doctors as they discussed the condition of the remains and decided which portion of the skeleton would have to be ground up in order to extract the DNA. It was usually a finger or toe—a body part that would unfortunately be missing from the final product. A small price to pay, Scarrow thought.

"All of your apostle selections are interesting," Coyotl said. "Some of them I didn't know a lot about, like Timur and Mary. But so far, I've found them all to be... worthy. And Elizabeth. Her, I really like."

"Don't get too close to any of them, Coyotl. Friendships and relationships will interfere with their training and orientation. I've noticed the way you're coming on to Mary. Satisfy your sexual appetite somewhere else." He took his eyes from the monitor and looked at his chief of staff.

Coyotl gave him a wicked smile. "I think Mary would be an amazing conquest."

"My apostles are off limits."

"Why?"

"When you lay down in a viper pit, you are destined to get bitten."

"We want to try something slightly different this time." Dr. Blakely sat in an expansive dining room with Scarrow, Coyotl, and the rest of the team as they dined on African lobster tails and grilled scallops with Cabernet Sauvignon flown in from Argentina.

"The outcome will not change?" Scarrow asked.

"Of course not. We are way beyond the experimental stages. Although no two regeneration procedures are ever exactly alike, our techniques have proven as reliable as performing a routine organ transplant."

"So what do you want to do differently?"

"Normally, once the DNA is extracted from the sample, we sequence it to recreate the individual's genome. From there we can create a complete set of chromosomes based on the sequence information. Then we package the set of chromosomes into a liposome."

Blakely stopped to take a sip of wine. "Next we irradiate human embryonic stem cells, or H-E-S cells, to eliminate the cells' DNA then fuse the liposome with the stem cells to introduce the corpse's chromosomes. From there we simply expand the H-E-S cells and screen them for a normal complement of chromosomes by standard karyotyping. Next we expand the H-E-S cells, hydrate the corpse with cell culture media, seed the cells into the corpse and let the H-E-S cells use the extracellular matrix scaffold to regenerate the various body tissues. When we incubate the corpse the H-E-S cells will attach, grow, and differentiate into the appropriate tissue—"

Scarrow held up his hand. "Plain English."

"Of course, sorry. We want to form the circulatory system first. We believe this will be a more efficient method and will save time as well. We will start with the heart in order to distribute the nutrients throughout the body. We'll manipulate or treat the H-E-S cells to make heart muscle and endothelial cells. From there, we'll continue formulating the cells to become skeletal muscle and attach to the existing skeleton or regenerate what's missing."

"So no more missing parts?"

"Right, Javier. That's the big difference and a nice side benefit. Our patient doesn't have to go around with a missing toe or finger. We'll formulate cells using our rapid regeneration procedures to make the various organs such as the lungs and liver, grow them in three-dimensional molds of human organs, and finally, we'll treat cells to become nerves to control it all." He smiled proudly and took another sip of wine. "And as before, we'll then revive the patient in the same manner as an ER doctor revives someone in cardiac arrest."

"I trust all of you completely to make the right choices in accomplishing this task." Scarrow acknowledged each man around the table. "You and your amazing team have not let me down, Dr. Blakely."

"Nor do we intend to. You have given us the challenge of a lifetime. A chance to do what most thought was only the domain of science fiction novels. You have given us the opportunity to rebuild a human being from the dust of death. Something each of us is dedicated to, but our research would otherwise be forbidden. You have provided an arena in which we can do the research and experimentation that is needed to extend life and heal those suffering. There is such stigma and so many so-called moral issues surrounding human replication and stem cell research. But here in Azteca, we are proving that it can be done."

Scarrow fought back a smile, knowing that this magnificent medical team had no idea of his grander plan—not just to save human lives, but to literally save the world. "Much like the phoenix rising."

"Exactly," Blakely added. "Just like the phoenix."

"I'm pleased you're continuing to improve the process and are not afraid to try new things. It fortifies my belief I have made a good choice in bringing you all together." Scarrow leaned forward in his chair, his expression serious. "And on that same note, I want to push ahead with two unique requests. First, I would like you to give this latest patient, the one called ten-eighty, the ability to speak in multiple languages."

Blakely turned to the CEO of the electronics firm that designed the *Engage* implant device. The man nodded. "It will take awhile, but it can be done with a bit of reprogramming."

"Good. But my second and biggest challenge to you is to give the subject a unique facial structure."

One of two reconstructive plastic surgeons replied, "*Any* specifications or just to our fancy as you've allowed us to do with the others?"

"Oh, no. I have something specific in mind this time." Reaching into his briefcase sitting on the floor by his side, Scarrow removed a folder. He slid it across the table toward the plastic surgeon. "I want you to make the patient look like this."

The doctor opened the folder and studied the photograph of a man's face. With an expression of shock mixed with wonder, he stared at Scarrow. "You must be joking."

TIGRESS OF ČACHTICE

2012, MIAMI

"LISTEN ..." SENECA HESITATED, stumbling over how to refer to her father.

"Start with Al. Maybe one day we'll work up to Dad."

"I don't think so."

"You don't need to go through all this alone. Let me help?"

She shook her head, agitated that he attempted to slip so easily into a fatherly role. "You haven't heard a thing I've said." She went to the door to open it.

"I can see my way out." He moved in her direction, stopping next to her. "Listen, little one, I'm not here to complicate your life. There's much more to all this than you realize. I'll give you some space to hash everything over in your head. But I'll be back in touch."

"Just go."

"I left my card on the kitchen counter. My cell number is on it. Call anytime." He turned and walked out.

When the door closed she headed to the kitchen and poured herself a dose of Seagrams VO, neat. It burned all the way down in two gulps. She poured another shot and took a sip. That should help. Moving back into the living room, she settled into the couch cushions, rolled her head, feeling her neck and shoulder muscles resist with tension—the ever-present reminder of her Mexico City injuries.

Al's parting words gave her an idea, not about him, but about Mexico and finding out who was responsible for Daniel's death. If she could come up with some plausible story to continue the project with her boss at *Planet Discovery*, she could keep trying to track down who had killed Daniel. She retrieved her purse and dug through it coming up with the small business card holder. Flipping through the cards she finally held onto one and pitched the others on the couch. She figured TV *Mexicali* might be the only possible route.

She dialed the number for the Mexican television network. "Can I please speak with the remote production director?"

"*Un minuto, por favor.*"

The line switched to an audio live news feed when she was put on hold. Several minutes passed before a man said, "*Éste es Enrique.*"

"You are the remote production director?"

"Yes." He answered with a slight accent. "Can I help you?"

"I hope so. My name is Seneca Hunt. I'm the journalist who was in Mexico City covering the excavation of Montezuma's tomb. Unfortunately, as you know, there was the terrible explosion. I lost all of my audiotapes of the interviews I did with the archaeologist, Dr. Bernal. I was wondering if TV *Mexicali* had salvaged anything.

Anything at all. Maybe something that was sent electronically or uploaded before the explosion."

"We were disappointed that we did not recover anything, and we did not have any data transmitted back to the studios prior to the incident."

Seneca looked at the card again. "Do you know how I can get in touch with Carlos Moctezuma? He was a tech assistant at the location shoot."

The line was silent for a moment. "Señorita Hunt, I'm sorry... it is our understanding that you were the only survivor."

Seneca touched her hand to her mouth to hush the surprise in her voice. "Oh, my. I didn't know. I thought Carlos left before the explosion. Please give my condolences to his friends and family." Slowly she settled the receiver into the cradle. Carlos had been her last hope for copies or backups of the tapes that might contain some obscure clue tucked away in them that could lead to those responsible for the bombing and why. Something she missed or didn't seem important at the time. But this was turning out to be a dead end.

Curling her legs under her, she drank half the shot of whiskey, then rested the side of her head on the back couch cushion. Things were going from bad to worse. Daniel was gone. Her mother's care was less than satisfactory. Soon, she might be out of a place to live. Her luggage was lost. Her father showed up out of the blue. And nothing remained of her notes and interviews.

This might be a good day to just go back to bed. Seneca started to rise, then noticed a new message on the answer phone. She hoped it wasn't another from her father. She clicked the *play message* button, then hung her finger over *erase.*

"Hello, Ms. Hunt. My name is Matt Everhart. You don't know me but I'm a fellow writer. I read on the Internet about what happened to you in Mexico. Listen, the reason I'm calling is, well, it's probably just a coincidence, but thought you might be interested in what I recently discovered at Čachtice Castle in Slovakia while doing research for my next novel. I'll try calling you again later, or you can give me a call. I live in the Keys so I'm not that far if after talking you'd like to meet. My cell number should be on your caller ID. Bye."

The end-of-message tone sounded, followed by the time and date. Matt Everhart. The name was vaguely familiar. She had seen his novels in the local bookstore, she believed. What in the world was he talking about—some castle in Slovakia?

As she listened to Matt Everhart's message again, her curiosity piqued.

She clicked through the recent caller ID numbers, found his and pressed *Talk*.

He answered on the fourth ring. "Hello."

"Mr. Everhart, this is Seneca Hunt returning your call."

"Oh, hey, thanks." He sounded out of breath. "Sorry, you caught me on the treadmill. Hang on." A moment later, he returned still breathing a bit heavy. "Thanks for calling me back."

"Is this not a good time? I can call later." Maybe she should have taken a nap before calling, the effects of the Seagrams were kicking in.

"No, it's fine. I was just trying to run away from a T-bone steak I ate last night. My doctor says I can't run from a bad diet, but I try."

Seneca laughed. "You certainly have me curious as to why you called. You mentioned you're a writer. I have to apologize right up front. I'm familiar with your work, but have to admit I haven't read your books."

"No apology needed. I'm not offended."

She thought he sounded sincere, even a bit humble. That was nice—not a celebrity with an inflated ego and an attitude to match.

"You said in your message that you had uncovered something while doing research in ..."

"Slovakia. You might think this a little crazy, but I thought it interesting enough to give you a call. I read on the Net about the terrorist attack in Mexico. The initial reports, or maybe they were rumors—I guess you'll know better—say that the tomb was minus an emperor."

The way he spoke, it was obvious he didn't realize that Daniel Bernal was her fiancé. He would have offered his condolences at least and spoken a little more solemnly. But that was probably a good thing or the combo of conversation and liquor might have sent her on another crying jag. "That's right. There was no funerary jar. No remains of Montezuma."

"I was in Eastern Europe a couple of months ago doing research on serial killers for my next book. Ever hear of Elizabeth Bathory?"

"No, I don't think so." She wondered what he was getting at. Maybe he was a kook, and she was going to regret returning his call.

"Bathory was a scary lady. A countess, actually. She was known as the *Blood Countess, Tigress of Čachtice*. The legend is she killed hundreds of girls and young women, then bathed in the blood of virgins to retain her youth. She was never tried in court, but she was kept walled up in several rooms inside Čachtice Castle until she died. They buried her in the cemetery nearby, but the villagers were so distressed they moved her to her birthplace at Nagyecsed in Hungary where she was laid to rest in the Bathory family crypt. I spent some time at the castle ruin and then went off to visit Nagyecsed and the crypt. As it turned out, several days before my arrival, her tomb was broken into."

"Dan, I mean, Dr. Bernal, the dig master in Mexico, said he didn't suspect grave robbers."

"I understand. That's what initiated the connection between my Elizabeth and your Montezuma. My call is about what wasn't stolen."

FIREWORKS
1899, CHICAGO

GROVES STARED OUT THE window of his eighth-floor suite at the Congress Hotel and watched groups of revelers blowing party horns, shouting, and singing along the windy, snow-covered Chicago sidewalks. Although there were still four hours to midnight, hundreds were already gathering in the park to watch the New Year's Eve fireworks. The new century was about to begin.

He also saw his reflection in the glass. The image looking back at him was an enigma—a mystery that ate away at his every waking hour.

Why wasn't he aging? Why couldn't he die?

He had long since resorted to using theatrical makeup to add subtle shadows under his eyes and hollows in his cheeks. There wasn't much he could do to add creases in his face, but he toyed with the makeup enough to create the illusion of shallow wrinkles and furrows. He had a number of expensive short beards and long-haired wigs, both salted with gray.

The constant deception eliminated any chance of a normal life. Through the years, Groves had his share of women, but he avoided marriage and children. And that took care of having to explain away his masquerade. The only person he had kept a long-term relationship with was Charlie Pykes, his business partner. But recently Charlie had passed away from the scourge of the terrible Bright's disease. On his deathbed he had asked Groves, "What's your secret?"

"You taught me everything about making money, Charlie. You're my secret."

"No," Pykes had said, his voice barely above a whisper. "Not the money. What's your *secret*?"

Groves didn't answer but simply patted Charlie's hand and watched the old assayer close his eyes forever.

After Charlie's passing, Groves became more reclusive, obsessed with protecting his secret. For the past ten years he had studied elocution and learned to read and write, all of which were necessary to perpetuate his secret. He couldn't forever be the uneducated cowboy, Billy Groves. Yet there were times he enjoyed slipping back into that persona. All his studies had paid off. He could be William or Billy, whatever pleased him or the situation demanded.

He was now directing his finances and business dealings long distance through a staff of attorneys and managers assembled with Pykes's help. Once a year, he traveled to Chicago to attend the board of directors meeting for Groves Consortium—his holding company whose investments covered mining, timber, railroads, metalworking, oil exploration, and shipbuilding. Investing his original Apache treasure and selling most of the ancient artifacts to private collectors had amassed a great fortune for him. He kept a few of his favorite pieces as a reminder of the strangest day in his life—the day he was swallowed up by the earth only to rise from the dead.

A knock on his hotel room door made Groves turn away from the activity on the street below. Standing in front of a mirror, he adjusted his tuxedo, fake beard, and wig before answering the door.

A bellboy saluted. “Mr. Groves, your friends have assembled and are awaiting your company.”

“Much obliged.” Groves handed the young man a two-dollar silver certificate.

“Thank you, sir.” He motioned for Groves to follow.

They made their way downstairs and across the lobby to the ornate Italian-designed Pompeian Room.

As Groves entered, a group of a dozen men standing near a stone fireplace turned in his direction. One of them, a short, round man with a pale complexion came forward, his hand outstretched. “Mr. Groves, so nice of you to join us.” He went to a whisper. “There is some treachery afoot with our newest partner, Colin Black.”

“Thank you.” Groves followed his senior vice president to the middle of the gathering.

“Gentlemen.” The man’s voice boomed. “May I present Mr. William Groves, our chairman, who has just arrived this afternoon by way of his private rail coach. Let’s welcome him to the Windy City.”

As they applauded and stepped forward, Groves greeted each board member. A few were new, including Colin Black. “Welcome to the board, Mr. Black.” He shook the man’s hand and noticed that Black appeared younger than expected, and from his VP's warning, Groves intended to be cautious. It would not be the first time an unscrupulous newspaper or worse, a competitor, had tried to slip inside Groves Consortium for an exclusive story or to steal trade secrets. "I understand you're the new director of Ashland Coal and Coke?"

"That's correct, sir." Black pumped Groves's hand. "It's a pleasure to meet you."

"I look forward to your P and L presentation, Mr. Black. Maybe you can tell me all about what it's like to mine coal in West Virginia."

The VP waved over a waiter. "Get Mr. Groves a Tennessee whiskey." He turned to the gathering. "Gentlemen, if you will excuse us." He led Groves a few paces away. "I highly suspect that Mr. Black is an impostor."

"How's that?"

"After we purchased Ashland four months ago, I received a letter from their general manager. He said that Mr. Black would be their representative, joining us here in Chicago."

"So?"

"If you'll remember, when you and I visited the property prior to the acquisition, Mr. Black was out of town, so neither of us met him."

Groves nodded.

"In the letter, it also mentioned that Mr. Black was a victim of an industrial accident in which he lost his left arm at the elbow, but would not need any special accommodations."

Groves glanced over at Black who was chatting with a fellow board member and gesturing with his left hand. "Must be a miracle."

After dinner Groves and his board moved into the hotel's German Room, a spacious lounge decorated in the style of a Munich pub. The men assembled in large leather chairs while puffing on *Partagas* cigars brought up from Havana and sampling the *nose* of fine French Calvados brandy they sipped from seventeen-ounce snifters. Groves listened intently as each identified the biggest mountain they would have to climb to survive in the twentieth century. When they were done, Groves announced he was retiring to his room for the evening.

He left the group and headed for the ornate Otis elevators in the rear of the lobby.

A bellboy approached. "Mr. Groves. A telegram just arrived for you." He handed Groves a brown envelope.

"Much obliged, son." Groves reached into his pocket, removed two dollars and gave it to the bellboy. Alone inside the elevator, he opened the envelope and read the single sheet. The message was from the manager of Ashland Coal and Coke. *Sorry to inform you Mr. Black has met an untimely demise. Stop. Sheriff suspects foul play. Stop. Will mail PL statement to your office. Stop.*

He folded the telegram and placed it in his coat pocket. Getting off at the eighth floor, he was walking down the hallway when he heard muffled steps coming from behind on the thick carpet.

"You, sir, are a charlatan."

Groves turned to see Mr. Black standing a few paces behind. "I beg your pardon."

"A man who disguises his identity is a fraud." Black came closer. "I've found you out. You're an impostor."

"I think you've had too much to drink." Groves started to turn away. Black was on the right track, but a little confused. He *was* William Groves. "Now, if you'll excuse me."

"So you don't mind me informing your company that you are not William Groves but an impostor?"

"That's ridiculous. Why would you make such a claim?"

"I saw your ... paraphernalia. All the tools of deception you use to disguise yourself."

Groves felt a bubble of fear burst in his chest. "I don't know what you're talking about."

"When you were in West Virginia several months ago. I was the manager at the Kanawha Hotel where you stayed." He bared a toothy grin. "I knew you were a rich man, and I went to your room to pocket a few trinkets that could fetch me a small bankroll." His smile grew larger. "But when I saw all that makeup, those wigs and beards, I knew I had hit the jackpot. There were more dollars to be made than by petty thieving. And here I am. You should be happy that I'm willing to keep your secret."

"If you want to speak of impostors, Mr. Black, perhaps you would be so kind as to explain if you had anything to do with the suspicious death of the real Colin Black."

Black gave him a sly wink. "You got me. What can I say? One imposter to another. So, you know the game."

What kind of fool was this man? Groves thought. This was no game. "What is it you intend to do?"

"That would be your choice."

"Are you attempting to blackmail me, sir?"

"I would prefer to call it an insurance premium."

"And how much is the premium?"

Black lowered his voice. "Why don't we say one hundred thousand dollars?"

Groves studied the man for a moment, perplexed by Black's stupidity and naïveté. "Go enjoy the New Year's fireworks, Mr. Black. I'll give you my decision in the morning." He turned and walked away.

Groves peeled off every item of his masquerade. Standing naked in front of the sink, he scrubbed the makeup from his face. Then he strode over to the closet and dressed in a homespun woolen, collarless shirt, a pair of denim pants, and a worn, fringed leather jacket. Propping his black felt hat atop his head, he swiped the brim and took a last look in the mirror. No trace of William Groves, chairman of Groves Consortium remained. There was just Billy Groves the cowboy, who then reached into his luggage and removed a small caliber pistol. Mr. Black was in for a different kind of fireworks.

TONGUE OF THE OCEAN
2012, BAHAMAS

SCARROW WATCHED ELIZABETH ENTER the water from the dive platform mounted on the stern of the 120-foot *Phoenix Explorer*. He treaded water nearby waiting for her to work up the courage to swim in the Caribbean Sea at night under a moonless sky. Her previous dives, while training and afterward, had all been with the sun high overhead. Tonight, all that lit the surface was the swath of the Milky Way painted silver across the heavens.

Scarrow always had his yacht's captain kill the floodlights when he did night dives so he could appreciate the mystery and majesty of the ocean. Even after so many wall dives, it still chilled him with fear almost to the point of paralysis—a reaction he rarely felt anymore without extreme activities like this.

"How do you feel?" Scarrow spoke into the ultrasonic transceiver built into his full facemask. The starlight glistened off the neoprene skin of Elizabeth's wetsuit. Even in the dim light, he saw that her eyes were wide with excitement.

"Javier, it's wonderfully frightening. My heart is racing."

"Turn on your lantern." He flipped the switch on his hand-held underwater light.

Elizabeth obeyed, and their two beams took on the appearance of Jedi lightsabers in the inky void.

"Are you ready?" He was going to take her deeper than ever before. Even though they would only be able to stay down for around twelve minutes, it would be worth it.

"I am."

"The bottom here is about fifty feet." He dropped beneath the surface, adjusted his buoyancy, and with smooth, strong leg motions propelled himself into the darkness. Elizabeth's beam let him know she was right behind.

"Look at all the fish." Her light beam reflected off a school of cigar minnows as they darted past.

"Once we get to the bottom, we have only a few hundred feet to swim before we come to the edge. There the floor drops to six thousand feet—a sheer vertical wall. We'll descend to a ledge one hundred twenty feet down from the surface. You must remain alert and attentive to your dive watch and air gauge. We've talked about the symptoms of nitrogen narcosis. It's easy to become overwhelmed with the beauty of the wall and think you can go deeper or even dispense with your regulator."

"I will."

"Enjoy what you are about to see." He pulled a Cyalume light stick from his belt and held it up. "Once we get to the ledge below, I'll break this open. You'll be amazed at the spectacular light show it produces as the chemicals disperse in the water."

"I can't wait, Javier. You have given me a new life with so much to explore. I can't express how grateful I am."

The sandy bottom appeared in Scarrow's beam. He leveled off and waited for Elizabeth to join him. Motioning forward, they glided in tandem above the bottom.

A few moments later, Scarrow heard a gasp from Elizabeth as they reached the edge. The reaction was always the same from anyone he brought here—total shock. Appearing as if a giant knife had sliced away the ocean bottom, the floor below them disappeared. Like two eagles soaring out over a majestic cliff face, they dropped into the abyss known as the Tongue of the Ocean.

Scarrow sat in a chaise lounge watching Elizabeth as she seemed to glide across his master stateroom aboard the *Phoenix Explorer*.

Elizabeth stood in front of the dresser mirror and slowly opened her white robe, letting it drop to the carpet. She studied herself—the body of a beautiful young woman still glowing and flushed from her hot shower.

He watched as she caressed her breasts, then ran her hands across her flat stomach flaring out over her hips. "I hope you are pleased?"

"I am." She angled sideways and admired her profile. "How could I not be pleased. You have given me a new life and a new body in which to live it."

"If you are satisfied, then so am I."

"I still don't understand what you ask of me. What could I possibly give you that would be worth this … miracle?"

"You have certain talents, and that is what I seek as payment. You possess the drive and dedication I need to fulfill my ultimate goal—I cannot do it without your help and the assistance of your fellow apostles."

"I'm sorry, but I don't understand."

"Soon, all will be revealed, Elizabeth. All I ask of you and the others is that you do what you enjoyed so in your previous life."

SACRED FIRE
2012, BAHAMAS

SCARROW GATHERED HIS CORE group in the conference room of the sprawling Azteca pyramid. Seated around the large, oval, cherry wood table were what he liked to think of as his disciples—his most devoted staff. Each was barefoot and dressed in simple gray robes with a rope belted at the waist. Their attire was in sharp contrast to Scarrow's. He wore an elaborate layered mantle of purple and gold, along with hand-tooled leather sandals, ornate gold bracelets, and other gem-encrusted jewelry.

Suspended on the wall behind him was an imposing replica of the Mexica Sun Stone, the Eagle Bowl—the original recovered during Mexico City's main square excavation in 1790.

Coyotl handed out the agenda while Scarrow gave everyone a few minutes to digest it before calling for their individual departmental reports.

"Dr. Blakely, would you like to go first?"

"Subjects' vitals and general health are all within normal limits. Psychological and environmental indoctrination have shown positive results in developing the desired personality characteristics."

"I thought all that was locked in and predetermined by genetics," Coyotl said. "Isn't that why these specific individuals were chosen as apostles?"

"You're correct to a degree. Genetics plays a strong role," Dr. Blakely said. "But our genetic makeup only predisposes us to express certain behaviors. Environment and experiences also influence the development of personality traits. Our subjects have been limited to only the experiences we have provided. The combination of genetics and our programmed experiences are producing the desired results."

Blakely turned to Scarrow. "As I said, we are seeing evidence of precisely the characteristics you seek. The interesting component is observing the uniqueness or quirkiness of each individual—how they respond to certain stimuli and situations, the levels of impulsivity and aggression. We continue to monitor certain neurochemicals and enzymes, such as serotonin and monoamine oxidase. One interesting fact we have obtained is that all our subjects have the 7-repeat in the DRD4 gene, which in previous studies indicates a propensity for novelty or risk-taking behaviors."

"Repeats?"

"It doesn't matter." Scarrow motioned to Coyotl. "We don't have to understand."

"Sorry, I don't mean to be talking in *sciencease*," Blakely said. "A repeat is a DNA sequence that, well, simply repeats. That's all it is. It's one of quite a few mutations. If you have the 7-repeat in the DRD4 gene, chances are you are more of a risk taker and exhibit more novelty-seeking behaviors than those with other repeats, other mutations."

"So what is the bottom line in lay terms?"

"Our most current analysis, Javier, indicates that we have successfully combined all the factors necessary to give us the specified results. And on schedule. No delays. We expect all subjects will complete processing within our original timeframe."

"Excellent." Scarrow glanced over the metal brazier sitting in the center of the table. A stainless steel venting hood descended from the ceiling to hang above the brazier, drawing away the swirls of smoke. He felt the heat of the sacred fire, and he thought back to when he had lit this fire in 1960, the night when the gods had finally answered his requests, and he began laying the groundwork for his plan. The time was nearing to light the Eternal Flame again, the 52-year cycle was coming to an end just as the calendars prophesied. All must be in place by the fall equinox, a traditional day of ritual of his people. Then he could be assured that his task would be complete by December 21. His apostles would have dispersed and begun their work of harvesting the hearts of the Sweet Flowers. The gods would be pleased and catastrophe averted.

After several other reports covering fund raising, Phoenix Ministry preparations in various cities, and other business, Scarrow dismissed the group, asking only that Coyotl remain. When it was just the two of them, he said. "Have you taken care of the last witness?"

"Soon. I'm going to Miami right after this meeting."

"How did you find her?"

"Very easily. Once we intercepted her luggage before it left Mexico City, personal items inside helped us establish where she lives. One of our disciples slipped into her apartment to search for any other evidence of the Bernal interview she might have hand-carried on the plane. He found nothing, but we decided to listen in on her phone conversations for a few days to see what she told her magazine editor. She has not spoken to him yet, but she had a conversation with a writer about other tomb robberies. She's going down to the Keys to meet with him to discuss it."

"Then we have two potential targets. How do you intend to solve the problem?"

"They have plans for a boat ride. I believe we're going to have the perfect opportunity to make use of our newest technology. The latest Groves Avionics prototype drone is waiting at the Homestead Research Center. We'll use it to eliminate them both. As far as the authorities are concerned, it will be a sanctioned FAA and military-approved training exercise. Once the mission is complete, I'll return immediately."

"I caution you to avoid trying to kill a fly with a bazooka. How will this appear as anything other than a brazen attack on innocent victims?"

"It will be seen as a terrible tragedy," Coyotl said. "A horrible malfunction of a new weapon still under development."

"And the aftermath?"

"We predict an investigation and most assuredly a multi-million-dollar wrongful death lawsuit against Groves Avionics. We'll settle out of court, and it will all go away. The price of doing business as you're fond of saying."

"I need you back here to manage the apostles. We can't afford to have you gone too long. Their training and orientation can't be interrupted. You realize this should have been taken care of in Mexico City?" Scarrow's glare was stern. "We must close every door that could possibly allow someone a glimpse into what we are doing, no matter how insignificant it may seem. The world wouldn't understand what we are about to do." With a motion of his hand, he signaled that the discussion was over.

As the two left the conference room, Coyotl said, "By this time tomorrow night I will have shut the last door."

THE LORELEI
2012, FLORIDA KEYS

SENECA LOWERED THE CONVERTIBLE top on her C70 to feel the sea-scrubbed air whirl around her. The Overseas Highway hadn't changed much since she'd traveled to Key West a few years back to do a piece on Fantasy Fest. The only difference was the conversion of a large portion from two into four lanes. The rest was typical Keys panorama, plenty of motels and hotels, charter boats, restaurants, and gift shops. Despite growth, there were stretches that managed to hold onto a laid-back mystique and slow-moving lifestyle that withstood the rush of the outside world. Like it had been when she was a kid.

When Matt Everhart invited her to come to Islamorada with the promise of a delicious dinner and a starlit boat ride, she declined, not feeling up to going anywhere or doing anything. But after thinking about it for a few days, she finally changed her mind, called him back, and accepted. There was always the outside chance it could lead to an angle for a story that would satisfy her editor, but more importantly let her continue investigating who was responsible for taking Daniel from her. Certain that no one would understand how she could take off for a place like the Keys so soon after losing Dan, she decided not to tell anyone about the overnight trip. This was not a weekend vacation escape, nor was she interested in explaining herself to others. All she knew was that she wasn't going to let her grief keep her from uncovering every stone, pursuing every hint of a possible lead. If she could find who had murdered Daniel, then maybe she would allow herself some selfish time to lie in bed and cry for days on end.

The drive reawakened in her how much she missed being on the water. Seneca scanned the radio stations until she found something that matched the scenery, not her dark mood. The Caribbean music brought back memories of times when she'd come to the Keys as a child with her mother. Good times. Brenda was a free spirit, and Seneca's recollections were of blazing sunsets, thatched tiki bars, fishing trips, and her mother dancing to steel drum music on a moonlit beach.

They had spent a lot of time on the water. Brenda loved the ocean, and once when they lived in a small apartment near the Intracoastal Waterway in Fort Lauderdale, Brenda had saved up enough money to buy a boat. It was an old, rundown, mahogany Chris Craft with a small cabin and aging inboard. But to Brenda and Seneca, it was the *Queen Mary*. Many evenings they'd cruise into open water around dusk to watch the stars come out. Brenda told endless stories during those boat rides, but sometimes they just sat in silence staring at the heavens and ocean. Seneca supposed that was why she had such a fondness for being on and near the water. For an instant, she wondered how different it would have been to be raised in a family with a mother *and* father.

"*Why Don't We Get Drunk and Screw?*" Jimmy Buffet's voice filled the car, and the lyrics brought a smile to Seneca's face. *God, how long had it been since she felt like smiling.* She wished life was just as simple as the song title.

Seneca passed through Key Largo, and just short of a half hour later pulled into the parking lot of the Key Lantern Motel in Islamorada. It was advertised as one of the most reasonably priced motels around—nothing fancy, just clean, friendly, and casual.

After checking into her room, she flipped open her phone, found Matt Everhart's number in her contacts and called.

"There's a wonderful little spot on the Gulf side called the Lorelei," he said after thanking her for coming. "Why don't I pick you up around six? Where are you staying?"

"No, that's okay. I might do a little sightseeing. I'll just meet you there." She didn't want to be stuck with someone she knew little about. If she wanted to call it a night, having her own car made it easy.

"That's fine. You'll know it by the Mermaid sign. Around marker 82. Bayside. Great outdoor dining and live music. I'll get a table on the deck outside." He paused a moment. "Or would you rather eat inside?"

"By the water would be wonderful."

"Just look for a guy wearing a University of Florida shirt. If we're lucky we'll get a real show on the horizon when the sun goes down."

"Sounds perfect." She needed a real show right about now.

Surprisingly, the Key Lantern was next door to the Lorelei, but Seneca didn't especially want Matt to know where she was staying.

The motel was exactly as advertised—nothing fancy, but clean and comfortable. Maybe she should do a travel piece on it and some of the other budget motels in the area for a little extra income. Her editor didn't mind her doing freelance work for non-science magazines. She might even get a reduced rate or free stay out of the article. Seneca made a note to speak to the owner before she checked out.

Instead of walking to the restaurant, she drove the short distance. Dressed in a white blouse, ankle-length skirt, and sandals, Seneca stepped onto the Lorelei's open deck portion of the busy restaurant. She scanned the tables, her eyes coming to rest on one with a single occupant wearing a blue UF polo shirt.

He saw her, and she waved.

Matt rose as she approached and outstretched his hand.

"Ms. Hunt?"

She had seen the author's picture on his website before she left her apartment and thought he was nice looking, but he was more than that in person. Appearing to be in his late thirties, he had a shock of thick, nearly black hair, rich coffee-colored eyes, an even, light suede tan on the angular planes of his face, and stood at about six feet or a tad over, she guessed. The UF shirt was tucked into khaki cargo shorts, and he wore a pair of worn boat shoes, maybe Sperry Top-Siders. He was obviously living the Keys lifestyle.

"Call me Seneca."

"You're just in time, Seneca." Matt gestured to the west and the spectacular sunset that was building. "Just enough *smathering* of clouds to make it interesting. It isn't the most clear days that make the most dramatic sunsets."

She wondered if *smathering* was a real word or if he just made it up. No matter, it fit perfectly. "You promised, and it looks like you're going to deliver."

"Thanks again for coming. I'm anxious to hear about what happened in Mexico. So far, all I know is what I read on the Internet and the little bit you told me on the phone."

The waiter strode over to take their drink order. Matt spoke up. "Two margaritas on the rocks." He glanced at Seneca. "With salt?"

"Absolutely." She sat back, realizing the calming effect of the ocean and the onset of the vibrant sunset were helping her to slow down and relax. It was nice to be away from the city. Taking a deep breath she began relating the Mexico experience including a description of the tomb. Finally, she said, "Dr. Bernal was my fiancé."

Matt reeled back. "Oh, man. I'm so sorry. Nothing I read mentioned that. I wouldn't have sounded so cavalier. I would have been more sensitive when you first declined my invitation. Oh, God, what you must have thought of me."

"I realized you didn't know."

"I am sorry."

"It's okay. Really it is."

Matt kept shaking his head at his ignorance.

Seneca began another conversation to help bail him out. "So let me tell you what Dan thought. He was so intrigued with the fact that Montezuma's remains were not there, yet the grave didn't appear to be robbed because all the valuable grave goods were still there. All kinds of pottery, gold, and gems, even what appeared to be a small reliquary that he theorized was possibly a gift from the Spanish. The burial shroud that should have wrapped Montezuma's body before cremation was crumpled on the ground. And Daniel was puzzled as to why there was no funerary jar."

"I don't blame him for being perplexed."

"His basic questions were, why weren't the artifacts stolen if the grave had been broken into in the past, why was Montezuma's burial shroud still there, and where were his remains."

"Those are precisely the things that captured my attention. Just like what wasn't taken from Elizabeth Bathory's grave that captivated me. Like your fiancé, I was fascinated by the goods left behind in Montezuma's tomb. It seemed like an interesting coincidence—Bathory and Montezuma, that is."

"I did some reading up on Bathory and wow, you *are* right, she was a real piece of work. Pure evil."

"That she was. I told you the local villagers so reviled her that they didn't want her buried in their cemetery. Instead, they moved her to her birthplace. I went there to do some more research, and that's when I found out her grave had recently been opened. Not robbed, mind you—at least not in the traditional sense. Even though she was despised, old Liz was still of royal lineage and so she was buried with a few of the family jewels—a necklace, broach, and several rings."

The waiter brought their drinks. "Are you ready to order?" He looked at Seneca.

"Oh, my, I haven't even looked at the menu."

"If you like fish," Matt said, "I suggest the whole yellowtail. I've had it here before and it's excellent."

"Then it's the yellowtail." She closed the menu.

"Good choice. And for you, sir?"

"Prime rib, rare."

The man nodded and scooped up their menus.

"Prime rib? With all this scrumptious seafood?"

"I eat my share. But now and again I've got a hankering for beef."

"Didn't you say on the phone that you were trying to jog away from a steak?"

"I'm always on the run from something."

She realized he had an infectious smile. Like Daniel's.

"Usually it's a group of religious extremists who think my books are heresy or blasphemy."

"Really? You mean people actually confront you?"

"Some folks take my writing way too seriously. That's why I decided to live in a place that's out of the way. It takes a commitment to come all the way down here looking for me."

She liked that Matt was not pretentious. He didn't try to impress her. He seemed personable and down to earth.

"You were telling me that they buried Elizabeth Bathory with her jewelry?" She saw that Matt noticed the engagement ring. Seneca touched the diamond. "I haven't been able to take it off yet. It's on my checklist of things to do. I just haven't gotten to it."

Matt nodded in understanding and paused a moment before continuing. "My point is that a grave robber loots graves for valuables, not old brittle bones. Even though Elizabeth's crypt had been opened and her remains taken, whoever did it left behind her valuables. It didn't make sense to me. Then, out of nowhere I caught the story about Montezuma's tomb. Of course the initial news accounts didn't say too much about how all the grave goods had been untouched and that Montezuma's remains were nowhere to be found. The media focused on the fact that there had been a local terrorist bombing, probably drug-gangs or fanatical political faction-related. But I thought the real story might be bigger than what the news played up. Just a hunch, but I had to wonder if there was a connection somehow."

"Maybe. But what would Elizabeth Bathory and Montezuma have in common? What could be the thread that links them? After all, they're separated by continents and what, a hundred or so years?"

"I've thought about that, too, but there *is* one link. Think about it."

Seneca glanced at the blazing sunset over Florida Bay before turning back to Matt. "That the only things missing from their graves are their remains."

REVELATION

1962, RENO, NEVADA

"THERE'S A STORY GOING around that you got yourself a room full of Spanish treasure hidden in the basement of this hotel." The call girl straddled Groves as she pumped him deeper into her. Between grunts, she said, "Honey, you gonna show me your treasure?"

"What do you think I got shoved up inside you? That's the best treasure you gonna get—long and hard." Groves watched her breasts bounce as he gripped her hips—their bodies dripping in sweat. She bent forward letting her long hair hang down and rake his chest.

This one was unquenchable, he thought—the best so far. It was the third time that night they had screwed since his men had sent her up from the casino. He knew she had no idea he was William Groves the billionaire, only that he was the wealthy mystery guy living in the private penthouse.

Groves was working on his personal goal to bang a different woman every night. It was one of the hundred challenges he set for himself out of utter boredom. So far he had not missed a night. But he was no less bored.

After all, since finding the treasure eighty-six years ago, he'd made more money than the gross national product of most countries. He owned more corporations than he could keep track of or even remember. His accountants told him he had over a half-million employees worldwide. He had faked his own death in 1919 followed by faking the deaths of his *son* in 1937 and *grandson* in 1960. To the outside world, he was William Groves IV, great-grandson of Billy Groves, the cowboy, and considered by the media and business world as an eccentric billionaire recluse, just like his father, grandfather, and great-grandfather.

He ran Groves Consortium from behind an impenetrable curtain of privacy armed with a battalion of attorneys and security experts. No one knew or would have believed he was really the same cowboy that stumbled across the Apache treasure trove in 1876, died from the wound of an arrow, was buried by an earthquake, and rose from the grave.

Groves lived anonymously in the penthouse suite of the plushest casino and resort hotel in Reno—one of over a dozen castles, country estates, mansions, and hotels he owned throughout the world. Growing tired of the hassle of moving between them, he had made the Reno penthouse permanent, having lived there for more than five years. Each day he gazed out over a world that might as well be an alien planet for he could never set foot on it as a normal mortal. He had long forgotten the meaning of freedom.

While those around him grew old and passed away, he lived on in the body of a thirty-seven-year-old Arizona cowboy, fresh from a Mexican shootout in Santa Ana. Whether his immortality was a blessing or a curse, he had no idea why he was chosen or how. There were times he wanted to test his immortality. He would take a pistol, cock it, and hold the tip of the barrel to his temple, but he never had the *cojones* to pull the trigger.

Groves was a man who possessed everything and yet had nothing. His latest method of passing the time was to drink heavily and fuck as many whores as possible. But even as he did, he knew the thrill would soon wear off. He spent less and less time allowing himself to be seen or dealt with as William Groves and more and more behind-closed-door time, like tonight, as plain old Billy, the skin he was most comfortable in.

Suddenly, Groves thrust upwards and shot his load into her. "How's that for buried treasure?" His speech was slurred from so much booze.

She rolled off. "You're a damn fire hose, baby." Her words were equally distorted from hours of drinking everything in his penthouse bar in between going at it like rabbits.

Groves struggled to slide off the bed and get to his feet. His legs wobbled as he navigated across the master bedroom to the bath. Standing over the toilet, he leaned forward, bracing himself against the wall while he took a piss. She was the best one this week, he thought. He'd have his men pay her double for the best piece of ass he'd had in a long time. A thousand should do it.

"Come on, baby. Show me that treasure."

Groves turned to see her propped against the door frame, her naked body still glistening from their sexual workout.

"I just gave you all the treasure I've got." He staggered toward her, and they fell into each other's arms, barely able to stand. "You drained me dry."

"I know you got gold and shit hidden around here somewhere," she whispered as she bit his earlobe. "I've heard the rumors. How else did you come up with enough money to buy this hotel? Come on, baby. Show me."

It was something few had ever seen. If he showed her, he would be breaking his own rules. But what the hell. She was so drunk that no one would believe her anyway. And that's if she would even remember tonight and what she was about to view.

"You have to promise to keep it our little secret." He took her by the arm and led her across the room, stopping long enough to grab each of them a bathrobe. Neither could walk in a straight line, but with a lot of effort, they wound up at the entrance to an elevator—not the one leading to the private casino entrance and parking garage but a small lift big enough for two or three people. Inside it, she had to hold on to him to keep from falling.

They descended twelve stories before coming to a halt. No other floors had access to this elevator—its shaft completely encased in concrete and steel plates. When the door opened, what lay ahead was a short hallway ending in an imposing vault-style door.

After a few paces, they stood in front of the big, brushed bronze door. "Turn your back for a minute."

Obeying, she looked away as she leaned up against the wall. "Holy shit, I'm dizzy."

Groves worked at remembering the combination to the triple locks. He got it wrong the first time and hesitated, knowing if he mucked it up three times in a row the vault would automatically seal itself for twenty-four hours.

He shook his head, trying to clear the murky shadows induced by so much alcohol. Finally, he turned the combination wheels again. A moment later, a series of clicking sounds let him know the bomb-proof door was ready to swing open.

"This way." He guided her by his hand on her waist.

They entered the darkness of the vault. Groves flipped on the lights. The room was about the size of a two-car garage. It contained heavy floor-to-ceiling iron shelving lining the perimeter and two rows running down the middle. What was left of the Apache treasure—about a third by Groves's estimate—was there. Most of the gold and silver was long gone. What remained were several art objects and odd military and ancient Mexican and Indian pieces. Though he had liquidated the bulk of those types of articles, there were still a few chests filled with rare coins and one modest pile of bullion. And there were millions in US currency. One should always have cash on hand.

Groves stood back and watched as she moved around the room, her eyes wide in wonder. She seemed to want to touch every surface, especially anything that sparkled. "This is the sexiest place I've ever seen." She picked up a handful of coins and rubbed them across her breasts through her open robe. "How much is this all worth, honey?"

"No idea." He held on to the corner of a shelf.

"What you gonna do with it all?"

"Keep it so I can bring beautiful women like you down here to play with it."

"Check this out." She placed two coins on her nipples like pasties.

Groves yawned. *Time to cut this short and send her on her way. It had probably been a mistake to bring her down here, anyway.*

"What's this?" She pointed to a small silver chest on the bottom of a shelf.

Groves strained to focus on what she indicated. "Shit, I forgot about that one. Never did figure out why it was in with this batch. Held on to it just because it's a memento from a special day in my life. Guess the box is worth something."

"So what's in it?"

"It's been a real long time, but if I remember, just a piece of cloth with some guy's picture on it. I remember that he's got feathers sticking out of his head."

"Can I look, please?"

"Sure, what the hell. Then we've got to go."

She opened the lid and looked inside. "You're right, just an old cloth."

"Like I said, a picture of some guy who liked to wear feathers. Maybe he was an Indian chief. Probably not worth a dime."

Reaching in, she lifted the cloth, unfolded it and held it so the light struck the surface. "Wow!"

"What is it?" he asked, growing impatient.

"I thought you said it was a guy with feathers."

"It is, isn't it?"

Holding the cloth by the corners, she turned it so Groves could plainly see the face on its surface. "No, honey, it's a picture of you."

REBIRTH

2012, BAHAMAS

Scarrow stood in the twilight of the genetics lab—the glow of the computer screens and electronic gear softened the hard-edged coldness of the room. His eyes scanned the body resting on the stainless steel table a few feet away. A stark white sheet covered the corpse from the neck down. The surgeons kept the room chilled, but Scarrow didn't mind. He was on fire with excitement.

This would be the creation of his ninth apostle—three more to go. And although he had witnessed his hand-picked team of physicians perform the miracle of rebirth before, the power and magnitude of the event besieged him. He truly believed that this task had been handed to him to bring back into the world the grandeur and glory of his empire. That was what separated him from Groves—why Groves had lost touch with reality—a lack of purpose. Scarrow was being allowed a chance to put all things right by rebuilding what had been destroyed. But unlike the time in which he ruled millions before watching his nation conquered by the Spanish army, today he had the power to avenge his people and his gods. Soon he and his final twelve apostles would follow in the Aztec tradition and hold in their hands the still-beating hearts of those being sacrificed in the name of restoring the delicate equilibrium of the universe.

The magnitude of it all caused Scarrow to feel his pulse race. To remain calm, he took in a deep breath.

He chose each apostle for their intense dedication to a cause and commitment to achieving their objectives at all costs, including the willingness to take human life if need be. In return for Scarrow's gift of rebirth, his apostles were dedicated to him, obligated and grateful. They would go out into the world and carry on his mission. And once complete, their reward would be to break the chains of mortality and live forever.

Scarrow stood beside the table and gazed at the body. Dr. Blakely and his team had done well. The face bore an expression of peace and serenity. He touched the man's forehead. The skin was cold and lifeless. Scarrow's hands no longer trembled as they did with the rebirth of the earlier apostles. At this point, he knew exactly what to expect once life flowed back into the body. The color would come to the skin as it warmed. Then the first breath would cause the chest to rise. There would be movement under the eyelids and sporadic tics in the limbs, a slight parting of the lips, a flaring of the nostrils. The male apostles had experienced erections during rebirth while the females exhibited a flush to their cheeks. Finally, the most glorious moment of all—their eyes would open and look upon the face of their life giver, their savior, their god.

Excitement rolled through him at knowing what was about to take place. He said a prayer of thanks that he had been chosen to resurrect the Kingdom of the Sun. In his past, human civilization had already been destroyed four times—four suns—the first sun annihilated by jaguars, the second sun destroyed by great winds, the third by fiery rain, and the fourth by a great flood. He and his apostles would appease the gods with an abundance of human sacrifice, and the time of the fifth sun would continue.

Turning, he nodded to the team of surgeons standing nearby. The room immediately flooded with white light as the high intensity lamps over the operating table blazed to life.

"It's time," Scarrow said and stepped aside.

INDIGO SKY
2012, FLORIDA KEYS

"I COULD REALLY GET used to this." Seneca watched the swaths of red, tangerine, violet, and gold swirl across the sky as the sun sank into Florida Bay. "Daniel would have loved this place. He'd be telling me to listen to the rustle of palms and taste the brine on the southeasterly breeze. You're so lucky."

Matt watched her and smiled. "Yeah, I have to put up with this most every night. It's the price you pay to live in paradise." He started to speak, but gave her a few more moments to muse over the beauty of the setting sun. "I did some more poking around on the Internet after we talked. Made some phone calls, too. I came across an instance of another empty tomb, actually, two more."

"You're kidding?"

"Ever heard of Emir Timur?"

She shook her head.

"He was a fourteenth-century warrior and emperor, also known as Tamerlane, who founded the Timurid Empire. Tamerlane was buried in a mausoleum in Uzbekistan. The building was recently undergoing restoration, and when his tomb was opened, they discovered it was empty." He paused as the waiter brought their dinner.

"Mmmm, looks delicious," Seneca said as the plate of baked yellowtail snapper was placed before her. "Your prime rib looks yummy, too."

"Can I get you folks anything else?"

Matt glanced at Seneca. "I think we're good." He realized he was somewhat taken with her. From her voice on the phone, he hadn't pictured Seneca Hunt quite like the woman sitting across the table. She seemed almost delicate and reserved, yet there was a gleam in her eyes. And her eyes smiled as much as her lips. She was quite attractive.

Seneca took a bite of the snapper. "It doesn't just look delicious, it tastes even better."

"I've never gone wrong with that recommendation."

"Getting back to Mr. Tamerlane, let me guess—when they opened his tomb the grave goods were still there, but no human remains."

Matt nodded. "Tamerlane was supposedly related to Genghis Khan and was likely the most influential military leader in central Asia during his time, despite the partial paralysis of his left side. That's actually how he got his name—Timur, the Lame. As emperor, he was entombed with an impressive array of military and imperial garb along with other valuable objects, all of which were still there. Only his bones were missing."

Matt cut another piece of meat, stabbed it with his fork, and put it in his mouth European style, tines pointing down.

He motioned toward the horizon. "I don't think an artist has ever captured on canvas that deep indigo at the moment the sun disappears. It doesn't last long except in your memory. I'm a romantic in case you haven't guessed."

"I wish I were more so. I should stop and notice things like beautiful sunsets more often. No, I take that back. I do notice sunsets, but only when they relate to what I'm writing. Most of the time, I get so focused I might as well be wearing blinders to nonessential details like the color of the sky the instant the sun goes down."

"Ah, but as a journalist, you appreciate the whole canvas. That's all that really matters. The ways you and I write are not that different—we both deal in details. It's just that most of mine are over-embellished to create a scene that doesn't really exist. I see it playing out in that little movie in my head, and I've got to describe it with enough details that the reader sees the same movie." He grinned. "Plus, fiction or fact, if you live down here, sunsets are hard to ignore."

"You should write something for the Chamber of Commerce. At least get them to put you on retainer."

"If my book sales dry up, I'll have that to fall back on." He laid down his fork. As much as he'd like to continue in a direction that would reveal more about her, he thought better of it. After all, she was a professional writer and had traveled all the way down here to learn about the tomb robberies. Not to go on a blind date.

"Back to Tamerlane. Interesting guy. He led his armies across western and central Asia, leaving the population decimated by systematic mass slaughter and genocide. And yet he managed to maintain a great appreciation for art and literature. He was a military genius who loved to play chess to improve his battlefield tactics."

Seneca washed down more fish with her margarita. "He does sound interesting, but I think tying him to Montezuma is farfetched. You mentioned two empty tombs. Who's the other?"

"I'm not sure it's related at all—just a notion. Do you remember a story in the news a month or so ago about some vandalism that occurred over in London in Westminster Abbey?"

"Actually, I do recall something about Queen Mary's grave being defaced. AKA Bloody Mary, same as the drink."

"Right, but I also heard that the drink originated with a waitress named Mary who worked at the Bucket of Blood Bar in Chicago. There are a lot of theories. But most everyone associates the name with Queen Mary. And for good reason. As a Catholic, Mary gained the nickname because of her persecution of Protestants during her five-year reign. A lot of people were burned at the stake, including a former Archbishop of Canterbury and a former Bishop of London. Oh, and here's an interesting side-story. When you were a kid, did you ever recite the nursery rhyme 'Mary, Mary, quite contrary'? That's our Mary, some say."

"So her grave was vandalized. What's the connection?"

"I've got a buddy at Scotland Yard that I use as a source from time to time for verifying my research. That was one of the calls I made today. I asked him for details on that event since it has to do with a tomb. Apparently, what was not released to the public for security reasons is that her tomb was broken into and the remains removed. The details weren't released to the public because of the outcry it could cause. If the authorities can't protect the tombs of the former queens of England in Westminster Abbey, how can they protect the United Kingdom?"

"So what really happened?"

"Mary shared a crypt with her half-sister, Queen Elizabeth I. Someone broke into the tomb and stole Mary's remains. They left Elizabeth's bones untouched."

Seneca ate in silence for a moment.

"I can't be certain there really is something to tie all these events together or if it's just my overactive imagination. After all, I write fiction for a living."

"I don't see a clear link between Tamerlane, Queen Mary, and Elizabeth Bathory. And where does Montezuma fit in?"

"I didn't make a connection at first, either. Then it occurred to me that besides their remains being stolen, there was one other common denominator."

Now it was Seneca who laid down her fork and waited for his point.

"They're all, in their own ways, mass murderers. Montezuma was responsible for sacrificing eighty thousand in a span of four days during the dedication of his temple. Tamerlane slaughtered close to seventeen million during his military campaigns. Elizabeth Bathory murdered over six hundred girls and young women. That earned her the title of the most prolific female serial killer of all time. And Queen Mary, well the number of her victims pales compared to the other three, but it's still impressive. She sent more than three hundred Protestants to be burned at the stake and will forever be known by her colorful nickname."

"You put Montezuma, Tamerlane, and Mary in the same category? They weren't serial killers like Bathory."

"Yes, but they're all mass murderers, no matter how you look at it. Different motivations, but the result was the same."

"But with Montezuma, you have to consider the culture and the times."

Matt sipped his margarita and peered over the salted rim at her. "You have to take that into consideration for all four, not just Montezuma. In each case, they were driven by what they believed to be righteous and justified. It doesn't matter what *we* think is just and right."

"This could be my next story. If I follow-up on this, it might allow me to keep tracking down Daniel's murderer or murderers? I won't rest until I've done that." She looked away, toward the water for a moment, then back at Matt. "That's what keeps me going. It's the only reason I get up in the morning—to nail whoever killed Daniel." Seneca swept her hair back as if recomposing. "So, I can present all four of these *mass murderers* to my editor and pose the same philosophical question we just discussed."

Matt was impressed with her determination.

"I could equate it with today's world leaders, tyrants, and fringe zealots. This would make sense—at least from a feature story standpoint."

"Certainly has possibilities."

"Sorry. So much for talking. Our food is getting cold. Let's eat."

Some time later, with their empty plates collected, the waiter returned, and Matt insisted on signing the check. Afterward he stood and went to Seneca, holding the back of her chair as she got up.

"Thanks for making the trek down here and keeping me company," he said. "I hoped you might find these empty tomb stories as interesting as I do. I plan to make use of it in my next book."

"You may not realize it, but after the disaster in Mexico, you might have just given me a huge boost. The trip was well worth it. And I got to meet a new friend. Could I call you if I need any more info?"

"It would be my pleasure." As they stepped into the parking lot, he hoped she would call him, especially once she had healed from her recent tragedy. He would have pursued seeing her again, but the timing was wrong. At least he would offer to take her on the promised boat ride.

"You up for that spin out on the water? On a night like this it really is quite wonderful when the bay is lit only by the stars. It's a little windy but we can tuck in behind a mangrove island so we don't rock so much."

"That would be lovely, Matt, but—" Seneca came to a sudden halt. "You've got to be kidding me. Jesus Christ, why won't he just butt out?"

"What is it? What's the matter?"

Seneca didn't answer. Instead she marched over to the Mercedes SUV with the orange fog lamps.

THE MEETING
1981, WASHINGTON, DC

"No matter what they say, it isn't true I flew that." The crowd roared with laughter as Ronald Reagan pointed to the Wright Brothers' plane.

Groves watched the president from the side of the stage, fifty feet away. Reagan ran his hand down the front of his heavily starched white shirt from throat to abdomen. Maybe the new president was more comfortable in boots and jeans rather than white tie and tails, Groves thought. He looked down at his own glossy black, patent leather shoes and razor-creased tux, and longed for boots and spurs, too. Even with all the success they had both experienced, the simple fact was they were just cowboys at heart.

President and Mrs. Reagan waved to the packed crowd of party goers gathered inside the National Air and Space Museum—one of nine inaugural balls spread across the nation's capital.

Reagan is almost giddy, Groves thought. And he should be. A few hours earlier, he became the fortieth president of the United

States, and a short time later received word that the fifty-two American hostages held by Iran for the past 444 days had been freed. It was a great day for Ronald Reagan and America.

Groves knew the president's schedule called for him to stay ten or fifteen minutes at each event, and by all indications, he was preparing to leave. With a proud Nancy on his arm, Reagan, still waving, turned to exit in Groves's direction. Surrounded by a contingent of Secret Service, the group started moving as the hall erupted in thunderous applause and cheers while the orchestra played a rousing "Hail to the Chief."

Accompanied by a half-dozen of his own security personnel, Groves watched as a White House aide moved toward Reagan. Getting his attention, the aide leaned in close and spoke into Reagan's ear. The president gave him a nod of acknowledgment and continued waving to the crowd. When the presidential party finally arrived at the stage exit, they halted. The president broke away and strode over to Groves.

"William, I'm so pleased you came." Reagan extended his hand.

"How could I say no, Mr. President?"

"Mr. Groves," Nancy Reagan said as she joined her husband.

The president pumped Groves's hand. "You're the spitting image of your father." He turned to Nancy. "How long ago did we last see his dad? Had to be twenty or so years ago when we had Billy out to the ranch. Boy, time sure passes quickly, especially when you get to be my age." The president stared at William for a moment then shook his head and uttered a small amused chuckle. "The resemblance is uncanny."

"I hear that a lot."

"Won't you join us?" Mrs. Reagan asked. "It's going to be quite a night."

"I wish I could, but I'm afraid I have some other commitments."

"Then let's plan on you visiting Nancy and me at the White House real soon."

"It would be my honor."

"I intend to hold you to it." Reagan turned to the group of supporters standing a few feet away. "Take a good look, my friends. You rarely get a chance to see one of the great American entrepreneurs, William Groves the Third."

As the supporters seemed to realize who Reagan referred to, they broke into applause. The wall of camera flashes became blinding.

Reagan shook Groves's hand once more. "Thanks again for coming, William."

Like the rush of a great wind, Ronald and Nancy Reagan, along with their aides and the Secret Service, swept out of the hall.

As a group of reporters sprang toward Groves, his personal security surrounded him and started moving in the opposite direction of the president's party toward an exit corridor. When it became obvious that they would not have access to the billionaire who was becoming more and more a recluse, the press spun an about-face and hustled to catch up with the presidential party.

A few moments later, Groves and his men emerged into an underground parking garage. Waiting for him was a black limousine, its motor running and an assistant standing beside the open side door.

As Groves approached, he smelled the cloth that the assistant had saturated with rubbing alcohol and held out for him. This had become a ritual over the last several years. When in public, Groves avoided touching doorknobs or shaking hands with people, but when he had to, those acts were followed by serious hand cleansing. He couldn't afford to become debilitated with a sickness that would make his life miserable but never kill him.

Groves took the cloth and scrubbed his hands with it before dropping it in the disposal bag also provided by his assistant. "What's this?" Groves said as the man handed him an envelope. "The gentleman insisted I give it to you."

Groves tore open the envelope and read the embossed script on the business card. *Javier Scarrow, Spiritualist. Expert on Mexican Culture and Antiquity.*

"Don't know him." Groves flipped the card over. As he read the handwritten message, a surge charged through his body like an electrical current. His legs suddenly felt feeble, barely strong enough to hold him up. Groves wiped his perspiring brow, feeling almost like the time he awoke to find himself buried alive in the mountains of Northern Sonora. It was hard to breathe.

His voice was charred with unexpected dryness. "Where is this man?"

The assistant motioned in the direction to Groves's right. He turned to see a tall man in a suit and overcoat standing near the entrance to an elevator. He had a dark complexion and a close-cropped mustache and beard. His hair was as black and gleaming as his obsidian eyes. In an instant, Groves recognized the face—a face he had gazed upon so many years ago inside the Apache treasure cave.

KILLER WHALE
2012, FLORIDA KEYS

SENECA SMACKED HER PALMS on the hood of the Mercedes SUV. The parking lot light shone through the windshield revealing that there was nobody inside.

"All right, where the hell are you?" She turned in a circle raising her arms in the air. "I know it's your car. Why can't you just leave me alone instead of lurking out there in the shadows, you son-of-a-bitch. What did you do, skulk in the dark like some kind of stalker and watch me eat? I don't want anything to do with you. Is that so hard to understand?"

Winded and shaking, she stomped back toward Matt.

"You all right?" His face bore an expression of complete confusion.

"Sorry. I know you must think I'm a lunatic. I'm just so furious." She heaved out a sigh. "It's my father. Well, not exactly—not a father I ever knew. Long story. I don't want to bore you." She looked back. "That's his car over there."

Two couples leaving the restaurant stopped to stare in Seneca's direction.

"I'm so sorry for pitching a fit in the middle of the parking lot and making an ass of myself in front of someone I just met who graciously paid for my dinner." She looked at Matt apologetically. "I'm really sorry." She gave him her most sincere smile. "I hope that boat ride invitation is still good?"

Seneca followed Matt's 911 Carrera, taking her own car. After several minutes his blinker flashed and they turned onto a street that ran parallel to a canal. At the end of the street, Matt braked, and a moment later a white wrought-iron gate in front of a house opened and automatic security floods flashed on. The actual living quarters of the house were elevated. Parking, storage, and a covered barbecue and patio were ground level.

Matt pulled his Porsche into the parking spot below the house and got out.

Seneca stared at the pale yellow house with its white shutters and metal roof. She loved the old Key West–style architecture. The floodlights revealed a wraparound veranda with a white railing.

She got out of her car and walked toward him. "I think I'm in the wrong part of the writing business."

"It's my sanctuary. I bought it several years ago when the bottom fell out of the real estate market. The owners were anxious to sell, so I got a steal of a deal. I never could have afforded it when the market was at its peak. It's my home, my office, my getaway. Come inside for a sec while I get the boat keys." He started up the steps with Seneca trailing.

"Here we are." Matt opened the door and ushered her into a great room with sliding glass doors stretching across the length of the opposite wall. They opened to the veranda at the rear of the house.

"Would you like anything to drink? And if you need to use the restroom, it's the door there to your left."

"I'm fine, thanks."

"I'll just be a minute. Have a seat."

Seneca sank slowly onto the leather sectional. Everything she saw was stylish but moderate by what she thought were most people's standards. There wasn't much furniture, just enough to be functional. Straight clean lines and a very masculine nautical theme. No clutter like her apartment. Daniel would have liked it.

As she observed the rest of the great room, one thing that most intrigued her was the horizontal wood paneling. It begged to be touched. Just as Seneca rose to go get a closer look, Matt reappeared.

"Ready?"

"Yep. Can I ask you a question first? What kind of wood is this? It's got so much character. I love the red stain in the grain."

"It's reclaimed pine from an old Vermont covered bridge. I had it put in after I bought the house. The only modification I've made." Matt ran his hand down the wall. "A little on the rough side, but…"

"I like it a lot."

"Me, too."

"Is it okay if I leave my purse?"

"Oh, sure. No need to lug it on the boat."

Matt led her down the back stairs and flipped on a couple of switches at the base. The backyard and dock burst into view. A jet ski sat atop the floating drive-on dock and a Boston Whaler was moored at the end of the pier.

"Sariel?" She noticed the lettering on the side. "Interesting name."

Matt held her hand as she stepped off the dock into the Whaler. "The main character in my series. She's an angel—literally. You've got a unique name. Is it a family name?"

"No. My mother was kind of a hippie. Well, not kind of. She was a full-blown hippie and women's rights activist. My name comes from the 1848 Seneca Falls Convention in New York and a reformer named Elizabeth Cady Stanton. My full name is Seneca Cady Hunt. And, FYI, Hunt is my mother's maiden name."

"I think it's great to have a name that means something."

A sliver of a crescent moon hung in the sky as Matt started the Whaler and slipped away from the dock. His house was at the mouth of the canal so it took only a few minutes to leave the "no wake" zone and head west into Florida Bay.

Matt accelerated the twin Mercury outboards. The boat porpoised for a second on the choppy water, then got up on plane. Soon they were racing across the dark water.

Seneca grew more relaxed, the tension gliding away, leaving her stalking father behind with the diminishing glow of the Upper Keys. There was nothing quite like being on the water, she thought. It put things in perspective. The splendid stillness and the absence of daily distractions.

"There's a cabin if you want to look around?" Matt had to yell over the wind and roar of the engines. "It's got a small galley and head. The berth sleeps two." He switched on the interior lights.

Seneca opened the hatch and peered inside. "Looks like you've got everything you need." She noticed the reduction in the boat's speed.

"I'm going to slip us up behind that mangrove island to keep out of the wind so we won't rock so much."

She closed the hatch. With the boat in neutral, Matt flipped a switch on the control panel, causing the electric winch to lower the anchor. A moment later, she felt it grab and swing the boat around.

"Chill time." Matt turned off the engines and moved to the stern. "Come sit back here so the T-top doesn't interrupt your view."

Joining him, she sat on the padded bench and gazed up. "I've been living in Miami for so long and its city lights, I've forgotten the absolute beauty of the night sky."

A whooshing noise close by startled her. Then a smile of recognition broke over her face. "A dolphin taking a breath, right?" But she didn't need Matt's confirmation. "I can remember when I was a kid being out on the water with my mother. Some days it was so quiet we could hear the dolphins breathe. No splashing, just breathing. We'd hear them before we saw them."

"If we get lucky, we'll see shooting stars." Matt pointed. "Now there's a beautiful sight."

Seneca saw a half-dozen twinkling lights the size of stars on the horizon forming a long line from west to east. They seemed to be moving, but very slowly. "What are they?"

"It's called the string of pearls. Those are airliners lined up on their approach to Miami International. Tonight the line stretches way out over the Everglades."

"I guess you need to be this far away to appreciate it."

"On a clear night like this one, you can—"

She turned to him. "Something wrong?"

Matt leaned forward. "Must be my imagination." He continued to stare intently into the blackness of the night sky. "How peculiar, there it is again—something moving across the sky about twenty degrees off the horizon. You can see it block out the stars for a few seconds."

"Where?"

"One o'clock."

Seneca strained to see. "Yes! I can make out its outline. Kind of like an airplane but no lights."

He stood and cocked his head to the right. "Or sound. I've never seen anything quite like it. It's sort of cigar shaped."

They were now standing elbow to elbow. "Shaped more like a flying killer whale."

"You're right. But it's impossible to judge how big or how far away it is."

She cupped her hand to her ear. "Matt, I do hear something—like a beating sound, but really soft and muffled."

"Yeah, now I hear—"

Suddenly the Boston Whaler buckled and shook, chunks of fiberglass, metal, and plastic shooting through the air as large-caliber rounds ripped into the cabin.

In almost the same instant, Seneca felt Matt grab her shoulders and shove her over the side.

FACE TO FACE
1981, WASHINGTON, DC

"We have a mutual friend." Scarrow sat in the back of the billionaire's limousine as it sped along Independence Avenue. The two men had just left Reagan's inaugural ball at the National Air and Space Museum and were headed to Washington National Airport.

Scarrow didn't scare Groves, there had been others like him before—those hell bent on extortion. A handful down through the years discovered the tiny cracks in his façade when they caught him in an unguarded moment without his specialized makeup and facial prosthetics. Fools like Colin Black who paid for their greed with their lives. Each one had suffered an untimely demise or mysterious disappearance. Unlimited funds could buy anything.

But even though this man didn't intimidate him, Groves knew in his gut that Scarrow was different. He felt it from his first glimpse of the man's face in the parking lot.

He pushed a console button and the soundproof divider separating the passenger compartment and the driver closed. Staring at the handwriting on the back of Scarrow's business card, he read aloud, "I know the secret of your longevity." He looked at Scarrow. "Explain yourself."

"It needs no explanation."

"You say you know the *secret*. What secret is that?" That's what intrigued Groves. No one had ever claimed to know *how* this had happened to him. Hell, he didn't even know. But suddenly there was this new thread that he couldn't quite untangle. He'd seen Scarrow's face before all right, only back then it was more primitive looking and he wore a crown of feathers. It was the imprint on the piece of cloth in the silver chest. And then, that night in Reno the hooker held up the cloth and Scarrow's face had been replaced by his own.

Was that old scrap of cloth the link to what had happened to him? That made no sense.

All these years, he had hidden under layers of lies, masquerade, and deception. Had someone—this stranger—actually discovered the secret to what caused him to remain ageless? The idea of Scarrow being able to explain how his *condition* had happened would be nothing short of a blessing. And a relief. Once he understood, there was the possibility the weight might finally be lifted from his soul, a weight that tried to suffocate his every thought. Growing more apprehensive, Groves wiped his palms on his pants legs.

"Who is the mutual friend you mentioned?"

"Veronica."

Groves' mind sifted through current and past acquaintances, close and distant. There were so many women he'd known down through the years and thousands in his many corporations. It was possible some were named Veronica, but none of any importance came to mind.

"I don't know anyone by that name. This is all a mistake, a misunderstanding. I think you have me confused with someone else. I don't know this Veronica person, and I don't know you."

"How old are you, William? You don't mind if I call you William, do you?"

"My age isn't any of your concern."

Scarrow leaned in close. Almost in a whisper, he said, "By my estimates, you're around one-hundred forty." He smiled broadly. "But you only look like you're in your late thirties." Looking smug, he added, "How'd I do, William?"

Groves's palms turned clammy. "What do you want?" He lowered the pitch of his voice to sound as menacing as possible, not wanting Scarrow to think he felt threatened. After all, this man could be bluffing—a lucky guess, an outside bet in order to swindle money out of him.

"You're probably thinking that I'm here to blackmail you or intimidate you or in some way take advantage of your situation." Scarrow seemed to relax as he leaned back into the plush seat. "Let me assure you, it's the farthest thing from my mind. You see, William, we not only have a mutual friend, we also share a common set of unusual circumstances."

"I doubt that." Groves laughed nervously. "You're just another scam artist—"

"Oh, William. Have a little faith. I'm probably the only person on the face of the Earth who understands your gift. It *is* a gift, you know. To help answer your concerns, let me tell you my story, first." He rubbed his chin as if organizing his thoughts. "I received the gift four hundred and sixty-one years ago—way before you did. I'll leave the details for a future discussion, but I'll tell you that it was at a time of great turmoil. I was the leader of a vast nation facing the peril of an invading army threatening to destroy our culture and civilization. The commander of the enemy forces displayed a swatch of cloth which he claimed bore the image of his god. He told me that the cloth was a priceless relic known as the Veil of Veronica. He said it originally belonged to a holy woman who used it to cleanse the sweat and blood from the face of a condemned man on his journey to be executed. William, the face I saw embedded within the threads of the veil was of the great prophet and rabbi, Jesus Christ."

He paused as if to let the story sink into Groves's mind.

"The one who showed me Veronica's veil told me of Christ's crucifixion and resurrection. It occurred to me that, because of the miracle of the face appearing on the cloth, there might be a connection between it and Christ's rising from the dead. So, in a brief moment when I was alone with the veil, I decided that if it conveyed some magical power, I, too, wanted to be like Christ and have the power to rise from my tomb. In desperation, because I knew that I would soon be taken prisoner and put to death, I touched the veil to my face just as Veronica had done to the rabbi. After my cruel execution I found myself wrapped in a burial cloth—and most astonishingly alive inside my tomb. My closest attendants may have returned at some point to cremate my body.

But I had risen from the dead and escaped. That began my endless search for the veil. I knew that by touching it to my face I had been given immortality."

Groves shuddered. Like an avalanche of memory, he saw himself standing in the Apache cave staring at the face of the man with the crown of feathers. Then he remembered what happened next.

He used the cloth to wipe the sweat from his own face.

"Tell me, William, the first time you gazed upon the cloth, whose face did you see?"

"Yours." Groves could only manage a whisper.

"And whose face is on it now?"

THE LESSON
2012, BAHAMAS

An abundance of stars filled the Caribbean sky and thin wisps of cirrus clouds curled around a crescent moon as Scarrow looked out from the ceremonial terrace atop Azteca. Although the lights on the horizon were from distant Bahamian hamlets, he so yearned for them to be the home fires of his beloved city of Tenochtitlan and the boat lanterns that were once scattered across Lake Texcoco. Flickering around the perimeter of the temple roof, torches filled the breeze with a pungent smoky haze.

In the middle of the terrace stood a single, knee-high trapezoidal stone slab. It was designed so that when the *xochimiqui,* or captured warrior, was stretched out upon it, his back would naturally arch.

Scarrow searched the faces of the current nine apostles as they watched from the opposite side of the slab. Each wore decorative, floor-length cloth sheaths that hung down the front and back. Scarrow was dressed in a similar manner but also wore a crown of feathers that pointed toward the heavens and a wide, hand-tooled silver belt on which was depicted the Aztec Fire Serpent of Time. Upon his feet and those of the apostles were leather sandals with strands of thin golden rope that wound around their legs to their knees. Bracelets, earrings, and necklaces of turquoise and silver hung from their bodies. And in his hand he held a trowel-shaped, black obsidian knife with a leather-bound handle. Torches bathed the sacrificial altar in shimmering golden light.

"We have allowed our universe to become out of balance." He knew there were modern scientific explanations of the imbalance, of how on December 21, 2012, many ancient calendars predicted calamity. Scientists calculated that the Earth would be in exact alignment with the sun and the center of the Milky Way Galaxy. The whole mantle of the Earth would slide, resulting in the shifting of the magnetic poles. The result would be global devastation. It didn't matter what scientific terms were used or what modern geophysicists projected. His advisors and other ancients prophesied the same day as cataclysmic. And that day was quickly approaching.

He continued. "We have little time to reverse the gods' discontent. But we will. We will restore universal harmony with our own hands and pay them our endless debt. Tonight you will witness the setting free of the *tonalli,* the animated spirit that lives within our blood. When we experience great fear, it concentrates in the heart. This is why our gods hunger for the human heart, for without the sacrifice of the spirit and the consumption of the *tonalli,* they will command the total destruction of our world. Tonight we will ensure that *Tonatuih,* our sun god, is appeased."

With a nod, he watched two apostles enter a nearby antechamber and return escorting a young bronze-skinned man. The man's hands were bound behind his back, and he was blindfolded and gagged. Coming to stand beside the stone slab, he was made to face Scarrow.

"Are you ready to offer up your *tonalli* to nourish the great war god, *Huitzilopochtli,* and to *Tonatuih,* the god of the sun?"

The young man shook his head as he tried to pull away from the grip of the apostles. His muffled pleas could be heard through the gag as he struggled.

Scarrow signaled for the man's bindings to be cut. With two additional apostles assisting, they grasped the man's arms and legs, forcing him to lie back onto the slab, its shape causing his chest to thrust upward.

His breathing became rapid and shallow, his head darting about in terror. Scarrow pulled the blindfold away. The man jerked his head to each side, staring with wild eyes at the audience around him, then back at Scarrow. The apostles pinned his arms and legs.

The man raised his head to speak. But before he could utter a word, Scarrow stabbed the knife into the victim's abdomen, sliced upwards and thrust his hand inside the wet, red wound. He reached up, beneath the diaphragm, and a second later the victim's head collapsed, hanging over the back of the slab. Scarrow withdrew his hand and raised it, gripping the still-beating heart with its ropes of blood vessels and tissue trailing. "His spirit is with the sun."

He spread blood on the victim's lips, then paraded the glistening organ before everyone. Next, he turned to tread a few steps to a stone carving of *Tonatuih*, the Aztec sun god. The god's fixed eyes stared out menacingly as if searching for his next meal, mouth open wide, tongue in the shape of the sacrificial knife, protruding through bared teeth, ready to savor the next offering. Carved on either side of his head were claws grasping a human heart. Scarrow shoved the still-quivering organ into the stone mouth, mashing and grinding it into the opening until all that remained was a smear of crimson blending into the scarlet-painted face.

He returned to the sacrificial stone slab. "Soon, you will choose your own honored *xochimiqui* to give up their *tonalli* spirits in order to preserve and renew our world. That time draws near as you prepare to go forth to your homelands and make ready for the final days of the old world and the new beginning." He smiled at each one. "When we are done here tonight, we will feast upon what is left of this flesh and celebrate what the *xochimiqui* have given us."

Memories flooded back to him of almost five hundred years ago when he stood atop the ancient Templo Mayor watching his priests perform this sacred ritual so many times. Tonight, he was not a priest, but he *was* the teacher of those he called his apostles—his new priests. He had deliberately chosen the final number to be twelve, imitating the Christian faith. After all, was this not the same as the Christian communion—the sacrifice of body and blood? There were still three more apostles to resurrect, but all were within his timeline. He was the new messiah and would prove it beyond any doubt. In addition to his apostles, the Azteca disciples—not his chosen twelve, but still his devout staff of followers—would help prepare the way for him and his Phoenix apostles. He knew the time was approaching when the fulfillment of human sacrifice would return, and the gods would find favor with him and all his work. This was why they had chosen him to receive the special gift of immortality.

"Let us continue the lesson," he said.

A moment later, the next *xochimiqui* was led from the antechamber to the altar stone—this time a young female. As she tried to struggle and fight, Scarrow watched the apostles cut the straps that bound her hands behind her back. Then they stretched her across the slab.

Standing over the *xochimiqui*, Scarrow took the still-dripping knife and offered the blade to his apostles.

"Who will be first?"

MANGROVES
2012, FLORIDA BAY

BLACKNESS ENGULFED SENECA. THE impact of the water drove the air from her lungs and she took a choking gulp of saltwater. With arms thrashing and reaching, she broke the surface and sucked in a breath.

"This way!" Matt was yelling. "Get away from the boat!"

As she tried to find her bearings, she glanced over her shoulder. The long black object they'd seen moving against the stars hung in the sky nearby, its rotors almost perfectly silent.

How can that be? Where is the noise?

She could plainly see it was a small black helicopter, maybe twenty feet long or less. No windows or lights.

Where is the pilot?

And yet, even though she saw the spinning rotors, they made only a muffled whopping sound.

A quick burst of flame erupted from underneath its body as more projectiles slammed into the mortally wounded Boston Whaler.

Flames burst from the boat's cabin, sending orange and red fireworks shooting out over the chop.

"Swim to the island!"

A beam of light flicked on from a round pod mounted under the nose of the machine and lit up the boat.

"They think we're still onboard," she said.

"Dive underwater!"

Seneca dropped beneath the surface, breast stroking, coming up only briefly when her lungs burned so fiercely that she had no choice. Her long skirt strangled her legs, making it impossible to swim—her sandals had already slipped away. To escape, she had to lose the skirt. Grabbing the elastic waistband, she yanked down and kicked it off.

She surfaced to snatch a quick breath and locate the dark mass of the island. The beam of light swept across the water behind her as if sniffing for a trail. As she went under again she heard another volley of shots impact the boat and felt the concussion of an explosion—the fuel tanks must have ignited.

Seneca struggled, her legs thundering under the surface, her arms taking wide, forceful arcs, using up her precious oxygen.

Then a bump against her thigh.

Sweet Jesus.

A shark? It had to be. It felt big. She knew how abundant they were in these waters this time of year and their need to prowl the shallows for baitfish, especially at night. She and her mother had hooked ten-foot-long, two-hundred-pound lemon sharks and bull sharks in no more than three feet of water not far from here. The water was warm, and sharks were plentiful.

Oh God, oh God. She swam hard.

Maybe it was just a piece of driftwood or the dolphin she heard earlier taking a breath. She tried convincing herself it was the friendly Flipper in a lame effort to lock down the terror. Her heart hammered against her chest as if it might explode with the next beat causing her arteries to rupture from the force of blood pulsing in her head.

Kicking and sweeping the water back with her arms, she kept below the surface until she felt her feet snag the sand. At this point she had no choice but to expose herself to the helicopter attack and run for the island. She shot up and staggered forward. Looking back, she could no longer see the helicopter. With its black form and stealth rotors, it could be coming around for another assault and she wouldn't know it until the bullets tore into her.

The flames ate at the twenty-six-foot Boston Whaler—she smelled the caustic smoke as the synthetic materials burned.

Reaching ankle-deep water, Seneca dropped onto her hands and knees. When she looked up she saw that just to her right a narrow creek ran through the island like a watery tunnel. In the bare light she caught a glimpse of several pairs of eyes staring back at her. Raccoons, she supposed. Finally, she was able to stand on wobbly legs—her muscles cramping from the frantic swim.

Seneca wished she still had her shoes as she crossed the stubble of mangrove sprouts before reaching a muddy spot on the edge of the island where the suction swallowed her feet. She knew her bare soles would be no match for the hidden edges of coral and shell lurking in the dark.

A swarm of mosquitoes rushed to attack, invading her hair, her nostrils, her eyes. She swatted and spat as she scanned the blackness for Matt. There wasn't enough light from the claw of moon to see more than a few feet. The smoldering mass of burning boat in the distance was no help.

Seneca bent forward and put her hands on her knees, trying to catch her breath.

"Matt?"

No answer.

FIREBIRD

1981, SOMEWHERE OVER THE MIDWEST

"How DID YOU FIND me?" Groves and Scarrow sat in the wood-paneled office compartment inside the private Boeing 727 as it streaked westward across the heartland of America.

"I became mildly suspicious in 1937 when I saw the news of the death of your son in the papers." Scarrow took a sip of tea from the bone china cup displaying the gold Groves Consortium logo on the side. "I was living in Spain at the time teaching Latin American history at *Universidad de Barcelona.* You know, it's ironic that they never knew I was teaching from firsthand experience. Anyway, you see, William, I have a photographic memory, and I recalled reading the news of your death back in 1919. Because of your stature in the world as a leading industrialist—I believe the press referred to you as the Invisible Titan—I remember feeling regret that I never had the opportunity to meet you. So when I saw the picture of your departed son, something caught my attention. It wasn't the amazing resemblance so much as the way the face stared out at me—the look of mistrust in the eyes, the glare of reluctance at having to be exposed to the public. It was the same expression looking back at me in the mirror every day of my life.

"I dug through the university archives and found your obituary photo in an old copy of the *Chicago Herald*. Holding it next to the photo of your son, I realized it was more than an uncanny resemblance—it had to be the same person. But without undeniable proof, I chalked it up to being so desperate for answers that I was grasping at ghosts. Then when your grandson passed away in 1960, once again I found myself staring at a familiar face. My gut told me I may have found what I had sought for so long."

"I regretted ever having my picture taken at all," Groves said. "I knew each time I did, I was leaving evidence—a trail somebody could eventually follow. But in those early days, I also never realized I'd have to fake my death and assume the identity of my own son, much less my grandson. I kept out of the way of photographers for over fifty years. But, I knew this day would eventually come." Groves leaned back in the plush executive chair as he felt the plane course correct. "I still find it hard to believe you put this all together based on a few old photographs."

Scarrow laughed out loud. "Oh, no, William, it was way more than that. In 1960, I was a senior research analyst for the Smithsonian Institute. My specialty, as you know from my business card, is Mexican culture and antiquity. I had unrestricted access to the Institute's research and records facilities along with those of other government agencies. My superiors believed I was working on a side project—an unauthorized biography of the industrialist William Groves. That's how I was able to amass a detailed, sometimes day-by-day record of a certain Arizona Territory cowboy named

Billy Groves. I must tell you, William, your amazing rise from a penniless cowboy who showed up in a dusty border town with some Spanish gold pieces to become one of the richest men in the world makes quite a story. You undoubtedly have a natural knack as a business visionary. It's well documented how you've found mere germs of ideas and managed to grow them into international success stories. My compliments to your amazing ability to make money. So to answer your question, no, it was more than the photographs. It took me years, actually decades, to put it all together. But I did, and here I am, your new partner."

"Excuse me!" Groves sat up with a start. "What the hell do you mean, partner? I offered to let you on my airplane so I could hear your story. I was fascinated, nothing more. But we have no partnership. As a matter of fact, we have no relationship at all. I admit, your story is intriguing and I sympathize that you share the same condition as I do. But that doesn't prove anything. Once this plane lands in Phoenix, we'll part paths, Mr. Scarrow. I'll go to my winter home in the desert, and you'll go to wherever you came from. And I can promise you that we will never meet again."

"It's interesting that we are going to Phoenix." Scarrow paused to finish his tea. "Are you familiar with the legend of the mythical phoenix firebird?"

Groves was annoyed that Scarrow seemed to ignore his rebuff. He had never met a man so in control, so calm, so focused. "Somewhat. What does it have to do with anything?"

"According to Egyptian and Greek mythologies, the phoenix was a bird with a tail of gold and red plumage. It lived for about five hundred years. At the end of its life, it would build a nest of twigs. Then it would set fire to the nest and become consumed by the flames. Soon after, a new phoenix bird would rise from the ashes to begin the next five-hundred-year life-cycle."

"That's all well and good. But I don't get why you're telling me this fairytale."

"Let's just say that I'm the phoenix about to end my life-cycle. I need to build my nest and rise from the ashes."

"And what's that got to do with me?"

"You have the means for me to complete my life and begin again. You have what I need to rise from the ashes."

"Which is?"

"Veronica's veil."

RED SQUARE
2012, MOSCOW

As Dr. Josef Mengele stood inside the west portal of the Cathedral of the Archangel, he removed his fake mustache, bushy wig, and thick-rimmed glasses, revealing the perfect likeness to the man Scarrow had the plastic surgeons create. He slipped his disguise into the side pocket of his crisp gray suit coat. Mengele glanced at the faded fresco overhead depicting the mass baptism of the Russian people during the reign of Prince Vladimir the Great. It was hard to see since the only lighting came from scattered security lights—the giant chandeliers were shut down hours ago once the last of the tourists left. The Italian Renaissance–inspired, onion-domed church was among the many cathedrals, palaces, and government buildings nestled inside the Kremlin.

Taking an extra moment to adjust his tie and straighten the lapel pin bearing the flag of the Russian Federation, he nodded to the phoenix disciples flanking his sides. Dressed in black suits and bearing the small Presidential Security Service emblem on their lapels, the two men acknowledged that they were ready.

In unison, with Dr. Mengele trailing slightly, the trio started across the echoing marble floor of the five-hundred-year-old church toward the expansive, floor-to-ceiling iconostasis that stretched across the back wall. They passed numerous sarcophagi of Russia's rulers, from Grand Duke Ivan I to Mikhail Romanov, the founder of the Romanov dynasty. As they approached the wall of icons, a soldier on solitary guard duty saw them and rushed to intercept.

"Halt! The cathedral is closed." He pulled a flashlight from his belt with one hand while he removed his pistol from its holster with the other. He glanced at the Security Service emblem on their jackets. "Present your identification, please."

The trio paused.

Shining his light into the faces of the three men, he stopped on Mengele. He took a step forward, his jaw dropping as his eyes grew large. "Mr. President? I—" The hand holding his gun sunk slowly to his side. "I don't understand. What are you ..."

"Get the light out of my face!" Mengele spoke just above a whisper. The *Engage* wireless electrode implanted in his brain was programmed with several languages including English and Russian. It had translated the guard's words into Mengele's native German and allowed him to answer in Russian.

"I'm so sorry, Mr. President. I never expected to see—"

"I'm here on a matter of state security and I need your assistance." Dr. Mengele took a step forward and placed his hand on the guard's shoulder. "What is your name, son?"

"Dmitry, sir." The young guard's voice was filled with uncertainty. "Corporal Dmitry Sabonis."

"Are you related to our glorious Soviet gold medalist?"

The soldier nodded. "A distant cousin, Mr. President."

"Something to take pride in, corporal." He leaned in close. "Can I trust you to keep my mission in strictest confidence?"

"Of course, sir." The guard snapped to attention. "I am here to serve at the pleasure of the President of the Russian Federation."

"Good. Then take us behind the iconostasis to the private chapel. I need to see the tomb of the Grand Prince of Moscow, the first Tsar of all Russia, Ivan the Terrible."

As the last notes of Tchaikovsky performed by the Moscow Symphony Orchestra faded into the night and the stage went dark, a single spotlight shown on the figure of Javier Scarrow. He stood in the center of the sweeping glass and chrome stage. Clothed in a bright orange and blue robe, he gazed upon sprawling Red Square just outside the walls of the Kremlin. In the far distance, banks of floodlights illuminated St. Basil's Cathedral, making it appear like a nighttime attraction in a Disney theme park. Between the cathedral and the Phoenix Ministry pavilion, a crowd of half a million devoted followers hung on every word Scarrow said as his voice, along with that of the Russian translator, boomed through the thundering speaker system and his face appeared on rows of giant TV screens lining the Square.

"Welcome." Scarrow reached out his arms as if to embrace the throng. "Tonight, I bring you a message of hope, of peace, of joy, of balance and harmony, because we are all of one world, one universe, and one spirit. Many years ago a great leader, Tecumseh, Chief of the Shawnee nation of Native Americans spoke these words. 'Brothers, we all belong to one family; we are all children of the Great Spirit; we walk in the same path; slake our thirst at the same spring; and now affairs of the greatest concern lead us to smoke the pipe around the same council fire.

"'Brothers, we are friends; we must assist each other to bear our burdens.'" Scarrow paused to let the translation catch up to him and to give the audience a dramatic moment to reflect.

"Tecumseh's words hold true to this day. When I quote his words, express his vision, and speak of the Great Spirit, I speak to you of the collective deities of Islam, Judaism, Buddhism, Christianity, Animism, Hinduism, and Zoroastrianism, and other great religions, there is a common theme that connects us all. For the Hindus, there is the belief in *Brahman,* the underlying universal life force, and *dharma,* that there are three paths for maintaining world order, balance, and harmony.

"In Animism, there is belief in a spiritual realm which humans share with the universe. In Zoroastrianism, there is a supreme creator of the universe.

"I could continue on and on with each, but you, beloved brothers and sisters, already see the pattern. We are one in the universe. We use different words, but we say the same thing. And always there is the cosmic dualism, the struggle for balance, the struggle between what we perceive as good and evil."

Scarrow paused again and reached his arms forward to the crowd. "One world, one universe, one spirit. We are one!"

Applause rang out across the square and the crowd repeated, "We are one! We are one! We are one!"

"In our blindness and greed as humans, we have separated ourselves, drawn profound lines between groups, not divisions that the universe created, but that we humans saw fit to define ourselves as one better than another. We have not honored the universe, the deities that we all say we worship. We've given them all different names and say they belong only to our group. My group of Hindus. My group of Christians. My group of Jews. And now we pay the price." His voice rose. "The recent disasters are evidence of our universe convulsing. The massive earthquakes in China and Chile, the tsunami in Hawaii, the volcano in Yellowstone National Park in the United States, the horrendous flood in the Czech Republic. Do you believe these are just normal, that these disasters are a natural course of events? Not so, my brothers and sisters. These recent calamities have been of proportions of greater magnitude than we have experienced before."

Scarrow drew a deep, chest-inflating breath. His voice came softly and forlornly. "We have damaged our world... our universe... and it is in the throes of agony. We have abused our resources, scarred the very earth with our mining and deforestation, raped our flora and fauna to extinction. Mother Earth is in great pain." The pitch of his voice dropped even lower, plaintiff and melancholy. "And we have gravely wounded one another."

Scarrow punched up the tone. "But we do not have to continue along this path. We can mend the wounds, heal the scars. Find peace and joy, and bring harmony and balance back to the universe. We can know one another, see beyond the shallowness of the color of our skin, the shape of our eyes, and recognize ourselves as brothers and sisters. We have the same beliefs and messages. We are of one world, one universe, and one spirit. We are one. Extend your hand to the brother or sister next to you. Grasp hands in a renewal of peace and harmony, a promise to the universe that we are remorseful for our ways, and we praise what it has provided. We will move forward, rising from the ashes of the destruction we have brought on, rising from the ashes of our despair just as the phoenix bird rose from his ashes. Extend your hand and with it your love for one another. Our Phoenix Ministry is the promise of a bountiful future and at last, peace and harmony and balance in the universe, and it is incumbent upon us to make great sacrifices to that end. And we will, because we are one!"

The crowd responded with cries of affirmation, repeating again and again, "We are one!"

Patiently, he waited for the crowd to calm. Then his voice became melodic as he brought back Tecumseh's words. "'Brothers, we all belong to one family; we are all children of the Great Spirit; we walk in the same path; slake our thirst at the same spring; and now affairs of the greatest concern lead us to smoke the pipe around the same council fire.

"'Brothers, we are friends; we must assist each other to bear our burdens.'"

After a short pause, Scarrow said, "I will show you the way. I will show you the truth. I will show you the path." Slowly, he began the chant, "One world, one universe, one spirit. We are one!"

Red Square resounded with the voices of the frenzied mass, some shouting, some weeping, some with arms waving in the air, others falling to their knees. A flush of warmth filled Scarrow's chest. He had them. This was the beginning.

BLINDED

2012, FLORIDA BAY

THE BUTTRESSES OF THE red mangrove prop roots made it appear as if the trees were walking in the water on spindly, tangled spider legs. There wasn't much solid ground to the island that Seneca could make out in the darkness, mostly mud and mangroves.

She searched for any sign of the helicopter, but saw nothing overhead except a vast spray of stars. Turning toward the bay, she called for Matt again. No response. She swallowed hard, imagining he was seriously injured… or worse.

Struggling to free her feet from the suction of the mud, she worked her way toward the protective cover of the mangrove trees. Maybe the creek bottom was sandier with less mud, she thought, and headed in its direction.

The water deepened to thigh high as she reached the mouth of the creek and the leading edge of the mangrove forest. As she took a step, the side of her foot slid against something sharp. "Damn it." She yelped as the salt water seeped into the fresh cut.

Seneca felt the top of a knot of roots for any unsavory critter that might be using the spot for a resting place.

No snake or lizard or crab. No anything, thank God.

Using the slippery scaffold of barnacled roots she climbed up to where she could sit clear of the water, but not without receiving tiny slits in her soles.

Jesus, what had happened? Who was shooting at them? And what was that black helicopter that seemed to be straight out of a James Bond movie? Who were they trying to kill? She certainly had no enemies that would go to this extreme. Maybe it was the religious whackos Matt told her about? The ones who objected to his books and called him a heretic. But they sounded like random screwball radicals, not a group that had access to a high-tech helicopter with large caliber weapons.

The cut on the side of her foot burned. Unable to see in the dark, her fingertip probing revealed the ragged edge of broken skin and her warm sticky blood slowly dripping into the creek. She thought of that *bump* against her thigh she felt while swimming to the island. If it was a shark, at least she was safely out of the water and not sending a bloody invitation to dinner.

A sudden forceful yank on her leg sent her splashing into the shallow creek. Seneca scrambled to right herself, wiping the water from her face.

"Quiet," Matt whispered. His powerful hands pulled her down into the water beside him.

Stunned, Seneca stared at his shadowy face as they crouched in the creek. "Matt! What's going—"

He put his finger to her lips, then pointed to an opening in the mangrove canopy.

"Is it them?"

Matt glared at the sky.

Seneca trained her eyes on his line of sight and listened. Above the breeze through the mangroves and the gentle gurgle of the creek, she heard it—the faint sound of rotor blades.

"How will they see us without a spotlight?"

"Infrared sensors. They don't penetrate the water effectively. Keep your body submerged. Move along the creek until we get near where the raccoons were feeding. Swim zigzag and stay under as long as you can. When you get near the raccoons, ball up under the mangrove roots. Understand?"

Seneca nodded, and Matt signaled for her to go. She could only guess how far the animals were from them and wasn't sure how long it would take to swim the distance. She didn't understand why he wanted her to do this, but he must have a reason.

After swimming for over a minute, she figured she had reached the right spot, and raised her head out of the water. Her rough calculation had been good. Just a couple of yards away she saw the eyes of the raccoons and their silhouettes when they moved. They didn't dart away, so her presence hadn't seemed to startle them.

Matt emerged beside her. He took her hand and pulled her from the middle of the creek closer to the mass of roots where the raccoons were. "Squeeze under the roots, they'll break our outline," he whispered. "Whoever is watching the images may mistake us for just more raccoons."

When they were under the cage of mangrove roots, he wrapped his arms around her and held her still, their faces just barely above the waterline.

A muted rotor sound caused her to look up. Through a break in the trees she saw a portion of the stars disappear as the black machine passed overhead.

The eeriness of the shadows, the sound of water coursing through the maze of roots, the thought of her wound sending a trickle of blood to the open water, worsened her already unnerved state. She remained as still as possible, praying the raccoons didn't flee.

Seneca strained to detect the sound of the rotors but heard nothing other than the ripple of the water and the wind. Then, in the distance came the high-pitched hum of a boat engine. As the moments passed, it grew closer. At least the creek was so narrow where they hid, almost nothing short of a kayak or canoe could get to them.

She wondered if they should attempt to get to the mouth of the creek again and hail the passing boat, even though the chances of them being heard or seen in the darkness were remote. But she quickly reassessed that option. What if it was the same bunch that attacked the Whaler? No. She and Matt would wait. Once the sun came up, waving at a passing fisherman would be the best bet. But not now, not with the black helicopter so close.

The sound of the boat grew stronger, and Seneca was certain it cruised as close as it could get without running aground.

She glanced at Matt. But before she could say anything, the engine slowed to an idle.

Suddenly, a brilliant beam of light penetrated the tangled mangrove island scattering the raccoons and blinding her.

THE CONVERSATION
1981, SOMEWHERE OVER THE MIDWEST

GROVES SAT ALONE IN his office aboard the private 727. His personal assistant had informed him that a call was coming in from his Asian regional director, and Groves had asked Scarrow to excuse him while he took the call. He watched the tall Mexican stand and leave, and wondered what would happen once they landed. How would this awkward meeting come to an end? It was obvious Scarrow had an agenda in mind—although he hadn't defined what he meant by being *partners*. Groves was sure the man would show his cards before they parted ways. He supposed it would come down to a simple case of blackmail or extortion. That kind of threat was manageable—usually with the blackmailer meeting an untimely demise.

After finishing the call, he sat staring out the window at the tops of the moonlit clouds thirty-eight thousand feet above the sleeping countryside. What started as a miracle in the Apache treasure cave had, over the years, transformed into a curse. It haunted him every waking hour and crept right into his dark dreams.

It's one thing to want to live forever; it's another to have no choice.

Immortality had come with a heavy toll of loneliness, isolation, fear, paranoia, and a hundred other demons.

Although Groves was rarely seen by anyone, including his support staff, he kept them well compensated so they would resist being enticed or bribed to reveal insider info on their reclusive boss. His closest business associates lived lives of opulence exceeding what it would take to betray Groves.

In allowing Javier Scarrow to approach him, Groves realized he had taken a huge risk and began to think it immensely foolish. He never should have let Scarrow on board the flight, but there had been no time to linger in Washington and hear the man out. He certainly couldn't ignore the stranger, not after the shock of the man's handwritten note revealing the knowledge of his *secret*.

Groves consoled himself in the fact that at dawn they would land in Phoenix where he would wish Scarrow farewell then be whisked away to his Arizona desert retreat. With any luck, he would never see the man again. It was just a matter of a few more hours.

Groves left his office and wandered through the forward compartments to the lounge. He found Scarrow sitting on a velour couch, reading a copy of *Time*—a giant dollar sign on the cover representing the economy with the headline, "Reagan's Biggest Challenge."

"I hope your call went well." Scarrow closed the magazine and laid it aside.

"All problems stem from money, and money is the solution to all problems." Groves went to a well-stocked bar and poured himself a whiskey over ice. "Want a drink, Mr. Scarrow?"

"I'd hoped you would call me Javier. And I'll have what you're having."

Groves handed Scarrow a drink, then sat opposite him on a matching couch. He was fascinated with the fact that someone else shared his secret. If nothing else, he was eager to hear what it was like for this man to have lived for almost five hundred years. "So you were some kind of king?"

"I am Emperor Motecuhzoma Xocoyotzin, ruler of Tenochtitlan."

"In English, please."

"Modern history refers to me as Emperor Montezuma II, ninth ruler of the Aztec nation."

Groves nodded as he tried to recall his basic Mexican history. "You lost a war with the Spanish—a conquistador named Cortés did in your people, right?"

"Yes."

"Now here's what I don't understand." He took a sip of his whiskey. "There were a lot of you people, a helluva lot more than Cortés could have brought along on his ships. So how'd you manage to get your ass kicked by a few hundred men?"

"It was a complex situation. We suffered from historical and physical issues that accelerated the Conquest."

"Like what?"

Scarrow held up his fingers as he recited a list. "A raging smallpox epidemic, thanks to the Spanish. Our own religious belief that our defeat was foretold by eight omens that came before the arrival of the Spanish. Our mistaken belief that Cortés was *Quetzalcoatl*, our god-king who was prophesied to return and reclaim his city. And of course our goal in battle was different—in war we took prisoners rather than killing the enemy. And not least of all, our weaponry was good, but no match for armor, guns, and cannons."

"Back up there a minute. I don't get it. Why would you want to take prisoners instead of killing your enemy?"

"Our captives were used to satisfy our gods. It is nobler to die by sacrifice to the gods than in battle. Once captured, they go willingly."

"Sounds like you still believe in that plan—that you're still at war."

"I do believe it, and in many ways, we continue fighting a battle, one that will have profound impact on us all."

"Let me ask you another question. Isn't it true you cut out their hearts, and that you people were cannibals?"

"William, to give you a simple *yes* answer would be like me saying it's true that Christians receive communion because they're hungry. To fully understand the Aztec practice of human sacrifice would take more time than we have here tonight. But I promise that there will come a time when you do understand and approve of the practice."

"Well, I can't imagine justifying cutting out the heart of a person who's still alive, only much less eating another human being. In my book, that's deviant. Actually, it's murder and it's sick, plain and simple."

"How many years did it take for you to come to the realization that you were different? In fact, immortal? And if you had to explain it to someone, without them experiencing it themselves, could they possibly understand? For that matter, it was only a few hours ago that you learned how you actually received the gift of immortality. So trust me, understanding human sacrifice is complex for anyone to grasp, but it is possible."

"If you say so." This conversation was getting stranger by the moment, Groves thought. "You claim it was that cloth, the veil, that brought you immortality. And yet, you said that it is the one thing you need from me. If you've already received its power, why do you need it now?"

"There will be twelve others that will someday deserve to be rewarded by the gift of the veil. I need it to prepare for their coming."

"So how do you even know I've got it?"

"Of course you have it, William. You've already confirmed it."

"Sorry, but you've lost me."

"Nineteen years ago? Reno, Nevada? Remember the hooker you took down into your underground vault?"

Groves studied the aircraft's ceiling while he tried to recall his years in Reno. Suddenly, he remembered. The woman's claim of rumors about him having a *treasure*. Her insistence that he show her the vault. He was so drunk that he violated his own rules. There had been no rumors. She was there for a reason. Groves rubbed the sweat from his face in a feeble attempt to hide his anger and regret.

Taking a deep breath to recover, he said, "Okay, answer me this. Why me? Why did it happen to me—and you, for that matter?"

Scarrow let a slow, all-knowing smile seep across his face. "Because we were chosen."

What the hell was he talking about? Groves thought. "By whom, and for what? This is getting way over my head now." He stood and paced, rubbing the back of his neck, sloshing his drink over the rim of his glass.

"You need to relax and listen. Why don't you sit back down and take a few deep breaths. What I have to tell you is good news, not bad. Please, sit."

Damn it! Groves admonished himself. He had allowed Scarrow to glimpse a brief lapse of self-control. This man, this stranger, had managed to worm his way into a private world—one Groves had spent decades building a rampart around to keep people out. How could he have let this happen? What was different about this man that he so easily blinded Groves? He had to regain his composure. No more slipups. No more losing control. "This had better be good." He returned to the couch.

Scarrow placed his drink aside. "I did not use the word *chosen* lightly. Just as the Christ was chosen by the creator of the universe, so have you and I been chosen. Christ was given the gift of immortality so that he could rule over his kingdom forever. You and I have been chosen to make sure there is an eternal universe in which kingdoms like his can exist."

Groves laughed out loud. "That's the most ridiculous thing I've ever heard. I have to tell you, Mr. Scarrow, I don't think you're playing with a full deck."

"Do you doubt your inability to age, William?"

Groves hesitated before shaking his head.

"How many times were you dealt a deadly wound and survived? You bear the scars of bullets and arrows, and yet you beat all the odds and are sitting here today. Would you care to see the five deadly dagger wounds inflicted upon me by my Spanish captors? Without the veil, my ashes would still be entombed beneath the cobblestone plaza in Mexico City."

"No need." Groves held up his hand. "I'll take your word for it."

"Do you grasp the fact that you received the gift through the power of the veil in the same manner in which the Christ was able to suffer the deadly wounds of his Crucifixion and then rise from the dead? Did you not also rise from the dead?"

Groves simply watched Scarrow as uneasiness coursed through his veins. Comparing his resurrection to that of Jesus Christ was unsettling. In a somewhat weak voice, he said, "I'll grant you all that. But I still don't get the chosen part. And for that matter, what do you mean by suggesting we become partners?"

"I could say it was destined, but I don't think you would accept that on its own. So, I will explain in terms you will understand. I believe there are things we can do for each other that would justify a partnership. The whole is greater than the sum of its parts, as they say."

"Mr. Scarrow—"

"Javier."

Groves nodded, but was not ready to settle into a first-name basis with this man just yet. "Since you've spent so much time and energy tracking me down and learning everything about me, you already know that I have an immense amount of wealth and power. Groves Consortium is made up of hundreds of corporations that deal with everything from food processing to oil exploration. I even own a company that makes rocket engines for the space program and another that develops secret military technology. If I never made another dollar, I'd still have a shitload of money."

He sat his drink down on a glass table. "Now you add to that the fact that I'm probably going to outlive everybody on earth that's alive today, except for maybe you." He leaned back in the soft cushion, content that he had regained control of the conversation and would soon dismiss this man as an opportunist and maybe even a scam artist. "So, Mr. Scarrow, enlighten me. If you were my partner, what could you do for me?"

Scarrow stared across the space between them with an expression that nearly paralyzed Groves. The confidence the cowboy had felt a second ago evaporated.

Scarrow leaned forward, his face stern and hard, his eyes conveying a compelling and regal manifestation Groves had never witnessed before. "William, over the years you've made amazing business contracts that, at the time, seemed crazy and foolish to those around you. Little did they know that in your madness was brilliance, for a hundred years later, those crazy deals would reap millions. You have an ability to turn everything around you into profit—literally a Midas touch. But unlike King Midas, you *started* with gold and turned it into more gold. Now, here's your problem, as I see it. Your life may be filled with riches and treasures, but we both know you're not rich, not in the spiritual sense of the word. Yes, you can buy whatever you want—no price is too high. You've proven that thousands of times. But once you have your newest possession or conquest, how does it make you feel? Are you happy? Content? Fulfilled?"

Groves wiped away a thin film of perspiration that had returned to his forehead.

"Of course not. You're not only a prisoner of your own success, but you're held captive by what you consider a curse. You confirm it every time you look in the mirror. What I can do for you is to prove that your encounter with the veil was not a curse but a blessing, an amazing opportunity. No more hiding behind a wall of secrecy. I can take you to a level of spirituality you've never experienced before, a higher plane of consciousness, an enhanced experience of life. I will show you that finding the Veil of Veronica was the luckiest day of your life. And what I can do for you no one else on earth can do."

Scarrow paused and gave Groves an insightful nod, almost like he could read his mind, like he truly knew and understood how meaningless and empty Groves's life was. As much as Groves wished this man to go away, to vanish from his sight and take his tempting words with him, he was compelled to find out what Scarrow offered. Otherwise, he would regret it forever.

"All right, Mr. Scarrow, you have my attention. What is it you can offer me that I cannot achieve on my own?" As he waited for an answer, he felt a chill crawl up his spine.

"I can make you into a god."

The dawn washed the city orange as the sun rose over the Goldfield Mountains. Having just touched down, the Boeing 727 slowed and taxied toward the sprawling Groves Avionics complex in the northeast corner of the Phoenix Sky Harbor International Airport.

Scarrow watched the arid landscape slip past while the plane crisscrossed the tarmac to a private hangar. He knew he had only a short time left before the aircraft would come to a halt, the doors open, and he and his host disembark. So far, Groves had responded as predicted, at least up until the point he offered him the ultimate temptation—to become like him, a god of the universe. It was a lot for the man to absorb and process in a short time. But watching the cowboy-industrialist from a distance for so long, he was convinced that this was the time in Groves's *long* life that he would be most vulnerable and receptive. Living an exhausting life of hiding, masquerading, deceiving, and constantly fabricating lies had chiseled away at Groves. He was terrified of being found out, of becoming a sideshow freak for the world, to be poked and prodded by scientists and psychiatrists for all eternity. He had gone to extreme lengths to prevent that. Groves was clinging to the final vestiges of sanity, so very precariously balanced on the edge of the ravine where reality and fantasy flowed as one river of thought, no longer distinguishable. A promise of something extraordinary, something beyond anything his fortunes could buy—it had to be his salvation. For Scarrow offered Groves a life of prestige and glory to match his immortality. He was sure the cowboy would come around. There was still time. But time was not infinite. The day of doom approached.

To stop it, he must prepare for the coming of the Phoenix Apostles.

THE SAD NIGHT
1981, SOUTHERN ARIZONA

THE GROVES AVIONICS HELICOPTER hovered over the helipad inside the walled compound of the rambling ranch house located about forty miles north of the Mexican border. Standing on his terrace, Groves watched the aircraft descend and throw up a cloud of dust and sand. He imagined its lone passenger had glanced out the side window on the final approach and saw the gouging scar in the earth on the horizon—what was left of the Cornelia copper mine. Groves had invested heavily in the open-pit mine in 1911 and watched it produce more than six billion pounds of the mineral before the operation shut down in early 1980 as copper prices plunged.

Apprehension swept through his body as he watched the rotors spin down and the side door open. A moment later, Javier Scarrow appeared framed in the doorway.

Two weeks prior, Groves and Scarrow had parted ways after their flight across the country from Washington to Phoenix. The result of their discussions of immortality, the veil, and their shared situation caused Groves many sleepless nights. The day after the arrival home, he had made a clandestine trip into the nearby town of Ajo. Venturing beyond the walls of his compound was something he rarely did without heavy security and a disguise. But on this occasion, he slipped away from the compound, driving himself into the small town to the Catholic church. It was Sunday, and he sat in the back pew during the sparsely attended evening Mass. His eyes roamed the walls, stopping to marvel at the stained glass windows.

When the service was over and most of the parishioners had departed, Groves walked the outer aisles, finally finding what he wanted. He came to stand in front of the Sixth Station of the Cross. This was the one that interested him.

Like the other thirteen Stations lining the walls, the Sixth Station was a simple wooden plaque hanging between two windows. It depicted Jesus carrying a cross. Beside him stood a woman holding a piece of cloth. Appearing as if she held a portrait, there was a man's face pictured on the cloth.

"Good evening." A voice came from behind Groves.

Turning, he saw an elderly priest approaching, dressed in black trousers and a short sleeve shirt with a Roman collar. He had a full head of salt-and-pepper-colored hair and the swarthy skin common to the area's Mexican population.

"Hello." Groves nodded.

"Welcome to the Church of the Immaculate Conception. I'm Father Miguel."

The priest extended his hand and Groves shook it. "Butch Mills. Nice to meet you."

"I've not seen you in church before, Mr. Mills. Are you new to the area?"

"Passing through."

"Well, we're happy you dropped in. You seem quite interested in the Stations of the Cross?"

"Mainly this one. Can you tell me about it?"

"Of course. It depicts the story of how Saint Veronica used a portion of her clothing, probably her veil, to wipe the sweat and blood from the face of Our Lord and Savior Jesus Christ as he carried his cross to be crucified."

"A friend lent me some books awhile back. Said I was a pagan and needed to get some religion." Groves pulled at his chin as he looked down with a perfectly executed embarrassed grin. "Guess he was probably right about that. Anyhow, that's how I first heard about this Veronica and her veil. But then I went to the Bible and tried to read about it. No luck."

"Actually, there's no reference to the story in the canonical Gospels. I suppose the closest might be the miracle of the woman who was healed by touching the hem of Jesus' garment. That's in Luke, 8:43–48. She was identified as being named Veronica. But the story you see before you, portrayed in the Sixth Station, is more legend than fact."

"I saw a picture of a huge statue of Veronica that's in St. Peter's Basilica. I also found references to a ton of paintings of the woman and that event." He pointed to the wooden plaque. "And you said she's a saint. Why all the fuss for someone who's only legend?"

"Many legends are based on fact, Mr. Mills. We in the Church believe that whether Saint Veronica was a real person or not, she exemplifies the compassionate side of mankind. And her veil is an example of God's love. The lesson being taught is that for those practicing compassion, they will be rewarded. In her case she was rewarded with the imprint of Christ's face on the cloth."

Groves scratched the top of his head. "But there's no proof that the veil really existed?"

"I'm neither an historian nor an expert. But I believe that because of what some things symbolize, they are best left to faith. If we gain knowledge and grace from the story of Veronica and the veil, and that knowledge helps us lead a better Christian life, then it doesn't really matter if it's true or not."

"Did her wiping the face of Christ with the veil have anything to do with his rising from the dead? I mean, could the cloth have had some kind of magical powers or something?"

Father Miguel laughed. "Of course not, Mr. Mills. Christ rose from the dead because he is the Son of God. The Veil of Veronica had nothing to do with it."

"And you're sure about that?"

"As sure as we're standing here."

"Where can I find more information on the woman and the veil?"

"I'm afraid there isn't much hard evidence you can research. Just the legend. Sorry."

"Not your fault. Thanks anyway."

Groves nodded a farewell to the priest and headed outside to his Jeep. Legend or not, he was going to dig up enough information on the Veil of Veronica to make a decision whether to bring Scarrow to him and discuss this whole Aztec god-thing or dismiss the man entirely.

Over the next week he had phoned contacts inside the Mexican government trying to find out if there was any record of Montezuma coming in contact with the veil. At first, his sources produced nothing of value. But then he got an interesting report of a passing reference in an obscure diary of a Spanish soldier who accompanied Cortés to Mexico. It stated that there was a religious icon given to Cortés by Diego Velázquez de Cuéllar, governor of Cuba. The officer referred to it as *imagen verdadera* which meant *true image.* However, there was some doubt it was the veil because the Vatican claimed to be in possession of the relic until at least 1608, then it was questionable as to whether it disappeared or not. And the timing would have been all wrong. Cortés left Cuba in 1519 while the veil was still alleged to be in Rome. Some believed the Vatican exhibits a fake copy so as not to disappoint those who make a pilgrimage to see its annual public display. Also, the relic could have disappeared or left the Vatican before 1608. The diary stated that on the night of June 30, 1520, just after the death of Montezuma, the Aztec army rose up in retaliation against the Spanish. Loaded down with gold and treasure plundered from the imperial palace, the soldiers attempted to escape the city. Most were slaughtered; a handful fled north into the mountains where rumors said some of the treasure was hidden away or stolen by mountain Indians.

Groves's source did mention that over the years, Aztec treasure taken by the fleeing Spanish soldiers surfaced as far north as New Mexico and Arizona.

The diary never said for sure what had happened to the relic, only that it was probably stolen during the infamous and bloody *La Noche Triste;* The Sad Night.

BLUE LIGHTS
2012, FLORIDA BAY

MATT TURNED AWAY FROM the blinding beam of light.

"Oh, my God, they found us." Seneca raised her arm to shield her eyes.

"Come on." Matt bolted to his feet, expecting to hear the ear-splitting bursts of automatic gunfire at any minute. He grabbed Seneca's hand and pulled her along, running farther upstream, but the water was nearly to his groin now. The tide was coming in and all they managed to do was to struggle, fall forward, then clamber to stand again.

They had to get away, had to make it around the bend up ahead in the creek to escape the light. If whoever was on that boat fired in their direction, chances were good that at least one of them would be hit. He slogged through the water and felt Seneca fall again. He turned to help her up when a sudden brilliance illuminated the sky and turned the mangroves to daylight.

Seneca gasped. "Are they shooting?"

"No, it's just a flare." He stood beside her, and she threw him a look of concern.

"Who are they?"

"Shh. Sound carries over water," he whispered. "I can't see anything with that damn light in my face."

A voice boomed out from the boat through a loud hailer.

"United States Coast Guard. Is anyone in need of assistance?"

The voice then spoke in Spanish, and Matt assumed it was the same statement and question.

"Do you believe them?"

"I don't know," he said. "But they've got us in their sights and they haven't fired."

Seneca sank into the creek. "What should we do?"

Matt dropped down beside her. "If they're the good guys, how in the hell did they even know we were in trouble? This island blocked the boat from the wind, but it also hid us from the mainland."

"Then maybe they're not—"

The bullhorn rang out again, repeating the same message.

"I don't think we've got much choice," Matt said. "They can take us out right where we stand if they want to. This island isn't that big. Staying here won't do us much good. Plus, I'd sure like to know what the hell's going on. We won't find out standing here."

"Do you need assistance?" the bullhorn voice called across the water. "*¿Alguien necesita ayuda*? We can't get any closer. You'll have to swim to us."

Matt shielded his eyes with his hand trying to get a look at the boat. "Get that light out of our eyes!"

The beam arced away.

"I can't make out the craft," Seneca said, "but I see flashing blue emergency lights."

"I see them, too, but anyone could fake that. Let me go first. If it's safe, I'll call back to you. If not, head upstream and hide in the mangroves."

"If they're the bad guys, they'll find me as soon as the sun comes up. I'd rather meet them head on. I'm going with you." Her decision took her by surprise and Seneca wondered if maybe she *had* inherited some of her mother's genes.

"Let's hope it's really the Coast Guard. Are you ready?"

She nodded, and side-by-side they trudged along the creek, then through the mud to the bay and swam toward the boat and the flashing blue lights.

As they approached, the spotlight focused on them once again, and Matt prayed it was not so a gunner could take aim.

Finally, as they came alongside, Matt saw the vessel more clearly. Over the side of the boat's orange foam collar, a man extended his arm to help Seneca up. Matt watched her grab the hand. The man in the boat began lifting her.

"Bless you." She sighed, then looked up and recoiled.

THE LIST
1989, EL SEGUNDO, CA

THE SPOKESMAN IN THE IBM-blue business suit stood at the podium in the Groves Aerospace press room. After completing the obligatory welcome and appreciation remarks, he spieled off a short bio of the man he was about to introduce. "It is my pleasure to present the new president and CEO of Groves Consortium, Mr. Javier Scarrow."

There was a rustle of whispers and paper as Scarrow shook the man's hand then took his place at the microphone. "Good afternoon, ladies and gentlemen." He thanked the spokesman for the flattering introduction and expressed his appreciation to the members of the press corps. He waited for everyone to settle before pointing to the AP reporter. "I'll take the first question."

"Will Mr. Groves be joining us today?"

"I'm afraid not. But be assured that I speak on behalf of our chairman, William Groves IV, in all matters concerning the Consortium and Groves Aerospace."

The reporter gave an expression that seemed to imply he had heard that excuse many times before. "As you know, Mr. Scarrow, there are anti-nuclear groups concerned over what they perceive as an unacceptable risk to the public's safety with the upcoming October launch of the Galileo spacecraft. Mainly, their issue is with Galileo's RTGs."

"We are well aware of their objections. To address those concerns, let me ask our senior RTG project engineer to say a few words."

Scarrow stepped aside as the scientist came to the podium. He was partially bald and wore thick framed glasses. "For those of you who don't know, RTG stands for radioisotope thermoelectric generator—there are two onboard the unmanned Galileo spacecraft. Groves Aerospace, in partnership with NASA, helped design the RTG units. It was determined that because of the distance between Jupiter and the sun, solar panels would be impractical as would be large, bulky batteries. RTG technology was chosen for its efficiency and compactness."

The reporter remained standing. "But, sir, the anti-nuclear groups are seeking a court injunction prohibiting Galileo's launch based on a fear that because the craft carries plutonium-238, an accident could cause harm to the atmosphere, possibly resulting in human injury or death."

Scarrow joined the engineer. "RTGs have been used for years in planetary exploration without mishap. The Lincoln Experimental Satellites launched by the US Department of Defense had seven percent more plutonium on board than Galileo, and the two Voyager spacecraft each carried eighty percent more plutonium."

"Yes," the reporter insisted, "but the activists point out the tragic crash of the Soviet Union's nuclear-powered Cosmos 954 satellite in Canada in 1978, and the 1986 Challenger accident as having raised public awareness of the possibility of a dangerous spacecraft failure. Also, Mr. Scarrow, no RTGs have ever been aboard a craft that will swing past the Earth at as close a range and high speed as Galileo's gravity assist trajectory required to propel it on its mission."

"We still believe, based upon our extensive safety studies, that the small amount of plutonium carried aboard the spacecraft poses no threat to the atmosphere, our planet, or anyone on it." He turned away from the reporter. "Next question?"

"Javier, did they bring up the legal attempts to stop the launch? Don't they understand that we've done the research? That there's no real danger?"

"Relax, William. All the questions were handled fine." Scarrow spoke to Groves on the car phone as the limousine moved north through traffic along Lincoln Boulevard.

"Did they ask why I wasn't there?"

"Of course. They always do. And once I apologized that for health reasons you couldn't make it, the subject wasn't brought up again. We agreed that you don't have to take part in any more day-to-day busywork. That's what you have me for and the hundreds of others assisting me. You worry too much. Let me handle the heavy lifting. You relax and enjoy that beautiful view of the Palisades."

"I know we made that decision. I just feel like I'm losing touch with what's going on in my … our companies."

"You won't lose your touch, I promise. I give you a full briefing every morning, you know that." Scarrow glanced out the window as they passed Marina del Ray. Then he opened the folder on his lap. A sheet of paper displayed a list of names along with a short biography of each. He studied the list while he spoke. "William, are you taking your medications? You're not skipping any are you? You have to build up your immune system. You know how easily you can contract an infection or cold. Did you take your pills today?"

"Yes, I took the damn pills. I'm getting tired of this place. I want to move. Where can we move?"

"You live in a mansion in the Pacific Palisades that rivals the Hearst Castle. It would take you a month to sleep in every room." Scarrow realized that Groves was getting more and more eccentric with each passing year. That was good, but Groves's idiosyncrasies required constant maintenance. They had already relocated four times since Scarrow took on the management of Groves Consortium. First it had been from Arizona to a remote Greek island. From there, it was to another island off the coast of Thailand, then the Campania vineyard near Naples, and finally back to the US and a mansion in the Pacific Palisades.

"Why do you want to move again?"

"I'm bored. And the air is filthy. I need clean air like back in Arizona."

"All right, William. Where would you like to live this time?"

"Are there any castles for sale in Germany?"

"I'm sure there are."

As Scarrow spoke, he came to the end of the list and now focused his attention back to the first name: Herod the Great. Roman king of Israel. Regarded as a madman who murdered his own family and a great many rabbis. Responsible for the Massacre of the Innocents. Died 4 BC. Believed to be buried in the Holy Land east of Herodium near Jerusalem.

Perfect.

RESCUE

2012, FLORIDA BAY

Seneca was anxious to be out of the black water. And though at first she had shrunk back into the murkiness when she saw the face of the man who leaned over the boat to assist her, she quickly acquiesced.

"Give me your hand!"

The beam of light once again swept by and temporarily blinded her. She reached up, and at first grasp the man's strong hand clamped around her wrist. She locked on by returning the hold and was hefted up over the orange collar of the vessel, sliding belly first and toppling ass over teakettle onto the deck.

Matt was hoisted next and made his entrance much more in command than she had. Seneca thought she must have looked like the proverbial fish flopping in the bottom of the boat while Matt appeared more like a male gymnast performing a smooth pommel horse routine. She wiped the water from her face and swept back her hair.

"Thanks," Matt said. "Are you guys—"

"So is this really the Coast Guard or a kidnapping?" Seneca had an icy bite in her tone.

Matt looked at her, confused.

Swabbing her face with her palms, she looked up at the man who had helped her aboard. She made a wide sweep with her arm from Matt to her rescuer. "Matt Everhart, Al Palermo."

Matt's face was still ridden with confusion.

"My father."

Coast Guard officer Sawicki handed Seneca and Matt cups of coffee. Moments earlier, he had given her an orange jumpsuit to cover her blouse and panties—the outfit usually reserved for Cuban and Haitian refugees who were taken into custody. Al declined the beverage and sat in a nearby chair in the station office.

"So you say my father is responsible for our rescue?"

Al winked at Seneca, but said nothing.

"More or less." Sawicki sat behind his desk. "As a matter of fact, I didn't believe what was happening at first." He glanced at Palermo as if asking for an okay.

Al's expression deemed a positive response, so Sawicki continued. "I got an emergency call from the Commandant, Admiral Charles Burke." Sawicki scanned their faces and appeared disappointed in their reactions. "You do realize the admiral now leads the largest component of the Department of Homeland Security? So, you just don't get a call from the Commandant of the US Coast Guard every day. Any day for that matter, so you can bet it got my attention. The admiral said he had knowledge of a vessel in trouble and that a man," he pointed to Al, "this man as it turns out, would be requesting our help at any minute, and that we were to give our swiftest and most thorough response without question. Then he hung up. Just like that. I don't think I had the receiver back in the cradle yet when Mr. Palermo showed up in my doorway. We scrambled, as ordered, no questions asked. The glow on the horizon gave us pretty clear direction, but Mr. Palermo also gave us some GPS coordinates. You know the rest."

Seneca glared at her father. "GPS coordinates? How? What's going on?"

Before Al could answer, Matt said, "I'd like to know who the hell shot up my boat. I want somebody to pay for that."

"Were they trying to kill us?" All the mystery was making Seneca's anger boil.

"I think we deserve explanations, Mr. Palermo. Look, I don't want to interfere with some father-daughter thing you two have going, but I lost a $100,000 boat tonight and damn near got killed, and you seem to be the guy with all the answers."

"I'm just a dad looking out for his little girl." Al spread his hands in a gesture of innocence.

"Bullshit!" Seneca swirled the coffee in the mug before depositing it with a thud on Sawicki's desk. "Don't you have anything stronger than this? I think I could use a real drink." Plowing her fingers through her hair, she stomped over to her father. With her arms folded, she glared at him. "Who the hell *are* you?"

FOR SALE
1998, MEXICO CITY

SCARROW STOOD ON THE crowded sidewalk along Calle del Carmen and studied the survey map. He had contracted three different Mexican land surveyors to pinpoint the specific location, and all three came to the same conclusion within a few feet. Folding the map, he crossed the street and entered Los Sanchez, a small taco stand and souvenir shop located a block east of the ruins of Templo Mayor.

"May I speak to the owner," Scarrow said in Spanish to the man behind the counter. The shop was filled with tourists, buzzing conversation, and the aroma of chili pepper and fried cornmeal. The man called out to a gray-haired elderly Mexican who had just entered the shop from the back, his arms full of boxes.

The old man sat the boxes down and approached Scarrow. His eyes were milky, and his skin blotched from age and too much sun. He walked with a limp.

"I am José Sanchez, the owner. What do you need?"

"Javier Scarrow. I was wondering if there was a place we could talk in private?"

"As you can see, this is a busy day for us. If you would like to buy something, any of my employees can help you."

Scarrow leaned forward and spoke so only Sanchez could hear. "I only need a few minutes. I'm willing to make it worth your while."

The store owner gave him a look of suspicion.

"Only a few moments, I promise."

With a hesitant wave, he motioned for Scarrow to follow through a swinging doorway into the steamy kitchen; the source of the heavy aromas. They moved up a narrow stairway to a second-floor landing. A large open area served as storage for dry goods and merchandise. Lining a number of wooden shelves, Scarrow saw miniature models of the Mexico City Metropolitan Cathedral and a number of Aztec souvenir trinkets including a small replica of the Mexica Sun Stone. It was a good reproduction, he thought. In the corner was a desk cluttered with stacks of papers and more novelties.

"What do you want?" Sanchez stood beside the desk and turned to face Scarrow.

"Does your store have a basement?"

Sanchez gave Scarrow another look of skepticism and shook his head. "I don't understand the purpose of your question. And I told you, I'm very busy. So if you don't mind—"

"Does it?"

With a deep sigh, Sanchez said, "Yes, there's a basement." He motioned to the stairs. "That's all the time I have—"

"I want to buy your store."

"I'm afraid it's not for sale."

"At what price would it be for sale?"

"You don't understand, I'm not—"

"Name your price."

Sanchez looked at Scarrow with an expression of total confusion. He shrugged. "I really have never thought of selling…" He turned and went to the chair behind the desk. Sitting, he rubbed his face with his hands. "I don't know, it's been in my family—"

"How does twenty million sound?"

The old man's mouth dropped open, and his eyes grew wide at Scarrow's words. It was obvious the wheels, however old and worn, were turning in his head. Finally, he stood. "Pesos?"

"Dollars."

BLACK OP

2012, FLORIDA KEYS

Matt Everhart poured two shots of whiskey over ice and took it to Al Palermo who sat in one of the lounge chairs on the veranda overlooking the bay. After leaving the Coast Guard station, they had gone to Matt's place to talk. Seneca still wore the orange jumpsuit, but Matt had changed out of his sodden clothes into jeans and T-shirt.

"How about you, Seneca? If you don't want hard stuff I've got beer or wine."

"Whiskey is perfect. On the rocks, please."

"Why don't you just bring her a glass of wine?"

"Whiskey," Seneca restated.

Seneca straightened and breathed out a loud, disapproving huff. "I'm an adult and can decide what I want to drink, how much, and when. And besides that, you have no stinking right—" Too frustrated to continue, Seneca settled in the chair.

She watched Matt through the open sliding glass doors, certain that he couldn't have missed the crossfire between her and Al.

Matt returned and handed the drink to her with a napkin wrapped around the bottom.

"Thanks, Matt. So, Al, you told us at the Coast Guard station that you would explain about yourself later. Well, it's later, so explain."

"Not a 'thank you, Dad,' first? 'Glad you saved my life, Dad.' Something like that would be nice."

"Thank you, Al. Matt and I are grateful you saved our lives. How's that?"

"It'll do for the time being."

"The floor is yours."

Al took a sip of his drink and smacked his lips. "I'm retired. But I've maintained good friends in the business over the years. They do me favors when I need them."

"Oh, for Christ's sake." Seneca groaned. "You're unbelievable. Why don't you just talk straight and stop with all this mumbo-jumbo vagueness. I think I deserve that."

Al sipped his drink again, taking his time. "You're right." He stood and faced her. "I spent my life working for the government. Intelligence gathering."

"CIA?" Matt said.

"Not exactly, but close enough."

Seneca put her face in her hands, shaking her head. "Unbelievable." Looking up, she rolled her eyes. "What does *not exactly* mean?"

"In pedestrian terms, I worked for an organization not known to the public."

"Black op?" Matt said.

"You could say that."

"I hate to feel stupid," she said, "but covert operations aren't my forte. What is black op?"

"Black ops are highly secret covert operations," Matt said before turning to Al. "Correct me if I'm off base and have put the wrong spin on this, but black ops are usually ultra secretive because they often involve activities that are questionable in regards to ethics and legality."

Al confirmed with a half-nod half-shrug and raised brows. "No, no, you've got the spin right. But unlike the black operations of the military, my group was strictly into gathering information, conducting research, and putting the results into a form that could be used by the government."

Seneca laughed. "I don't believe you. No way could you and my mother have ever had a relationship. She'd have never gotten involved with someone who had that kind of background. Impossible."

Al cupped his drink with both hands. "In a way you're dead on. Guess I'm going to have to do a little more explaining."

"Guess so."

"I first met your mother at Woodstock. The decade of the sixties was a strange time for the country. A time of upheaval and turbulence. The Civil Rights Movement, the Cuban Missile Crisis, the Cold War, nuclear arms race, the Chicago 7, Charles Manson, Students for a Democratic Society, the assassinations of JFK, Bobby Kennedy, and Martin Luther King, Jr. It was a time of enormous contrast. The Peace Corps, the Bay of Pigs. Vietnam, the

Beatles. The Texas tower sniper, the first artificial heart, landing a man on the moon.

"I was a few years older than Brenda and had already graduated from college. Not only had I graduated, but I'd been recruited by the FBI. My job at Woodstock was to pose as just another hippie and keep a watchful eye. There were quite a few of us there for surveillance. The government had reason to be on the paranoid side with all the unrest. So much was going on back then. Anyway, I met Brenda while undercover. I really liked her, which to me came as a surprise since she was so far left and I was so far to the right. Maybe there's truth in the saying that opposites attract. But of course she didn't know my real mission. I didn't tell her. We spent three days together, then it was over. She went back to school, and I went back to the New York field office.

"Seven years later we met up again, quite by accident, at the Democratic National Convention in seventy-six. Again, I was on the job, but not with the FBI. A year earlier I'd become a part of the organization I remained with until retirement." Al smiled at his daughter. "Brenda and I got pretty serious over the next several months. She possessed such a remarkable free spirit, like some kind of real-life sprite. It was impossible not to be drawn to her. I was so spellbound by her that our political differences didn't matter to me. For what it's worth to you, I loved your mother. Always have. And you're the best thing that came out of that. I wanted to marry her, but before I could do that, I knew I had to tell her the truth about me." He sat back down. "I did, and you can imagine her response. She accused me of betraying and lying to her. She wanted no part of me—refused to identify me as the father on your birth certificate. Refused any and all of my pleas to have some part in your life. And that's the way it's been ever since."

A sudden wooziness crept over Seneca, and she closed her eyes recalling all those memories of reading and treasuring his letters, sleeping with them under her pillow, holding them close as if she were embracing the father she didn't know.

"Are you okay?" Matt asked.

She opened her eyes and nodded, then turned to Al. "Is that what you meant by me not knowing the whole story?"

Al gave her a warm smile. "That's most of it."

CHATROOM
2012, FLORIDA KEYS

It was close to midnight as Seneca looked out over the dark water from Matt's veranda. The evening had been an eventful one, to put it mildly. At last she felt herself unwinding a little at a time.

The gentle breeze was enough to keep the temperature comfortable, and the calming sounds of the surf were welcome to her ears. She brushed a strand of hair from her eyes. Al Palermo had made a good case. Knowing her mother like she did, Seneca could find truth in his story about Brenda not wanting anything to do with him after learning he had been lying to her. And her mother never would have tolerated a man whose political ideals were directly opposed to hers, whether she was in love with him or not. Maybe that's what had soured and sealed Brenda's opinion of men.

She turned to Al sitting beside her. "I still don't understand why you've decided to force yourself into my life now."

"The last time we met I asked you how your mother was doing. I knew she wasn't well. It was a question of concern, not small talk drivel. I thought I should step up and try to fill in for her in some small way. I could never replace her, nor would I want to. Your mother was a unique woman in so many ways. Her quirkiness and uniqueness were part of her allure. I've never known anyone like her."

"You could have *stepped up* when I was a kid. This reconnection you want seems like pity … no, more like guilt. Surely you've got to understand why I feel the way I do." Seneca stroked her upper arms as if chilled. "It's almost like you've gone from one extreme to the other—having nothing to do with me for years and suddenly stalking me the next. And how did you know I'd come down here, anyway? Were you following me?"

Al took the last swallow of his drink. "No. But if I had been tailing you, you wouldn't have known it unless I wanted you to. I'm good at what I do."

"So I take it that you wanted me to see you when you followed me from MIA?"

"Let's just say I was building up to our first meeting. And when I left your apartment the day I showed up uninvited, I attached a small homing device on your car."

Seneca's face flushed. "You did what? You've got no right—father or no father. I'm a grown woman." She blew out a frustrated breath, shaking her head. "I can't believe it."

"What I don't get is how you knew the boat was in trouble." Matt leaned against the veranda's banister.

"I didn't." Al glanced up and pointed into the night sky. "The stars told me." He smiled at them, then seemed to realize neither understood. "Okay, let me back up a bit." He looked at Seneca. "While I was waiting for you in your apartment that day, I took the liberty of listening to your answering machine. I noted Matt's phone number. So, when you left the Lorelei's parking lot earlier tonight, I ran a reverse phone number check and got Matt's address." Al waved his hand in the air. "I know, I know, Matt, you're going to tell me that your number is unlisted. Trust me, nobody's number is truly unlisted. Then I gave the address to a friend, he got the GPS coordinates, fed it to the satellite, and presto, he's got a bird's-eye view of your house. He sees your floodlights come on, then follows your boat's running lights. He tracks you out the channel into the bay. When he notified me that the boat was on fire, I jumped in the car, put in a call to Admiral Burke, and hauled my ass to the Coast Guard station. The rest you know."

"Seems a little excessive," Seneca said. "Not the best way to establish a great relationship with your daughter. Way too much drama and cloak and dagger?"

Al stood and walked through the open sliding glass doors to the bar. "May I?" He lifted the bottle of Jack Daniels and motioned to Matt.

"Help yourself."

Al poured a shot in his glass and drank it down, then poured one more before rejoining the two on the deck. "Because of the position I held at my…job, the names of my immediate family are always on a security watch list. Even though your last name isn't Palermo, you're still listed as my daughter."

"Why am I on a watch list?"

Al brushed the pad of his thumb over his lips. "Well, there's always a slim chance that my family might be at a slight risk of retaliation against me for some things I've done."

"This just keeps getting better." Seneca shook her head. "I don't see you for thirty-three years, and yet the whole time, I'm at risk because you pissed off some terrorists or Communist or whoever?"

"I said the risk was slight."

Al gave Seneca a smile like the one a dentist gives a patient when he says there may be a slight discomfort in what happens next.

"Gee, that's reassuring."

"We randomly monitor Internet chatter. We don't always know who the individuals are, but certain chatrooms are hangouts for some very unsavory characters. In one of those rooms, your name came up."

"Came up? In what way?"

Al knocked back the Jack Daniels. "Can you think of anyone who would want you dead?"

TWO THORNS
2012, MOSCOW

"Apparently, the guard was on drugs." The mayor of Moscow sat beside Scarrow in the VIP box of the Bolshoi Theatre. His English was perfect, and Scarrow could only detect the slightest accent.

"When they found him," the mayor continued, "he was barely conscious and hallucinating, prattling on about the president himself being the one who defaced the tomb of the tsar. Such an embarrassing state of affairs that we can't get dependable young people to perform even the most simple of tasks."

"Drug abuse is rampant across the world, not just here." Scarrow watched the last of the two thousand patrons of the arts enter the grand Russian theater and take their seats. "So all that was missing were the last remains of Ivan the Terrible?" He turned to Coyotl beside him. "Can you imagine?"

"Yes," the mayor said. "Seems odd doesn't it? Almost deviant." He waved a finger in the air. "But you can be assured the police will get to the bottom of this and recover all that was stolen. Desecrating the final resting place of our great tsars will not be tolerated."

As the house lights dimmed, he turned to the man next to him, the one Scarrow had introduced to the mayor as the Phoenix Ministry Brazilian liaison. "You know, speaking of the Russian president, without your mustache and glasses, and perhaps a shorter hairstyle, you might bear a close resemblance to our president."

Dr. Mengele smiled. "You're not the first to say so."

The long-range Gulfstream G650 with the Phoenix Ministry insignia on its side streaked across Poland en route to Paris, its twin Rolls-Royce engines pushing it at just under Mach 1. The setting sun cast a fiery blanket across the tops of the clouds as Scarrow drummed his fingers on the small mahogany desk.

"I'm confused." He spoke to Coyotl, who sat facing him. "You were able to locate, attack, and destroy the boat using the Groves Avionics stealth helicopter drone, and yet the woman and her friend escaped?"

"We don't have all the details yet."

"The only detail that's important to me is that she is still alive." He shook his head in frustration. "We already knew she was going to meet this novelist so they could compare their knowledge of the tomb robberies. Now, to make matters worse, you tell me that while monitoring the emergency channels, we confirmed that someone alerted the authorities to rush to their rescue. This is becoming a bad dream. If you had done your job to begin with, there would be no surviving witnesses from Mexico City and hence no collaboration with this other writer. Now we are faced with multiple problems instead of just one. I'm starting to have my doubts about you and your talents."

"Forgive me, Javier."

"You must understand that there's no room for errors, poor judgment, or failure at this stage. The very idea that this insignificant woman could stand in the way of averting the most earth-changing event in human history is beyond belief." Scarrow rubbed the back of his neck to relieve tension. "What was her name again?"

"Seneca Hunt. I'm sure we can take care of this minor distraction and move on.

"First, I want to know everything there is to know about her and her writer friend—past history, acquaintances, habits, everything. We must find a way to eliminate these two thorns in my side as quickly and discretely as we can. We must see to it that no one else surfaces to threaten the Ministry. We can't be sidetracked again. This woman and the writer must be dealt with. And if there is someone else involved that might be helping them, then we need to find that out as well. The bottom line is that they need to disappear."

From across the narrow aisle of the eight-passenger executive jet, Dr. Mengele folded the copy of *Berliner Zeitung* and set it aside. He glanced over at Scarrow. "Perhaps I could be of service."

TARGET

2012, FLORIDA KEYS

MATT RAPPED ON THE guestroom door. "Do you have everything you need?"

"Yes, thanks." Seneca answered from inside the bedroom as she fastened the last button of Matt's striped pajama top. "This works great as a sleeping shirt. Looks brand new."

"It was a gift. See you in the morning."

"Good night." As she listened to his footsteps fade down the hall, she was casually curious as to who might have given him the pajamas. He hadn't mentioned anyone special.

Matt was generous to put her and Al up for the rest of the night—what there was left of it. She was exhausted and ready to grab a couple of hours sleep before driving back to Miami. Once home, she figured she would research on the Internet and do some hustling, then in a day or two she might have a lead, a small thread to follow, to get to the bottom of who was responsible for Daniel's death, and she might also have something to pitch to her editor. But her father was going to have to leave her alone.

Al told Matt earlier that he would get a hotel room, but Matt talked him out of it.

She hadn't fancied going back to the Key Lantern. Not that she was afraid; it was just that she was on edge with everything that had happened. She would be better off with the security of knowing others were there with her rather than driving to the motel in the middle of the night and staying alone in the room. And Al asking who might want to kill her had rattled Seneca. When she pressed why he would ask such a question, her father had been vague, blowing it off. So when Matt insisted on her staying the night in one of the guestrooms, and after she uttered an unconvincing excuse to decline the offer, she readily gave in to his prodding.

Seneca pulled down the spread and slid into the double bed. The sheets were wonderfully cool and soft. She had showered and washed the salt off her body and out of her panties and bra, hanging them both on the deck railing outside the guestroom in the warm night breeze. There wasn't much to them, so she was sure her undergarments would be dry in no time.

As her head nestled into the down pillow, she breathed in a clean, sun-drenched fragrance as if the linens had been line dried, but the pillowcase was much too soft for that—line drying added a fresh scent, but sometimes made the fabric stiff. Slowly her eyes closed, letting the scent saturate her, coaxing forth trickles of childhood memories of running and hiding between the billowing sheets on the backyard line before helping her mother bring them in to fold. The past was full of such treasured moments.

Seneca's eyes opened as another thought skidded into the spotlight on the stage inside her head—thoughts about another time in her more recent past. Not hidden nuggets of childhood moments, but more like poisoned darts stabbing her every time they shot into view. Daniel dying in her arms, so desperately trying to breathe, fighting back the pain, his shuddering as the icy fingers of death slowly and torturously took him.

Those were the images and thoughts that persisted until she finally fell into a dreamless sleep.

———

The sun sparkling through the slats in the plantation shutters awoke Seneca. The light was bright, way beyond the light of dawn. "Oh, damn." She kicked off the sheets and sat up. Overslept!

The wood plank flooring creaked as she stepped from the bed. She glanced at the clock radio on the way to the deck outside her room. Six minutes after eight. She'd wanted to be on the road way before now.

Seneca grabbed her underclothes and scrambled into them and the orange jumpsuit. Still shoeless, she padded to the kitchen already hearing Matt's and Al's voices. She finger-combed her hair, doing her best to look less of a mess. She couldn't wait to get back to the motel, brush her teeth and change into her real clothes.

Al sighted Seneca as she made her way into the room. "Ah, good morning, sunshine."

"Morning."

Al and Matt sat at the table sipping what smelled like a strong coffee blend, *The Miami Herald* divvied up between them.

"Like a cup?" Matt looked up from his reading.

"Any chance of a Diet Coke? That's my morning eye-opener of choice."

"Maybe." He got to his feet. "Let me check the pantry."

"Want the headlines or the food section?" Al scooted two folded sections of the newspaper across the table. "Sit a minute. I'm surprised the phone didn't wake you earlier."

"I was dead to the world." She took a seat.

Seneca heard the pop top open as Matt returned. He poured a Diet Coke over ice in a glass as he talked. "The Coast Guard called and said it had been determined that the incident with my boat was an accident. It was a military trial of some new type of secret drone helicopter that went haywire. I hope the military is willing to pay me for my loss. I loved that boat."

"Thanks." Seneca took the glass when he held it out. "I can imagine the red tape that's going to involve."

"Probably." Matt returned to his seat.

Al seemed to study her face. "How long do you plan on staying down here in paradise?"

"I'm going back just as soon as I get my stuff from the motel. And Matt, I hope you really don't mind if I call later in the week. I'll probably think of a dozen questions about the empty tombs."

"No problem." He took a sip from his coffee mug.

"So you think there's something to these tomb robberies—the missing remains?" Al said.

"I'm hoping. A story about someone stealing the bones of the most notorious mass murderers in history should perk up the ears of my editor." Her voice choked. "And Daniel deserves it."

He sat back as if digesting what she had said. "Hmm. Interesting. You sure you're ready to go headlong into work?"

Seneca drew in a breath. "Listen, last night you said someone picked up my name in a chatroom being monitored by your … organization. Maybe it has something to do with Daniel's death. Why didn't you explain in what context my name was mentioned?"

"That's because I don't know the context. The information gathered is top-secret intelligence. For one of my old chums to even alert me that he'd seen your name is extraordinary."

"Are you being deliberately vague?"

"No, I'm being honest. I'm retired, no longer part of the unit. My friend could get in some mighty hot water for leaking it to me. What he told me was sketchy."

"Is there any way you could get more information from him?"

"Not without a really compelling reason. That's why I asked you if you knew anybody who might like to see you on the other side of the turf." He folded the sports section and placed it on the table. Al's tone turned serious. "Somebody has made you a target. So, I'll ask again. Do you know anyone who would want you dead?"

"No. Who would want to kill me?"

TONIGHT SHOW
2008, BURBANK, CA

As they came back from the break, the floor director counted down Jay Leno. "My next guest is the former president and CEO of one of the largest corporations in the world, and now the charismatic founder of the highly publicized and amazingly popular Phoenix Ministry. Please welcome Javier Scarrow." Leno stood and walked from behind his desk to greet Scarrow as the *NBC Tonight Show* band played and the audience broke into applause.

Scarrow, dressed in a black custom-tailored suit, shook Leno's hand, then went to stand in front of the guest's chair. He waved to the audience before sitting.

"Welcome. Good to have you with us."

"It's a pleasure, Jay." Scarrow unbuttoned his coat then crossed his legs, smoothing the creases in his pants. "I've looked forward to being here."

"You have a new book out called *The Grand Alignment*." Leno held up the book for the camera. The cover showed Scarrow dressed in a red and black robe with his arms extended as he gazed to the heavens. Behind him was a picture of a stylized, pyramid-shaped structure gleaming in the sunlight, over which floated various planets and stars.

"I read your book over the weekend, and I have to admit, I found it fascinating. Obviously, many others have, too. It's been number one on the bestseller list for ..."

"Ten weeks."

"And I understand it's already been translated into forty languages. So congratulations on your success."

"The message is compelling, Jay, and I believe the time is right for us all to think about universal balance and alignment."

"So before we get into the basis for your Phoenix Ministry and how you intend to change the world, tell us about your background. I mean, you spent a number of years as head of Groves Consortium, right?"

"Eighteen."

"How was that? Working with a recluse like William Groves? There's been so much written about him. What's he really like?"

"It's an understatement to say that William Groves is truly bigger than life. As was his father, grandfather, and so on. The company that was started back at the turn of the last century has been responsible for so many innovations and life-transforming technological advancements. It's hard to know where to begin. Space exploration, medicine, energy, and so much more. Whenever he finds a worthy idea, no matter how small, he funds it until it became a success. William is an extremely powerful and persuasive individual who knows what he wants and how to get it. But it's important to remember that being one of the richest men in the world, he has to be conscious of his safety and security. So despite all the rumors you hear and read, he is a perfectly normal human being who totally enjoys and cherishes his privacy. We have to respect that."

"Yes, but is it true that he won't allow anyone to touch him, that he makes his support staff wear surgical gloves and masks when they're in the same room with him? Kind of reminiscent of Howard Hughes, wouldn't you say."

Scarrow laughed. "Unlike Howard Hughes, William has a medical condition that makes him susceptible to infections that would be minor inconveniences to most of us, but could be potentially life threatening for him. So he does take all necessary precautions."

"And you're still helping to run the company?"

"Not on a daily basis. Our ministry takes up most of my time now. I stepped down last year as the president and CEO, but I still serve on the board and as a personal advisor to William."

"What got you interested in the concepts you profess in your book?"

"Since you've read *The Grand Alignment*, you know that I stress the importance of universal harmony. By that I mean that as creatures of the same universe, in order to achieve happiness and fulfillment, we must all be in synchronization in our thoughts and in our actions. We must be as one in our goals and objectives, and stop isolating ourselves in different sects. I don't believe we are meant to separate ourselves from others. That breeds hatred when our true endeavor is just the opposite. We must have a vision that looks beyond the present, beyond our little niche and cocoon, and be able to chart a map of the future."

"In your book, you stress a non-religious belief."

"Correct. I'm not talking about religion, but a belief system that lets us all focus on the same goals. All the great prophets have delivered the same message of loving one another and the act of giving of oneself."

"So you don't support one religion over another?"

"No. If the common goal of all the world's religions is universal welfare, why do we need so many? Why not set the goal that we must achieve harmony in our lives and come together as one to attain it without being labeled under the banner of one religion or another?

"After all, aren't the basic instincts of all people the same—the striving for peace and brotherhood? Isn't this the core of all religions? It's what ancient Indian philosophy calls dharma. All that's needed to be in balance with our surroundings is to have a well-developed life science which produces harmony between body, mind, and soul. A higher truth.

"Everything in creation vibrates. Our thoughts vibrate and are sent out into the universe. Our objective is to attune our vibrations. All of us want better, happier lives, but too many of us don't know how to bring that about in our daily existence. We think those things manifest in possessions and riches, but where has that gotten us? What have we given back to a universe that has sustained us since man first walked the Earth? We must strive to come together, to give back, and mentally bring all of nature in alignment. We must be one in our universal thoughts. We must be as one."

As he paused, the audience broke into applause.

Jay grinned into the camera. "Wow, that's got a definite, woo-woo, New Age ring to it."

"That's an interesting term. But the fact is, there's no more of what you call woo-woo than any present or past religion practiced around the world. We are talking about a new way of thinking, not a new religion. And this *is* a new age. It's time to change our way of thinking. In one instant, one singular moment in time, we have the ability to annihilate the human race. Why have we worked so hard at discovering the perfect way to destroy ourselves? A new age has arrived, and we must change if we want to survive and not become the next extinct species. I believe that it's time to let go of that old attitude."

"Well said." The audience erupted in applause. Jay waited for them to settle down. "Now, you also say in your book that everyone needs to make sacrifices. I think you touched on that when you mentioned *giving back.* Can you elaborate a little more on what you mean?"

"By sacrificing, I mean giving up something in our lives. No matter how much or how little we have in our lives, there's always a portion we can give back to the universe. Whether it's money or time or prayer, we can give something back that will then be passed on to the collective universe which serves us all. The yield of our sacrifices will be reaped by generations to come." Scarrow turned and looked at the audience.

"There's certainly nothing wrong with that concept." The applause built again. "So where do you head from here? I know you're gearing up for a two-year world tour. I understand your destinations span the globe."

"Yes, our first stop is going to be Munich, Germany, followed by Saudi Arabia, and then on to the Holy Land."

“So you weren’t kidding about working with peoples of all faiths. What are we talking here, Buddhists, Muslims, and Jews?”

“And Christians. As I said, Jay, the Phoenix Ministry has nothing to do with religion. Some of our largest groups of supporters are already established in those countries.”

“Amazing. Well look, I know you’ve gotta run. We wish you the best of luck.” He held up the book one more time. “It’s called *The Grand Alignment* and it’s in stores now. Javier, will you come back and see us after you’ve finished your two-year road trip?”

“I’d be delighted.”

They shook hands.

Leno pointed at the camera. “Okay, don’t go away. After the break, Alicia Keys performs right here.”

Groves sat in the darkened bedroom suite atop the *Burj Al Arab* Hotel in Dubai and stared out of the smoked plate-glass windows overlooking the Persian Gulf. He had been watching the satellite feed of the *Tonight Show*. When it went to a commercial, he aimed the remote at the television and pushed the off button. As he leaned back in his chair and rubbed his face, he whispered, “What have I done?”

BODY SNATCHERS
2012, MIAMI

Seneca sat at the writing desk in a corner of her bedroom waiting for her desktop computer to finish booting. She'd have much rather been settled on the couch with her laptop and a Diet Coke. But the laptop was among the items lost in the Mexico City bombing. She rested her forehead in the heels of her hands, elbows propped, staring at the keyboard. Where was she going to get the money for a new laptop, another camera, her mother's care? Her email program opened, and she looked at the scrolling list of new messages. Moaning about her situation wasn't going to get her anywhere but into a funk. The best thing to do was make an all-out effort to patch something together for her editor.

She scrolled through the emails, deleting most as spam, opening a few, and skipping the ones she would read later. Just as she was about to close out she heard the familiar ping that alerted her to new email. It was from Matt.

She clicked on it.

Hi Seneca,

Hope you got home safe. I was sitting here trying to work on my book but have been distracted, replaying our ordeal. I have to say, you are a truly amazing lady; that was clear the moment I met you. You certainly proved it during—what should we call it—our mangrove adventure. We are lucky to be alive! When I think of that and then all you have been through, I don't have much to complain about. The loss of my boat is trivial compared to you losing your fiancé in Mexico. I'm sure he's proud of you and your courage in getting through the terror of last night. I'm honored to be your friend.

I've been thinking about those tombs and the missing remains, and I really believe we might be on to something. It just seems like too much of a coincidence.

Anyway, hope to hear from you soon.

All best,

Matt

Seneca hit the reply button.

Great to hear from you, Matt. Yes, I arrived safely. Driving in Miami was a breeze after this weekend's "mangrove adventure." Talk about being in the wrong place at the wrong time! I'll have a great story to tell during dinner conversations.

I'm going to do some digging myself about the tombs. I just sat down at the computer to get started.

Thanks for your kind words. They mean a lot.

Talk to you soon.

PS. I'm proud to call you friend, too.

Seneca reread her message before hitting the send button. Daniel would have liked Matt, she thought.

She deliberately switched her thoughts, not allowing herself to dwell on Dan. The best thing was for her to pour herself into her work and let that absorb her.

"Okay, then."

She Googled *famous grave robberies* and found over ninety-seven thousand results. Most of the first sites were about Egyptian tombs, but as she dove deeper into the Web she found more interesting morsels, like the numerous attempts to steal Abraham Lincoln's remains. The body had been moved seventeen times to stop repeated attempts. Finally, in 1900, his coffin was buried ten feet underground in a cage and encased in four thousand pounds of concrete. Well, yeah, she thought, that ought to put an end to it.

Seneca ran across other grave robberies of famous people, like Oliver Cromwell. His grave had been desecrated, and all of his teeth and some of his hair were stolen.

The next site was more grisly. Its focus was on a present-day, ghoulish and macabre industry that was booming. Apparently with the phenomenal growth in biotechnology, pharmaceutical industries, and transplant surgeries, there is a huge global demand for body parts, which in turn spawns a growing unlawful trade in them. This new industry in the illegal trafficking of body parts was shocking. One detective described his job of opening coffins to verify the contents and finding bodies with missing skin, bone, tendons, and organs. Typical was plumbing pipes substituted for missing bones and sawdust filled empty abdominal cavities.

The more Seneca read, the more astounded she became. One of the most alarming accounts was what became of Alistair Cooke's remains. He was ninety-five years old when he died of lung cancer that had metastasized to his bones. This morbid ring of body snatchers paid funeral directors $1,000 per corpse, and then sold the remains to tissue-processing companies. The documentation accompanying Cooke's remains had been altered, changing his age and also falsifying his cause of death as a heart attack. Even the spelling of his name had been changed. Alistair Cooke's brittle, cancer-ridden bones were sold for $7,000. They had been disarticulated, fragmented, and some portions ground and pulverized to be used in a variety of orthopedic procedures, transplants, and oral surgeries, which horrifyingly endangered the recipients' lives. It is suspected that his diseased remains may reside in fifteen to twenty people, depending on the procedure.

The article went on to say that the primary demand for illegal body parts came from the United States, but the list of other countries was extensive.

She scanned a few more articles, stunned at each, especially when she found information that it was easier to ship a private refrigerated truck full of human heads than a truckload of frozen chickens across state lines. After all, the latter needs government inspection.

Seneca sat back mulling over the possibility that maybe the tomb robberies were all about selling body parts for money. Or bones, anyway. If so, what did that have to do with the Mexico bombing? And that angle wasn't going to help her sell her story idea to her editor. Simply by surfing the Internet there were clearly enough articles and documentaries out there on the subject. She needed a new twist. Why not take Montezuma's treasures if money was the motive? Why go to such trouble with his tomb and Elizabeth Bathory's and the others? Could the price of body parts exceed that of the gold and gems in Montezuma's tomb? That was hard to believe since it involved bones that were hundreds of years old. And wouldn't any local graveyard be an easier target. There were thousands of remote cemeteries across the globe that could be robbed without immediate discovery.

Seneca drummed her fingers on the desk as she ran through what she and Matt had discussed.

Startled, she jumped when the phone rang.

"Hello."

"You'll never guess what just came over Reuters." It was Matt. He didn't wait for her to answer. Excitement filled his voice. "Ever heard of Maximilien Robespierre?"

"Sure. The French leader of the historic Reign of Terror."

"Right. And founder of the Cult of the Supreme Being. A man so despised that when the state executed him, they guillotined him face up so he could see his death coming."

"And?"

"His remains were recently discovered stolen from the Catacombs of Paris."

BAND OF BUTCHERS
2012, MIAMI

SENECA SAT IN THE Air France waiting area of Miami International Airport and people-watched. The majority of the passengers around her conversed in French. It was such a fluid language, she thought. Much more lyrical than English. She had intended to learn an additional language or two to assist her in her writing and travels. Being around Daniel had helped her with conversational Spanish. He encouraged her all the time to use it. She twirled her engagement ring around her finger.

She felt uneasy moving on with her life so soon after losing Daniel and knowing that others were going to judge her. But they didn't understand. Daniel *was* the reason she kept going, the only reason. She would avenge him first. She had the rest of her life to mourn. As every day passed, the trail grew colder. Besides, Daniel had a different take on what people did when someone died. He refused to attend funerals, not out of disrespect, but like her, he abhorred the thought of death and what he considered the morbid celebration of one's passing. His famous saying was that he intended to live as long as he could so he would be dead as short a time as possible. Unfortunately, his mantra didn't come true, but it did rub off on Seneca.

She glanced at her watch. Fifteen minutes until boarding. Matt was late. The drive up from the Keys was always a gamble. Looking up, she saw him coming toward her through the crowd of travelers—forest green, long-sleeved T-shirt tucked into jeans, a knapsack slung over his shoulder—he waved as he approached.

"Hey, lady." He bent and planted an affectionate kiss on her cheek before dropping into the seat beside her. "Sorry to be late. My insurance agent was faxing over some papers for me to sign for settling the payment of the boat loss. Had to wait for that or there would be a delay in getting a check."

"So Groves Avionics is really paying for a new boat?"

"Looks that way. And the amount they offered will buy a much nicer one than the one they shot up."

"Speaking of Groves Avionics, is William Groves still alive?"

"I'm pretty sure he's still around. But he's a recluse. I don't think anyone has seen him in years."

"Anything I've ever read or heard about him paints him as a very strange bird."

"Actually, I believe the current William Groves is the fourth generation of strange birds, each one more eccentric and secretive than the last. You should do a feature story on him. Might be interesting to meet the most famous man the world has rarely seen."

"I doubt I'll ever get near him, but it's not a bad idea to try." Seneca made a mental note to look into doing a piece on the guy the media called the Last Tycoon.

"I'm glad you decided to take this trip. I know it's a hard time for you."

Seneca glanced at her ring finger. "It's rough. But I'm struggling to move on. I have to." She looked at Matt. "This trip means more to me than just my job. I have my own agenda as well."

"I understand. Good for you."

"I appreciate that."

They sat in silence for a moment, then Matt spoke. "So, what's the game plan once we land at Charles de Gaulle?"

The momentary sense of heaviness let go of its hold on her. "We get in around eleven in the morning. I've requested early check-in at our hotel. That way we can rest up for tomorrow night. My magazine has arranged for a special after-hours tour of the catacombs. A sister publication in Paris has lined up a guide that will take us to the area where the robbery took place. And we're allowed to take pictures—something that's normally forbidden. I lost my Nikon in the Mexican explosion, but I brought a digital point and shoot—eight megapixels. Had to max out my card to get it. Better than nothing. So anyway, we have dinner, then go meet the guide and head for the tunnels."

"I hope you don't mind me asking, but are you okay moneywise with this trip?"

"Normally, I wouldn't be. But Al showed up with airline tickets in his hand and insisted I take them. They were nonrefundable. I felt kind of funny accepting them—but, what the hell. He's doing everything he can think of to make up for lost time."

"I'm surprised he didn't want to come along."

"Oh, he wanted to, but I told him I really needed to take this whole father-daughter thing slow and easy. Having him on a roundtrip transatlantic flight would be way too much at this stage. He was considerate."

"I think he has the best of intentions, Seneca."

She shrugged.

Matt swiveled in his seat to partially face her. "So what's the big news you promised on the phone this morning? I've been wondering about it all the way up here."

"Let's wait until we get on the plane."

"Come on, just give me a hint. It's the least you can do after what we've been through."

She spoke just above a whisper. "There are more tomb robberies than we thought. A lot more."

The Boeing 747-400 achieved cruising altitude, and the seatbelt sign switched off. It was already getting dark over the Atlantic as the flight attendants started moving the refreshments carts down the aisles. Matt sat at a window seat with Seneca beside him. He turned away from the window. "Okay, time's up. Tell me everything."

"As you know, my long-lost father showed up in my life after no communication all these years. Now he's calling me almost every day. He wants to help us in any way he can. So he called some of his buddies in his hush-hush black ops fraternity and got information on past tomb robberies where it involved a famous person and only the remains were taken."

"Does he think there's anything to make of it?"

"Not really. He said there's no obvious threat from someone collecting old bones. He added that at worst, it was ghoulish and creepy, but not a threat to anyone. Still, he was eager to help."

"He's right, it is creepy. So what did he come up with?"

She bent over and pulled a folder from her carryon bag. "I just hope all this pans out and we find a connection to Montezuma's tomb. Then we'd know who was responsible for the explosion in Mexico—we'd know who killed Daniel and the others." She sat up and opened the folder. "Okay, not including the Aztec Emperor, there have been eleven other tomb robberies over the last two years that fit our criteria. We've already discussed Bloody Mary, Elizabeth Bathory, and Tamerlane. And we're headed to Paris to investigate the missing remains of Robespierre. That leaves seven more. This whole thing seems to have started about twenty-four months ago when the unmarked grave of Ilse Koch was opened and her remains removed. The grave was in an unattended prison cemetery in the small town of Aichach, located not too far from Munich."

"I don't remember anything about that in the news."

"Other than locally, it wouldn't have attracted much attention outside Germany."

Matt appeared in thought for a moment. "Ilse Koch. Wasn't she a Nazi at a concentration camp?"

"Wife of the Buchenwald commandant. Among other things, she had inmates with interesting tattoos killed so that their skin could be made into lampshades for her home. Totally drunk on power and sadistically cruel toward the prisoners, they called her the *Bitch of Buchenwald*. She was one of the first prominent Nazis to be tried by the US military. A war crimes tribunal sentenced her to life in 1947. She committed suicide by hanging herself at Aichach women's prison in 1967."

"Human lampshades." Matt shook his head. "You can't make up stuff like that. Okay, she definitely qualifies for our ever-growing club of mass murderers. That leaves six more. Let me guess. Ted Bundy?"

"I'm afraid Ted would be small potatoes in our band of butchers. No, our next missing body belongs to a guy who caused the death of so many people, their corpses floated on the Nile River in quantities sufficient enough to clog the Owen Falls Hydro-Electric Dam. Before he was through, he was responsible for the deaths of over three hundred thousand people."

"Idi Amin Dada?"

"You're really good. He was forced to flee into exile in 1979. He fell into a coma and died in 2003 at King Faisal Specialist Hospital in Saudi Arabia. He was buried in a simple grave in Ruwais Cemetery in Jeddah. Six months ago, his body was discovered missing from the burial plot."

"Okay, he definitely qualifies." Matt chewed on his lower lip as he seemed to digest the information so far. "That leaves five. Who's next?"

She referred to her notes. "Remember King Herod the Great from the Bible? He was responsible for what's known as the Massacre of the Innocents. He ordered the execution of all young male infants in the region to avoid the loss of his throne. This was after the Magi dropped by on the way to Bethlehem and told him about the newborn King of the Jews. Some accounts claim that the number of babies slaughtered was over ten thousand. His tomb was discovered by an archaeologist from Hebrew University a little over a year ago at King Herod's winter palace in the Judean desert about twelve kilometers south of Jerusalem."

"Let me guess—only his remains were missing."

"Correct."

Matt shook his head. "Unbelievable. And number four?"

Seneca watched the gleam of excitement showing in his eyes. "Remember during our dinner at the Lorelei when you told me about Tamerlane and you said he was supposedly related to Genghis Khan?"

"Yes."

"Eighteen months ago, an international archaeological dig team uncovered what was believed to be Genghis Khan's palace in rural Mongolia. Soon after that, they found his tomb. It had recently been opened and resealed. Lots of grave goods were still inside. But..."

"His remains were missing."

"You got it."

"How does he fit into our specs?"

"Similar to Tamerlane." She scanned her notes. "For instance, in Iraq and Iran, he is looked on as a genocidal warlord who caused enormous destruction to the population. The invasions of Baghdad and Samarkand resulted in mass murders—portions of southern Khuzestan were completely destroyed. Among the Iranian people, he is regarded as one of the most despised conquerors along with Alexander and Tamerlane. Same thing in much of Russia, Middle East, China, Ukraine, Poland, and Hungary. Genghis Khan is reviled as a mass murderer who committed untold crimes against humanity."

"Your father outdid himself with this research. You know, I feel like Casey Kasem counting down the top ten hits. And number three is?"

"Slobodan Milosevic. He unleashed wars in Bosnia and Croatia, creating two million refugees and left a quarter million dead with his ethnic cleansing. In 2006, while he was being tried for crimes against humanity, he died in his prison cell of a heart attack. His body was returned to Serbia for burial. Eight months ago, maintenance workers found his grave opened and his body missing."

The flight attendant came by and filled their drink order. Matt waited until she moved on down the aisle. "I'm finding this fascinating."

"Hold your fascination for the next one."

"What are we up to?"

"Number two." She looked at her notes again then back at Matt.

He gave her a "tell me" expression.

"The Nazis were so infamous that they've given us two members of this club. Number two is none other than the Angel of Death himself, Dr. Josef Mengele. He performed cruel and grotesque experiments on camp inmates at the Nazi Auschwitz-Birkenau concentration camp. There's no telling how many were sent to the gas chambers as he stood on the train platform inspecting new arrivals and directing some to the right, some to the left, his white coat and white arms outstretched evoked the image of a white angel.

"After the war he escaped to South America, where he lived under the name of Wolfgang Gerhard. He drowned while swimming at a beach in Brazil in 1979. In 1985, authorities exhumed his body so forensic tests could be conducted to prove his identity. After that, the São Paulo Institute of Forensic Medicine stored his bones under heavy security in anticipation that some fringe group might want to steal the bones of one of their folk heroes. Recently the Institute discovered a break-in. A special safe holding only Mengele's remains was found empty."

"Do they suspect one of the fringe groups?"

"So far, none have claimed responsibility or bragged that they have his bones."

"And the last one on the list?"

"I've saved the best for last. This next robbery has to take the prize for the most brazen and bold. Can you imagine the balls it would take to steal the remains of the Russian Tsar, Ivan the Terrible, from inside the Kremlin?"

"My God, when did that happen?"

"Two weeks ago. And here's the wildest part of all. A guard on duty the night of the robbery claimed the thief was none other than the president of Russia himself."

Matt sank back in his seat and counted them down on his fingers. "Montezuma, Bathory, Tamerlane, Bloody Mary, Genghis Khan, Mengele, Koch, Milosevic, Herod, Amin, Ivan the Terrible, and now Robespierre. Twelve members of our band of butchers. What do you think it all means?"

"It's either the most ghoulish prank in history or we're sitting on some kind of time bomb."

MASS GRAVE
2012, PARIS

"THANK YOU FOR MEETING us so late at night," Seneca said to the man that *Planet Discovery Magazine*'s sister publication had arranged to escort her and Matt into the catacombs. They stood on the sidewalk along Avenue du Colonel Henri Rol-Tanguy just outside a red brick building with a large unmarked metal door. The traffic had thinned from the daytime rush.

"This is the best time," the guide said. He unlocked the door and motioned for them to follow him down a flight of stairs. "No one to disturb us. Besides, where we're going, it's always night." He was maybe five-foot-eight with a thick mustache and dark hair combed straight back that accented a narrow, taut face. He wore a black leather jacket over a sweater, heavy work gloves, and dark trousers that appeared as if beneath them there was some kind of knee padding. In one hand was a large battery lantern—a backpack hung on his back like a camel's hump.

At the bottom, a small gallery led into a dark tunnel. Running along the upper left-hand side of the tunnel's arched ceiling was a bundle of thick electrical cables. A string of light bulbs spaced too far apart created a soft circle separating one black patch of tunnel from the next. The dank smell irritated Seneca's nose as the chilly dampness seemed to creep into her skin.

"I guess they don't spend a lot on electricity down here," Matt said, a few paces ahead of Seneca.

"No need." The guide said, still leading the way inside the tunnel. "This area is mainly for tourists, and the less light, the more dramatic their experience." He paused for a moment and turned to face them as he spoke. "Where we're going, there is no light, for the dead have no eyes."

"That's nice," Seneca said under her breath as she flipped on the switch to the flashlight the guide had given her. Matt had received one as well.

Again the man paused. "Save your batteries. You're going to need them later." Forging ahead, he said, "The catacombs are what's left of *les carrières de Paris,* the quarries of Paris, dating back to the Romans. During the late seventeenth century, the city cemeteries became overwhelmed with bodies causing disease from improper burials, open mass graves, and decomposing corpses. So it was decided to relocate all the bodies into the tunnels." Again he paused and glanced back. "We will soon be surrounded by the remains of seven million Parisians."

The trio came to a junction. As the guide motioned toward the right, Matt pointed to the other tunnel and asked, "Where does that one go?"

"That is one of many entrances to a honeycomb of rock quarries estimated to be three hundred kilometers long. No one goes into that maze unless they wish to remain forever lost below the city. We go this way, not too far."

To Seneca, the gravel sounded like walking on kernels of corn. Like the previous tunnel, this one was cold, damp, and poorly lit.

"This is the *Ossuary of Denfert-Rochereaux*," the guide said as they came to the end of the passage and entered a room whose ceiling appeared to be held up by a series of fat, square columns painted with white geometric designs. "You are about to be greeted by a million sets of bones."

As the guide shone his light around, Seneca saw human bones stacked from floor to roof, forming a wall whose thickness was impossible for her to judge.

"My God," she whispered with a gasp as her eyes followed the endless wall of brown bones—neatly stacked layers of human femurs separated by a quilted layer of skulls and then another of bones. Moving from one room to the next, the staggering number of remains overwhelmed her. "I never imagined this."

"No one does," the guide commented, leading them slowly past thousands of the dead. "It's ironic that just below the streets of the City of Lights is the largest mass grave in history."

"I've read about it," Matt said, "but nothing prepared me for this."

"This way." After a number of bone-filled rooms, the guide led them to another series of crypts, these filled with small-bone heaps piled shoulder-high like autumn leaves.

Water dripped steadily from the ceiling and echoed around them. "I don't understand something," Seneca said as they entered the next room.

The man halted to wait for her question.

"There doesn't seem to be any rhyme or reason to this place. How could anyone possibly know that specific remains were missing? Especially a single individual among millions?"

"There are a few individuals who have a special resting place. It was only several years ago that Robespierre's was identified." He motioned for them to follow, leading the way through a series of chambers whose thick walls were again constructed of bones and skulls reaching to the roof. "These are the bodies from the riots in the *Place de Greve*, from the *Hotel de Brienne*, and from the *Rue Meslee*. They were placed here in 1788." Finally he stopped. "Here we are."

Before them, Seneca saw a wall of large bricks, each one bearing a name. Near a far corner, a brick and the surrounding mortar had been removed leaving open a dark, empty cavity.

The guide pointed. "There is the crypt you seek, the final resting place of Maximilien Robespierre. In 1794, Robespierre was guillotined without trial. His corpse and head were both buried in the common cemetery of *Errancis* but were later moved here."

Matt stood in front of the hole in the wall and shined his light beam inside. Seneca joined him as they peered into the blackness. There were a few scraps of cloth and a layer of dust and dirt. Other than that, the small crypt was empty.

"Were any other crypts disturbed or opened besides this one?" Matt asked.

The guide shook his head. "This has never happened before. Highly unusual for anyone to want a handful of old bones, don't you think? Why bother to open a crypt?" He made a sweeping angelic gesture with his arms. "There are plenty of others to choose from if all they wanted were bones."

"Have the authorities determined any suspects?" Seneca asked.

"No," the guide said. "Nor are they spending a great deal of time on it. There are many other more important crimes to investigate."

"Then I guess we've seen all we need to see," Matt said.

"Oh, but you've yet to see the real catacombs. The true underbelly of Paris."

"What do you mean?" Seneca said, turning to stare at the guide. To her shock, he held a gun aimed at her chest.

"What's going on?" Matt said, his eyes fixed on the pistol.

The man pointed his light beam toward an entrance to another tunnel a few yards away. A jail-like iron gate protected the opening. "That way," he ordered. "Your final tour is about to begin."

LOST
2012, PARIS

"What do you want?" Seneca was surprised at how shaky and thin her voice sounded. Her heart tripped at the sight of the gun in the guide's hand. "I don't have much money with me, but you can have it. Here, take my credit cards." She reached for the latch on her hip pack.

"Did you bring us all this way just to rob us?" Matt asked.

The man laughed. "That would be overly dramatic, wouldn't it?" He waved the gun at Seneca. "I'm not interested in your money." Aiming the beam of his lantern toward the tunnel entrance, he produced a set of keys and unlocked the metal gate. It shrieked from rust and corrosion as he opened it. "Let's go."

"If you're not going to rob us, what's this all about?" Matt said.

The explosion of the gun blast was deafening in the confined space. As a reflex, Seneca ducked only to find that the man had fired into the floor beside where she and Matt stood. Shards of gravel sprayed her jeans-covered leg. The surprise effect of the boom worked. She was ready to do whatever he demanded.

"Okay," Matt said, moving to shield her. "We get the message."

"Next time I won't aim at the floor. Now move!"

Entering the new tunnel, Seneca turned to see the guide relocking it from the inside. As he followed, he alternately jabbed the muzzle of the gun into one of their backs if they slowed. When they tried to speak, he demanded they remain silent. Once he stopped them for a moment. Seneca glanced over her shoulder to see him pull a piece of paper from his backpack. Shining his light on it, he studied it carefully.

"Let's go," he ordered.

There were no lights overhead like before, making it apparent to Seneca that they were venturing off the approved tourist route. Unlike the tunnels they left behind, the floor became uneven and littered with debris, trash, and chunks of rock. She followed Matt, carefully stepping over what seemed like an endless scattering of old wood and pieces of stone lying in the narrowing path.

After many hundreds of zigzagging yards, they came to a junction of three tunnels. Someone had painted a white stickman skeleton figure on the wall with an arrow pointing to the right.

As they paused, Seneca heard the crinkle of paper from behind. A moment later, the man said, "Go left."

Following his order, Matt led on and soon passed a break in the wall. Illuminated by their three flashlight beams, Seneca saw a large cavity filled with bones and skulls. Different from the areas they had seen earlier, these were not stacked in an orderly fashion, but appeared to have been dumped inside the cavern like heaps of refuse.

The rock-walled artery rambled on around sharp, jagged corners and down inclines only to start back up again, sometimes in angled slopes and other times as crude stone steps.

The guide stopped often to check the paper, and the farther they traveled, the more Seneca believed that this was not going to end well. There was a good chance she and Matt might be the next residents of the catacombs among the millions of human remains scattered along the miles of tunnels and countless chambers. Her research had told her that there were almost as many miles of passages in the catacombs as there were streets above ground in Paris. No one knew for sure how many entrances there were to the tunnels. Over the years, most had been found and sealed. Some tunnels extended to a depth of more than three hundred feet. Few remained accessible.

Why was the guide doing this? Was there a connection between the tomb robbery and their kidnapper? If he wasn't the real guide arranged by her magazine, then who was he? Why did he need what was probably a map?

"Which way?" Matt asked as they came upon another juncture.

"Straight," the guide said after checking the paper.

Seneca aimed her flashlight ahead. The ceiling dropped down to form a crawlspace barely three feet high. And the floor was covered in human bones. "You can't be serious?"

"Dead serious." He jabbed her again with the gun barrel. "Give me your flashlights." He took the lights, turned them off, and placed both into his backpack. "Now, start crawling."

Matt crouched, then got on all fours and started forward.

Seneca gingerly lowered herself and touched her palms to the brittle bones, hearing some splinter and crack as she put weight on her hands. Below her knees, the crunching sounded to her like the snapping of dry branches in a forest. Revulsion paired with fear reared up inside her.

The guide switched off his lantern. "Go until I tell you to stop."

After navigating the passage and moving across the blanket of bones for over half an hour, Seneca's hands and knees were torn and bruised. She now understood why the man was gloved and realized the reason for the knee padding beneath his trousers. She whimpered when the heel of her hand came down on a sliver of bone that pierced her skin.

Finally the guide turned on his lantern. Ahead was a tunnel high enough for them to stand.

Seneca recoiled. The tunnel was alive with rats, some nearly the size of a cat.

"Keep going!"

"Can we have our flashlights back?" Seneca asked, crawling behind Matt into the larger chamber. When she stood, her stiff and aching back slowly uncurled.

"They're of no more use to you." The man emerged behind them from the crawlspace.

"Come on, be reasonable," Matt said. "Take away our lights and we're as good as dead."

"Now you're catching on. Start walking." He aimed his light down the tunnel so they could see where they were headed, then again plunged them into darkness.

In the blackness, their pace was slow. Seneca could hear the scurrying of the rats all around. The guide directed them through more passageways, twisting and turning, walking over dry bones or slogging through knee-deep water or slippery mud. As if to quickly check their location, he flashed on his lantern and looked at his map. But in the next instant he extinguished it, leaving them in total darkness, compounding their confusion and disorientation.

After what seemed like another half hour had passed, feeling along the wall in order to keep trekking forward or to navigate a corner, Seneca reached ahead and grabbed the back of Matt's jacket. She tugged on it, causing him to stop.

Turning around, she faced the darkness behind her and listened. "You aren't there any more, are you?"

No response.

"He left us," she said. "The guide, or whoever he was, is gone."

Seneca took Matt's hand, hearing nothing but her own breathing, the pounding of blood in her ears, the scuttle of the rats, and the distant drip on water. They were alone, engulfed in the eternal blackness of the catacombs.

HALLOWEEN
2012, PARIS

Seneca clenched Matt's hand. It was a small comfort but she was grateful. "Should we try to follow him?"

"Quiet," he whispered.

They waited in silence for five, maybe ten minutes—no way for her to be certain.

"I wanted to make sure he wasn't just waiting in the distance or coming back," Matt said.

"I don't understand. Shouldn't we have tried to go after him?"

"No. Even if we had, he knows the way and would have quickly out-distanced us. Remember, he's got a map. We don't even know how long he was gone. We made dozens of turns through so many different tunnels, we'd never catch up or even know if we were headed in the right direction."

"How could he have known so many details when we first started out, then needed a map later."

"He could have taken the regular tour for the tourists. It wouldn't be hard to learn a few facts to sound authentic."

Seneca felt helpless and a bit uneasy talking to blackness. And it was blackness beyond anything she had ever experienced. There was no point of reference other than Matt's voice. The total lack of sight had already eroded her courage. "Why did he do this to us?"

"It has to be connected to the tomb robbery. After all, he knew exactly why we came here. And I find it impossible to believe that he was the real contact arranged by your magazine. This guy didn't want our money. He wanted us ..."

"Dead?"

"I was going to say lost, but down here that's the equivalent of dead." Matt sank to the floor and guided her down beside him. They sat on the sandy floor with their backs to the wall. "Here's what worries me. Did you notice all the graffiti on the walls and the trash covering the floor once we first left the tourist areas?"

"Yeah, tons of it."

"The last few times the guy turned on his light and I could see our surroundings, the amount of graffiti had diminished. Only a scattering here and there. And very little trash. We kept going on for quite a ways after that. After the crawlspace I didn't feel much litter at my feet—the beer cans and bags of trash like from before. That means the cataphiles may not come into this area often, if at all."

"Cataphiles?"

"Despite the catacombs being off limits except for the tourist section, the tunnels are a popular attraction for underground urban explorers. At night they descend into the underground through manholes, abandoned railway tunnels, basements of derelict buildings, deserted metro stations, wherever they can find an opening.

Most are teens or college age. It's an obsession for them. The locals call them cataphiles—literally lovers of the catacombs. Cataphiles play a constant game of cat and mouse with a team of underground police who patrol large portions of the tunnels looking for them. The kids get fined a few Euros and just show up again the next night or following weekend."

"But isn't that good news?" Seneca said. "Doesn't that mean that we could be found by the cataphiles or even the police?"

"It would be good news except for two things, and that's what's bothering me. The lack of the graffiti I last noticed and the absence of litter tells me we're in an area not frequented by anyone for some reason. And to add to that, it's the beginning of the week, the night with the least amount of underground explorers. Our friend knew exactly what he was doing. He brought us to a secluded section on a night with the fewest visitors."

"Now I understand why he didn't just shoot us. If our bodies were discovered with bullet wounds, it would obviously be murder and result in a police investigation. But if we die of an injury or simply become lost until we starve to death, it would be chalked up to a couple of stupid American tourists who wandered off into the Paris underground and never came out."

"Listen," Matt said as a distant rumble shook the ground around them.

"What was that?"

"Might be a nearby metro tunnel. The problem is, low frequency sounds are omni-directional. There's no way to know for sure where they originate. We could think we were headed toward the source only to find it was from the opposite direction."

She heard it again, this time more distant. Then there was only the faraway dripping of water.

Matt said, "In my research, I read about a guy who worked at the Val-de-Grace hospital. One night he left his post and descended into the quarries on a mission to steal from the wine caves of the monks of Chartreux. It was 1793 when he went missing and they didn't find his body until 1804. Apparently, he was discovered holding a large ring of keys and was lying a few yards from an exit. Presumably, his candle went out, and he wandered for days before dying of thirst."

Seneca felt a chill colder than the constant fifty-two degrees of the tunnels claimed in the tourist brochures. She started to tremble, and as she did, Matt responded by slipping his arm around her shoulders and pulling her closer. "What should we do?" she asked.

"I think our best bet is to try to work our way back in the direction we came. If we can find the crawlspace, maybe it'll lead to the area that has more traffic."

"But we must have passed dozens of other tunnels and bone-filled rooms and holes in the walls. He had a friggin' map. We've got nothing. We could think we're going in the right direction while we're headed off to an even worse place."

Matt gave out a nervous laugh. "I'm not sure we could find a worse place. The guidebook calls the catacombs the Empire of the Dead."

"Thanks for that cheerful thought." She felt tears forming. "Maybe one of us is a bad luck charm." There was a long pause. Then she said, "It's the second time someone has tried to kill us."

"You're right. I never believed it when they said the incident on my boat was an accident. And the helicopter manufacturer's attorney was way too quick to agree to settle out of court."

"Now that this has happened, I think it's what we're investigating that's gotten us into trouble."

"The tomb robberies."

"Right. That's the common thread. After all, there's no connection prior to us meeting in the Keys. And don't forget the bombing in Mexico while I was covering what's looking more like a tomb robbery." The chilling fingers of panic were starting to work their way up her spine. "Three attempts on my life. I think that makes me the bad talisman."

Matt snuggled her closer. "It might have been just you in Mexico, but now it's *us*. Someone is stealing the remains of mass murderers for a specific purpose and they don't want *us* finding out what it is. That's why there was the explosion in Mexico, why they shot up my boat, and that's why we're sitting here in the dark with little chance of finding our way out. I think we're starting to get too close to the truth, and they want us out of the way."

"If you're right, they've done a good job of getting the message across to me."

"Think you've got enough for a story now?"

Seneca chuckled, appreciating his attempt to lighten up the moment. "I hope I get a chance to write it."

The distant rumble shook the ground again.

"You ready to try and find a way out?"

"Yes," Seneca said, and started to get to her feet, but Matt held her arm, pulling her back.

"Can I ask you a question?"

"Of course," she said.

"Do you like Halloween?"

"Well, sure, at least I did when I was a kid. It was one of my favorite holidays. But I'm not feeling the love right now. I've got all I can take of being spooked."

"Halloween is still my favorite holiday. I go all out decorating my house every year. In addition to handing out candy, I always have a big bag of glow sticks, and I give one to every trick-or-treater so they'll have a safe night collecting their candy."

"That's really sweet, Matt, but is this the appropriate time to be telling me? I think we should leave Halloween chat for some sunny day at the beach or something. Know what I mean?"

He didn't answer. Instead, Seneca heard what sounded like him digging into his jacket pocket. Next was a crackling sound like he was opening a candy bar wrapper. Then a snap and shaking sounds.

Suddenly, the space around them came to life in a soft green glow.

"Happy Halloween," he said with a broad grin.

GRAFFITI

2012, PARIS

"How many glow sticks do you have?" Seneca asked as Matt held the light-emitting plastic tube in front of them and started along the tunnel back the way they had come. The chemiluminescence from the stick painted their immediate surroundings a pale lime green.

"I packed them thinking they might come in handy in the dark of the catacombs. The good news is, I have two." He moved cautiously along what was once a quarry shaft that probably dated back to the Romans.

"What's the bad news?" Seneca held on to the back of Matt's jacket as they gingerly made their way across the rough, uneven floor.

"Each one lasts about a half hour. Unfortunately, there's no way to turn them off and conserve the light. So if we don't find our way out of here in about an hour, we're screwed."

"Then we need to move as fast as we can."

"Just remember, if we get injured, even having the light stick won't do us much good."

"Yes, sir."

It was about thirty minutes later by Seneca's calculations when they came to an area of the tunnel partially flooded with ankle-deep water.

"You remember this?" Matt asked.

"Sort of. After the crawlspace, I was completely disoriented. I know we passed through water, but I can't swear this was the same place."

"Damn." Matt shook the glow stick.

"What's wrong?"

"We're losing it. I probably should have waited to activate the stick until we got to the crawlspace."

"You did what you thought was best. Let's just keep moving."

She tried to sound confident, but she could tell the stick was dimming. The green glow made everything start to look the same to her—endless rock walls and scattered debris. For all she knew, they could be going in the wrong direction and heading deeper into the maze of tunnels. It seemed that all she could think about was the story of the guy who died in the dark a few yards from an exit. They didn't find his body for eleven years. She was wandering through the Empire of the Dead. Was it just a matter of time before she and Matt joined their ranks to become another set of bones among millions?

They paused as Matt shook the stick again. This time it seemed like his effort only made the light diminish faster.

"Take a good look around," he said. "We need to keep going as far as we can before I activate the other glow stick."

Seneca took a hard look at the details of the tunnel up ahead, but the fading glow stick only illuminated eight or ten feet in a circle around them. And even as she tried to see what lay ahead, the light faded like a candle at the end of its wick. "Let's just keep going. There's nothing else we can do."

"Okay. Watch your head. The ceiling drops down in places."

With a tight grip on Matt's jacket, Seneca sloshed through the cold water. Soon, she felt the floor incline, and once again the path became dry and crunchy.

"A few more yards, then we'll stop," Matt said.

A moment later, she felt Matt halt and drop down against the wall, pulling her beside him.

"Are we having fun yet?" he asked as she heard him toss the glow stick across the tunnel. It hit with a soft thump. Like taking its last breath of life, the plastic tube glowed dimly before dying.

She reached out and took his hand. Seneca had taken his hand earlier, too. She hoped he didn't mistake it as a romantic gesture, just that it made her feel safe. "I only met you a week ago and so far I've gotten you into more trouble than I've ever been in my entire life. You're a good person, Matt."

"I'm just another of your satisfied customers," Matt said. His words were lighthearted. "But I think I'm more the culprit than you give me credit."

"Thanks for trying to make me feel less guilty. And I appreciate your humor."

"Truth is, I don't want to cry in front of a pretty lady like you. I guess I'm trying to apologize. If I hadn't called you, you'd probably be catching some rays around your apartment pool right now."

She squeezed his hand. "So tell me again why you're coming along on this quest?"

"Are you kidding? If we make it out of here alive, this is all going into my next book. I wouldn't miss this for the world. And the travel is tax deductible. Plus, we're in this together. As far as we know, we are the only people in the world who have stumbled onto this tomb robbery story. We've got to make an effort to get to the bottom of it."

Seneca raked her hand through her hair. "Frankly, none of it makes sense. We're talking stealing old bones here. What if it's a perverted attempt at some global scavenger hunt? The winner gets to sleep in Grant's Tomb or something equally twisted. There are a lot of sick people out there. We may be chasing nothing more threatening than an international fraternity prank."

"Now that would make quite a plot. Gamma Sigma Kappa frat brothers hunt down journalist and writer so they don't fuck up their college initiation. That should land me a lead story on *The Daily Show* with Jon Stewart. Of course I'd have to give up my writing career and become a greeter at Wal-Mart." He started fumbling in his jacket. "Time to light the way."

"Know what? Rather than using the glow stick, how about saving it for an emergency?"

"What do you propose? Trying to go on in the dark is slow and risky."

"I've got a better idea."

"I hope it involves a giant floodlight."

"Actually, you're close." She dug deep into the side thigh pocket of her cargo pants. Her fingers found the smooth metal surface of her compact digital camera. Carefully, she removed it, knowing that if she dropped the camera in the pitch blackness of the tunnel, it could be lost forever.

"So don't keep me in suspense. Do you have a flashlight hidden away?"

"Sort of. Remember on the plane I mentioned that I bought a digital point-and-shoot for the trip? I've had it all along. But it was just now that I realized we could use it to help find our way out of here."

"The flash would be blinding. We could never use it as a flashlight."

"Of course not. But we could take a picture with the flash and then look at it in the LCD display. It would show us what's up ahead for maybe twenty or so feet. The battery is good for hours, and the memory card holds tons of pictures."

"Damn," Matt said. "I gotta hand it to you, that's brilliant. Have you ever used the camera before?"

"No. I bought it at the gift shop at the airport. I took a quick look at the directions and figured I'd have time to practice with it at the hotel, but I forgot about it until we were leaving to go meet the . . . guide, or whatever he was. I've never taken a picture with it. But how hard can it be?"

"You're certain there's a battery and memory card in it?"

"Yep, brand new."

"Then let's give it a try. Know how to turn it on?"

"Yes, that much I remember from the quick start guide."

Seneca fumbled with the camera for a moment until she found the tiny power button. The rectangular LCD on the back of the camera glowed slightly and displayed a few small function icons like battery strength and red eye reduction.

"Okay, I think we're ready. Let's get up so we can move as soon as we study the photo."

"Good idea," Matt said. He stood and helped her up beside him. "Now, we need to cover our eyes or the flash will be painful."

"Got it." She held the camera out at arm's length in the direction she hoped was where they needed to go. "Are you ready?"

"Yes," he said. "Do it."

"Here we go. Three, two, one."

Even with closing her eyes and holding her left hand over them, she saw the white flash around the edges of her palm and through the skin of her lids. An instant later, the blackness returned.

"You okay?" she asked.

"No problem. Let's see what we've got."

Seneca held the back of the camera toward them and found the button to review the photo. The LCD displayed the image of a stone wall. It was overexposed with little detail other than white blotches caused from the flash being so close.

"You need to swing to the left about twenty degrees and try it again," Matt said.

"I also need to keep my feet in place when I've finished taking the picture so I can make any adjustments."

"Good idea."

"Let's try it again." She found the button that switched the function from photo review to taking pictures. Holding it extended in her right hand, she said, "Ready?"

"Ready."

Covering her eyes with her left hand, she pushed the button, and the flash went off.

"You good?" she asked.

"Fine."

"Then let's take a look."

Seneca shifted the function to review. Holding the camera between them, she watched the image appear.

"Holy shit!" Matt said.

"Oh, my God, there's someone there."

Seneca felt a cold blade of fear rip through her as she glared at the image. Standing ten or so feet in front of them was a woman. She had long hair flowing down around her shoulders and was dressed in what looked like a loose white gown, like a choir robe. Her arms were outstretched.

"Hello?" Matt called. "Anyone there?"

"Can you help us?" Seneca said. "Hello, please say something. Help us get out."

She looked at the image again. The woman seemed to be poised, calm, and serene, as if in a tranquil garden or church. She looked almost artificial like a mannequin or a painting.

Matt slipped his arm around her waist and whispered, "Stay calm. Maybe it's just graffiti—something painted on the wall."

She let out a long sigh and a tiny nervous laugh. "Of course. We're standing here like a couple of dopes yelling at a painting. I gotta tell you, that scared the shit out of me."

"It's probably like the skeleton man we saw painted on the tunnel wall coming in. Remember?"

"You're right. Now that we know there's a painting of a woman on the wall in front of us, let's take a deep breath and try it again."

"I'm ready."

"Cover your eyes. Here we go."

Holding the camera in front of her, she put her left hand over her eyes and squeezed them closed. "Three, two, one."

Like before, the soft white glow of the flash still made it through her lids. "Okay, let's see what we've got."

Pushing the function button caused the LCD screen to produce the latest image. Seneca screamed and let the camera slip from her hand as the face of the woman filled the display.

"Shit!" Matt said. "She's standing right in front of us."

WRITING ON THE WALL

2012, PARIS

"Are you there?" Seneca reached to try to touch the woman who had appeared in the picture, her words sounded strangely high-pitched, like a squeaky door. She felt her pulse pounding in her neck and temples. "Please say something."

"Can you help us find our way out?" Matt said. "We're lost."

His voice doesn't sound much better than mine, Seneca thought. She felt his arm still hugging her waist, reminding her of how secure she always felt in Daniel's embrace. The memory quickly passed with the gravity of the moment.

"Please speak to us," Matt said.

No response from the blackness before them.

For a good thirty seconds, they stood in silence, only the sound of their breathing filled the eternal night of the catacombs.

"Are you all right?" Matt whispered.

"Not really. I'm pretty freaked out." She felt him pull her tighter to him, and she appreciated his support, both mental and physical.

"Let's find your camera."

"Hang on." She bent until her fingertips touched the damp, sandy floor, praying the camera had not been damaged when she dropped it. It was not around her feet, so she ran her hand over the floor in front of her. Nothing.

Matt got down beside her on hands and knees. A few seconds later, he said, "Got it."

They stood, and he reached to find her hand, carefully placing the camera in her palm.

Seneca brushed off the dirt from the metal surface and located the power button. She pressed it, but there was no response. Perhaps it was on, she thought, and pushing the button had just turned it off. Pressing the button again brought the same result.

"We may have a problem here. It won't turn on."

"Probably jarred when it hit," he said. "But those cameras are pretty rugged. Try again."

She did with no success.

"How about reseating the battery and memory card?"

"Good idea. Now if I can just remember how to open the compartment on the bottom. It's hard enough when I can see what I'm doing."

Seneca worked with the tiny release on the bottom that protected the battery and memory card slots. A few seconds later she managed to open and remove both, then placed them back inside and closed the door.

"Here we go," she said.

Pushing on the power button, she sighed as the LCD display glowed slightly. The original overexposed photo of the wall appeared.

"We lucked out," Matt said. "Now advance to the picture of the woman. I want a closer look at her."

"Frankly, I don't ever want to see that woman's face again."

Seneca pressed the forward button but nothing happened. The photo of the wall remained in the LCD.

"Where's the picture of the woman with her arms outstretched?"

"Let me try going in the other direction." She pressed the reverse button. "Looks like the only picture on the card is the first one I took. The two of the woman are gone."

"Well, I know it wasn't our imaginations. The pictures were there."

"Agreed, but they're not now. I don't know what to tell you."

"Let's try it again. This time, without dropping the camera."

"I didn't do it on purpose. When it looked like she was standing right in front of me, I panicked."

"I understand. Let's just take another picture so we can get moving."

"Fine." She realized they were both getting edgy. Being trapped in the Catacombs of Paris was not something either of them had to deal with every day.

She pressed the function button preparing the camera to take another picture. "You ready?"

"Yes," he said, "but this time, blinded or not, I'm going to keep my eyes open. I want to see firsthand what's in front of us."

She held the camera out at arm's length and covered her eyes. "Three, two, one."

Flash.

"Oh, shit!" Matt said.

"What is it?" Seneca asked as the darkness instantly enveloped them.

"That hurt big time."

"Did you see anything?"

"Yeah, a supernova. Now I know what it's like to stand about ten feet from the sun."

"Any graffiti?"

"I'm not sure. Know what could have happened—maybe you accidently zoomed in on the picture of the woman when you took the photo. That's why her face filled the frame."

Seneca suddenly felt embarrassed that she had come close to a panic attack from looking at graffiti on the tunnel wall. And the close-up of the face could easily have been her fault. "You're right. I probably pushed the zoom button by accident. Sorry."

"So let's see what you got this time."

She pressed the function button and the LCD display turned on. This time there was no woman—painted or otherwise. Just a wall that appeared to be twenty or so feet in front of them.

"You sure you're aiming in the same direction?"

"As sure as I can be. If you think you can do better, have at it."

"I wasn't criticizing, just asking."

"Sorry," Seneca said. "This place is definitely getting to me."

"Let me see the new picture again," Matt said.

She held the back of the camera toward the sound of his voice.

"There's definitely some graffiti on the wall. See the writing?"

Holding the display closer to her face, she said, "Yeah, I see it now."

"Can you make out what it says?"

"No, but I remember from the quick start instructions that I can zoom into a picture once I've taken it. Let me try."

She worked with each button causing menus to appear and the function icons to change. Then success. The image changed in the display, and the graffiti became bigger and clearer.

"Now you should be able to read it," Matt said.

"It says *destroy the veil by fire.*" She turned to Matt, his face barely illuminated in the faint light of the display. "Any idea what that means?"

He repeated the words written on the tunnel wall as he studied the image on the LCD. "Sounds like a cataphile took one too many hits from whatever he was smoking down here."

"None of the graffiti we've seen has made any sense." She pressed the zoom-out button and examined the photo again. "Looks like there's a turn in the tunnel to the right just past the wall with the writing. Let's make our way to that point, then take another picture."

"I'll lead the way. Grab on to my jacket."

Turning at the wall with the graffiti, Seneca followed Matt along the bend in the tunnel. After a dozen slow-going steps, they stopped. She oriented herself parallel to the wall and extended her arm with the camera aimed forward.

"Ready?" she asked.

"Do it."

A moment later, they stared at the photo in the LCD display.

"More of the same," Matt said. "But the ceiling looks pretty rugged and somewhat lower. We need to be extra careful."

"Lead the way," Seneca said, holding onto the back of his jacket. She extended her other hand above her head as the ceiling dropped, causing them both to stoop while they made their way forward.

Ten photographs later and what Seneca figured was a few hundred yards along the tunnel, it was time for a break.

"Something tells me we're not going in the same direction we came," Matt said as they sat.

"I agree. None of the pictures look familiar."

"I'm tempted to pull out the other glow stick, fire it up and see how much distance we can manage to cover—"

"What's wrong," she asked.

"Maybe it's just my imagination."

"What?"

"I swear I just heard someone laugh."

Without being told to do so, they both remained still and silent—Seneca holding her breath. A minute went by, then two.

"Yes!" Seneca said. "I just heard it."

"Any idea from which direction it came?"

"No, but I'll bet it didn't come from where we just did."

"I say, let's light up the glow stick and see if we can find who's down here with us."

Seneca stood and waited for Matt to unwrap the stick. Soon, their surroundings became visible, this time painted a pastel yellow. With Matt in the lead, they moved along the tunnel as it zigzagged below the Paris streets.

Rounding a turn in the passage, Matt stopped. He turned to Seneca and whispered, "Smell that?"

She nodded. "Marijuana."

"And it's close by. Let's go."

Again they continued down the tunnel, Matt's arm extended in front as he gripped the glow stick.

Making another sharp turn in the passage they entered a spacious chamber. Two men sat on a small limestone bench. They wore headlamps and looked up in unison, illuminating Matt and Seneca. The lights formed beams through a thin gray fog of smoke.

Seneca saw that one of the men held a can of beer. With a laugh, he raised it in a toast and said, "We have company."

The other man blew smoke into the air before saying, "Five Euros they're lost."

"Yes," Seneca said, "we are desperately lost. Can you help us?"

"A sucker bet," the first man said. "Of course we can help you. But first you should join us for a beer and a buzz." He reached into a nearby backpack and produced two cans, holding them in an offering gesture.

"No thanks," Seneca said.

"Or me," Matt said. "But thanks anyway"

They walked forward until they stood in front of the two men.

"Whatever," the first man said, stuffing the beers into the backpack. "At least take a moment, relax, and enjoy the solitude of the Empire of the Dead."

Seneca and Matt sat on a nearby stone bench. "We're kind of anxious to get out of here," Seneca said.

"I'm Nightcrawler," the first man said, ignoring her comment. "This is my friend, Nomad. Welcome to our cozy underground abode. And who might you be?"

"Seneca, and this is Matt. You both speak English. Are you Americans?"

"Expats," Nomad said. "We moved to Europe many years ago. We're teachers at a local university but like to come down here once a week or so to get away from the real world."

"Well, we're sure lucky to have found you," Matt said. "So you can show us the way out?"

"Sure," Nightcrawler said.

"How far are we from an exit?" Seneca asked.

The two men looked at each other and laughed. Then Nomad pointed to his right and said, "About twenty feet that way."

DEAD-END

2012, PARIS

Nightcrawler and Nomad guided Seneca and Matt out of the catacombs by way of a sewer access culvert that led to an abandoned railroad tunnel. From there they thanked the two expatriates before making their way across an open field and along a few quiet neighborhood side streets until they were able to flag down a taxi. It drove them to a police substation a couple of blocks from where they were staying at the *Hotel du Lion*. After meeting with an investigator for a brief fifteen minutes, they walked the remaining distance to their hotel. Moving across the lobby, they came under intense scrutiny from hotel security. Their muddy clothes and scraggly appearance caught the eye of the staff and guests alike.

After cleaning up and getting dressed, Matt came to Seneca's room where they placed a call to Al and reported their catacombs experience.

Seneca gave Al the French sister publication information and a description of the guide, and he promised to call back within the next few hours.

While they waited, Matt and Seneca ordered room service. After finishing their dinner, Seneca curled up on the bed and slept while Matt sat on a nearby couch and watched a French version of *Jeopardy*.

The ring of her cell phone jarred her awake.

Matt got to her phone first. "Hello."

Seneca groggily sat up. "Is it Al?"

Matt nodded. "Here she is."

"Hey, it's me. I'm putting you on speaker." She pressed the icon for the speakerphone. "What did you find out? Any idea who the man was who kidnapped us?"

"First off," Al said, "the official guide who the magazine arranged to take you into the catacombs said you called and canceled. Now we know that wasn't you. Other than that, not much else. You said you talked to the police? What was their take on the incident?"

"They said we were lucky to make it out without getting seriously injured," Seneca said, "and they reminded us that it's illegal to go down there in the first place. Almost like they didn't hear a word we said about the kidnapping at gunpoint. And since we had no proof that any of it actually happened, I'm not sure they even believed us. The investigator cautioned us on the consequences for giving a false statement to the police. Unquestionably they were not interested in doing any follow-up."

Matt went to stare out the window at the lights below. "Al, what do you really think is going on here?"

"At first, it looked to me like the Mexico City bombing and the helicopter incidents were just an unfortunate coincidence. But now you add getting marched into the catacombs at gunpoint, and things start to look a little more suspicious. Then there's that intel about Seneca's name in the chatroom. There are some other small traces I'm getting bits of info on, but not enough to make any declarations. But I can tell you this, I don't like it."

"What about the list of tomb robberies your colleagues dug up—pardon the pun?"

"Interesting and undoubtedly bizarre, but I'm not sure. Even though I still don't see a direct connection, the evidence is enough to raise questions. If there's a tie-in to the robberies, then whoever is stealing those human remains doesn't like you guys nosing around. At this point, I would suggest that for your own safety you return home and get back to your normal routines. Butt out."

"You know I can't do that," Seneca said. "Nobody else is trying to find out who murdered Daniel and the others. This series of tomb robberies is my only lead."

"Look, I think you have a serious problem. Somebody wants you dead. All I'm saying is try to eliminate the motivation for that in any way you can. Let me and my buddies keep investigating."

"I thought you said they could get into trouble helping you out now that you're retired."

"I still have a few connections here and there. You let me worry about it."

Matt said, "Al, what about the fact that all the remains belonged to, for lack of a better definition, what most would consider mass murderers? What do you think about that?"

"Again, fascinating but not worth risking your lives over. What can someone possibly do with their bones? Now if they were somehow bringing them all back to life, well, that would be a whole different story."

"The fact that they're trying to stop us is exactly why we need to keep going," Seneca said. "Not only might this have the potential to help uncover who is responsible for Dan's death and add valuable research for Matt, but the mere fact that someone wants us to stop investigating is a red flag that there's something *to* investigate."

"Okay," Al said, "let's say for argument's sake that you're right. What's your plan? Where do you two go next? The list of robbery locations is all over the map—South America to Europe to the Middle East. Are you going to try guessing where the next one will be? That gives me a headache just thinking about it." There was a long pause. "So, have you even got a plan?"

Seneca looked at Matt and shrugged. "We're still brainstorming."

"Even more reason to catch the next flight. I've taken the liberty of arranging for a company to move your stuff to the new place you and Daniel had put a deposit on. It'll all be done by the time you get back."

"Al, I've already explained to you that I can't afford that condo on my salary. I have to find a cheaper place."

"No, you don't. I'm your father and as far as I'm concerned, you've just had a little setback. That's where you wanted to live and that's where you're gonna live." His voice was strong and stern, rattling the small cell speakerphone. "So get your tickets and head home. There's nothing more for you to see or do in Paris. It's a dead-end."

Seneca shook her head as she glared at Matt. "Al, when you said you had taken liberties, you really meant it. I don't know whether to say thank you or hang up on you."

"Listen, little one. Don't be cutting off your nose because of pride."

Matt gave her an encouraging smile and nodded in favor of her father's advice.

"I suppose you're right," she said. "If someone wants me dead, there's no sense in me being bullheaded and letting them have their wish. I'll text our flight information to you as soon as we have it."

"Good. In the meantime, I'll keep looking for a connection to all this from my end."

"Oh," Seneca said, "there is one more thing. While your spy pals are doing their digging, have them see if they can figure out the meaning of a phrase we came across."

"What is it?" Al asked.

"Destroy the veil by fire."

2012, BAHAMAS

Coyotl shifted his weight in the club chair. His palms left a slick of perspiration on the leather when he moved his hands from the armrests to his lap, and he felt the same cold dampness accumulating on the backs of his thighs, moistening his trouser legs. Scarrow had summoned him to the Azteca library from his afternoon duties of working with the apostles. Coyotl assumed this was not going to be a friendly chat.

Scarrow sat opposite Coyotl on a matching leather couch, the brass nail heads as hard and cold as Scarrow's eyes.

"Have you ever really taken a close look at the quality, the perfection of every feature and appointment in Azteca? Examine the flooring, Coyotl. Exquisite wenge wood, clear grade, no blemishes of any kind. Some believe it has mystical powers. That's why it's been used for hundreds of years in its native Africa to make ceremonial masks and statues to honor the gods."

Coyotl kept his eyes cast down, understanding that Scarrow's mood was as dark as the color of the brown floor.

"And the rugs. They are not just any rugs. They are authentic Persian rugs, made from silk and kurk wool shorn from the chest and shoulders of mountain lambs. They have as many as one thousand knots per square inch. The dye mellows with age and the rugs improve over the years. A good Persian rug can last for a hundred years ... they say." Scarrow glanced from one rug to another as he spoke, almost as if he were admiring works of art on a museum wall. He paused before fixing his glare on his chief of staff. "Perfection. But nothing lasts forever, does it?"

Coyotl raised his head, knowing his eyes didn't hide his fear.

Scarrow continued. "Attention to perfection is important to me. I don't tolerate anything less. So you can see I am having a problem, my friend."

The blood flowing through Coyotl's heart felt as if it had clogged and jammed. "But I am not responsible for Paris!"

Scarrow stretched back against the couch. "Ah, your comment tells me that you clearly understand my concern."

"Yes, Javier, I do, but I'm trying to clarify what happened."

"Did you not escort the apostle Mengele to Paris?"

"Yes, but—"

"Then it *was* your responsibility."

Coyotl squirmed, a bead of perspiration tracking down his spine. "I didn't devise the plan. You made the decision for them to be abandoned in the catacombs. I even warned that it was not foolproof."

"And that was your responsibility, to see that it *was* foolproof."

Coyotl felt the urge to stand and pace. Instead he replanted his palms on the armrests, feeling his fingers curl over and clench the leading edge. "That was impossible. I don't know how they found their way out. They were taken so deep in the labyrinth it would have taken a miracle."

Scarrow steepled his fingers and tapped them against his lips, seeming to pause in thought. "So you're telling me it was also a miracle that they survived the assault on the boat in the Keys? And the bombing in Mexico City? How could anyone have survived that? You believe they were all miracles?"

"The Hunt woman and her companion have had extraordinarily good luck. All the plans had shortcomings. You chose strategies that had a risk of failure because of the design—to make them look like accidents. Why not just outright kill them both? Shoot them. Make it look like a carjacking or a robbery or some other random act of violence. But just get it done. Sometimes simple is the best choice."

"Only under the right circumstances." Scarrow stood, drawing himself up to his full height, a scowl sweeping his face. "You don't understand. Perhaps no one *can* understand. The Phoenix Ministries is the result of my life's mission. The task I have been given weighs heavy on my shoulders. Out of everyone who has ever lived, I was chosen. I can't fail, because if I do, it's the end of mankind. There will be no second chance. We are within days of fulfillment."

"Javier, we can only attempt to understand and empathize. I believe in you and am completely dedicated to you and the mission of the Ministry. But perhaps you need to consider a less complicated solution to this problem so you can move on with your work."

"If Seneca Hunt and Matt Everhart are killed in a way that would invite a police investigation, it would put us in grave jeopardy. I can't afford even the most microscopic link that could lead to me or my purpose. One miscalculation on our part—one single infinitesimal inkling or suspicion—and these two individuals will unravel everything. However we choose to eliminate them must not open any type of police or government probe."

Scarrow walked across the room, pulled back the drape and looked out the window to the green blanket of pine forest beyond. He spoke softly, almost to himself. "The woman already has knowledge that could destroy us. She just doesn't know it."

THE JAGUAR SLEEPS TONIGHT

2012, PARIS

"I COULD DO WITH a few more hours sleep," Seneca said, resting her head on the seatback as the taxi pulled away from the hotel and headed to Charles de Gaulle Airport.

"You can get some rest on the plane," Matt said, sitting beside her. "It's a long flight."

"My internal clock will be all screwed up by the time we get to Miami."

"It'll take a day or two to straighten out. Right now I can't tell if I'm so overtired I don't feel it anymore or if I'm getting a second wind."

"Lucky you."

"Speaking of luck," Matt said, "Al's been a godsend. He's opened doors we couldn't even knock on—not to mention the fact that he saved our lives."

"I know you're right, but his sudden appearance in my life hasn't been so easy for me. I suppose I haven't been very receptive to him. It all looks great from your point of view, but my perspective is a tad skewed."

"Maybe you should make a concentrated effort to let your resentment go. All those negative feelings have negative impacts."

Seneca rolled her head in the other direction.

"Sorry," Matt said. "You're right. My point of view doesn't have baggage tethered to it. I apologize for going where I have no business."

She turned back. "It's complicated." Then she smiled. "But I'm working on it. That's more than I can say for the Paris police. For God's sake, we were kidnapped and left to die under their city. You'd think they'd at least make an effort."

"I bet they have tourists lost down there every other day. Even though so much of the catacombs are off limits, people break the rules all the time. They're probably sick of us. And then the French do have a reputation for not liking anyone, especially Americans. I wonder if they could work up any appreciation if all Frenchmen watched the first thirty minutes of *Saving Private Ryan.*"

Seneca laughed at the recollection that sprang into her head. "Fuck the French. That was one of my mother's colorful quotes. Whenever she had a disagreement with someone and decided to go ahead and do things her way, that was always her response. Probably something she heard her father say after coming back from the war."

"Are you going to feel safe in Miami?"

"Safe as anywhere I guess. At least the new apartment has better security. It's gated and staffed with a real person. The security folks buzz around on golf carts day and night. But I suspect that if whoever these guys are that want to get to me, they'll find a way."

"Do you have a gun?"

"Dan bought me a handgun about a year or so ago. He made me go for firearms lessons, but other than that, I've never used it. Guns scare me."

"You might want to brush up and take a few more classes. I hate to recommend carrying a weapon, but I think your father's instincts are right, especially after what's happened here."

"In order to figure out who it is, first we've got to figure out why. I keep going back to the beginning—Mexico City and Montezuma's tomb. But the one little bump I keep stumbling over is that there was no evidence that Montezuma's tomb had been broken into, at least that we could see, unless it was way back in the historical record. The other tomb robberies you and Al came up with are recent—within the last two years. That one fact breaks the pattern. So what's the connection? I can't get a handle on it."

"Maybe you just didn't see where the breach was in the tomb. It's just too much of a coincidence—Montezuma's tomb is where all this started."

"The more I think about it, the more I'm convinced that someone wanted *everybody* involved at that dig site killed. Somehow I survived, so I'm still a target. What could make someone want everyone at Montezuma's tomb dead?"

"Maybe they considered disturbing the tomb to be the ultimate desecration, and they wanted to make a point. An excessive way of doing it maybe, but still getting the point across."

"But if the intent was to drive home a message, wouldn't someone have spoken up and claimed responsibility by now? Their message is no good if they don't reveal the reason for the bombing in the first place. Nobody has come forward. And why continue to hunt me down? That just doesn't fly."

"Nope. You're right."

Seneca's cell chimed. The caller ID displayed *unknown caller*. She tapped the green answer button on the display.

"Hello."

A gravelly voice that sounded as if a hand was intentionally muffling it came from the phone. "I know who you are. They want you dead."

"Who is this?" She put the phone on speaker.

"Just do what I tell you," the voice whispered.

Seneca strained to hear over the road noise. "Speak up, I can't hear."

"Find El Jaguar."

"I don't understand."

The voice changed to song—a familiar tune with the words slightly changed. "In the jungle, the Jaguar sleeps tonight." The voice returned to the muffled tone. "Sleep well tonight."

"No, wait. Who are you? Talk to me."

The end-of-call beep sounded.

"Damn."

"What the hell was that all about?"

"I have no idea."

As the classic view of the Eiffel Tower shooting up from the Paris skyline came into view, the chorus of "The Lion Sleeps Tonight" played over and over in her mind.

Scarrow sat beside William Groves's bed in the penthouse suite of Azteca, his hands clasped, wondering what was going on in the eccentric cowboy's head.

Moments earlier Scarrow had received a call from his director of security informing him that a suspicious call had been made by someone in the complex. That call urged him to pay a visit to the small surveillance center where he listened to a phone tap recording. Scarrow didn't trust anyone, not even those close to him. So all phone conversations were monitored.

After reviewing the recording for the third time, Scarrow launched the Internet browser on one of the computers and started a search for information on psychoactive drugs—commonly called *truth serums*—drugs that made recipients lose inhibitions and become communicative, freely sharing their thoughts and then forgetting they had even had the conversation.

Once he found what he sought, he picked up the phone and called Coyotl's office. When his chief of staff answered, Scarrow said, "Find out which one of the doctors has the most experience with anesthesia and tell him to meet me in the penthouse. And tell him to bring sodium thiopental."

"Is there a problem?"

"Not if I can help it."

There was a moment of silence. "Of course, Javier."

Within thirty minutes the physician arrived and administered the sodium thiopental as per Scarrow's order. "And I want you to up the dosage of his regular meds from now on," Scarrow ordered.

"But..."

Scarrow shot the doctor a fierce glance.

The doctor shrugged. "Whatever you say."

Scarrow leaned close to Groves's ear. "Are you awake, William? I only need you to answer one question. Tell me, who is El Jaguar?"

LADY SMITH

2012, MIAMI

Seneca left her new apartment and drove along Old Cutler Road, heading to Park View Nursing Home. Huge banyan trees lined the road; fashioning a lush green canopy overhead and a forest maze of aerial roots hanging from branches to the ground. Every time she drove this route, she was always in awe of the beauty of the seemingly ever-expanding branches. No wonder banyan trees were supposed to represent eternal life.

The words *eternal life* cued unnerving dark images and thoughts. Seneca took one hand at a time off the steering wheel and wiped her sweaty palms on her jeans. *Why couldn't death be swifter and less terrorizing?* She supposed that even someone guillotined had final perceptions. The brain didn't die instantly, did it? There had to be a second of realization. She'd never really thought about death before Daniel.

Now it haunted her like a shadow.

Seneca forced her concentration back to the traffic.

She kept watch in her rearview mirror, having become overly suspicious. She'd already decided that if she thought she was being followed or threatened, she would call 911 and drive straight to the closest police station. She was uneasy about being out and about, but no one except Al and Matt knew of her new apartment location. She'd make a quick visit to her mother, then head back home.

To make good use of her time, she fumbled for her cell phone in her purse to call her editor. She removed the Lady Smith and placed it on the passenger seat, then grabbed the phone and glanced at it long enough to bring up the menu display and her contacts list. A few moments later she listened to an out-of-office answer phone message asking if she would like his voicemail. She snapped the phone closed, intending to call back later.

Al had taken care of the move, just as he promised. But everything was still in boxes except for the gun Dan had bought her. Al must have found it and thought that under the circumstances she might want to start carrying it right away. The small Lady Smith and ammunition had been on the kitchen counter when she arrived from the airport.

Shortly after getting home the previous evening, Seneca had opened several of the cardboard containers brought over by the movers Al had hired. He did a great job of labeling the boxes, and she had no trouble locating those that contained most of her necessities. Then she opened one that was filled with Daniel's things—text and reference books, his notebooks, and correspondence with other academics. Seeing his possessions had taken the wind out of her as surely as a blow to her gut, slamming home the devastation of losing him.

After the encounter with his possessions, she hadn't felt like unpacking anything else. So she changed into a tank top and shorts, stayed barefoot and pulled her hair back in a pony tail. Then she'd poured a glass of merlot and sat on the balcony staring out at the blue water of Biscayne Bay.

She and Dan had fallen in love with the apartment because of the view. She sipped the wine and watched the sailboats and power racers move like carnival targets across the horizon until the darkness reduced them to nondescript running lights. With eyes clouded in a blur of tears, she left the balcony, climbed onto the bare mattress in her bedroom and slept.

Feeling somewhat refreshed the next morning, Seneca showered, dressed, and stopped at a McDonalds for breakfast before heading along Old Cutler. The ride was surprisingly enjoyable, not counting the brief gloomy thoughts. She finally pulled into the parking lot of the nursing home. With the gun clutched in her hand, she sat for a few minutes surveying her surroundings. When she felt certain that no one had followed or threatened her, she packed the handgun in her purse, got out of the car and went inside.

Her footsteps echoed down the hallway as she approached her mother's room. The empty sound of her footfalls created a thought. There was no such thing as a nursing *home.* They were nursing *institutions.* Homes were warm and cozy, didn't smell sterile and, in a home, footsteps didn't echo. Homes had walls filled with photographs and art, and the sound-absorbing comforts of furniture, rugs, and curtains.

This was no home.

Seneca rapped lightly on the door to her mother's room. Even though the door was ajar, she still felt that it was the courteous thing to do. Brenda had already been deprived of a lot of her dignity and deserved the common courtesy of an announcement that someone was about to enter the room.

"Mom?" She peeked around the edge of the door. "Are you decent?"

Expecting to find her mother sitting in the chair watching television, instead she saw an empty chair and a bed neatly made. On the stand by the bed was a box of chocolate-covered cherry cordials. Seneca wondered who they had come from. She tapped on the bathroom door. "Are you in there, Mom?"

No answer.

As she headed to the nurses' station, a chilling thought formed. Had someone taken her mother? Perhaps the same people who tried to kill her?

She quickened her pace. "Excuse me," she said when she reached the u-shaped counter. The young nurse she'd had the confrontation with the last time looked up from her computer.

"Can I help you?"

"My mother. She's not in her room."

"Which room is that?"

"Brenda Hunt. I don't remember the number."

"Oh, yes. She's in the community room."

"The community room?"

"She has a visitor—a gentleman."

Seneca's breath caught as she felt the side of her handbag for the reassurance of the Lady Smith.

THE LETTER

2012, MIAMI

SENECA SPRINTED DOWN THE hall in the direction of the community room. She pushed open one of the double glass doors and entered the nearly empty gathering room, immediately scanning for her mother. There were two old men at a table playing dominoes and a group of women at another table playing Mah Jongg. A male attendant sat on a folding chair appearing to be absorbed in watching a talk show on the television. No sign of Brenda.

Seneca's eyes panned the room again, stopping on the plate-glass picture window and two people sitting outside on the lawn in the shade of a grand live oak. Though they were some distance away, she was sure the one in the wheelchair was her mother, and the other person sitting on the concrete bench beside her looked like Al.

Seneca located the exit on the far side of the room but it was locked. She supposed that was a good thing because of the number of residents with dementia who might wander off. It wouldn't be hard to slip out unnoticed right under this attendant's nose. He was so engrossed in the television show that he hadn't even realized she had come in the room.

Seneca came to stand beside the attendant, and after getting his attention asked him to open the door for her.

Grudgingly he got up, keys jangling as he made his way to the door and unlocked it. He never said a word, just put the key in, turned it, and walked away.

"Gee thanks," she said.

As she approached, Al looked up and waved. *It really is him*, she thought.

"Hello," Seneca said, bending and kissing her mother on the cheek. "Wow, you are enjoying the outdoors today. It's been a long time."

Brenda smiled but there was an emptiness that lingered in her eyes as if her brain struggled to make connections. She seemed to become a little agitated, wringing her hands and cocking her head.

"It's Seneca," Al said. "Our ... your daughter."

"Well, I know who she is."

"Have a seat." Al patted the bench.

Seneca took both her mother's hands in hers. "You're having a good day, aren't you?" Then she sat beside Al. "I didn't see your car in the parking lot. I would have noticed."

"I parked in the rear. You should have checked that out. Don't be sloppy."

Feeling a little foolish, Seneca said, "And what brings you here?"

"I heard our girl was being naughty and not eating, but I know her secret." He smiled at Brenda. "Don't I?"

Brenda smiled back. "This nice man brought my favorite candy."

Seneca felt her eyes sting as she nearly teared up. Brenda didn't have a clue who Al was. And her mother had just pretended that of course she knew who Seneca was and never even really processed it.

"And what did I make you do to earn those cherry cordials? Hmmm? You remember." He pretended to hold something to his mouth and nibble.

Even with the hint, Brenda had forgotten.

"I am so proud of her," Al said. "She devoured a fresh bagel with cream cheese and a glass of orange juice. Then we decided it would be nice to take a stroll. Get some sunshine and fresh air. I promised she could have those candies when we go back. I knew they were her favorite. Always have been."

"Well, I am proud of you, too," Seneca said.

"Have we met before?" Brenda asked, quizzically staring at Seneca.

Without even a blink, Seneca answered. "Yes, we have."

"I thought you looked familiar. I'm not as good with faces as I used to be."

Her mother's voice was as raspy as ever, and her fight for air just as desperate, but Seneca detected a lilt in her voice, a hint of happiness and appreciation of the moment.

"Is this your young man?" Brenda asked, nodding toward Al. "Isn't he too old for you, honey?"

Seneca laughed and Al chuckled right along. Seneca said, "We're just friends. He's old enough to be my father."

Seneca tossed her keys on the kitchen counter and put her purse there as well. This was the first time she had visited with her mother and come away with a smile. Even though Brenda had no idea who she or Al were, Seneca hadn't come away depressed. She was certain that somehow, the joy that Al had brought to her mother in their younger years had today found some neurological pathway, maybe old and frayed but still intact, to make a tiny connection again. All those years Brenda denied loving her father was bull. It was clear that her mother loved Al so deeply that even Alzheimer's couldn't erase it. What a waste of two lives, she thought. Her mother threw away her chance at happiness. So stubborn.

Bra-burning Brenda.

Flopping on the couch, Seneca dragged the box of Daniel's belongings toward her and parked it at her feet—the one she'd opened earlier. She took out the book that was on top: *Mortuary Practices of the Windover Bog People.* She flipped through it, stopping on the pictures and their captions. One in particular she found interesting enough to read more about. A backhoe operator had discovered human bones in a peat bog. The remains were burials from more than seven thousand years ago. The preservation was so complete that the archaeologists found brain tissue and sometimes complete brains, though shrunken to about a third of their normal size, inside the skulls. Still the brain hemispheres and convolutions were clear. Amazing, she thought.

Seneca continued sifting through the box. From the larger box she lifted an open shoebox filled with letters and envelopes.

The first letter was written in an extravagant hand and in Spanish. She translated words now and again and kind of got the gist of the letter. It was a friendly letter describing some new and exciting find, but she wasn't sure of what. But then she came to the signature, and it stopped her cold. Of course, this might be someone who could help. If there were some connection between Montezuma's tomb and all the others, he just might have the answers or lead them in a direction. Daniel certainly had faith in him. She looked at the return address on the letter.

Roberto Flores.

And then she stared again at the elaborately scrawled signature.

El Jaguar.

THE ELEVEN
2012, BAHAMAS

The 120-foot *Phoenix Explorer* slowed as the captain brought the bow around to face the white beaches of Andros Island three miles away. Scarrow stood on the stern deck watching the dawn build on the horizon over a flat ocean. He wore his highest order of ceremonial robes and a gold crown crested with long, green quetzal feathers. He recited an ancient Aztec chant in his native *Nahuatl* tongue. Only he understood the words, but the cadence and the tone were clear, and the essence of the chant absorbed all those who listened.

With Coyotl beside him, Scarrow turned to address his eleven Phoenix apostles, each dressed in the traditional robe of an Aztec priest. He marveled at each face that had been sculpted by the plastic and reconstructive surgeons.

Through months of indoctrination, they had studied their own previous lives, and he often saw them staring in the mirror as if searching for a hint of memory. How odd a feeling that must be, he thought—being told you were a great leader or person who wielded tremendous power and yet having no recollection of it. To reinforce their former personas, Scarrow called them by their given names, the names he now spoke, his voice strong and deep.

"Maximilien, Ivan, Josef, Elizabeth, Mary, Timur, Slobodan, Khan, Herod, Idi Amin, and Ilse. You are about to witness not only the beginning of a new day, but a new dawn for mankind, for our world and the universe. Through the human sacrifices you will soon carry out, the precious life blood will flow from the bodies of the *xochimiqui* and into the mouth of *Tonatuih.*

Scarrow turned his back and swept his arm in a great arc across the horizon while gazing at the rising sun. It glowed like the reflection of a gold ingot in the bright light.

He turned slowly, a move orchestrated to enhance and build anticipation. He knew how to enthrall and how to stir the ardor in men and women. As Montezuma II, he had perfected such performances, and today he recaptured that godlike feeling, mesmerizing his apostles as he faced them again.

"Grave sacrifices were made so that man could live in a world endowed with lush forests and vegetation that burst forth with sweet nectar to taste, exquisite color for our visual pleasure, and the delightful miracle of fruit to take the hunger from our bellies. We are blessed with the rain that sweetens the waters of our lakes, rivers, and streams, and the splendid bounty harvested from the sea. Every stone, every animal, every grain of sand, every blade of grass vibrates in harmony so that we may live an abundant life."

He paused, sweeping his gaze from apostle to apostle with eyes that burned beneath hooded lids. He lowered the volume of his voice to make them strain to hear his message, to force them to listen intently.

"Before our time, the bones of the ancestors were brought back and were bled over by the gods—by whatever name you call them, Buddha, Allah, Yahweh—and the new humanity was created. The birth of the Fifth Sun. Yet we give no true thanks for the shedding of their blood, their grand sacrifice. We say it in empty words and prayers, but not in our deeds, not in acts of proof. It has been a long time since man was genuine with his praise and appreciation, and the universe tires of serving an ungrateful people. You are special ones chosen because you have experienced dedication to a goal or ideal so powerful that you allowed your passion to consume you. That is why you are here. That is why you live again.

"There remains only one left to join us, one whom I especially savor to bring into this ministry as *my* final apostle. When your number is twelve, we will be complete. And upon the coming day of glory when I prove to all the world that we are its only hope and salvation, you will commence your work. Draw on those talents you used in your previous lives to bring mankind to an understanding and acceptance of its responsibility so that life will go on. You will have the power to choose those most worthy. Let their blood flow through your hands. Feel the warmth of their spirit. Take life so others may live."

Scarrow stopped and surveyed his apostles, letting the flame inside him smolder in his eyes.

"Who stands with me at this moment without prejudice or doubt? Who amongst you will be the first to go into the world to prove your loyalty even before I reveal your final reward?"

Instantly, before another apostle's foot could move, a black man stepped out of the ranks. "It is I," he said. "His Excellency, President for Life, Idi Amin Dada Oumee."

Scarrow smiled. "And so it will be, Your Excellency."

EL JAGUAR
2012, WEST COAST OF PANAMA

"ISLA DE SANGRE MEANS Island of Blood, right?" Seneca asked.

Captain Mali Mali nodded. He was a tall, skinny, dark-skinned man with a shaved head. He stood at the helm of the twenty-eight-foot sport boat as he steered it across the Gulf of Chirique to the island thirty miles from the mainland.

"And does it get its name because of the penal colony?" She held on to the railing next to him.

"No, probably from the Spanish in the 1500s. The prison was built in 1919. But many *los desaparecidos* shed their blood there. So it is a good name for a bad place."

"*Los desaparecidos*?" Matt asked.

"The disappeared ones." The captain crossed himself. "They were the thousands who vanished under the dictators Omar Torrijos and Manuel Noriega. Many are buried in the unmarked graves near the old prison while others were dismembered and fed to the sharks." He smiled at Matt. "There are many sharks."

Seneca gave Matt a concerned glance. She hoped they knew what they were getting themselves into. After finding Daniel's letter among the contents of the box of his belongings, she had contacted *Universidad de Las Americas* in Mexico City to find out where Professor Flores had retired. All Daniel had said was that the professor moved to some jungle island. She'd finally spoken to someone at the university who knew exactly where Flores was. He lived on an island off the west coast of Panama.

Seneca was determined to follow-up on the mysterious phone call suggesting she find El Jaguar. It only took one call to Matt for him to jump at the chance to continue the quest of the tomb robbers. The following day, the two flew to Panama City and drove to the coastal town of Santa Catalina where they sought transportation out to the island to find Flores.

They had been on the water for just over ninety minutes when Isla de Sangre appeared on the mid-afternoon horizon and stretched across the bow of the boat. They were about to dock at the wharf once used for receiving prisoners and supplies. Once a Panamanian penal colony, Seneca had been told its fearsome reputation helped to discourage visitors and preserve the island's pristine condition, which remained almost completely undeveloped outside the bounds of the prison camp.

"I got the impression from the lack of boats available for hire that no one likes coming out here," Matt said.

"The people have superstitions about the old prison," Mali Mali said. "So having two charters within a week pay me to take them to the island is very unusual. Two days ago, I brought another man across."

"Maybe it's going to become a hotspot for tourists," Matt said.

"That would be good for my business, but it's doubtful that will happen. There are only a handful of people living on the island—a few former prisoners and a couple of fishermen. They choose to live there because it is so isolated. They don't like visitors."

"Do you know Professor Roberto Flores?" Seneca asked. "He's retired and lives on the island."

The captain hesitated.

"Some call him El Jaguar," Matt added.

"Oh, yes, of course, El Jaguar. He is a very smart man. He stays in a small cottage near the old prison."

"So you've met him?" Matt asked.

"I have drunk with El Jaguar many times. He is a dangerous man to bet against if you think you can out drink him." As he spoke, Captain Mali Mali made a motion as if chugging from an invisible glass. "You will find that he does not like strangers. El Jaguar can disappear into the rainforest as quick as the cat for which he is named."

"Well, we hope he won't disappear on us," Seneca said. "We're going there to visit him."

The captain reached down and opened a cabinet door beneath the helm. He removed a liter bottle of *seco*. "You will make friends with El Jaguar if you give him this."

"What is it?" Matt asked.

"This is his favorite drink. Made from distilled sugarcane. He likes it with a bit of goat's milk. *Seco con leche*."

"Thank you." Seneca took the bottle, holding it up to the sun to look through the clear liquid. "How much do we owe you for this?"

"Nothing. It is a gift for my friend. Tell him it is from Captain Mali Mali, and depending on his mood he will quickly invite you into his cottage or aim his pistol and shoot you. Either way, the *seco* will help to ease the pain."

Seneca glanced at Matt. "Good to know."

The captain finessed the boat up against the dock and secured it with the bowline. He helped Seneca step onto the wooden planks, then steadied the vessel while Matt climbed off.

"If you're going to see El Jaguar, take the road that runs up from the beach." Mali Mali pointed to a dirt road running among the coconut palms. "Follow it for a few miles until you come to the old prison. His cottage is a half mile or so beyond."

"You'll be back early tomorrow morning?" Matt asked, confirming that the captain understood their agreement.

Captain Mali Mali jabbed his index finger toward the sky. "Weather permitting. Good luck with El Jaguar." He cast off the line and backed the boat away from the wharf. With a quick wave, he swung it around and headed out of the protected horseshoe-shaped cove toward the open ocean.

They watched for a moment before walking along the uneven planks of the pier toward the beach. When they arrived at the road, they turned north in the direction Mali Mali had indicated and entered the jungle along what must have once been a heavily traveled route. Now it was nothing more than two parallel ruts with knee-high weeds down the middle. Dense jungle bordered both sides. The call of a macaw and the shrieks of howler monkeys echoed through the foliage around them, and a rather large iguana wandered across the road a hundred feet in front.

"I have a sound machine at home I use to sleep to," Seneca said. "This is so much better, and it's in stereo."

Thirty minutes later, the first of the prison buildings came into view—bulky concrete structures that appeared to grow out of the red dirt and thick underbrush.

"Looks like the jungle is wasting no time reclaiming this place," Seneca said.

Vines and branches twisted and intertwined with rusting iron bars covering the windows. Perched atop the building, an egret gave them a wary eye, then took flight, disappearing over the jungle in the direction of the ocean.

They approached what looked like it was once the main building; a large sign over the doorway read *Penitenciaria*.

Moving past the building, two more crumbling block buildings came into view, each made up of three stories with rows of abandoned cells. The roof had long since rotted away and collapsed. Small lizards scurried across the hot concrete floors and scrambled up the sides of the graffiti-covered walls; messages from former prisoners that included a giant red heart and a drawing of Christ on the Cross with the words *Jesús es nuestro Salvador*—Jesus is our Savior.

"Doesn't look so menacing now," Matt said, "but I can imagine what must have taken place here over the years."

"Especially with that. Take a look." She pointed across the road to an area appearing to cover about an acre. It was enclosed with a waist-high concrete wall. Even with the overgrowth of weeds and brush, she could see hundreds of mounds.

"Looks like graves—unmarked graves. Captain Mali Mali wasn't exaggerating. A lot of men died here."

"It's the catacombs on a much smaller scale." Seneca squinted her eyes in the bright sun. "That's interesting. This place was closed down ten years ago and yet one of those graves looks fresh."

"Plus, there are two newly dug open graves," Matt said as they moved past the cemetery. "The undertaker business must be booming."

Ten minutes later, they came to an expanse of bright green, recently cut grass dotted with coconut palms, avocado and mango trees, and banana plants. Seneca saw a few goats and chickens wandering around a brightly painted yellow house. A wood-planked walkway extended from the road to the front porch. As she watched, a scarlet macaw flew over her head and landed in one of the avocado trees.

"This must be the place," Matt said and led the way along the wooden walkway.

As they approached the porch, Seneca called out, "¡*Hola*! ¿*Esta alguien en la casa*?" She waited a moment then called in English, "Hello, anyone home?"

Only the sound of the jungle answered. There was no response from inside the house.

"Maybe he's not home," she said, watching the front door for any movement.

"¿*Qué quiere usted*?"

Seneca and Matt turned at the sound of the voice to see a man standing beside one of the thick-trunked palms. He was a tall and bulky black man wearing a straw cowboy hat, a T-shirt that bore the Coca-Cola logo, cut-off denim shorts, and black flip-flops. He had a closely cropped black beard and his eyes were hidden behind what appeared to be a pair of women's gold sunglasses. In his right hand was a pistol aimed at them both.

WHITE AND BLACK
2012, ISLA DE SANGRE

"*¿Es usted el jaguar*?" Seneca said, raising her hands.

"*¿Americanos*?" The man took a step forward.

"Yes," Matt said, also raising his hands. "Do you speak English?"

He nodded.

"Professor Roberto Flores?" Seneca asked.

"Who wants to know?"

"I'm Seneca Hunt from *Planet Discovery Magazine* and this is my friend and fellow writer, Matt Everhart. We need to speak to you."

"I am Flores." He motioned to the bottle in her right hand. "What is that?"

"A gift from Captain Mali Mali. He said it's your favorite. *Seco*."

A fleeting look of uncertainty slid over Flores's face. "*Seco,*" he repeated, the word seeming to stumble as it came off his tongue.

"Right. Of course." Flores lowered the gun and shoved it in his waistband. "I get few visitors so I must be cautious."

"We understand," Matt said. "Captain Mali Mali mentioned the two of you are good friends."

Flores moved past them. "Inside, out of this heat."

Following the man into the cottage, Seneca gave Matt a questioning glance. Flores was not what she had expected.

"There are some cups over there." Flores motioned to a cupboard above an old porcelain sink.

Seneca glanced around the sparse cottage interior as she retrieved the cups, each one a different design and color. The house appeared to consist of two rooms; the one they were in and, from what she could see through a partially opened door, a bedroom. The floor was constructed of wood planks worn dark with age. Near the sink was a metal-legged table with a Formica top in a yellow daisies pattern. There were four folding metal chairs, all dented and rusting. The walls were covered with a tightly woven thatch similar to grasscloth and were decorated with dozens of paintings of tropical birds and flowers. In the middle of the room facing the large window overlooking the lawn and distant jungle was a vinyl recliner. On a table beside it rested a seashell ashtray with a miniature Matterhorn of cigarette butts. A plastic, battery-powered radio also occupied a portion of the tabletop.

Seneca set the cups on the Formica table. When she was seated, Flores opened the bottle of liquor and poured an inch into each cup. He raised his drink. "To a successful visit. I hope I can give you whatever information you need."

They clinked their cups. The alcohol burned Seneca's mouth and caught in her throat. She stifled a cough, then swallowed.

"Wow, not for the meek of heart." She wiped her lips on the back of her hand.

Flores drained his cup before placing it with a thump onto the tabletop. The strength of the *seco* seemed to get to the professor as well. He cleared his throat and snorted. "What do you want?"

"Do you remember a student of yours—Daniel Bernal?"

Flores seemed to ponder the question for a moment. "Of course. Daniel was one of my most promising golden nuggets. Much natural talent. How is he?"

Seneca thought she could answer the question without choking up. She almost made it. "He … he's dead, Professor Flores."

"Really? I'm sorry to hear that. His death will be a great loss to the field of archaeology, no doubt." Flores pushed his cup to the side, done with the liquor, but offered Matt and Seneca another drink. They declined. "What happened to him?"

She thought his response somewhat stiff and on the edge of being cold and apathetic. Daniel had given her the impression that he and Flores had been close, and there was evidence of that friendship in the letters she came across in Dan's belongings. "He and I were engaged to be married. He was on a dig in Mexico City, and I was there covering his discovery of Montezuma's tomb. There was an explosion—possibly a terrorist's attack. Daniel and his team were killed."

"Terrorists?" He leaned back in his chair, his gaze drifting up to the ceiling. "Murdering an archaeologist? That's disturbing." He looked back at Seneca. "I'm sorry for your loss. How long ago was this?"

Flores still seemed distant and uncaring. Where was the emotional response to losing a friend?

"A few weeks." She felt her eyes moisten, but managed to keep it from going any further.

Flores shook his head. "Now that I think about it, I do remember something on the radio about an explosion in Mexico City. So, what does that have to do with me?"

"We're investigating a series of tomb robberies occurring over the last two years," Matt said. "They involved the burial remains of numerous historical figures. In many cases, including the tomb of Montezuma, valuable grave goods were left behind, only the remains were taken."

"We're trying to see if there is some connection between these robberies in order to identify who is responsible," Seneca said. "And to answer the question of why are the remains being stolen in the first place. We came to you because we received a tip that El Jaguar might know what this is all about."

"A tip?" Flores smiled. "It seems my reputation is widespread. Who gave you the tip?"

"We don't know," Seneca said. "Only that we should seek the answers we need from El Jaguar living in the jungle. We contacted your university and found out you were retired and living here."

"Why *do* you live here?" Matt asked. "If you don't mind me asking."

"Solitude. I enjoy the isolation."

"Well, you picked the right place." Matt gave a shallow laugh as he looked around the room.

Seneca couldn't dodge the feeling that there was something wrong, but she didn't know what. She stood. "Professor Flores, it was a long boat ride and I need to use your restroom."

He glanced toward the bedroom. "In there."

She grabbed her backpack and headed for the bedroom, closing the door behind her. A single bed dominated the small room. Like the main room, the walls were covered with paintings of birds, flowers, and other island wildlife. In the corner was an old-fashioned water closet toilet with the tank overhead. She pulled down her jeans, squatted just above the seat, and relieved herself. As she did, she took in the other objects in the room. At least two dozen fishing poles and tackle occupied one corner. An old chest stood against the far wall, and a simple chest of drawers sat by the door, the drawers ajar, the top covered with books.

Then something caught her eye—a spot of red on the sheet hanging down from underneath a military green blanket that covered the bed. Finishing with the toilet, she pulled the chain on the tank to flush, yanked up her pants, and stepped to the side of the bed. Slowly lifting the blanket, she muffled a gasp with her palm as a large dark bloodstain appeared. In the same instant, she remembered something Daniel had mentioned about Professor Flores, something that had been scratching at the back of her skull since she first saw the black man in front of the cottage. Daniel had mentioned that his mentor always wore a wide-brimmed hat and long-sleeved shirt whenever he went outside. He'd had a couple of bouts with skin cancer and since the first round he always took precautions to guard his fair skin from the sun.

Professor Roberto Flores was not a black man.

UNMARKED GRAVE

2012, ISLA DE SANGRE

Seneca walked out of the bedroom with her backpack in one hand and the Lady Smith in the other. She stopped behind the impostor and raised the gun, pressing it into the back of his head.

"Who are you, and what have you done with Professor Flores?"

"Seneca, what the hell are you doing?" Matt jumped to his feet.

"This man is not Flores. In the bedroom, the sheets are soaked with blood. And Flores isn't black. Daniel said he is fair skinned."

The black man pushed back against the gun barrel as if daring her to shoot. "Don't be foolish. Why don't you tell me everything you know about the tomb robberies and I might allow you to live? Otherwise you'll never leave this island alive."

Seneca jammed the gun into his head. "I think it's the other way around. I'm the one pointing a gun at your head. Who's responsible for the tomb robberies? Who is trying to kill us?" She shoved the barrel hard against his skull. "And who murdered Daniel Bernal?"

Despite his bulk, the man was fast. In one fluid motion, he swung his right arm around as he pushed the metal chair backwards into her and jumped to his feet. Catching her forearm, he deflected the blast from the Smith & Wesson to the side of the table. Brittle Formica chunks flew in a spray.

Losing her balance, Seneca fell against the porcelain sink. She struck her head but was able to twist around in time to see the man pull his pistol from his waistband and take aim at her. In that same instant, Matt slammed one of the metal chairs across the man's back. The gun blast shattered the sink and was followed by a second from the Lady Smith causing the man to grab his chest.

Seneca watched a scarlet patch form on the front of the Coca-Cola T-shirt. A beat later, the man sank to his knees and collapsed beside her.

She scrambled out of the way as Matt grabbed the impostor's gun.

The man brought his hand up before his face looking in what appeared to be amazement at the blood dripping from his fingers. "It wasn't supposed to be this way."

"Who are you?" Seneca asked.

His eyes tried to focus on her. "He promised I would live forever."

"Who promised?" Matt knelt beside him. "Who are you talking about?"

"This was my second—"

"Second what?" Seneca said. "Did you kill Professor Flores?"

His stare burned into her. "There will be others. You are already dead."

Suddenly his eyes stretched wide as he fought to keep them open. His mouth fell agape and the crescent of pink inside his bottom lip paled to white while the outer portion blued. A shudder passed through the man, and he made animal-sounding grunts that seemed to come from deep inside. Then came a series of random twitches that intensified into what Seneca realized was a full-blown seizure. Brutally fierce muscle contractions assailed him, and the arrhythmic thudding of his body as it convulsed against the floor sent waves of nausea through her. The contents of her stomach rose, and she covered her mouth and fought back a gag reflex.

The man's eyes rolled back in his head so that only the whites showed as the seizure escalated. His extremities became rigid, shaking violently, and a trail of urine streamed down his pants. Soon, the tremors slowly subsided and finally disappeared.

Looking confused and glassy eyed, the irises of the man's eyes reappeared, and he peered up at her.

"Who are you?" she whispered.

At first he didn't answer as he struggled with the blood filling his mouth. But then he spoke, softly, with unexpected clarity. "I am His Excellency, Idi Amin Dada, President of Uganda."

His eyes closed and Seneca saw that his chest no longer rose and fell. The stench of defecation permeated the air.

Once darkness fell, it took ten minutes to push the wheelbarrow with the black man's body up the wooden walkway to the road heading back to the cemetery. Seneca led the way with a flashlight and shovel she found in Flores's cottage. The sounds of the jungle that she thought so comforting on their walk to the cottage now sounded menacing. They unnerved her as the volume seemed to be louder and harsher. And on a few occasions, she thought she heard the rustle of movement in the underbrush that sounded like it was made by a creature much larger than an iguana or tropical bird.

Still shaken, her hands trembled from what had just happened. She had shot and killed another human being. Her right hand continued to sense the cold dead weight of the Lady Smith, and the ringing in her ears lingered from the blast of the fatal shot.

Only a few weeks ago she was an excited bride-to-be, so in love that the world seemed to revolve around her every desire. Nothing could have derailed the fulfillment of her dreams, her love for Daniel or their happiness.

Instead of such bliss, she was trudging down a dirt road in the middle of the jungle on a remote island helping a man she hardly knew dispose of the body of someone she'd just killed. This was beyond a derailment; this was a head-on collision with disaster.

Who would go to such lengths to come to this distant place, murder Professor Flores, impersonate him, then try to kill her and Matt?

She already knew in her gut that this was not going to end tonight once they buried this man. Seneca recalled the dead man's chilling last words—that others would come, that she was already dead. If anything, it was only going to get worse until she exposed whoever was responsible for the tomb robberies. Otherwise, she would soon occupy her own tomb.

"Heads up."

"What?" she said.

“Keep the light on the road. You were wandering off course,” Matt said.

“Sorry.” She paused to turn and face him. “I was trying to figure out what the shit this is all about. It just so happens that I’ve never fucking killed a man before. Could you cut me some slack!”

“Yeah, well this is the first time I’ve buried a dead body, so do me a favor and shine the light in the right direction.”

“Thanks for your heartfelt concern.”

Matt lowered the wheelbarrow and wiped the sweat from his forehead. He came around and placed his hands on her shoulders. “We’re in this together, Seneca. Remember, they tried to kill me, too. The last thing we need is to start arguing or mistrusting each other. I know you’re on edge and upset. So am I.”

Realizing what he said made sense, she moved close and let him take her into his arms. Suddenly she was sobbing. Seneca found comfort in Matt’s embrace and felt guilty that she did, as if she were betraying Daniel. Still, she was slow to pull away.

“I’m sorry,” she sputtered through her tears. “I feel like I’m about to explode. I don’t understand why any of this is happening.”

“Neither do I, but we have to finish this business tonight before someone comes along and discovers what’s happened here.”

She nodded as he gave her a compassionate kiss on the forehead.

“Let’s go.” Matt returned to the back of the wheelbarrow. With a grunt, he lifted the handles.

They continued on until the ghostly forms of the prison buildings materialized out of the dark jungle. Seneca spotted the wall surrounding the old penal colony cemetery. She pushed open the entrance gate, its rusted hinges not wanting to relinquish its secrets. Matt maneuvered the cumbersome load through the opening.

They found the fresh grave and the two newly dug ones beside it.

"You think those were meant for us?" she asked.

"Yes, and I'll bet money the new one contains the body of the real Flores."

A few minutes later, the crunch and scraping of Matt's shovel blended with the croaking of the tree frogs and the drone of the jungle's night creatures.

A new unmarked grave was added to Isla de Sangre cemetery.

THE SCROLL

2012, ISLA DE SANGRE

Matt wiped the sweat from his face on the tail of his shirt. Near dusk he stood over the grave of the man who called himself Idi Amin. After burying the black man, he had filled in the second open grave beside it, the one most assuredly meant for him or Seneca. But not before throwing Flores's blood-soaked sheets and the black man's gun in first.

While he was finishing up the work in the graveyard, Seneca announced she was going to go look around the old prison buildings. She was still feeling queasy after witnessing the death of the man in the cabin and couldn't take watching his burial or, for that matter, being in a place whose only purpose was to accommodate the dead.

Reluctantly agreeing, he cautioned her not to enter any of the structures—their deteriorated condition was unsafe.

Tossing the last shovel full of dirt on the new grave, Matt looked in the direction of the prison. Twilight was giving way to night and there was no sign of Seneca. She'd been gone for quite some time and he began to worry.

"Seneca?" he called in a loud whisper. "Where are you?"

No reply.

Matt placed the shovel in the wheelbarrow and pushed it back through the cemetery gate. Leaving it parked beside the road, he had taken a few steps toward the main prison structure when he heard rapid footfalls—someone was running toward him from the direction of the prison. An instant later Seneca appeared, her flashlight beam scanning the ground in front of her as she ran.

"Matt." She was panting. "You're not going to believe it." Out of breath and barely able to speak, she halted beside him and pointed her flashlight back in the direction of the main building, the one that proclaimed *Penitenciaria* over the entrance.

"Believe what?"

She shook her head, and between heavy breaths, said, "It freaked me out."

"What?"

"Come on." Without waiting, she spun around and briskly walked the path to the first of the buildings a hundred feet off the side of the road.

"Are you going to tell me?"

"No, I'd rather show you instead."

Moving along the front of the building with its crumbling walls and overgrown sidewalk, she came to a long flat wall. Shining the flashlight beam on it, she said, "Remember the graffiti we saw from the road in the daylight?"

"You mean the big heart and the portrait of Jesus? What of it?"

"Check this out."

Illuminating the face of Christ, she let the flashlight beam drift down to a painting of a ribbon scroll just below the portrait. On the yellow ribbon were the words, *Usted debe destruir el velo por el fuego*.

She looked back at him with wide-eyed fascination. "Can you believe it?"

"You know I don't read Spanish. What does it say?"

"It says, 'You must destroy the veil by fire.'"

Matt took a step back. "You're kidding." He studied the faded lettering. The paint was chipped and weathered. It had been there a long time. "Okay, maybe it's a common saying or has some kind of special meaning to Catholics. Catholicism is the predominant religion in France and Panama."

She turned to him. "But in the tunnels it was in English."

She was right. But it could still be a coincidence. Why in English if it was written by a French Catholic? A little creepy, but nothing to be overly concerned about. "I wonder, what's this veil they're talking about?"

"I'm blown away. Do you realize that on two occasions we've run into this same phrase? And both times, it was when we were in danger."

"I admit it's crazy, Seneca, but it may be nothing more unusual than seeing a yellow happy face in a couple of places. I'm not sure if it really means anything."

"This is interesting. I'm the one who always needs the extra ounce of proof while you're the guy who professes to believe in UFOs and Bigfoot. Now I give you the strangest coincidence I've ever seen in my life, and you're blowing it off as nothing more than a happy face? I don't think I'll ever figure you out, Matt Everhart."

"I'll give you this much, it's a bit unusual. But I think what we really need to do right now is hightail it back to Flores's cottage, wait until morning, get to the beach to rendezvous with Captain Mali Mali, and put this island in our wake. Some obscure religious saying is the least of our problems."

"Fine." Seneca brushed past him and started back the way they had come.

Matt followed and caught up with her as she waited by the wheelbarrow. Without another word, she headed along the road toward the cottage. Matt took a last glance at the cemetery, then followed.

They walked in silence the rest of the way as insects came at their flashlight beams like Kamikaze pilots.

Approaching Flores's cottage, Seneca said, "I don't think I want to go inside."

"I don't blame you, but if you stay out here, you'll be eaten alive."

With obvious reluctance, she opened the door and went in. "What do you think Flores used for lights?"

"I remember seeing an oil lamp earlier." He shined his flashlight in the direction of the counter beside the sink. There was a lamp and a box of matches. A few seconds later, it gave off a warm, yellow glow.

Matt could tell she was miffed that he had not taken the graffiti more seriously. At least it had refocused her attention away from the killing of the imposter. He looked at her in the soft light of the lantern, strands of her coppery hair hanging loosely in her face. She tossed them back as she wandered around the room examining Flores's possessions. She kept her arms folded, reluctant to touch anything, almost as if she were in a museum. Finally she faced Matt. "What are you staring at?"

"Forgive me. I was just marveling at your courage. This is not a situation I would wish on anyone."

She rubbed her bare arms. "I feel like my skin is on fire. This whole situation is horrible and there's nothing I can do about it, nowhere to run. It's like we're stuck on the dark side of the moon."

"We just need to get through tonight. Tomorrow, we'll be gone."

"We need to tell someone about this. You can't just kill a person and walk away. We could leave a note or something explaining what happened?"

"To whom? There are no authorities here, only a handful of islanders who have no desire to bring attention to themselves or this place. Flores had a reputation for disappearing into the jungle. If someone ever comes looking and finds him gone, that's what they'll assume. And no one knows we were here."

"Captain Mali Mali does."

"True, but he doesn't know our names. We tell him the truth—Flores wasn't here."

Seneca stood staring at Matt, her arms now wrapped around herself. Finally, she gave a slight nod. "I guess."

"Seneca, it was self-defense. He was going to kill you … us."

It took a few moments of silence before her body seemed to relax as if some of the anxiety flowed out of her into the air. "We need to figure out the sleeping arrangements."

"Let's see if he has a change of sheets. You can have the bed, and I'll park myself out here."

"No way, fresh sheets or not. The mattress is bloody."

“Then you take the recliner and I’ll find something to make a pallet on the floor.” Matt opened the door to the closet in the bedroom.

After looking at the sparse clothing hanging on the rack, Seneca said, “I guess Flores wasn’t trying to make a fashion statement.”

Matt pulled a lightweight blanket from the overhead shelf.

She put her nose to it. “Smells like mildew.”

Matt opened the coverlet, fluffed it in the air, then folded it lengthwise into thirds. “It’ll have to do.”

Once they settled into their relative sleeping accommodations, Matt extinguished the lamp, then lay awake staring into the darkness of the room as the jungle night sounds drifted in. He lay awake for a long time, knowing Seneca couldn’t sleep either as she tossed and turned. Though she had tried to put it aside, he understood that killing someone deeply disturbed her. That and the fact that tonight she had gazed into her own grave.

———

“We’re going to be late,” Matt said as they passed the prison on the way to meet the captain. The sun was already beating down.

“Mali Mali will wait. It’s not like he operates on a big city bus schedule.” She turned and walked backward, facing Matt. “Besides, it’ll just take a second.” She stopped and pulled her small camera out of her backpack. “Come on. Don’t you want to see it again? Or are you afraid it’s turned into a happy face?” Her mood changed to a more solemn tone. “I think it’s important. Too much of a coincidence. Somebody wants us dead, so I’m not discounting anything, Matt.”

"All right." He followed her off the road through the weeds toward the buildings. They found their way along the front of the main structure until they came to the wall with the graffiti.

"There's the big red heart." She moved along the wall before stopping to point. "And the picture of Jesus."

Matt stood beside her as they both looked at the faded, crumbling wall. Finally, he said, "We must be at the wrong place."

"No, it was here. I remember it exactly. See, there's the ribbon scroll."

"So where is the thing about the veil?" He slowly read the words on the scroll. "*Jesus es nuestro Salvador.* Doesn't that mean *Jesus is our Savior* or something like that?"

Seneca nodded. "I don't understand. We both stood here and saw it last night."

"This place is covered with graffiti. I tell you, we're at the wrong wall." He checked his watch again. "Come on, we've got to get to the dock."

He turned and started back the way they had come. Behind him, he heard the click of the digital camera as Seneca photographed the wall.

Two miles later, they emerged from the jungle and saw the beach spread out ahead. On the horizon, a sport boat knifed through the breakwater. Captain Mali Mali waved as he brought the boat across the calmer water of the cove toward the dock.

"You think you've got enough for a story now?" Matt said.

Seneca shook her head. "I don't know what I've got anymore."

"So how was your visit with El Jaguar?" the captain asked as he assisted them into the boat.

"Unfortunately, we never found Professor Flores," Seneca said.

"That's too bad." Mali Mali grinned. "But I hope you didn't let the *seco* go to waste?"

Seneca shot Matt a look. "No, it went for a good cause."

"Still, it is a shame you couldn't find El Jaguar. He is a most interesting character. But quite elusive."

"All we can figure is that he's off in the jungle on one of his jaunts," Matt said.

"He has a habit of doing that. What about the other one—the black man I brought over two days before you?"

Seneca shook her head as she looked away. "No, didn't see him either."

"That's no surprise." The captain laughed as he pushed the throttles forward. "Many come here only to disappear forever."

THE PROMISE
2012, BAHAMAS

Scarrow waited in the shadows of the bedroom for Groves to awaken. The medical staff assigned to care for the recluse had alerted him that Groves suffered a blackout and had been found lying naked on the bathroom floor. A thorough examination found no broken bones or serious injuries. He had regained consciousness, and with the help of medication managed to sleep the rest of the night.

The room was cold enough for Scarrow to see his own breath. He shivered as he watched the frail form sleeping behind the gauze-like netting. As he often did lately, Scarrow wished there were some way that the effect of the veil could be reversed or canceled so that Groves would just fade away and die in his sleep. But he knew full well that no matter how incapacitated, sick, or mentally wrecked the cowboy got, he would never die.

The reality was that Groves had become a burden that grew heavier each day—the high maintenance required by the billionaire seemed to be a constant drain on Scarrow's valuable time. Ultimately, Scarrow had to make most of the decisions concerning Groves since the staff was only allowed limited access.

There was movement beneath the sheets. "Let me guess, Javier, you're standing there plotting on how you can do me in." The voice was weak and thin, and seemed to barely penetrate the darkness. "Isn't it ironic that doing away with me is the one thing you can't do?"

"Why would you say such a thing, William?" Scarrow sat in a nearby chair, the protective paper gown he wore over his clothes crinkling crisply. "I was worried and came to see to your comfort."

"Bullshit." Groves raised his scrawny hand to cover his mouth as he coughed. "You need me like a hog needs a bowtie. You've isolated me. I have no idea how my companies are doing. No newspapers, no television. For all I know you could have pissed away every last dime."

"If I had, do you think we would be here in this place? Have you ever had any reason to mistrust me? Have I ever given away your secret? No, William. Your companies are running smoothly and efficiently. There's no need for you to worry."

Groves's bony finger pointed at Scarrow. "Then tell me this, why do you keep me in this isolation chamber—this prison?"

"I don't keep you isolated, William. Your doctors have explained to you many times that your immune system is weak and susceptible to disease and sickness that could incapacitate you. Mostly your isolation is by your own design. Because of your medical condition you've become paranoid. After all, look at me." He drew attention to his gown and booties. "You had one of your own companies build this clean room—stainless steel walls, halogen lights that are washed down every day, a bank of ceiling HEPA filters, gel seals, negative pressure safety seals, and a dozen other specifications that protect you from the outside world. Your water is distilled and goes through two other purification processes as well as ionization to add antioxidants. All the windows are triple paned and heat sealed. And you wonder why there is no newspaper? Because a newspaper would bring millions of germs into this room. A television would require someone to install the satellite reception, which means a stranger would witness how bizarrely William Groves lives." Scarrow glared at him. "And you do live quite curiously, don't you think?" He sat silently a moment, letting Groves stew in his thoughts. "So, do you want me to have a newspaper sent up?"

Groves rubbed his temples with the heels of his hands. "I don't know why you don't understand. I can't die, and if I get a disease it won't kill me. I will just suffer with it eternally."

"Of course I understand. It is the same for me. But put all that aside. There's a bigger reason you stay away from the public. You know that. You are terrified that someone will find out your *secret*—if that came to the attention of the world and was spread across the headlines or the nightly news, you would be placed under the biggest microscope in history. You don't want that, and that's why we've been vigilant all these years to protect your privacy. Why are you questioning these things, now?"

"Why aren't you afraid, Javier? You should be." Groves emitted a grumble followed by another cough. "And who are those Frankenstein doctors you've got sneaking around? What the hell kind of monsters are they building down there in the laboratories? I'll wager it goes against God and man."

Scarrow leaned forward, resting his arms on his thighs, lacing his fingers. How many times had he explained? Groves's medications had negative effects on his memory, which often initiated problems, misunderstandings, and confusion. Groves had been intrigued with Scarrow's plan from the very beginning, buying in every step of the way. But there was no use in reminding him that they had been over this numerous times over the last thirty years.

"On the contrary. Oh, William, you will be so proud of this. You're giving a group of brilliant physicians and scientists an opportunity to research areas of medicine that they could not do elsewhere. And someday, when their work is presented to the world and recognized as the greatest advances in areas like reconstructive surgery and human cell regeneration, we will all share in their glory and accomplishments. And you, William, will be named as their principal benefactor, a man with unequaled foresight and vision. You will be the one who is responsible for bringing to the world miracles that up until now were only dreams. You will possess the ability to create life. Not only will you be the richest and most famous man in the world, but you will become what I promised from the start. You will become a god."

"Do I look like a god?" He started to laugh but could only produce a choking sound. "If I ever find a way to die, and I come face to face with the real God, he's gonna send me straight to hell for helping you create the abominations in this place."

"William, you have to trust me. Soon you'll—"

Scarrow reached into his pocket and removed the vibrating cell phone. "Yes?" He listened intently for ten seconds. "How did this happen?" He paused, looking at Groves. "I'll call you back." Standing, he shoved the phone back into his pocket. “I’m afraid I have to go.”

“Things aren’t going according to plan, Javier?” Groves laughed again which set off a coughing fit. “Life is full of disappointments,” he finally managed to say.

“Get some rest, William.”

Scarrow walked from the bedroom without looking back. He didn’t bother to strip off the disposable booties or paper gown as he passed through the stainless door and sterilization port. Standing in the hallway outside Groves’s penthouse suite, he clutched the phone so tightly that his fingers blanched white.

Pushing the speed dial number, he waited for Coyotl to answer. Using every ounce of willpower to harness his temper, he said, “What do you mean, he’s dead?”

GOSPEL OF THE ANGELS

2012, PANAMA CITY

"WHERE'S MATT?" AL ASKED as he walked into Seneca's room on the fourth floor of the Riande Granada Hotel in downtown Panama City.

"He called from his room to say he was going to pick up coffee and copies of the local newspapers. He wanted to see if there was any news about what happened on the island."

"There won't be." Al closed the door. "That place is about as isolated as it gets. The few inhabitants living there don't want any contact with the outside world. No news will come out of Isla de Sangre."

Still wearing the jeans and pullover she arrived in from the island the previous day, she made eye contact with Al and fought back tears. She wanted to stay strong but inside she was falling to pieces. Her father seemed to sense her torment and took a step toward her, reaching out his hands.

"I'm okay. Really, I'm fine. You didn't need to come all this way." What she wanted and needed was just what he was offering, a father's consoling embrace. In that safe place she could acknowledge that she had shot a man… killed another human being. But she couldn't make herself move.

Al took the initiative and put his arms about her. "I know, little one, I know." He patted her on the back as he held her. "Knowing you have taken someone's life isn't easy to live with. But you have to remember that he was there to kill you. What you did was clearly in self-defense. He could have just as easily murdered you and Matt."

"There were two open graves," she whispered, pulling back and wiping away her tears. "I know they were meant for us." Seneca sat on a nearby couch. Al sat beside her. "In my head I understand that his intent was to kill us. Even so, I don't think I'll ever get over this."

"I hate to ask you, but I think we have to go back to the island. You and Matt need to show me his grave. If I can collect some DNA samples and maybe get a good fingerprint, we might be able to get an ID on this guy."

"But that will mean involving the authorities. I'll be charged with murder."

"No, it means involving my buddies. They don't need to know the circumstances, just see if they can identify the man."

"Who are your friends? Who did you work for?"

Al hesitated, seeming to consider if he should answer. "It's better you don't know."

"I need to."

He rubbed his face as if fighting an internal conflict. "I was the director of a government group called ILIAD. Like I told you at Matt's place, they're a bunch of computer geeks who spend their time analyzing—"

There was a knock on the door. Al rose and answered it.

"Hey, Al." Matt had a couple of newspapers under his arm and held a cardboard carrier containing three large cups of Starbucks. "How was your flight?" He dropped the newspapers on the desk near the couch and handed out the coffee.

"Hurried but uneventful." They shook hands.

Matt nodded toward the newspapers. "I don't really read Spanish, but a quick glance through those turned up nothing about the island or a missing Professor Flores or a black man claiming to be Idi Amin Dada that I could see."

"I was telling Seneca that I doubt there'll be anything forthcoming. The few people who are on that island are there because they want to become invisible. The graves in the prison cemetery are unmarked for many reasons, that being one." Al returned to sit with Seneca on the couch. "We've got a great deal of ground to cover."

Matt said, "I'm ready for a lot fewer questions and a lot more answers."

"So, where do we start?" Seneca said.

"How about with the phrase you two gave me to investigate? The one you said was also painted on the penal colony prison wall."

"And?" Matt asked.

"First, let me say that the agency I formerly directed is not in the business of researching religious antiquity. But they are the best at researching anything. So it didn't take too long to come up with an answer. Although I'm told that it was obscure with a capital O."

"So it's something to do with religion?" Matt asked.

"Christianity."

"Explain."

Al told them the legend of the Veil of Veronica and its role in the Catholic Church. "But actually, there's no reference to Veronica or her veil in the canonical Gospels. I'm talking about the four Gospels—Matthew, Mark, Luke, and John—in the New Testament that we all studied in Sunday school. But those aren't the only Gospels, just the ones most people are familiar with, the ones that made it into the Bible."

Al picked up his coffee, shook the now-empty container, then placed it back on the desk.

"I can call down for more," Seneca said.

"Later, maybe. There are many other *gospels* that were not accepted into the canon for various reasons such as doubt over the authorship, the timeframe between the original writing and the events described, or the content was at odds with orthodoxy. Some of the non-canonical gospels were considered heretical by the Church. There were the Gospels of Thomas, Peter, the Infancy Gospels, Harmonies, Marcion's Gospel of Luke, the Gospel of Judas—"

"What? You're kidding?" Seneca said. "Judas?"

"Yes, and the list goes on and on. There are fragmentary gospels, reconstructed gospels, lost gospels—you get the idea. One of the more obscure and least known is the Gospel of the Angels. It first surfaced around the year one hundred, and no author was named, which is why it came under scrutiny and didn't make the cut."

"You're killing us here, Al," Matt said. "Get to the point."

"The Gospel of the Angels is an account of the role of angels throughout ancient religious history. For instance, there are detailed accounts of how the angel Gabriel first appeared to Daniel and later to Mary to tell her she was to give birth to Jesus. It tells the tale of the three angels that appeared to Abraham, and how God sent angels to lead Moses out of the desert—all in much more detail than in the Bible. There's the story of how angels announced the birth of Jesus to the shepherds, and how they ministered to Christ after his temptation in the desert. Lots of stories we're all familiar with, and some we're not.

"In particular, there's the story of how an angel appeared to a holy woman named Veronica. The angel presented her with a piece of cloth, a swatch the angel proclaimed to be cut from the robe of God, and instructed the woman to use it to wipe the face of the condemned rabbi Jesus Christ on his way to be put to death. Tradition has it that to reward Veronica for her compassion, Jesus left an imprint of his face on the cloth."

"Like the Shroud of Turin," Seneca said.

"If that's the veil we keep hearing about," Matt said, "what's up with this command to destroy it? I would think it would be considered a holy relic venerated by the Church."

"It was, and is. And that's the problem."

Seneca turned to Al. "So there was a Veronica and a veil?" She held up her hands. "But what does this have to do with the phrase we keep running into?"

“The angel commanded Veronica to destroy the veil by fire but only after Christ ascended into Heaven.”

“So?”

“She didn’t.”

DISTRACTION
2012, BAHAMAS

Scarrow burst into the Azteca conference room where Coyotl sat waiting. He stood stoic at the head of the table, his fists clenched at his side, his face burning from anger. He took in a deep breath. "How?"

"Shot," Coyotl said.

"He was sent on a simple mission. Kill them and dispose of the bodies." Scarrow struggled to not explode with rage. "Let me paint you a picture. We are dealing with a woman who writes articles for a science magazine and a man who makes up shit for a living. They aren't trained assassins, military commandos, part of the police SWAT team, secret agents, hired killers, gangbangers, or even members of the X-Men. And yet, they've managed to escape not one, not two, not three, but four attempts on their lives by one of the most well-funded private organizations in the world. They are either the luckiest two people who ever lived or we are totally incompetent. Which is it?"

"Well, Javier—"

"It doesn't matter. The answer is that they are amazingly lucky, and I must be surrounded by amateurs. We have lost an apostle. A cornerstone of my Ministry." Scarrow pressed the heels of his hands to his eyes and moved them in circles, massaging back the ache of frustration. "Media from around the world is preparing to converge on a single spot to watch as I make the ultimate sacrifice and prove beyond any doubt that the path of the Phoenix Ministry is the only one mankind can choose to avoid global disaster. Untold millions of dollars are being spent to make this happen. We only get one chance. There will be no do-over, no repeat."

Scarrow swiped his face with his palms. "And we are allowing two people—"

"Actually, three," Coyotl said softly.

Scarrow took another deep breath. "Yes, you are correct. Three people are standing in our way." He paused for a moment in thought. "Tell me what you know about our third friend. Give me details."

Coyotl referred to some notes in front of him. "His name is Albert Palermo. He's Seneca Hunt's father and a former director of a government agency. He abandoned the mother soon after she gave birth to the daughter and never returned. That is, until recently."

"Why did he come back?"

"He retired not long ago and it looks like he just wants to make up for lost time by getting to know his daughter."

"Impeccable timing, wouldn't you say?"

Coyotl nodded.

"What government agency are we talking about?"

"This was a tough one to crack. It took the resources of a number of Groves Consortium military contractors to finally piece together a basic profile. Palermo is the former director of a group called ILIAD—the International League to Investigate Alternative Defense. It's funded jointly by the US government and a number of allies. ILIAD was established during the Cold War as a think tank to deal with the Soviets, but now its function is primarily to find alternative means of defense against terrorism. And it controls a powerful network of intelligence-gathering technology."

"So his contacts at ILIAD are how he's been able to help her figure out the tomb robbery connections?"

"Yes."

"That's not good. It presents a new set of problems. We're going to have to stop our attempts to terminate her. Striking out at her or her father could initiate an investigation that might connect to us in some way. That would focus unwanted attention on us before we complete our task. We need a distraction to occupy her attention until after the grand event. At that point, she and the other two will become insignificant."

"What do you suggest?"

He went to stand before the replica of the Mexica Sun Stone on the back wall of the conference room. He could not afford to continue wasting precious time trying to deal with this threat. Suddenly, it struck him that he had been going about this in totally the wrong way.

He turned back to Coyotl. "Where is she now?"

"Still in Panama with Palermo and Everhart."

"Does she have any other family?"

“Her mother is alive, but incapacitated. She’s in an assisted care facility in Miami.”

“We must do two things. First create a need for her to return to her mother’s side.”

“How?”

“You said her mother was sick? See to it that she becomes sicker. Whatever she is suffering from, make it critical. Speak to our doctors if need be.”

“Consider it done.” Coyotl stood to leave but hesitated. “Javier, I have one more thing to say. Your choice for the last apostle is brilliant. It must be very rewarding for you.”

Scarrow smiled broadly, his anger dissolving away with the recognition that the one he chose was the most appropriate person for the role. “There is nothing sweeter than the taste of revenge, Coyotl.” He ran his palms over the smooth surface of the conference table.

“Do you intend to replace Idi Amin with another so the number is still twelve?”

“No. It’s too late. We will proceed with eleven. There’s no time to waste.”

“You said we need to do two things. What is the second?”

“You must bring Seneca Hunt to me.”

THE GHOST
2012, BAHAMAS

GROVES STARED INTO THE mirror, hardly recognizing the face looking back. What had become of the virile, rugged cowboy who once confronted bloodthirsty Apaches and fierce Mexican banditos? Where was the man who could outlast an endless string of whores each night and drink more whiskey than ten men anytime? What happened to the international industrialist and tycoon whose natural vision and shrewdness generated billions of dollars and the respect and envy of the world?

Scarrow had managed to reduce him to a ghost in the mirror.

Groves opened the front of his bamboo fiber robe and touched the scars—fading reminders of what should have taken him to the grave. No delusion. No hallucination. They were real. But he was no god as Scarrow claimed.

He backed away from the reflection and shuffled through the bedroom suite into the living room, shoving his hands deep into the pockets of the robe. The drone of the Australian didgeridoo sound machine and the smoke of sandalwood incense filled the air. Standing in front of the plate-glass windows that stretched across the entire wall, he pulled back the blackout drapes to look into the Caribbean night sky. He could see the ocean far in the distance and the starlight reflecting off its surface.

How many times over the years had he gazed into the star-filled heavens and questioned why he had been chosen to bear the curse of immortality. Over the decades, he had seen and done everything—experienced all there was to feel, smell, taste, touch. He had met the most famous and many of the infamous. If there were anything left to do or say or see, it was of little consequence now. What lay ahead seemed to hold no promise.

There had to be a reason, a purpose for him. No benevolent God could be so cruel as to condemn a man to a life of endless emptiness.

The ghost in the mirror gave him no answer.

Dressed in green scrubs, cap, and surgical mask, Groves moved silently along the corridor, its walls lit only by low-wattage night-lights. What the other residents in the huge pyramid building would consider a comfortable temperature, for Groves it was like walking in Death Valley. He missed the chill of his bedroom as the sweat from his frail body formed stains through the green cotton of the medical outfit. He feared becoming dehydrated before he could return to his room. But it was worth the discomfort to venture into the secret depths of Azteca.

This was his second middle-of-the-night excursion into the bowels of the building. The first revealed a series of sterile, white-walled medical chambers and science laboratories filled with racks and tables of high-tech equipment. In one room—which was nicely chilled and more to his liking—five corpses lay on pedestaled, stainless steel examination tables, their bodies covered with sheets. As he lifted each covering, he realized that the bodies were missing parts—some had various limbs amputated while others had been dissected. Voids appeared where internal organs were removed.

On shelves in a walk-in freezer, Groves found translucent heavy-duty plastic bags containing human body parts. The morbid sight was worse than the slaughtered Mexican Federales scattered on the floor of Renegade Pass so long ago. That had been gruesome, but this scene was ghoulish.

Tonight, he intended to explore the remaining rooms in the basement. As he passed a door that was ajar, he noticed a faint wedge of light flowing out onto the hallway floor. Groves hesitated, listening for any sounds. Hearing none, he gently pushed open the door. What he saw was a meeting room with a large table in the middle and chairs lining each side. Unlike a formal corporate conference room, this one was more of a workroom; the walls were covered with white dry marker boards. Scientific formulas and hand-drawn diagrams of the human anatomy filled most of their surfaces. At the end of the table, a woman sat reading what looked like a large textbook spread before her. She seemed deep in concentration.

As he stepped into the room, she looked up from the pages of the book and turned to gaze in his direction.

"Hello." She seemed not at all surprised to see him there.

Groves nodded as he took in her features. She had a somewhat plain face, pale skin with brown eyes, and a pointed nose. Her dark hair was long and flowed in curls down to her shoulders. She wore a bathrobe and slippers, and he got the impression that she had come here to read in solitude.

"Are you one of the surgeons?"

Groves nodded again and took a few steps forward until he had covered half the distance to her.

"I thought the doctors no longer had to work late. Are you one of those overachievers who put the surgeons to shame?"

Afraid to pull his surgical mask down, he spoke into it, feeling the hot moist backwash of his breath. "Yes, I'm working late."

"I don't remember seeing you around. What's your name?"

"Billy. Doctor Billy. I'm new."

"Nice to meet you. I'm Mary Tudor." She stood and extended her hand.

"My pleasure." He took several feeble steps in her direction. When he grasped her hand it felt small, and delicate, and warm through his latex gloves. "What are you reading there?"

She marked her page, then closed the book and showed him the cover. "It's the *Complete History of the British Empire*. I'm reading up on my heritage."

"So you're British."

"Through and through." She flashed a smile.

With a trickle of panic at being so close to someone who had not been sanitized and probably harbored millions, maybe billions of germs, he drew back toward the door.

"You all right?"

Groves nodded. "Are you visiting or do you work for Javier?"

"Well," she touched her chin with her fingertip, "I suppose both. I've been *visiting*, I guess you could say, for a short while before I travel to my homeland—England. There I will perform work for Javier."

"And what kind of work will you be doing?" Groves craned his head forward, his senses now highly attuned to every nuance of her face, eyes, mouth, and words.

"The most important work of all."

"Which is?"

"I am a Phoenix Apostle. My work is to save the world."

VERONICA'S LEGACY

2012, PANAMA CITY

Room service arrived and Matt poured a fresh cup of coffee for himself and Al.

Seneca sipped on a Diet Coke. "Al, how do you know that Veronica didn't destroy the veil?"

He pulled a small spiral pad from his pocket and flipped it open reviewing his notes. "After we zeroed in on her and her story, we started scouring all known databases including the hidden web."

"What's that?" Seneca asked.

"It's buried content that conventional search engines like Google and Yahoo don't pick up. The hidden web is over five hundred times bigger than the Internet and includes university reference libraries and other learning and research institutions."

"I didn't even know that existed."

Al smiled at her. "Most people don't. Anyway, piecing together the text from a number of ancient scripts in over a dozen languages including Greek, Latin, and Aramaic, we were able to form a fairly good picture of Veronica and her life, especially as it pertained to the relic."

He paused to stir cream into his coffee and take a bite of the breakfast pastry.

"In one account, we found that she was so overcome by the image of Christ's face on the cloth that she couldn't bring herself to destroy it as the angel had commanded. In fact, she hid it away until she neared the end of her life at which point she traveled to Rome and presented the veil to Emperor Tiberius. The next time it shows up is in the possession of the fourth pope, Saint Clement I.

"From there, we found little about the relic until the year 705 and the reign of John VII. There's a reference to it being present in the old St. Peter's when Pope John built what was called the Veronica chapel to house the veil. And the Vatican archives revealed that in 1011 there was a scribe who held the official office of *keeper of the cloth*. From then on, there are sporadic references to the veil and its presence in the Vatican.

"In 1300, Boniface VIII publicly displayed it during the start of what he called a Jubilee year, and the veil was referred to as one of the *Mirabilia Urbis* which means Wonders of the City. For the next two hundred years, Veronica's veil was regarded as the most precious of all Christian relics.

"Down through the following centuries, it was on public display during the feast of Saint Veronica and on Good Friday. But, in the early sixteenth century, the Church fell on hard times, and the veil was among many valuable objects sold by Pope Leo X to raise funds for a financially strapped Vatican. Holy Roman Emperor Charles V, King of Castile, became the new owner and later presented it to the Spanish conquistador Diego Velázquez de Cuéllar, governor of Cuba. The idea was for it to be carried throughout the conquest of the New World so that the savage Indians that were converted to Christianity could gaze upon the face of their Savior." Al paused to finish his pastry.

"And?" Seneca asked.

"End of the line. After that, there were a handful of fake veils showing up in various European churches. But there's no proof any of them are the real thing. As far as we could find, Veronica's veil vanished in 1517 while in the possession of the Cuban governor Velázquez."

Seneca sat in silence pondering the information Al had conveyed. "I wish we could have questioned Professor Flores. Somehow I just know from how Daniel spoke of him that he would have filled in a lot of gaps."

"He still might," Al said.

"How do you figure that?" Matt asked. "I'll wager that the professor is not only dead, but buried in that fresh grave on the island next to the guy who claimed to be Idi Amin."

"I'm sure you're right, Matt, but we also did some additional research on El Jaguar. He happened to be one of the foremost authorities on the conquest of Mexico, and when he decided to retire and head off into the sunset on Isla de Sangre, he bequeathed his entire collection of rare manuscripts and personal notebooks to the library at the Hospital de Jesús Nazareno in Mexico City."

"What's so special about that place?" Seneca asked.

"For starters, it's the oldest functioning hospital in the Americas. But more important, it was founded by the conquistador Hernán Cortés. His remains are buried in a vault inside the hospital chapel.

On a wall outside the building is a stone marker commemorating the spot believed to be the first meeting between Hernán Cortés and the Aztec Emperor Montezuma II." Al turned to Seneca. "Looks like you've come full circle."

"If I just knew the meaning of that circle." A thought occurred to her, and she went to her backpack searching its contents. Pulling out a folded piece of paper, she quickly scanned it, then held it up as if presenting a piece of evidence in a courtroom. "The circle gets tighter all the time."

"What have you got?" Al asked.

"It's your list of the tomb robberies. Do you remember who was the second name on the list?"

Matt and Al looked at each other. Simultaneously, they said, "Idi Amin Dada."

Seneca nodded as she looked at Matt. "Tell me that's just a coincidence."

He held up his hands in a sign of surrender. "Okay, I admit, that's hitting pretty close to home."

"So the remains of the African dictator are stolen," Al said, "then a man claiming to be Idi Amin murders Flores, impersonates him, and tries to kill you both. I can't help but believe this is all related, but there are still too many loose threads."

"It looks to me like we need to make a side trip to Mexico City on our way back to Miami," Matt said. "I suggest we get permission to look through Flores's collection."

"I can arrange for us to have access to the library," Al said. "The Mexican Secretary of Health is an old friend of mine."

"I'm not looking forward to going to Mexico City again," Seneca said. "But maybe if we can get some answers—"

Her cell phone rang. She took the call and listened intently. “Thank you, I’ll be there as soon as I can.” Ending the call she turned to Matt. “You’ll have to go to Mexico City by yourself.”

“What’s up?” he asked.

She faced Al. “My mother was rushed to Jackson Memorial Hospital this morning. She’s in the ICU.”

“What happened?”

“Pneumonia.” Seneca pressed the contacts icon on her phone and scrolled through her stored numbers. “I’ve got to get back to Miami right away.”

“Matt, you go on to Mexico.” Al put his hand on Seneca’s arm. “I’m going with you.”

“No, you don’t have to. I can manage.”

“I know you can,” Al said. “But I want to go. I’ll arrange for the tickets. Besides I want to make sure Brenda’s getting the best care. Maybe call in another doctor. I don’t care what it costs.”

Seneca turned and paced. She didn’t want to take any more handouts from her father, having already become more dependent on him than she wanted.

Al already had someone on his phone taking care of flight reservations.

Matt took Seneca’s hand. “Al only wants to help.”

She knew he was right.

“Is your mother going to be all right?”

Robbed of her voice as she choked back tears, Seneca closed her eyes and shrugged.

PICAROON
2012, MIAMI

After landing at Miami International, Seneca found her car and headed straight for Jackson Memorial Hospital. She and Al had managed to get on the same flight, but his car was located in a different parking garage. He was to meet her at the hospital. They had discussed Al staying behind and making a quick trip to the island to retrieve evidence from the dead man's body that might lead to his identification. But Al had said that could be postponed. After all, they knew the corpse wasn't going anywhere. Al would go back as soon as Brenda was stable or …

She didn't like to think of that.

It was at the peak of visiting hours and Jackson was crowded as she made her way down the hall on the second floor of the North Wing building. She stopped at the doorway to her mother's semi-private room. The good news was that her mother had been taken out of the intensive care unit that morning.

Occupying the first bed was a woman with long gray spidery hair, reminding Seneca of the Spanish moss that dripped from southern granddaddy oaks. Her pale skin was drawn tight over toothpick bones. Seneca caught a glimpse as she passed by the half-drawn curtain surrounding the bed, but it was enough to wrench a sad flash of sympathy from her gut.

In the far bed, her mother lay sleeping. "Mom," Seneca whispered, grasping the railing on the side of the bed. Brenda's closed eyes didn't blink, nor did she flinch at the sound of Seneca's voice. The papery skin of her frail arms bore multiple patches of deep purple bruises. Even the slightest, most simple trauma resulted in almost instant discoloration. Seneca knew that beneath the sheet and blanket, her mother's legs bore the same blemishes. Prednisone was a wonderful drug, but the bruising side effect made her mother look like she had been battered. Something as ordinary as a gentle bump against a table leg left its mark.

A snarl of tubes dangled from polyvinyl bags hung on a four-hook IV pole. Beeping, humming, and silent monitors tracked Brenda's vitals and blood oxygen saturation. Oxygen was delivered through another set of tubing, much like what Seneca used for her aquarium pump. Even with the extra supply of oxygen to her lungs, Brenda's every breath appeared labored, and was accompanied by a wet, rattling wheeze. Seneca noticed sourness in the air that even the vapors from antiseptics and medicines couldn't mask. A human odor that she imagined came from dying cells.

She circled the bed, touched her mother's cold cheek, then sat in the visitor's chair, deciding to wait there until her mother awakened no matter how long it took. She leaned her head back and closed her eyes.

God, dying is so awful.

A sick feeling spread from deep in her belly to her fingertips. Images and sensations flooded in, flickering past like an old movie reel. Chilly as the room was, in some crevice of her memory she felt the heat of Daniel's blood ooze through her fingers and spread over her, and the tackiness as it dried, then caked on her skin. A burst of light and then the vision of the last moment of the island imposter's life snapped into view—his body locked and violently seizing, the deathly whites of his eyes, the loss of control of his body functions, all playing out to the soundtrack of the rattle from her mother's breathing.

Knowing she was about to lose it, Seneca rose and went into the bathroom. She didn't want to wake her mother, and Al would be along any minute. He couldn't be that far behind her, and she would rather not be blubbering when he arrived.

Seneca sat on the toilet, folded her arms around her middle, and cried until she had drained the last drop of emotion. Standing, she moved to the sink while avoiding the mirror, leaned over and splashed water on her face. As she raised her head she heard a loud male voice.

"Brenda Hunt. Can you hear me? Wake up."

It wasn't Al's voice. *Must be the doctor*. She wanted to talk to him.

Seneca wiped the water from her face, and just as she put her hand on the door handle, she heard, "Where's your daughter?"

Cautiously, she put her ear to the door.

Her mother mumbled something, but she couldn't make it out.

"I'm a friend of your daughter. She was here. I must have just missed her. I went by her old place, but it looks like she's moved. Where is she living now? I want to visit her."

"Have you fed Picaroon?"

There was a pause, and Seneca knew the man had to be wondering what her mother was talking about. Picaroon was their pet African Grey Parrot years ago, named after the pirate word for *rascal.*

"Pica what?" The voice lacked all tenderness. "Look, just tell me where your daughter is living now."

"Picaroon. When he talks he sounds exactly like a person." Brenda's voice was weak and thin. "You'd never know the difference."

"Fuck," the man said, and Seneca heard what sounded like his fist connect with a hard surface. "This is useless." His footsteps were audible as he obviously stormed out of the room.

Seneca gently nudged the handle down and urged the door open. She peered through the crack, opening it a little at a time.

Brenda's empty eyes stared at her daughter as Seneca quietly came to the side of her bed.

Even though she was sure her mother wouldn't understand, Seneca felt the need to explain why she was leaving.

"I've got to go, Mom. I'm in trouble. When that man gets down to the parking lot he'll see my car is still here and come back looking for me." She stretched over the rail and kissed her mother's cheek.

"Do we have fresh fruit for Picaroon?"

Out of the corner of her eye, Seneca caught sight of movement. She turned, only able to see below the curtain guard. The pants and shoes of a man appeared as he strode in her direction. She ducked on the far side of the bed, crouching with every nerve fiber alive and firing panic.

SISTER ANGELICA
2012, MEXICO CITY

"WE HAVE BEEN EXPECTING you, Señor Everhart." The man offered his hand. "I'm Dr. Domingo, Chief of Administration here at Hospital de Jesús Nazareno."

"Pleased to meet you," Matt said as they exchanged handshakes. After arriving late that afternoon at Juárez International Airport from Panama City, he had checked into the Torre Lindavista Hotel before taking a taxi to the hospital.

"You must have friends in high places," Domingo smiled, exposing a line of well-shaped but yellow-stained teeth beneath a pencil-thin mustache. He was a few inches shorter than Matt, but heavier by at least fifty pounds.

"Why do you say that?" The odor of tobacco was strong, and Matt guessed the teeth discoloration was a result of years of smoking. He never understood how a physician could be a smoker.

"Access to Professor Flores's collection is almost always denied. It's usually reserved for graduate students working on their doctorates at the university. Most have to reserve time months in advance. You are the first nonacademic I can remember who's been allowed to see the Flores collection. And the permission was granted within hours."

"Then I am humbled at the privilege." They stood in Domingo's office on the fifth floor of the hospital administration wing. "Will you be assisting me?"

"No, I have to begin my rounds shortly. But I have an assistant who will." Domingo went to his desk and pushed a button on the phone. "Please summon Sister Angelica."

A moment later the office door opened and a woman Matt thought to be in her mid-thirties entered. Dressed in a nurse's uniform, she was medium height and trim with short black hair framing a cherubic face. But it was her dark eyes that seemed to catch and hold the light in the room that captured Matt's attention.

"This is Sister Angelica. She will be helping you with your research in the Flores's collection library."

"It's a pleasure, Señor Everhart." The nun extended her hand. "I've enjoyed all your novels and am looking forward to the next in your Sariel series."

"Thank you." She definitely had an appropriate name, he thought, since her appearance was quite angelic. "Do you read my books in English or Spanish?"

"English. As much as I'm sure the translations are more than adequate, I don't believe anyone can properly capture the original writer's style and nuances in a different language."

"I couldn't say. English is my only language. I'd be happy to sign your copies before I leave if you like."

"I'd like that."

"If you're ready, Mr. Everhart, Sister Angelica will show you the way back down and unlock the library for you."

"Thanks again, Dr. Domingo." The two men shook hands. "I appreciate your time."

"I hope you find what you're looking for."

Matt and Sister Angelica left the office.

"Let's catch the elevator back to the ground floor." She led the way down the hall. "The library is restricted, so you won't have any distractions."

"Great." Matt followed her to a bank of elevators. He hoped once they got to the library, the antiseptic smell of the hospital would diminish. "I really appreciate you taking the time to help me out. How long have you been with the hospital?" They entered the elevator.

"Five years."

"Are you from Mexico City?"

"No, Santa Monica. I was born in Southern California. My family is originally from Mexico, but my parents were both born in the United States. I grew up a typical American teenager who loved to surf and eat cheeseburgers."

The elevator doors opened on the ground floor with a hiss. "I'm curious as to why Flores would donate his collection to the hospital and not the university."

"It was an act of gratitude and appreciation. The professor's daughter was a near drowning victim—a waterskiing accident that left her in a vegetative state. She was cared for here for over two months until her death, which was just before Dr. Flores's retirement. He looked in on her every day."

"What about Mrs. Flores?"

"She passed away many years ago."

At the end of the tiled floor corridor, they arrived at a large wooden door. "This is the entrance to the Flores library."

Matt noticed that on the door was a sign with the words *No Entre* painted in gold script lettering. Metal strips and studs, tarnished and darkened with age, reinforced its ancient surface.

Sister Angelica removed a key from her pocket and unlocked the door. Inside, she flipped on a wall switch, and the room came alive with a set of overhead Spanish chandeliers.

The library was about thirty feet square and consisted of floor-to-ceiling shelves stocked with hundreds of books and manuscripts. The walls were rich, dark paneling and the floor a burgundy Mexican tile. Two desks sat in the middle of the room facing each other. On one rested a computer, monitor, and laser printer.

"Professor Flores had a huge collection of books dealing with the history and conquest of Mexico, most rare and irreplaceable. He also maintained thousands of personal journals and notebooks containing his writings over a thirty-year career at the University of Mexico. We are able to cross-reference and locate a great deal of the information he documented."

"That should make our job a little easier." Matt let his eyes wander around the room. "I'm envious of his collection. What's here is obviously invaluable to the history of Mexico."

"What exactly are you looking for?"

"To be honest, I'm not totally sure. But I have a pretty good idea where to start."

"Tell me." She motioned for him to sit at a desk while she took a seat at the one with the computer.

"I'm sure you're familiar with a sacred relic known as the Veil of Veronica?"

"Of course."

"Somehow I figured I wouldn't stump you on that one." When she barely broke a smile, he cleared his throat and continued, "Anyway, I have reason to believe that the Veil of Veronica may have some connection to the history of Mexico, particularly during the conquest of the Aztecs. I have a suspicion that the veil was brought to the New World."

"That's an interesting premise, but I was always led to believe the artifact resided in the Vatican. On what do you base your theory?"

For the next five minutes he relayed the story of the veil as uncovered by Al's research. He concluded with, "We've traced the relic to Diego Velázquez de Cuéllar, governor of Cuba who supposedly had it in his possession in 1517. That's where the story ends, and the veil seems to have disappeared."

"Then let's start with Velázquez. There should be a great deal of information available on him."

As Matt came to stand behind her chair, she brought up a search interface on the computer monitor and typed in the governor's name. A few seconds later, a list of links appeared.

"I thought so. There are many references to Velázquez. So let's associate the relic with his name." She filled in a few additional fields. "We'll put in *Veil, Veronica, relic, holy cloth, image of Jesus,* and a few others."

The return of links was quicker this time, and the list shorter. Sister Angelica scanned the links and clicked on a few. Because they were in Spanish, Matt took on the role of a bystander waiting for her progress report.

After scrolling through three pages of returns, she went back to the first page and reread one of the references. "Okay, this is really a stretch, but there's a manifest listing from one of the ships Velázquez furnished Cortés to sail from Cuba to Mexico. And it was in the year you mentioned—1517."

"What does it say?"

"Only that Cortés had among his personal items an object called a holy box or reliquary containing a sacred object. It was given to him by the governor."

"But we don't know what it was?"

"No, but there's also a reference to a diary of a Spanish officer who accompanied Cortés to Mexico. Apparently, there's a notation in the diary about a religious icon given to Cortés by the governor of Cuba."

"Now we're getting somewhere."

Sister Angelica made a note on a pad of paper, tore it off, then rose and walked to the bookshelves. "All of Professor Flores's books have been cataloged and stored in archival boxes." She ran her finger along a line of boxes about shoulder high. "Here it is."

She removed the box, opened it and checked the 3 by 5 identification card inside against the label on the box. Bringing it to the desk, she opened a drawer and removed a pair of surgical gloves. Pulling them onto her hands, she gently lifted the book—a small, dark leather-bound volume about the size of a passport, and a half-inch thick. She glanced at her notes, then, with great care, opened the diary. Using a desk knife, she separated the pages until she found the one she sought.

She read for a moment. "The officer referred to the relic as *imagen verdadera* which means true image."

"So it could be the veil?"

She turned to look at him and shrugged. "Maybe, maybe not."

"What's that?" Matt pointed to a piece of yellowed paper sticking out of the diary.

Sister Angelica used the desk knife to turn the page and expose a small sheet of folded notebook paper. "It might be one of Professor Flores's personal notes. Looks like the paper he always used, and I've found his one-page notes to himself stuffed in books before."

"Let's have a look."

She gently unfolded the paper. There were a few lines written in pencil. Sister Angelica looked at Matt with a broad smile. "It's Flores's handwriting dated 1981, and it says, *Call William Groves with confirmation of the Veil of Veronica*."

"William Groves?"

The nun looked up from Professor Flores's note. "Isn't he the billionaire industrialist?"

"Yes ..." Matt drew the word out. He was distracted, thinking it quite a coincidence that Groves Avionics was the one responsible for blowing his boat out of the water, and now here was Flores's note connecting Groves to the veil. Some thin fiber wove all this together. "Would it be possible to get a photocopy of that?"

"Of course." She rose and went to a copy machine on a corner table. "Do you think this is what you're searching for?"

"Maybe. It definitely fills in a couple of missing puzzle pieces." While he waited for her to finish making the copy, he said, "On my way in, I saw the stone on the wall outside the building commemorating the spot where Cortés and Montezuma II met for the first time."

"Yes, there is so much history beneath our feet. Inside the hospital chapel was the tomb of Cortés, the great conquistador. He died in Spain but his remains were eventually brought here. It was his request before he passed away."

"What do you mean that it *was* his tomb?"

She turned to face him. "You must not have heard."

"Heard what?"

"Two weeks ago, his tomb was broken into and his remains stolen."

BEGINNING OF THE END

2012, MIAMI

Seneca hovered behind the side of the bed as the man came to the opposite side. His voice seemed deliberately loud, and the words slowly spoken. "Brenda. How are you feeling? Breathing a little easier?"

Seneca heard the hum of the motors as the head of the bed began to rise.

"Can you sit up for me?"

This was not the same voice as the intruder who had been in the room minutes before. Seneca's taut shoulders relaxed—she was sure it was the doctor this time.

"Doctor?" She stood and fiddled with the small gold hoop earring in her right ear.

He seemed stunned by her sudden appearance.

"Sorry. I didn't mean to startle you. I lost my earring. I just found it on the floor as you walked in." She hoped the excuse didn't sound too lame or her nervousness give away the lie. "I don't think we've met. I'm Seneca Hunt, Brenda's daughter." She reached across the bed to shake his hand.

"Dr. Glaser. I'm consulting with Dr. Harris, the doctor at your mother's nursing home. I'm a pulmonary specialist."

"Dr. Harris? Dr. Liu is her doctor."

"I guess Dr. Harris took over some of his cases."

"Oh. Well, nice to meet you. How is my mother doing?"

"I was just about to listen to her lungs." He put his hand behind Brenda's shoulder for support. "Sit up for me."

Brenda gripped the bedrail and tugged herself forward to straighten.

"Good girl. Now, deep breath." There was a moment or two of silence other than Brenda's labored breaths.

The doctor leaned over and hopped his stethoscope from place to place on Brenda's back, appearing to listen intently. Shortly, he took the stethoscope from his ears.

"Okay, all done." He pushed a button and lowered the head of the bed to a partial upright position. "The nurse will get you up in the chair in a little while. Then you'll be able to look out the window."

"So, how is she?"

He didn't answer as he patted Brenda's hand. "Dr. Harris will be in to see you later." Then he turned his attention to Seneca and spoke softly. "Why don't we talk outside?"

Seneca followed him, scanning the hall in all directions, hoping the previous visitor hadn't returned yet. She needed to know about her mother, but she also had to get out of the hospital in a hurry.

"I'll tell you what, Alzheimer's or not, your mother is tough." He wrapped the stethoscope around his neck. "Day before yesterday I thought we were going to have to put her on a ventilator, but to our surprise she pulled out of it. Pneumonia can be extremely serious for someone with emphysema."

"Then she's going to be all right?" She glanced down the hall as she spoke.

The doctor's brow furrowed. "Ms. Hunt, you understand that this disease is progressive. It doesn't go away and doesn't get better."

His voice rang with compassion, and Seneca appreciated his sensitivity. She nodded.

"It will eventually be just too much for her lungs or too much strain on the heart. This was a close call."

She found herself whispering, "I know. I know." Seneca understood his drift. He didn't want to be so blunt as to say that her mother was drowning in her own fluids, that she wasn't going to be around much longer, that she's lucky she pulled through this episode and that things were only going to get worse—that this was the beginning of the end.

Seneca stood in the ladies room of the main lobby. She didn't dare go out to her car, sure that it was being watched. Where the hell was Al? When they parted at the airport, he'd said he was going to get his car and head straight to the hospital.

Seneca pulled her cell phone from her purse, pushed Al's name in her contacts list and put the phone to her ear. When she didn't hear it ringing, she looked at the display. *Call failed.* Damn. This building was like a fortress. No signal. Going outside and staying in the open while using the payphone would make her too vulnerable. She'd have to find another way to call Al. Perhaps a phone in one of the rooms.

Mustering her courage she left the restroom and headed to the elevator. Three women and a man joined her, waiting for the doors to open. Her pulse sped up. She had no clue what the man in her mother's room looked like. He could be the stranger standing beside her. There was no way of knowing.

When the doors finally opened, Seneca stepped inside and pushed the button for the third floor, deliberately avoiding the floor where her mother's room was. From hearing two of the women in conversation, she thought maybe they were together.

"Two, please," one of them said.

Seneca obliged, pressing the second floor button. The man said nothing and neither did the third woman. When the elevator stopped on the second floor, the two women friends got off. As the doors of the elevator closed, Seneca was grateful that she wasn't alone with the man. Still, she held her breath as the elevator bumped into motion. The ride to the third floor couldn't have taken more than five seconds, but it seemed an eternity. Not daring to look at him, she glared at the doors and slipped one hand inside her purse gripping the Lady Smith.

At last the elevator thumped to a stop, and the doors opened. Seneca shot out and headed down the hall taking a quick glimpse behind her. The man got off but didn't appear to be watching or following. He moved slowly, glancing from room to room as if searching for a particular number.

Seneca peered in several rooms, finally finding one with the occupant sleeping. The second bed empty. She crossed to the bedside stand near the vacant bed. Resting her purse on the bed, she removed her cell phone and recalled Al's number from the list, then dialed it on the hospital landline phone.

A sudden jab in her back made Seneca drop the receiver. She knew instantly what it was.

"Keep calm and no one will get hurt."

Seneca's breath caught, and her mind tripped over the voice from behind her.

It was a woman.

CHAMPAGNE

2012, MIAMI

SENECA DID AS HER assailant ordered and turned around, the face of the woman holding her at gunpoint coming into view. "You were on the elevator." She realized she'd been suspicious of the wrong person. "Who are you? Why are you doing this?"

"Quiet." The woman stole a quick glance at the sleeping patient.

Seneca cut her eyes toward her purse, thinking of the Lady Smith.

The woman must have noticed. She picked it up and looked inside. "Oh, my." She obviously spied the gun, then met Seneca's gaze. "As long as you cooperate, you won't get hurt and your mother will remain unharmed. Do exactly as I say. We're going to go down the hall and take the elevator back to the lobby. Then we'll walk out and get in a car waiting for us. No sudden moves or you'll never see your mother again. Got it?" She waved the gun. "Now, let's go."

Seneca nodded. She watched the woman drape a sweater over the small pistol while keeping it aimed at her. Then Seneca led the way out of the room with her assailant right behind.

They rode the elevator down with a young couple. From there, they moved across the expansive lobby and out the main doors to the hospital portico. Stopping at a trash receptacle, the woman disposed of Seneca's purse. "You're not going to need that."

A black limo sat waiting, and as they approached, a man emerged from the back.

"Hello, Seneca." He held the door open for her.

"Carlos?" Her breath caught as she stared into the face of the TV *Mexicali* tech assistant from the Aztec dig site.

"Call me by my Nahuatl name. I am Coyotl. Get in."

Trembling first from fear that was quickly replaced by anger, Seneca slid into the back seat and watched him follow and sit beside her.

The woman took the seat facing them. She tapped on the privacy window separating the passenger compartment from the driver, and the car started forward.

"Good job." Carlos nodded to the woman. "He's going to be pleased." He turned to Seneca. "I'd like you to meet my associate, Ilse."

Seneca's mind stumbled over the name. *Ilse—as in Ilse Koch, the Bitch of Buchenwald? It couldn't be. Ilse Koch was dead… as dead as Idi Amin had been before Seneca met him on the island.* "I don't understand any of this." She glared at Carlos and her fury spewed out. "Damn you! You murdered Daniel. Bastard!" She lurched, striking him with a solid blow to his cheek.

Carlos responded quickly, pinning her arms behind her and shoving her head to her knees. He rammed her wrists up, making her yelp with the pain. "Oh, that hurts doesn't it? I suggest you calm yourself, unless of course you don't mind a little pain." He nudged her elbows up again. "And I said to call me by my Nahuatl name. Coyotl."

Seneca bit down on her bottom lip hard enough she was certain she tasted blood. "Let go of me."

"How do I know you won't try that again?"

She nodded.

"Swear it on your dear Daniel's grave."

Seneca struggled not to attempt to rip away from him. "I swear." She couldn't bring herself to say *on Daniel's grave.*

Carlos slowly released his hold but only after giving one last thrust on her arms. "Sit up. Easy."

Seneca drew herself up and rolled her shoulders to help take the kink out. "What's this all about? Where are you taking me?" All she could think was that they probably needed to get away from any witnesses before killing her.

Ilse said, "Let's just say you've won a vacation in the Bahamas. Aren't you the lucky one?"

"Fuck you." Seneca immediately wished she'd kept her mouth shut.

"I like your spirit," Ilse said. "You remind me of myself. I'd prefer this to be a more civil trip. Things will go much better for you if you simply don't resist." She rested the gun in her lap as if making a point and removed a champagne flute from the onboard bar. "I don't see any reason not to travel in style. Champagne?"

Carlos lifted a bottle of Krug Brut and uncorked it, the foam washing over the lip of the neck. He poured a glass and held it out to Seneca.

She shook her head.

"Come on, don't be a party pooper," Ilse said. "Convince her."

He offered her the champagne again. "Have a drink in memory of your dearly departed."

Son-of-a-bitch, Seneca thought. Just the idea of joining him in a drink ignited a rage in her, but she didn't dare show it. She took the glass as he filled two more.

Seneca saw that they were coming to a stoplight. No way was she going peacefully. She needed some of her mother's gutsy strength right now.

"Cheers," Ilse said as the car came to a halt.

Seneca lifted her glass and threw the champagne into Ilse's face. In the same instant she twisted and reached for the door handle.

"That was a mistake." Ilse slammed the butt of her gun into the back of Seneca's head.

TRANSLATION
2012, MIAMI

AL REACHED TO THE passenger seat of his car and unsnapped the latches on his briefcase. He'd stored his cell inside when they took off from Panama. After leaving Miami International and promising to meet Seneca at the hospital, he had stopped for gas and to get some cash from an ATM. Seneca was probably wondering what was taking him so long. Maybe even talking herself into the notion that he had let her down again and decided not to come—that would be just like him, she would assume.

Palming the cell, he felt for the power button. As soon as the phone found the network, he heard a brief tone; a notification that he had voice mail. Al entered his code to retrieve his messages. There was only one. He heard a woman's voice in the background. "Keep calm and no one will get hurt," it began.

Al stomped on the accelerator and turned the volume up on the cell. He listened until he heard the woman say, "Now, let's go." Then silence.

Jesus H. Christ, why didn't I turn on my cell when we landed?

Al was only a few blocks from Jackson Memorial. Within a short time, he pulled up under the hospital portico and jumped out, bumping a man in a wheelchair and an attendant. "Sorry."

Bursting through the doors, he shouted at the woman behind the information desk across the lobby. "Call security. Now!"

Startled, the woman glared with eyes wide and mouth dropping open. Al had nearly reached the desk when a man in uniform darted forward and blocked him, one hand resting on the butt of his holstered gun.

"Hold it right there." The security guard punched the walkie on his shoulder. "Code yellow, main lobby."

"It's okay. I'm not a threat. My daughter's been abducted. Seal the hospital until it's been searched. They could still be in the building."

Al stood in the office of the hospital's chief of security. It had taken him more time than he wished to ease the minds of the security personnel and hospital administrator, wasting precious moments. But what was done was done. The window of possible opportunity had been missed, and there was nothing he could do about it. Even hearing Seneca's message that had automatically gone to his voice mail hadn't really convinced them she had been abducted. ILIAD had finally stepped in and not only squelched their questions, but also had arranged for complete hospital security clearance and access to anything Al requested.

Obviously impressed with Al's credentials, the security guard was now making every effort to appease and earn Al's respect to the point that it was embarrassing.

Al checked his watch, judging how much of the security video he would need to review. "Let me see the last hour from every camera."

The guard raised his thumb and extended his index finger to mimic a gun and pointed to Al. "You got it."

Almost instantly, the digital video disks jumped back one hour, confirmed by the burned-in time code. Each camera had a box in a grid on the large flat screens. There were sixteen boxes per screen and several screens that alternated just long enough for an observer to scan each. Al watched intently as the video replayed. His timing had been right, and in a couple of moments he saw the first shot of Seneca in the parking lot getting out of her car. "There. Pause it." He touched the car on the screen. "Get somebody outside and see if it's still there." He looked at his watch again. "That was forty-two minutes ago."

"Will do. I'll take care of it personally." The chief took over the video controls.

"All right, let's forward the video, please." A few seconds later, Al saw the image of Seneca in the lobby. "Stop. That's a good shot of her. Print that screen and make copies. Distribute them to every member of your staff who was on duty. I want them to look at her and see if they remember anything, no matter how trivial."

"I don't know if we can catch everyone. In ten minutes there will be a shift change for the nursing staff."

"Do whatever it takes."

The chief instructed one of the other security officers in the room and then returned to operating the surveillance controls.

The video displayed more images marching forward in time, from camera to camera—Seneca getting off the elevator on the third floor; Seneca coming back down the hall with a woman behind her; Seneca in the lobby; Seneca under the portico—

"Stop." It looked to Al like the woman trailing Seneca was disposing of something in the trash receptacle, maybe a purse. "Get somebody out there quick."

The man radioed the command.

"Pause it." Al looked at the image of a black Rolls Royce limousine stopping under the portico. "Slow mo, please."

A man stepped out of the car. Al couldn't get a view of Seneca's face, but she seemed to balk at seeing him, like maybe she knew the man. The woman turned, taking a look around and behind them. A good shot of them both. "Hold it. Get some stills of that man and the woman. Show those around as well."

The guard returned and proudly announced that Seneca's car had been located in the lot.

"Okay, start the video again, but keep it in slow motion." Leaning closer to the monitor, Al watched the limo pull away. "Yes. Freeze it right there. Perfect." He had a view of the license plate. "Zoom in." The numbers and letters came into focus. He held up his cell. "Do we have service down here?"

"Sure do," the guard said. "Repeaters get the cell signals into the security center."

Al placed a call to ILIAD and gave them the car's license plate number.

Another security guard entered the video surveillance room and plopped a woman's purse on the desk in front of Al. "Here you go."

The chief motioned toward the video monitors. "Want to see any more?"

"No, I think we've seen enough."

The hospital administrator came through the door. "Have you gotten everything you need?"

"I believe so." Al's cell rang. He flipped it open. "Palermo." He listened to the call from his contact at ILIAD for a minute or so, then closed the phone. Looking at the curious faces of those in the room, he said, "The tag was a fake. They must have anticipated the camera getting a look at it. But they didn't count on Seneca dropping the receiver and her call going through to my voice mail. That's the only lead we've got."

"Sorry there's not more to work with, Mr. Palermo." The administrator turned toward the door. "I'm heading back to my office. If we can be of any more help, just say the word."

"Thanks. I appreciate all your cooperation. Miami-Dade PD will be sending over a detective. He'll probably want to review the videos again."

"Not a problem."

Al heaved out a breath of frustration. "Excuse me, gentlemen. Need to make another call." He opened his phone and found the number in his contacts list. When he heard the phone ringing he switched ears.

"Matt, Al here. Listen, whatever viper's nest you and Seneca have gotten into is maybe even bigger than we thought. They've abducted her. I've asked ILIAD to get involved, and the police.

Maybe the FBI will be chiming in, but so far we haven't come up with anything."

"Shit. Is she okay?"

"Don't know. We've got them on video taking her from the hospital. We'll run some facial recognition programs, but unless the kidnappers are already in the system, it may be a dry hole. One thing I do know is whoever is running the show is well financed."

"Al, I was actually getting ready to call you. I've come across something and it looks like this is all tied to William Groves and Groves Consortium. You talk about somebody well-funded." He spent the next several minutes filling Al in on the Cortés tomb robbery, Professor Flores's notes with the reference to William Groves, and the connection to his boat being sunk.

"We might be getting closer to the who, but we still don't know the why."

"Any other clues?"

"Only that we found Seneca's purse. I've got it right here." Al opened the bag and began going through it. "Wallet, keys, brush, credit cards, and the infamous catacombs camera you told me about."

Al pressed the button to turn the camera on and hit the replay button. "And it still works." The last picture Seneca took filled the screen. He studied it. "Hold on a minute, Matt."

He remembered Seneca telling him about the graffiti on the island penal colony prison wall and how they couldn't find the same place the next day as they were leaving. She had wanted to take a picture. However, the shot she got was of scribble on the wall in Spanish that said *Jesus is our Savior*. But that's not what appeared in the digital picture.

Al looked at the guard's name badge. *Felix Moreno*. "Excuse me, Felix. Do you speak Spanish?"

"Yes, sir."

He held the camera out. "Take a look at this. Can you translate the writing for me?"

Craning his neck and squinting at the picture, the guard studied it a moment. "It says *you must destroy the veil by fire.*"

SWEET FLOWER
2012, BAHAMAS

SENECA OPENED HER EYES and found she was in the rear seat of a small passenger jet in flight. Out the window she saw the deep blue of the ocean meeting the pristine sky with a crisp line of demarcation along the horizon. Far below, a freighter left a foamy scar in its wake. A few smaller crafts dotted the endless expanse of ocean.

As she tried for a better look, vertigo set in, and a sharp pain made itself known on the back of her head. Reaching, she delicately touched the spot where the woman named Ilse had struck her. It was sore and tender, but no blood. Her hair was still damp from where someone had cleaned the wound; probably so she wouldn't soil the leather of the executive jet's seats.

Seneca looked at her watch.

"You've been sleeping for a couple of hours." Carlos looked up from a magazine in his lap; he sat in a backward-facing seat two rows ahead of her. The earbuds of his iPod hung from his neck. "We gave you an injection to keep you out for a while."

"Where are you taking me?" She tried to not move her head.

"I already told you." Ilse leaned around the seat opposite Carlos. "You're going on a Caribbean vacation."

"I've done nothing to either of you. Neither had Daniel. Why would you want us dead? Whatever the reason, it is all a terrible mistake."

"No mistake, my love." Ilse turned back around and wiggled into a more comfortable position. "You're the one he wants."

Judging from the Rolls Royce limo at the hospital and now the sleek, custom-appointed jet, she was obviously dealing with an extremely wealthy individual. On the forward bulkhead wall, she recognized the same logo that had been cut into the glass partition between the driver and passenger compartments of the limo, and engraved on the champagne flutes—the phoenix bird rising from flames. In a circle around the logo were the words, *Phoenix Ministry*. She had heard about the outfit on the news. What could a religious organization possibly have to do with this?

And what had happened to Al? He was supposed to be right behind her getting to Brenda's bedside. Maybe he'd been kidnapped, too, or hurt, or killed. The depth of her concern surprised her. Maybe she couldn't quite wrap her head around Al being her father, but she had gotten past the resentment she believed. Seneca hoped he'd only been delayed by having to get gas or something as equally mundane. Even if that were the case, it still meant he would be hard pressed finding her now. She was in a plane over the ocean with no idea of its destination.

Seneca studied Carlos, or Coyotl, or whoever he was. He seemed deeply immersed in the magazine article. His head bobbed slightly to whatever was on his iPod. In thinking back to Mexico City, she now realized he had acted squirrely from the moment she met him at the dig site. She assumed it was the pressure of the video shoot, but now she knew better. He planted the bomb that killed Daniel and the others. She was meant to be part of the death toll. And yet, she was spared. Why? Another surge of survivor guilt pained her. She supposed it didn't matter why she had survived; they were going to take care of that now.

Daniel's killer sat a few feet away, calmly listening to music and casually reading. What kind of person was this? Was there no remorse? She still reeled every time she thought of how she had managed to shoot and kill the man on the island, but she realized she would do it again to avenge Daniel.

"You can make this easy or hard." Carlos stood beside Seneca at the foot of the steps leading from the Learjet. "Go the easy route and you'll be treated with respect—there'll be no need for restraints. Choose hard and it'll be uncomfortable. Which is it?"

"Easy," she answered.

Seneca glanced around. They had landed at a small commercial airport in the Bahamas—a sign on the main building in the distance read, *Andros Town*. In addition to the modest terminal, there were a few aircraft service hangars with names like Bahamasair and Lynx Air International, and a scattering of prop commuters and private aircraft. She remembered coming here with her mother many years ago. By the looks of things, not much had changed.

"This way." Ilse walked ahead of Seneca and Carlos as the jet was being towed into an unmarked hangar. As at the hospital, a limousine awaited. This time it was a white Bentley.

Seneca watched the pine forests and farms pass as they left the airport and headed north along the rural two-lane road. Unlike the other tourist-destination islands in the Bahamas, Andros was the least populated. There were no big hotels and casinos, deep-water ports for cruise ships, or sprawling junk-filled gift bazaars. Instead, the attractions were angling for bonefish, diving the 140-mile-long barrier reef, and enjoying quiet seclusion.

Ten minutes into the drive, something caught Seneca's eye. The brilliance of the Caribbean sun flashed off an object that seemed to grow out of the forest to her left. It was a giant step pyramid with sides that glistened like highly polished black onyx. Soon, an imposing concrete wall etched with strange glyphs and symbols ran along the road. A few moments later, the Bentley turned off the main road toward an entrance gate and waited for a pair of large iron barriers to open. The now-familiar Phoenix crest adorned the entrance. She saw armed security guards motion the car to proceed. After a winding journey along a palm-bordered entrance road, the car pulled into a circular drive and up to the front of the six-story pyramid structure.

In the middle of the circle, Seneca saw a fountain; its centerpiece was a bronze-colored medallion whose surface bore a mixture of ancient Mexican Indian carvings surrounding a stylized rendering of the phoenix bird.

"After you." Carlos motioned to a pair of gilded doors at the base of the pyramid. Two men, dressed in brown jumpsuits similar to the ones worn by the security guards at the front gate, opened the doors as the three approached.

Inside, Seneca found herself in a grand entrance hall where the walls appeared to depict historic events of an ancient people—

Aztec, Toltec, or possibly Mayan, she guessed. The floors were of dark, heavily veined marble, and overhead, a lighting system focused on a suspended circular medallion like the one in the fountain outside. She recalled a similar carving shown to her by Daniel during their preparation for the Mexico City video shoot. She was now certain that the pictographs and glyphs, which seemed to be everywhere, were Aztec.

Standing in front of a floor-to-ceiling window a man appeared. The sun streamed through the glass, reflecting ribbons of colored light like a prism, the glare haloing him, his figure dark in silhouette. Seneca couldn't take her eyes from the man. Did she stand in the presence of a magician, wizard, prophet, messiah? Or madman?

Carlos was beside her. "May I present Javier Scarrow, the director of the Universal Phoenix Ministry."

In a low voice that expressed a sense of mystery and awe, he whispered, "Sweet Flower. Sweet *xochimiqui.*"

DNA

2012, MEXICO CITY

"THAT'S IMPOSSIBLE." MATT HELD the phone out as if he'd never seen one before. Shaking his head to clear his memory, he brought it back to his ear. "Al, I saw the prison wall that Seneca photographed on our way off the island. The scroll plainly read, *Jesús es nuestro Salvador.* I can still see it clearly in my mind. It was a bright and sunny day—there was no mistake."

He sat in his room at the Hotel Torre Lindavista. As he talked to Al, he reached in his shirt pocket and pulled out the copy of Professor Flores's note with the reference to William Groves.

"But you did say that you had trouble finding the wall that morning?"

"Al, I realize it sounds crazy, but if I didn't know better, I'd swear the lettering on the scroll somehow changed overnight."

There was a long pause. "That's crazy. I think you guys just got the wrong wall."

"No, you don't understand. The place was big, but not that big. We went to the exact spot where we saw the graffiti on the wall the night before. The only difference from the previous night was now it said, *Jesús es nuestro Salvador.* I suggested the same thing—that we were in the wrong place. Seneca would have nothing to do with that theory. She was certain. Finally, as I walked away, she took the picture."

"So you didn't actually see her take the picture?"

"I turned my back, took two steps and heard the click of the camera. Four, maybe five seconds tops. Give me some credit here."

"Sorry. Just covering all bases. I don't want to miss anything—no matter how minute. I'm upset with myself that I didn't go straight to the hospital. If I had, she'd still be safe. Twenty-twenty hindsight. Now she's gone, and I have no idea where she is or who took her. I just got my daughter back and suddenly she's taken away."

"Hey, you don't have to explain. I understand. How helpless do you think I feel? I'm thousands of miles away." Matt glanced at the note. "What do we do now? How do we find her? What about this Groves connection?"

"Is there a date on the note?"

"1981."

"So thirty-one years ago, William Groves wanted to know the history of the veil and how it got to Mexico. Where is Groves holed up these days?"

"No idea."

"Finding out should be easy enough. I'll call you back."

———

Matt showered and ordered room service, but was too troubled to eat. What could anyone possibly want with dead people's bones? Some of the remains were even thousands of years old. He'd heard of cultures and religious sects that put ground-up animal bones in drinks and food believing them to be aphrodisiacs or elixirs that would improve their sexuality or extend their lives. Voodoo and the like used human bones in rituals. Still, why collect bones from all over the world and go to such extremes? Were these remains handpicked?

Matt picked up his phone and scrolled through the recently received calls. He found the one he wanted and pushed talk.

When the hospital operator answered, he said, "Dr. Domingo, please."

A moment later, the chief of administration came on the line. "Dr. Domingo."

"Hello doctor. This is Matt Everhart."

"Ah, Señor Everhart, how can I help you?"

"Actually, I've got a technical question. I'm researching for my next novel. The theft of the remains of Hernán Cortés got me thinking about an idea. This may be out of your area of expertise, but can you tell me what can be determined from old bones like the ones stolen from the hospital chapel?"

"There are some basic facts that can be found from human remains. A few things come to mind. Sometimes it's possible to determine COD, sorry, cause of death. Things like trauma and cancers and evidence of certain illnesses can be found in bones. Also the manner of death might be determined. For example, knife cuts to the ribs or a bullet wedged in the spinal column might suggest how someone died. If the bone collection includes the skull or the pelvis, the sex of the individual can often be determined. In some cases, you can confirm that the deceased had certain types of diseases like syphilis or if they suffered from anemia. There may be lesions from tuberculosis or one might find confirmation of birth defects. Age can also be estimated based upon the different stages of afflictions such as arthritis. If the long bones are present, the height of the individual can be estimated. And bone density can even suggest race. Of course, there's the obvious DNA."

"Like determining if someone is related to another through their DNA?"

"Exactly."

"What about the kind of person someone was? I don't suppose you can discover anything about an individual's personality by analyzing their bones?" Matt figured he'd go in this direction because all the missing remains were from notorious mass murderers.

"We can get clues to the type of life the person led. We can look at where muscle was attached and tell if the muscles were well-developed from physical labor, or repetitive movement. Teeth can tell us a lot about the health and diet. But obviously, personality is centered in the brain. And even if you have the brain preserved, once it's dead, all traces of personality and memory are gone."

"It was just a thought."

"However, there are some interesting new studies out that claim personalities are determined from birth based upon our DNA."

"I'm not sure I follow."

"Well, let's say a person grows up to be shy and introverted. The latest studies in genetics claim that personality characteristics can be predicted by analyzing the DNA. So if a person is predisposed to be shy, it was probably determined from day-one by their unique DNA."

"But I thought a person's disposition was mainly shaped by environment. You know, if Hitler had been raised in totally different surroundings, he wouldn't have turned out the way he did."

"You would think. But the studies say that our DNA from birth sets the course of our life. And the theory is impossible to disprove because no one can be reborn and experience a different environment and upbringing. Hitler was what he was. There's no way to try raising him again and see if he would be any different. Of course I think there is some interplay between nature and nurture, but science is now finding that DNA plays a much larger role than we ever thought. If you are born a peaceful soul, so to speak, environment and experiences would probably not be enough to turn you into a violent murderer. You'd have to be predisposed to that type of behavior through your DNA. And vice-versa."

"*The Bad Seed*."

"Excuse me?"

"An old movie." A spark ignited in Matt's brain. Perhaps the remains of mass murderers contained more than decayed calcium and carbon. Perhaps they contained a code for personality and behavior. Could this be the motive behind the robberies? To capture that code and somehow use it?

"Señor Everhart, are you still there?"

"Yes. Sorry. Thank you very much, doctor. I really appreciate your help."

Matt hung up, his head still spinning with the thought. Was someone designing mass murderers?

DESTINED
2012, BAHAMAS

"What do you want with me?" Seneca didn't understand what this man was talking about. Why did he call her *Sweet Flower*? And what was the other word he uttered? Had she been abducted by some wacko religious cult?

Yes, she'd heard of the Phoenix Ministry, especially the attention it was getting in the media concerning all the speculation of what the highly anticipated *ultimate proof* event would be. It was scheduled to take place in Mexico on the fall equinox. Wasn't that only a few days away? So far the details were a well-kept secret. Such mystery only amplified the fervor; it seemed people wanted more of Javier Scarrow and his teachings.

Seneca hadn't paid much attention to the buzz. What little she did know about him was that his message sounded to her like New Age spirituality. She was always on the hunt for an exclusive, but since Scarrow and his Ministry already had so much media coverage, up until now she hadn't taken much interest. Maybe she should have been more inquisitive, she thought as she stood before the leader of the Phoenix Ministry.

"All your questions will soon be addressed." Scarrow moved out of the radiant backdrop of light and walked toward her—his gait powerful and confident.

For the first time Seneca saw his eyes, the color of coal. His skin was bronze, and his hair and close-cropped beard were as black as a raven's wing. Once out of the frame of light, he didn't appear so ominous, but rather handsome and sophisticated. She could understand his magnetism and appeal to so many.

The corners of his mouth turned up in a curious smile. "First, let's make you feel at home and comfortable. You are our honored guest."

Seneca followed Scarrow toward the doorway, but stopped short. He had to be crazy. It didn't make any sense. Who did he think she was, and what did he expect of her? How could this be the same man who had tried to kill her four times but now called her *Sweet Flower*? Honored guest?

"What is this all about?"

His gaze locked on hers, and Seneca felt rooted in place, spooked and confused by the serene smile that creased his eyes.

"All in good time."

After their brief meeting, Scarrow departed while Carlos escorted her up a spiral staircase to a second-story hallway lined with doors. Seneca couldn't help herself from thinking of this man, this Coyotl, as Carlos. That was who he was to her. She felt nervous and uncomfortable being so close to the man responsible for Daniel's death. He seemed to sense her revulsion and kept his distance.

Stopping at one of the doors, Carlos inserted a keycard in the electronic lock and ushered her in.

The room was a nicely furnished guest suite with private bath, king-size bed, dresser, armoire, desk, and nightstands. On the wall behind the bed hung a framed woven textile of brilliant colors and complex patterns. On one of the nightstands rested a small crystal decanter of water and a glass, both etched with the Phoenix Ministry logo.

Carlos filled the glass from the decanter and handed it to her. "I'm sure the aftereffects of the drug we gave you have left you thirsty."

Yes, she thought, her mouth and throat were dry. She downed the entire glass as Carlos watched.

When she was done he took the glass, set it back on the table, and moved to the door. "You should rest now."

Seneca heard the momentary buzz of the locking mechanism as he closed the door. Once his footsteps faded, muffled by the Oriental runner down the center of the marble hallway, she tried the door handle. Locked.

As she wandered around the room she noticed the data ports and phone jacks by the desk, but no computer and no phone. There would be no communicating with the outside world. Yet there were worse places she could think of to be held captive. Maybe Scarrow's intent was not to kill her. After all, wouldn't he have done that in Miami instead of going to all the trouble to fly her here?

She thought of Al. If he was okay, he would already be trying to track her down. There were the hospital security cameras. Maybe they caught Carlos or the woman on video. Or the limousine's license plate. Her car was still in the parking lot. They would locate it right away. Perhaps someone found her purse and turned it in to security. She prayed her father—

Seneca stopped herself, realizing she had actually thought of Al as her father. With it brought a mix of emotions. He had come from out of nowhere to suddenly be so important in her life. She felt a surge of hope that he and his friends at ILIAD would be all over her disappearance. It was just a matter of time before he figured out who kidnapped her and where she was being held.

That is, if Al was okay.

Seneca sat on the bed feeling inordinately drained and spent. She leaned back and allowed her body to discharge some of the tension and fear. A soft hum from overhead caused her to focus on the slow hypnotic motion of the ceiling fan. Her mind wandered from warm childhood memories of her mother and recollections of treasuring her father's correspondence, but quickly turned to darker thoughts—the panic at the mangrove island, the desperate isolation of the catacombs, and the sickening death of the impostor. The images slipped through her mind, finally settling on Daniel—his comforting smile, infectious laughter, and seductive touch. Then his last moments when she felt the flutter of the hummingbird drift away. Her eyes closed as she sorted her thoughts. Her body finally acquiesced, and she slept.

A knock at the door caused Seneca to struggle to sit upright.

"Yes?" Had it been a few moments or hours? There were no windows so she had no reference.

The door swung open.

It was Carlos. Her first thought was that she was dreaming because her mind seemed so fuzzy, but quickly realized she was not. Carlos was dressed in some sort of Indian garb—a black and red breastplate adorned with turquoise stones and gold trim. He wore leather band anklets with dangling shells. His hands were painted yellow. Two men stood behind Carlos, also dressed in similar breastplates and brightly colored loincloths with a hem with gold and jade. They each held a long, ornately carved wooden pole tipped with a narrow, ominous-looking blade. From pictures Daniel had shown Seneca in Mexico, she was certain it had to be Aztec.

"The water," she said thickly. "You drugged me."

"Come with me." Carlos motioned with his hand.

"Where?"

He helped her to her feet. She wobbled, but then steadied herself.

"He wants to see you."

He gripped her arm as they entered the hallway and walked to the staircase, the two men following behind them. At the bottom, they crossed the center of the grand entrance atrium where she had met Javier Scarrow and proceeded through a hall ending with a large door. It was intricately carved with images of birds, rabbits, snakes, fish, jaguars, monkeys, others she couldn't decide—some whose eyes seemed alive with emeralds and other gems. All were gilded.

Carlos pushed open the door and gestured for Seneca to enter. "Don't keep him waiting."

Pressing her palm against the door, it took all her strength to open it. Whatever they had given her in the water had sapped away her strength and balance. Overwhelmed by the sight, she took a few lethargic steps into the room, followed by Carlos and the two men.

The space lay dark and heavy with a smoky haze and a pungent spicy scent she couldn't place. A large metal brazier sat in the center of the floor with a wide copper-colored ventilation hood hanging above it collecting the smoke from a smoldering fire. Men dressed in the same manner as Carlos and his escorts lined the wall to her left. To her right were eleven men and women, their bodies painted black. Black hooded capes hung down their backs.

At the opposite end of the large room stood a massive stone throne, and poised before it was a man wearing a headdress of iridescent green feathers with accents of turquoise and red attached to a golden crown. He also wore a cape, this one of vibrant-colored feathers hanging down his back to the floor and draped around his neck and upper chest. He wore a decorative loincloth woven with golden thread and sandals with gold soles and straps that wrapped about his ankles. His left upper arm had a jewel-encrusted gold bracelet around it. Even with all the regalia, she recognized him as Javier Scarrow. The scene seemed surreal, amplified by whatever Carlos had put in her water.

"Do not gaze upon my face." Scarrow's voice was strong and filled the large room. "It is forbidden."

"What?" She was dumbfounded by his statement.

"Cast your eyes away from me."

She looked about the room, the movement making her dizzy. But she did notice that no one appeared to stare directly at Scarrow's face. She shifted her gaze to the fire in the middle of the room as her legs weakened. "I don't understand. Who are you?"

"I am Emperor Motecuhzoma Xocoyotzin, the ninth *tlatoani* of Tenochtitlan."

"Who?" Seneca's word came out distorted.

"Emperor Montezuma II, ninth ruler of the Aztec nation."

How about Javier Scarrow, insane Phoenix Ministry cult leader, she thought, the words in her head clearer than the ones from her lips. Forgetting his instructions, she glanced at him.

Scarrow stood beside the fire. He removed a small stone blade from his belt and drew it across his forearm, leaving a thin hairline slice in his flesh that quickly beaded with blood. Then he held his arm above the fire.

Seneca heard the sharp sizzle as his blood dripped onto the burning coals.

He looked hard at her. "You are offending me. I don't think that wise. I know this is difficult for you to understand, but because you are a captive with no knowledge of our ways, I am going to forgive your ignorance. Once you are prepared for your great task, then you will understand and accept your destiny. For of all gathered here, you are the most fortunate and privileged."

Seneca forced her focus from his face to his bejeweled and feathered cloak. "Why me?"

"You are chosen to be the first Sweet Flower. The first *xochimiqui*."

CONNECTING THE DOTS
2012, MIAMI

"GROVES IS LESS THAN an hour from here." Al sat on a barstool at the kitchen counter in Seneca's new apartment talking to Matt on the phone. He was surrounded by her still-unpacked boxes, and their presence reminded him even more of the temporary nature of life. His daughter had never gotten a chance to put her things away and start her new life without Daniel. Now, she was gone and may never get the chance.

"So he's in Florida?"

"No, the Bahamas." Al glanced at his notes taken a few moments earlier from his contact at ILIAD. "He lives on Andros Island in a heavily secured structure called Azteca. It's owned by Groves Consortium's former president and CEO, Javier Scarrow."

"The guy heading up that New Age movement?"

"Seems that Azteca is the headquarters for his Phoenix Ministry. Scarrow's the one holding those crusades all over the world. He's building a big temple right there in Mexico."

"Hang on." Matt picked up a tourist magazine from the bedside table. He flipped through a few pages. "It's northeast of the city near the Pyramids of the Sun and Moon. I saw on the news that there's some big event of Scarrow's getting ready to take place out there. He claims to be prepared to show undeniable proof that his teachings are the last best salvation for mankind."

"Lofty goals."

"Sure are, but his popularity and following are undeniable."

"Well, whether he's a savior or a scammer, he's got big bucks behind him." Al read off his list. "He's had huge rallies in France, the U.K., China, Germany. Even in Uzbekistan."

"Okay, we know he's connected to Groves. So what would tie him to Seneca's abduction?"

"And is there a link to the tomb robberies?"

"Wait a minute," Matt said. "Did you say Uzbekistan?"

"Yes, in the capital city of Tashkent. Scarrow was there for a two-day crusade. It drew thousands from all over the region." He heard the rustling of paper before Matt spoke again.

"Okay, Al. Bear with me here. You have a list of the Phoenix Ministry crusade locations, right?"

"I'm looking at it."

"When and where was the first?"

"Two years ago in Munich, Germany."

"According to the list you compiled for Seneca, the first tomb robbery was that of Ilse Koch two years ago. Did Scarrow have a crusade then?"

"Yes, with huge attendance."

"The second name on the list is Idi Amin. Was there a Ministry event in Uganda?"

Al looked at his notepad. "No, sorry."

"Okay, maybe my idea doesn't work after all."

There was a long pause and Al could almost hear the gears in Matt's head turning.

Finally, Matt said, "Where *was* the next major Phoenix Ministry event?"

"It wasn't actually a crusade like the other locations. It occurred in the Saudi Arabian city of Jeddah, along the coast of the Red Sea. Just a couple of days visiting with some of the royal family who happened to be there at the time and the local leaders."

"Yeah, but you know what? Idi Amin's remains were discovered missing from the Ruwais Cemetery in Jeddah, Saudi Arabia."

"I'll be a son-of-a-bitch."

Matt sighed. "I'll bet if we match them up, their major rallies will coincide with each tomb robbery."

"Let's try it," Al said. "Call out the rest of the robberies."

Matt continued down his list until he got to Josef Mengele. "The good doctor's remains were stolen from a forensics' lab in São Paulo."

"Yep, there was a crusade there."

Matt read the rest of the list, ending with Hernán Cortés.

Al said, "We've got two tomb robberies in Mexico City, and there's that huge Phoenix temple built where Scarrow's big event is scheduled."

"Okay, let's think about this. We have a direct connection between Scarrow, Groves, and the Veil of Veronica. We now believe that the group conducting the tomb robberies is most likely Scarrow and the Phoenix Ministry. No doubt their events were a means of getting them into each country—a cover to pull off the robberies. When they pack up their gear and leave, the stolen remains are hidden somewhere in their trucks."

"And we now believe that it's the same group that tried to kill you both, and probably the ones who abducted Seneca. But even with all the dots connected, we still don't know why or what the reason is for them to be stealing old bones."

"Actually," Matt said, "I may have a theory."

THE EMPEROR
2012, BAHAMAS

THOUGH SENECA DID NOT focus directly on Scarrow's face, she tracked him with her eyes. He backed away from the fire pit, and with a wave of his hand and a spoken word that she did not understand, dismissed everyone but her and Carlos. The procession was orderly and silent, except for the rustling of fabric and tinkling of shells.

When the room cleared, Scarrow seated himself on the throne. "Bring her."

Carlos clutched Seneca's arm and led her to stand just before the throne. He gently tapped her shoulder, letting her know she should kneel.

Seneca sank to her knees, sat back, and rested on her heels.

"Leave us." Scarrow waited in silence until the doors thudded closed behind Carlos.

Seneca found herself staring at his feet that were bound by leather sandals with gold soles. Such opulence. She remembered

Daniel commenting on the richness and magnificence of the way the Aztecs lived.

Finally, Scarrow spoke. "I maintain most of the old ways, the ancient rituals and traditions, at least in the presence of my apostles and disciples. But not always in the face of the rest of the world. They wouldn't understand. Much has changed over the last five hundred years. It took a long time for me to realize that I also had to make some changes if I wanted to accomplish my mission. The difficult part was finding the balance—the man the public perceives and contrasting him with my true self."

Scarrow removed the elaborate headdress, carefully resting it in his lap. He stroked one of the long green feathers. "This is not the original. That one rests in a museum. But one day it will be in its rightful place. Do you know the resplendent quetzal?"

She shook her head while thinking she sensed a bottomless pining in his voice.

"They are strikingly elegant birds with iridescent plumage. In mating season, the male grows a pair of long and beautiful tail feathers that form a train up to three feet. The quetzal is in danger of becoming extinct. It can't be caged and it dies in captivity. There's a lesson to be learned from this bird."

He paused as if in thought before beginning again in the same longing tone of reverie. "When Tenochtitlan was in its glory, before the arrival of the conquistadors, my people, the Mexica, had always kept the universe in balance. Our lives were filled with serving the gods who gave us life. It is time we returned to the ways that maintain such harmony. My message has found its way into many hearts around the world. It is what people want and believe is true and right. They are hungry for it, and they are mournful over the negligence and abuse we as a species have brought to this planet. I tell them what they want and need to hear." Scarrow put the feathered crown back on his head. "You may gaze upon me now. I want to see your eyes as I speak."

Through the smoky haze, the man on the throne wavered like a mirage, like heat eerily rising off pavement. She wasn't sure if the distortion was because of the drugs she'd ingested or if indeed she was witnessing something otherworldly.

He told her of how Cortés had produced the small silver chest containing the veil with the image of Christ imprinted in the fabric, and declared that it was the face of the Son of God who died and rose from the dead. How he then painfully watched the conquest and fall of his empire, and how in desperation he had secretly touched the relic to his own face. He knew he would soon die so he gave his priests special burial instructions. He reasoned that if the power of the veil was true, he would rise from the dead as Christ had done. As he told of his own resurrection his eyes seemed to be searching hers. "That night the conquistadors plundered our city. The only reason my tomb was not pillaged was because they believed the tomb to be sealed. They were unaware of the hidden entrance."

Scarrow spoke in such a compelling and fascinating manner that by the time he had finished, every cell of Seneca's being knew that what he said was true. Even though the story of the veil was mind-boggling, he had managed to dispel her disbelief. He transported her mentally to the world that he remembered in such rich detail and with such entrenched emotion that she now understood what Daniel had meant—that sometimes he thought he could journey to those ancient days by stepping through some fine filament of time and space. She was there with Montezuma, feeling the agony of his despair, the loss of glory, the finality of a people. Seneca had no doubt she was gazing upon Emperor Montezuma II.

"For many years I didn't understand what my mission was. But as time passed, I saw humanity losing respect for the Earth, which had once been as resplendent as the quetzal. Man has taken and not given back. We have gouged and scarred the soil, poisoned the air, destroyed the beauty of pristine lands, and fouled the water. And mankind has been proud of these things, even calling them great achievements. Now, modern science confirms what so many ancients predicted with their calendars and oral traditions. At the beginning I yearned for the return of my nation and the way we lived. But that was not to be. No, I was destined for something much more profound. Whatever man calls his god or gods, they are displeased with how we have become."

Seneca saw a great sadness in Scarrow's face, a deep and sincere grief in his eyes.

"It is time for mankind to unite and become stewards of this Earth and universe again, and to show our gratitude, not just speak of it. And we must do it soon, before life as we know it perishes because the Creator or creators have given up on us."

"But what does that have to do with me?"

"I don't know if you have knowledge of our ancient ways. So I'll tell you what you need to know. Life is *because* of the gods, they sacrificed themselves for humanity. It's a never-ending debt that we must pay back. Not since the days of my people has man *shown* his appreciation, his true thankfulness. Today, prayer is only empty words. We lived and practiced our gratefulness. When we went to war we didn't enter battle with the intent to kill. We took captives to pay the blood debt."

Seneca shuddered as she recalled the sight of the terrifying wall of skulls.

"On the battlefield the vanquished enemy submitted willingly. It was an honor to give themselves to the gods. In that manner, they perpetuated life. Everything—crops, rain, animals, stars, the moon, the sun, people—depends on keeping the universe in balance, which is accomplished by gratifying the gods. And so now we come to you. You were delivered to me. At first I didn't see. I only knew that you were the enemy. I lost sight of the old traditions and mistakenly sought to do away with you. But then came the revelation. I, who thought the old ways so important, had abandoned the basic principle of battling the enemy. Ours were ritual wars. Flower wars."

Suddenly Seneca understood why Scarrow had called her Sweet Flower. She was the captive enemy. He was going to sacrifice her all right—a sacrifice to his gods. "You mustn't do this."

"You will be rewarded in the next life. And until then you will be treated as royalty. You should be so honored to be the first, to begin the new era of peace."

Seneca rose to her feet and felt the blood rush from her head, leaving her swaying and her vision blurring.

"There is nowhere for you to go. Accept your destiny. Find pride in it."

She turned her back on Scarrow and ran to the door, finding it difficult not to stumble. She pushed it open and nearly fell, but Carlos caught her as she staggered through. Once she was stable, he led her away. Seneca glanced over her shoulder back through the haze. The Emperor Montezuma sat undisturbed and majestically regal on his throne.

Carlos nudged her along the hallway and up the stairs to her guestroom. "Is there anything I can get for you?"

She saw the full decanter on the nightstand.

"There is more *water* on the stand. You will need it to renew your strength."

"No. I don't want it."

"Drink or we'll have to resort to harsher means. It's less potent when you take the liquid. I think that's what you would prefer." He poured the water in the glass and gave it to her.

Seneca's gut instinct was to knock the water out of his hand and flee through the open door. But she knew she would never get outside the walls of Azteca before she was either captured or killed. She needed to stay alive until Al could come for her.

Reluctantly, she took the glass and drank. Dazed and traumatized, she dropped on the bed and listened to the door close.

When Seneca awoke she rolled to her side and turned on the bedside light, then looked at her watch. It was just after midnight. How in the hell was she going to get out of here? When and where did Scarrow plan to kill her? Someone had brought a tray of food—steak, lobster, and fresh steamed vegetables. Even a glass of wine. Though she was hungry, she was afraid to eat in case the food was drugged like the water. The effects of the earlier dose were still making her thoughts disjointed.

She longed for a shower, but that, too, was out of the question. If rescuers were on the way, she wanted to be ready, not soaking wet in the shower.

A faint knock on the door made her look up. She heard the buzz of the electronic lock followed by the door opening. Standing in the doorway was a figure clothed in surgical scrubs, mask, and gloves.

THE THEORY
2012, MIAMI

"So what's your theory?" Al could see a handful of sailboats on Biscayne Bay from Seneca's apartment as he stood in the kitchen and gazed out the sliding glass balcony doors.

From his Mexico City hotel room twelve hundred miles away, Matt said, "Remember when Seneca and I were in Paris talking to you on speakerphone discussing the motives for stealing the burial remains? You said that if they'd found a way to bring these mass murderers back to life—that would be a completely different situation?"

"Okay, I recall something like that. What of it?"

"That's my theory."

"Matt, I've grown to like you a lot. And I really appreciate how you've been there to protect my daughter. But I think you've been hitting the tequila a little too hard right now."

"I don't blame you for thinking I'm losing it. I know your comment back then was flippant, but stay with me for a second." Matt switched his cell to his other ear. "One of the things we keep asking ourselves is what anyone would want with a bunch of old bones. The question we really should be asking is what can someone do with those bones? More specific is what do the bones have that someone would want?"

"Like what?"

"DNA." Matt proceeded to go over the info Dr. Domingo had given him. "The one thing that all these missing remains have is they belonged to some bad-ass folks who were really into killing people. As a matter of fact, what they all had in common was a *passion* for killing. I think somebody wants *their* DNA for exactly that reason. I know it's a little fuzzy and needs some work, but my theory is that whoever is stealing the remains is retrieving the DNA from the bones and either performing some advanced scientific research, or possibly they've found a way to use the DNA to influence the behavior of others, or maybe even create a new human from their remains while maintaining and fostering their taste for killing."

"Why go to the trouble to get DNA from dead people if they're going to use it on others? Prisons are filled with killers. Getting a sample of their DNA would be easy. I don't see how your idea is possible. If you're suggesting human cloning, it's prohibited."

"Not exactly. It's in the courts all the time. Especially therapeutic cloning. Right now in the US, federal money can't be used to fund it. But there are private institutions that can do more, and there are parts of the world that don't have any restrictions or at least less stringent ones."

"I think you have an interesting premise but pretty farfetched. Plus, it would take highly advanced science and buckets of money."

"And do we know anyone with buckets of cash?"

"Well, yeah, I mean Groves certainly would be one of the few able to underwrite something like human cloning. But, Matt, the bigger question is, why. After all, this guy is a phantom. The last thing he wants is attention. You can bet he's not out to get a Nobel Prize or anything that would place him in the limelight. I think there are too many variables with your theory."

"Okay, I'll grant you that. I told you it needs work. But what about this New Age guru, Javier Scarrow? He's got access to Groves's fortune."

"What about him? From what I've caught on the news, he's preaching universal love, tree hugging, and flower power. A latent hippie." Al heard Matt give out a sigh.

"You're probably right. It's the only premise I could come up with, even if it is farfetched."

"I admit the whole thing has got me baffled, too. But the important issue we're faced with right now is to find Seneca and get her home safe."

"What are you going to do?"

"I've got my buddies at ILIAD working on getting more info out of the Bahamas. And the investigation of the abduction at the hospital is proceeding. They're treating it as a kidnapping. I hope to hear back from someone soon. I've been sitting here studying the list of Groves Consortium global holdings that ILIAD emailed me. It's endless. Since the turn of the last century, Groves has bought and sold over a thousand companies. Total profits since the consortium was established are estimated to be over a trillion dollars. They've invested in just about every type of venture you can imagine."

"I think we've beaten this horse long enough. I'm going to book a flight back to Miami for in the morning. Is there anything you want me to do while I'm still here?"

Al had highlighted a few names of properties on the consortium's holdings list. Most were multibillion-dollar companies that spanned the full spectrum of industry from science to manufacturing to military. But there was one in particular that caught his attention. One that didn't seem to belong.

"Actually, there is something you can check tomorrow before you leave."

"Name it."

"Do you like tacos?"

MIDNIGHT VISIT
2012, BAHAMAS

SENECA WATCHED THE MAN silhouetted in the doorway. He was tall and thin, but a surgical mask and cap hid his face and hair. He wore Latex gloves and medical booties. Stepping into the room, he closed the door.

"What do you want?" Her words were slurred from the effects of the drug. Why had they sent a surgeon?

"Seneca Hunt?" His voice sounded raspy.

She felt her muscles tense, ready to defend herself. But she doubted she could even stand.

"I'm the one who called you."

Seneca swung her legs over the side of the bed. "What?"

He put a finger to his lips. "Speak softly."

"What are you talking about? What call?"

"El Jaguar."

She rubbed her face still trying to clear her head. "That was you?"

Like an old phonograph record played too slowly, he sang and hummed in a whisper, "In the jungle, hmm hmm hmm hmm hmm, the Jaguar sleeps tonight."

"I don't understand. You work for Scarrow but you called me about Professor Flores?"

"About the veil."

"It has something to do with the tomb robberies, doesn't it?"

The man gave a tormented sigh.

"Are you a doctor?"

He tried to laugh but it quickly turned into a coughing and choking combination, and it took him a while to recover.

As Seneca sat on the side of the bed watching him, she realized that the drug came at her in waves. One minute she was nearly clear-headed, while a few moments later the room tilted and she fought to organize her thoughts. "You've got to help me get out of here. Please contact my father and tell him—"

"Too late."

Seneca thought he sounded apologetic—almost as if he regretted saying the words. She leaned forward as another wave of dizziness washed over her.

"Did Javier tell you his age?"

She nodded

"Believe him?"

She remembered Scarrow claiming he was Montezuma. But the drug played with her mind. Seneca closed her eyes and concentrated. "Please, just help me get out of here. He's going to kill me." Her throat tightened. "I don't want to die."

"The veil gave Javier eternal life." He took a few steps in her direction but stopped, almost as if he had second thoughts of getting too close. "And me."

"You mean the Veil of Veronica?"

"I accidently touched it to my face one-hundred-thirty-six years ago. And I'm still alive. But this isn't living. This is Hell." He pulled his mask down and let it hang below his chin.

"Who are you?"

"Just an old cowboy."

THE LAST DEAL

2012, BAHAMAS

SENECA GRIPPED THE EDGE of the nightstand staring at the man in surgical scrubs. "Tell me your name."

"William ... no, Billy Groves."

The billionaire industrialist? That was hard to believe. He appeared drained of life—gaunt and pale, and he reminded her of a figure made of wax. And yet, since their discussion began, she noticed that his voice grew ever stronger, his posture seemed a little straighter, and his eyes took on a faint glow replacing the emptiness.

"Mr. Groves, I want to believe you. And I think I did believe Scarrow, at least at the time, but you have to understand that what you're telling me is hard to get my head around. For me, at least, it's impossible to comprehend immortality. We're all faced with the inevitable fact that death will come someday. Thinking otherwise isn't rational."

"You can believe what you want. Would you like to see the marks where an Apache arrow ran me through from front to back, and where a gunslinger's .44 hit me in the gut. The scars are still there from wounds that should have killed me."

"I've always read that you were a recluse, that you avoid direct contact with others. So why are you here with me, a total stranger?"

"In the beginning, it was all about hiding my identity. Later, after I had a few bouts with some serious illnesses, I started avoiding contact with others. Even though disease can't kill me, I don't want to spend the rest of my life sick from some shit I caught screwing some whore. Then Javier came along. Said he was going to make me a god. Turns out all he wanted was my money and my power. And I don't want to be his kind of *god.* He got his doctors to prescribe medicines they said protected me from infections. That was bullshit. He managed to systematically isolate me from the world whether I wanted it or not."

Groves gestured to the room. "Like this prison. But I finally outsmarted him. I haven't taken those meds for a long time. That's why I can snoop around this place at night. He knows it—sees me on the surveillance cameras."

"Then he knows you're here and what you're saying."

"Nope. No audio, just video. He thinks I'm not in my right mind, so he doesn't care if I rattle around. I've gotten real good at acting crazy. Crazy like a fox. As far as being here with you, you're the only one who doesn't work for Javier. Everybody here is either one of his minions or the freaks he calls his apostles. Then he's got a bunch of followers he likes to call his disciples. You're the only one that I figured has no reason to betray me."

"Mr. Groves—"

"Billy." His lips showed a slight smile. "I'm starting to like you, Seneca Hunt."

"Okay, Billy." Seneca tried to stand but changed her mind as her head swam. "What's really going on here? Why are they stealing the bones of those people? Those mass murderers?"

"You think immortality is hard to grasp. What Javier is creating is diabolical, evil. He's Dr. Frankenstein."

"I still don't understand. What did you mean by the freaks he calls his apostles?"

"They're the ones he's brought to life from the stolen remains."

"That's impossible."

"I've seen them. Even met a few. Ever heard of Bloody Mary, the Queen of England? Ran into her the other night. Nice lady if you don't mind her penchant for burning folks at the stake. And somewhere around here is that Nazi bastard, Dr. Mengele, except he looks just like the president of Russia. It's a fucking three-ring circus."

"The woman who brought me here. Ilse. Is she one of the apostles?"

"Yep. Ilse Koch. She's a sicko."

"Was there a black apostle?"

"Scarrow hit the ceiling when he found out you killed Idi Amin. You caused him quite a setback. He thrives on perfection, and you upset his applecart. Then for some reason, he had a change of heart and decided it would be appropriate to make you his first sacrifice. Be afraid of him. He doesn't think like normal folks."

Seneca's hands turned clammy.

Groves moved a few steps closer. "He's got this grand plan to save the world and return it to the way it was five hundred years ago. He claims he can realign the cosmos to appease his ancient gods."

"What he preaches doesn't sound so menacing."

"Think again. To get what he wants, he's letting his apostles loose into the world to cut out the hearts of thousands of innocent victims—what does he call them—*xochimiqui*."

It was the word Scarrow had said to her when they met. Sweet flower, *xochimiqui*. Without thinking, Seneca ran her fingertips down her chest between her breasts, becoming acutely aware of her heart beating just below the breastbone. She pushed herself up onto her feet, but her legs felt like paper, her head like a bobble.

"He's decided to make you the first. He's going to slice out your heart and feed it to some stone-faced Aztec idol."

"I've got to get away. Please, you're my only hope. Contact my father. He'll come for me."

"Too late. He's taking you to Mexico at dawn. It's for his big event."

"Where are his apostles?"

"Already gone."

"What's going to happen to you?"

"Nothing. Along with immortality comes invincibility. Touching my face with that damn swatch of cloth condemned me to a life sentence—literally. It's a sacrilege against God. I would do anything to end it. I'm so weary."

"Why would these apostles do whatever he wants?"

"First he brought them back to life. If they carry out his plan, he'll reward them with the veil. They'll get a chance to live forever doing what they love to do—kill."

"Did he use it on them already?"

"No. His sick science brought them back to life. They can die—you already proved it. The most vicious mass murderers in history are heading back to their homelands to begin the slaughter. He told them to start with the homeless, the sick, the indigents. It doesn't matter to him—any human sacrifice counts. A heart is a heart to his gods."

Seneca realized that Groves hadn't coughed in the last few moments. Maybe talking to her helped him feel better, more confident.

"I'm so sorry, Billy. I wish I could do something to help you end your misery."

"Don't be worried about me. You're the one who's only got a few hours to live. I'd be making my peace with my Maker if I were you." He glanced as his watch and pulled the mask up over his face. "Time to go. They'll be making their rounds. Scarrow's not going to like that I paid you a visit. But what can he do? Kill me?"

"How did Scarrow get the veil in the first place?"

"From me. It was in a small silver chest I found among a horde of gold and valuables the Indians stole from the Spanish. It wound up part of an Apache treasure trove in the northern Mexican mountains."

"Why don't you get rid of the veil so he can't use it on the apostles?"

Groves shook his head. "It's not here. He told me he moved it to someplace safe years ago."

"You said it was in a small silver box and he hid it in a safe place?"

"Yep." Groves turned to leave.

Suddenly, a vision filled her head of a grainy image on a TV monitor. A small silver box sitting on a wooden table. Could it be that the veil was in Montezuma's tomb? That she had actually seen its container; what Daniel called a reliquary? He had said the Latin inscription meant *sweat-cloth* and *face*. And as the only living witness, that's why Scarrow tried so hard to silence her. No one must know of the veil's existence.

But how could the relic have gotten there? The tomb was sealed, wasn't it? She remembered Montezuma saying the only reason the Spanish hadn't stolen his grave goods was because they thought the tomb was sealed. They didn't know about the hidden entrance. And that had to be how Montezuma escaped after he rose from the dead.

"It's in his tomb." She blurted out the words. Her balance was shaky but she remained standing. "I've seen it. There has to be another entrance, one only he knows about."

Groves looked at his watch again. "Maybe." He started walking toward the door.

"All I ask is you contact my father. Tell him where Scarrow is taking me. He'll figure out a way to get the veil out of the tomb and destroy—"

Seneca's eyes widened. "Oh, my God!" She sat back onto the bed as the full realization became clear. According to Al's research, the angel had given Veronica a two-part command. The first was to wipe the face of Christ on the way to the crucifixion, and the second part was to destroy the veil by fire, but *not* before He ascended into heaven. Because, if Veronica had destroyed it before ...

"I know how to stop Scarrow *and* grant your wish."

"What wish?" He turned to her.

"To end the curse of the veil."

ZIRAGÁN BAR
2012, MEXICO CITY

MATT STOOD IN THE lobby of the Torre Lindavista Hotel and stared at the cell phone in his hand. He had been on his way to his room when he received an anxious call from Al. Something about Seneca being flown to Mexico. Al was rushing to the airport and catching a late flight out of Miami to Mexico City. Matt surmised that the only thing it could mean was confirmation of the connection between Seneca, Scarrow, and the Phoenix Ministry event. Al wouldn't arrive for several hours.

Matt approached the front desk.

"Yes, may I help you?" The clerk spoke with only the slightest of accents.

"How long does it take to get out to the place where the big television event is happening tonight? Out by the pyramids?"

"Normally it would take about forty-five minutes to get there. But tonight, it's impossible."

"Why?"

"The government has closed the highways and cordoned off the area. There are huge traffic jams. It's been all over the news. No one else is allowed in. If you aren't there already, you can forget about it."

Another roadblock, Matt thought. This time literally. If that was where Seneca was being taken, how could he and Al possibly get there? He took in a frustrated and angry breath.

"You can watch it all on the television in the bar." The clerk motioned to the entrance to the hotel's Ziragán Bar.

"Thanks." Matt nodded, then walked toward the source of music and voices drifting across the lobby. The inside of the Ziragán Bar was dark and crowded. It appeared to be mostly young adults, out for a Saturday evening. As he took an empty seat at the bar, he noticed a couple of TVs mounted around the room displaying news or sports shows.

He ordered a draft. While sipping his *cerveza*, he glanced up at a TV over the bar. It had switched from a soccer match to the live coverage of a large outdoor event. Although all the graphics were in Spanish, Matt recognized the name and logo of the Phoenix Ministry. Like dominoes falling, the networks started switching their feeds to a location in what appeared to be the middle of an expanse of land far from the city. Matt had previously read up on the location of tonight's event. It was being held among the sprawling remains of the pre-Columbian city of Teotihuacán abandoned long before the Aztecs came upon it. Built over two thousand years ago, Teotihuacán consisted of temple structures along its central Avenue of the Dead, including the Pyramid of the Moon, the Temple of the Feathered Serpent, and the imposing bulk of the third largest pyramid in the world, the Pyramid of the

Sun. Tonight they were all dramatically lit by untold numbers of floodlights.

Positioned between the two ancient pyramids was a sparkling modern building, also in the shape of a step pyramid, but only a fraction of the size of the colossal Sun and Moon structures. Its polished chrome and glass sides gleamed in the lights like a jewel in the Mexican desert.

Matt turned to a woman sitting beside him. "Do you speak English?"

She nodded.

"Can you tell me what they're saying?" He pointed to one of the TVs.

She listened intently, then translated. "This is some big religious event." Pausing for a moment as she watched, she said, "First, that Phoenix Ministry man is going to make a speech."

Matt watched the TV screen as Javier Scarrow spoke. He was dressed in a plain white robe and stood at the base of what was called the Phoenix Ministry Temple of the Universe. Before him, an enormous crowd gathered. It reminded Matt of a U2 concert he once attended, only bigger.

The woman took a sip of her beer as she listened. "He says he is going to take part in some sort of sacrifice."

"Sacrifice?"

"Yes."

"What exactly is he going to sacrifice?"

She shrugged. "He said he's going to have himself put to death—sacrificed to save the world."

Matt's skin turned cold as he watched the television. The woman either misunderstood or this guy was about to pull off some sort of elaborate scam. It was amazing what people could be led to believe.

"Are you sure?"

"I know it sounds crazy. But that's what he's claiming."

Does he intend to sacrifice Seneca, too?

"What's he saying now?"

She cocked her head. "Something about the alignment of the universe. That what he is about to do will prevent a major catastrophe."

Matt focused on the TV. Scarrow stood on a platform at the base of a double set of built-in stairs leading up the front of the temple. A group of men dressed in black robes appeared and surrounded Scarrow. Then, ever so slowly, a portion of the platform floor began to rise. A large circular object lifted out of the floor, its surface carved with what looked like ancient markings and symbols. Matt estimated that it measured about twenty feet in diameter.

"The announcer says it's a wood replica of the Aztec Calendar Stone," the woman said. "Some call it the Mexica Sun Stone, or more properly the Cuauhxicalli Eagle Bowl."

Matt leaned in close so he could hear her translations over the sound of the bar crowd. They were starting to pay attention to what was happening on the TV screens. Their voices rose as they reacted to the images broadcast live from Teotihuacán.

"What do the markings mean?"

"They tell of the ancient Aztec beliefs of when the world began and when it will end. It's very complicated."

"And when *will* it end?"

She pointed to Scarrow's image. "According to him, he says there are many ancient calendars that all point to December 21."

Matt pinched the bridge of his nose. "The old doomsday predictions about 2012. This guy has everybody in a frenzy over that impending date?"

"He says he's going to prove he is right. There will be no doubt after tonight. Even the most skeptical will follow him when the sun comes up in the morning."

Matt uttered something between a laugh and a sigh. "Not if he's dead."

The level of background noise in the bar grew even more intense. Apparently, everyone was reacting to what Scarrow had just said. Turning back to the broadcast, he saw why. The large circular object had risen and tilted back at about a 20-degree angle. Matt saw that near its lower half were what appeared to be two small shelves jutting out from the surface at a slight downward angle. With the help of the black-robed men, Scarrow stepped up onto the shelves, leaned against the wood, and faced the masses and cameras.

Then an amazing thing happened.

Scarrow outstretched his arms. Two men, now on ladders, climbed up to where his palms were exposed. They carried long, spikes and large hammers.

In an instant, the noise of the bar dropped to silence as the men positioned the wedged-shaped points of the spikes inside Scarrow's wrists and drew back the hammers.

"Are you shittin' me?" Matt said.

The hammers fell in perfect synchronization, and the bar patrons erupted in screams and gasps.

Two strikes of the hammers sunk each of the spikes into Scarrow's wrists up to the L-shaped heads. His wail of pain cut through the bar like a bullet.

With precision, both of the executioners dismounted the ladders. They moved to Scarrow's feet resting on the sloping shelves. Each took a spike in hand and placed the points against his skin and, with brutal force, drove the nails into the flesh, pinning both feet to the wood.

Another hush fell over the bar. With the black-robed men standing aside, the large circular Aztec calendar rose slowly until it was upright. Blood from Scarrow's wounds flowed over the ancient symbols, staining the wood red. His face, now filling the television screens, grimaced in pain as his eyes looked to the heavens.

Around the bar, Matt heard weeping and expressions of terror and disgust. Although he couldn't understand the language, it was obvious that the sight of a man actually being crucified had affected everyone in the room. He turned to find that the woman had left. He spotted her standing in a far corner, her hands covering her face as she cried.

"This is insane." Matt looked at his watch. It was a few minutes after midnight, and he sat helpless in the middle of a bar crowded with people reeling in shock. Was it already too late for Seneca?

ANONYMOUS CALLER
2012, MEXICO CITY

MATT STEERED THE RENTAL away from Benito Juárez International Airport and headed west toward the center of the city. Orange pools of light from the street lamps floated in the darkness along the avenue. He glanced over at Al in the passenger seat.

"I was going to try getting out to Scarrow's big event, but it was all over the news that the roads were blocked and the area sealed off. I would never have gotten near the place, so I watched it in the bar on TV. It was beyond belief."

"I can imagine. Well, actually, I can't. Other than that Mel Gibson movie, I've never seen anyone crucified."

"It's not pleasant." The traffic was thin in the early morning hour as Matt picked up speed. "It took him almost three hours to die."

"I'm surprised the networks would even broadcast such a thing."

"It's all about ratings."

Al agreed. "But I'm missing the point here. If he wants to save the world, why did he allow himself to be crucified?"

"Good question. After they took Scarrow down, an international team of doctors pronounced him dead. They hooked up a ton of medical equipment. There were no vitals whatsoever."

"You think it was some kind of illusion?"

"Anything's possible. But there were extreme close-ups of his hands and feet. You could clearly see the bleeding from multiple angles in high definition. The guy looked dead to me. There were millions of people watching and they even had a rep from every network as close-up witnesses."

"What did they do with him?"

"This is where it gets creepier. They took him down and put his body in some kind of clear plastic or glass coffin. The cameras are all aimed at it right now. When I left the hotel, there were no signs of life."

"So what's everyone doing out there?"

"Praying. Crying. Sleeping. I don't know. There's a huge mass of believers waiting for something to happen. Your guess is as good as mine."

"And nothing about Seneca?"

Matt shook his head. "Since you called, I've been trying to sort everything out. You were pretty frantic on your way to board the plane. Tell me again what happened?"

"I got a call from someone who said he had seen and talked to Seneca, and that she wanted him to contact me and tell me where she was. He claimed she was being flown down here and that she was in imminent danger. He said her captor is the Phoenix Ministry guy, Javier Scarrow—the guy who you say was just crucified. And the caller said that Scarrow intends to *sacrifice* her."

"What did he mean by that?"

"I pressed him for details and a motive, but he didn't divulge anything else."

"And you believe him?"

"What else do we have to go on?"

Al reached for his pocket as his phone rang. Glancing at it, he said, "Unknown caller." He pushed talk. "Palermo here." He listened for a moment. "Wait! What's this all about? Who are—"

Matt glared at Al. "What's up? Who was it?"

"Same guy. Said to meet him near Zócalo Plaza."

"For what?"

Al shrugged. "I don't know. Just that I need to meet him at five a.m."

Matt checked the clock on the dash. "Doesn't give us much time. Why won't he just come right out with it?"

"He must have his reasons."

"What if his reasons are to sidetrack us and delay any attempt to find and rescue Seneca? You don't know who the guy is or if he even talked to her. If Scarrow really has her, we should be busting our asses to find a way to get out there."

"That's another reason I tend to believe him," Al said. "He knows about the Scarrow tie-in. Plus, in his first call, he said he was the one who contacted Seneca in Paris with the El Jaguar tip."

"Yeah, and because of that, we almost got killed."

"It did lead to the Flores library and the connection to Groves. You gotta give him credit for that."

"Maybe. I don't know."

Al held up his phone. "Don't forget, he has my cell number. Who else but Seneca would have given it to him?"

"I still don't like it, Al. We need to find a way to get to Scarrow."

"I think we need to do what this guy says. He's our only key."

"And it could turn out to be a huge waste of time, time Seneca doesn't have."

"Either keep driving or stop and let me call a cab. I can't ignore the possibility that this guy knows where my daughter is and how I can get her back safely."

"Jesus, you have faith in some anonymous asshole who won't even tell you who he is and you completely disregard the fact that we've made a positive connection to Scarrow and Seneca's kidnapping? Common sense tells me, and I'm no super spy like some people in this car, that we ought to be doing everything in our power to get out to that Phoenix Ministry thing. Can't you and your big shots at ILIAD figure out a way to do that?"

Al reached over and placed his hand on Matt's shoulder. "Listen, I can tell you care a lot about her and you know I do. But one thing I've learned over the years is that in my line of work you can't let emotions dictate decisions. You have to keep a level head and evaluate the situation objectively."

Matt raked his fingers through his hair. "You're right, I do care about her." His voice rose in volume. "And I'm fucking afraid we're not going to get to her in time."

"Arguing won't solve anything. That's just squandering our time. We both want her safe. But the bottom line is, I'm her father and I'm going to make the call. Matt, all I can ask is that you trust me."

Matt slammed his palm on the steering wheel and blew out his breath in a long windy stream. "I just hope you're right." He turned onto a side street. "Zócalo Plaza is a big place. Did he give you any specifics?"

"That's another reason I think he's for real. Remember I told you about the report from ILIAD on the Groves Consortium property and business holdings? That there are hundreds, all large multi-million-dollar corporations and manufacturers? Except for one. Then I asked you if you liked tacos?"

Matt turned to Al. "The taco shop. Los Sanchez taco shop. The one I was going to check out?"

THE TUNNEL
2012, MEXICO CITY

MATT PARKED THE RENTAL on a side street near Zócalo Plaza. Getting out, he and Al moved rapidly across the cobblestones of the 240-square-meter plaza. It was well lit in the pre-dawn hour, but only a handful of others were out—most were street cleaners and employees heading to restaurants and bakeries to prepare the day's food.

The chilly air caused Al to zip up his light jacket as they passed the Metropolitan Cathedral and the ruins of Templo Mayor to the site where Daniel and the dig team had died. The area was located just beyond the main excavation and was surrounded by a wood and chain link fence that kept the area of the bomb blast sealed from the public. Notices in Spanish and English warned of no trespassing by order of the *Policía Judicial del Distrito Federal.*

Walking east from the ruins, they continued along a street that during the day would have been lined with vendors, locals out for the day, political activists, Aztec dancers, street musicians, and hordes of tourists. In the hours before daylight, it was empty and dark.

Just as they turned onto Calle del Carmen, a roar caused them to look up.

"Damn, he's low," Matt said as a helicopter streaked overhead just above the rooftops and disappeared in the direction of the Plaza.

"Had to have snagged a few TV antennas that low." Al turned and they continued south along the deserted street. Within a few minutes they stood in front of the taco and souvenir shop called Los Sanchez. A padlocked, metal roll-down door covered the entrance. By the looks of the graffiti, faded signs, and unkempt condition, the store had been abandoned for a long time. Of all the shops, Los Sanchez was the only one permanently boarded up—the rest appeared to be ready for the bustling crowds to come a few hours from now.

"Looks like it's been shut down for years." Al reached out and took hold of the lock, shaking it vigorously but with no indication it would give.

"He said to meet in the alley behind the shop, right?"

"Let's try down there." Al led the way along the sidewalk until they came to an alley. It was littered with black plastic garbage bags and stacks of cardboard boxes filled with trash. Even before they started down the pathway, the sickening stench of rotting food made the air almost impossible to breathe.

Two streetlights cast gloomy pools of light along the alley as they navigated to the rear of the shops. The smell of the garbage mixed with a variety of cooking odors, stale alcohol, and urine. It overloaded Matt's senses as he navigated around the heaps of trash and rubbish. At last, they entered a narrow alley running perpendicular to the first one and passed the back entrances to a number of businesses.

Matt turned on his penlight. There was no mistaking the rear of the Los Sanchez taco shop. Just like the front, it appeared to have been closed for quite some time. Graffiti and sporting events posters covered a metal door padlocked shut.

At the sound of voices, Matt switched off the light. He and Al backed in the depth of the shadows. They watched two men emerge from the rear entrance of a shop a few doors down and stand under a streetlamp. The glow of a struck match illuminated their faces as they lit cigarettes. Matt and Al remained motionless while the men chatted and smoked their cigarettes twenty feet away.

Eventually, one of the men noticed them and called out. "*¡Hola!*"

Al gave them a half-hearted wave and staggered slightly as if he had drunk one too many *cervezas*. Then he unzipped his pants and started pissing on the wall. Matt quickly followed his example. One of the men laughed. A short time later, a gruff command from inside the store forced the men to grind their smokes on the pavement and head back inside.

Al motioned down the alley in the direction they had come. "We've got a visitor."

Matt squinted in the darkness until he finally saw the figure of a man almost totally hidden in the low light.

The stranger walked toward them until he was only a few feet away. Tall and lanky, he was dressed as a cowboy: jeans, boots, a suede and fleece vest over a long-sleeved plaid shirt, a Stetson, and carried bolt cutters and a flashlight. To Matt, he appeared abnormally thin and fragile—his face almost skeleton-like. His skin was pale and papery. Only his eyes held any reflection of life inside.

"Are you Al Palermo, Seneca Hunt's father?" His voice sounded like it came from a cheap transistor radio, weak and slight.

"I am."

The cowboy pointed at Matt. "Who is he?"

"Matt Everhart. I'm a friend of Seneca's."

"They blew up your boat."

"You know about that?" Matt glanced at Al then back at the stranger. "Where is Seneca? Can you help us get her back safely?"

"She's in a bad place."

"Who are you?" Al asked.

He didn't answer. Instead, he handed the bolt cutters to Al. "Cut it."

Hesitating for a moment, Al took the tool and severed the lock.

The cowboy kicked the door with the toe of his boot, and it cracked open. A few seconds later, the three stood inside the dark interior of the Los Sanchez taco shop.

Matt quickly shone his penlight around the room. They were in a storeroom lined with metal shelves. There was also a food processing work table, sink, a mop and bucket, numerous cardboard boxes filled with rubbish and trash, a small walk-in freezer—everything in a general state of disarray. Discarded papers and flattened boxes cluttered the floor, and the air was heavy with decay and the smell of mildew. A flash of a rat moved through his light beam. Everything looked as if it had been abandoned quickly and not touched in years.

Al faced the cowboy. "So what's the deal? Why did you tell me to meet you here?"

The cowboy ignored the question. He pointed to a wood door on the wall next to the freezer. That one also had a padlock. "Cut it, too."

Al obeyed, and with a forceful snap of the bolt cutter handles, the lock broke. He pulled open the door.

The cowboy moved beside Al and switched on his flashlight aiming the beam into the darkness. There was no storeroom or closet on the other side, just four steps leading down to a platform. The steps turned and continued down. He turned to Matt. "You go first."

Matt led the descent, finding that past the platform eight more steps ended in a small basement. Al and the cowboy followed.

The basement smelled of damp dirt and old stone. Similar to the restaurant above, the room was cluttered with junk and discarded objects. Matt saw a neon Pepsi sign, stacked restaurant tables and chairs, more boxes filled with dust-covered newspapers, and wooden crates of empty soda bottles.

Once they stood at the foot of the steps, the cowboy pointed his flashlight. "Check under the stairs."

Matt noticed a mound of dirt and chips of stone debris underneath. He moved closer and found a portion of the floor and a section of the wall had been dug away revealing a four-foot-deep opening. The hole had a floor of cobblestones resembling the ones surrounding the Templo Mayor ruins. Off to one side was the entrance to a narrow tunnel.

The cowboy stood beside him. "It's down there."

THE TOMB

2012, MEXICO CITY

"You want us to go down *there*?" Matt thought about the catacombs as he aimed his light into the dark hole in the basement floor. Someone had dug it out, exposing a set of stone steps leading to the entrance to a tunnel—a narrow tunnel. From where he stood, it looked like he would barely be able to squeeze through. That is, if he even tried.

"No. Just you. It'll take someone spryer than me or your pal, here." The cowboy stood beside Al. "Want to save her life or not?"

"What's down there that's so important?" Matt examined the area around the hole and spotted a shovel and pickaxe. But the excavation had not been recent. Like everything else in the boarded-up restaurant, the tools were covered in dust and dirt.

The cowboy gave Matt a *get-going* nod. "Follow the passage. There's a chamber at the end. Somewhere in the chamber is a small silver box with a Latin inscription on top. Bring it to me."

"What's in it?" Al asked.

"Your daughter and I made a deal. I deliver what's in that box to her, and she uses it to end my pain and destroy Scarrow." He turned to Matt. "You're wasting precious seconds."

"Destroy Scarrow?" Matt said. "He's already dead. I watched him being crucified on TV."

The cowboy laughed. At least that's what Matt thought it was. But not a laugh of joy.

"Trust me, Scarrow is very much alive. Go." The word set off a hacking cough as the cowboy covered his mouth and bent over.

Taking a last look around, Matt climbed into the four-foot-deep hole and shone the light down the steps into the tunnel entrance. The walls and ceiling were stuccoed, the floor dirt. His light only penetrated for a few feet, but he saw that the tunnel had suffered the same effects as many other ancient structures in Mexico City. Having been built over what was once a lake bed, the soft clay soil had caused many buildings including the Metropolitan Cathedral to slowly sink. The uneven floor and walls of the tunnel gave it a warped appearance and confirmed that age had taken a toll on the passage. There were also signs that water had seeped into the tunnel in the past. The floor was damp, and the walls bore watermarks where flooding might have taken place. He remembered Seneca saying she had asked Daniel why Montezuma's tomb was not flooded. His answer was that the tomb was originally built above ground, same level as the temple—the Spanish constructed the city on top of it and all the other Aztec structures.

He could see that the width of the passage was narrow—his shoulders would rub both sides, and he would have to bend to proceed along its length. He squatted at the entrance and wondered if this was really such a good idea. Whispering a prayer that what lay ahead would not involve floods, earthquakes, or rats, he took his first step into the tunnel.

Matt felt like a hunched-over old man. He couldn't look up because of the low ceiling, so he moved slowly, examining the uneven floor as he went and feeling for any protrusions that could scrape his head. Twenty feet beyond the entrance, the tunnel made a slight bend to the right and sloped downward. The floor was spotted with small chunks of stone, probably broken off from the constant traffic and centuries of construction overhead. And after another fifty feet, the passage took a hard left turn. A short distance ahead, Matt saw three steep steps leading up into a rectangular space just big enough for him to fit through. On the far side of the space was blackness.

With great care, he climbed into the void. Then he aimed the light into the darkness beyond.

What he saw caused him to suck in his breath.

It was as Seneca had described—exactly what she and Daniel witnessed on the video monitor. He had just walked through an ancient corridor leading to Montezuma's tomb.

Shining the light around the chamber he saw Aztec artifacts and art objects, the altar, and the burial shroud lying on the floor beside it. The beam of light finally came to rest on a single object sitting atop a wooden table.

The silver chest.

RESURRECTION II
2012, ANCIENT CITY OF TEOTIHUACÁN

Seneca wanted to keep sleeping and ignored the tug on her arm.

"Get up." The voice was harsh.

Her eyes opened to narrow slits, and she groaned in protest.

"The sun will be up soon."

After the medical team had declared Scarrow dead, she was led into the interior of the Temple of the Universe and locked in a room. The drugs had her so groggy she'd happily lain on the bed and drifted off.

The man shoved a hand behind her neck, lifted and pulled her by one arm, helping her sit. "Let's go. Can you walk?"

Seneca wasn't sure.

When he pulled her to her feet, her knees buckled, and the rush of blood leaving her head made her think she was about to faint. She slumped, but he stopped her from collapsing. Little by little her legs regained their strength, and the dizziness that had swamped her dissipated.

The escort took her elbow and guided her out of the room and to the exit in the back of the temple.

As they came around the side, he kept her in the darkness, out of the floodlights shining on a transparent dome. Scarrow's body lay inside on what looked like a hospital gurney. A white sheet covered him up to his neck. Two monitors, on stands placed near his head, trailed leads, one that ran under the sheet and another set that ended in a web of electrodes attached to his head. Neither monitor showed any activity.

Javier Scarrow was dead.

She remembered his crucifixion and the agony he seemed to go through. For hours he had suffered. Numerous times, he prayed in a language she could not understand. Though his disciples asked several times if he wanted to discontinue, he had refused. And then finally his head had sagged to his chest. His death was confirmed by a medical team. Never leaving the view of the cameras and the mass of believers, his body was bathed, dressed in a clean white robe, and placed inside the clear dome coffin. The doctors attached probes to his body and then the dome was closed and sealed air-tight.

Cameras aimed at the coffin projected the live image on enormous screens placed in various locations so that the mass of people could watch and witness every detail, just as they had witnessed his crucifixion.

That was hours ago. Now Seneca glanced to the east. A thin golden strand of light hugged the horizon line where night and day converged.

Sunrise.

A sudden stirring of the onlookers made her look back at the dome.

"There it is again!" a voice rang out above the commotion that now poured from the crowd.

A tiny blip traveled across the screen of the EEG display. Then another. And another. Followed by a stream of waves on the heart monitor, peaks and valleys. Electrical activity in the heart and the brain.

The roar of the spectators ricocheted around the ancient city and off the walls of the pyramids.

As she watched the medical devices detecting the return of life, she was awestruck. Everything Scarrow and Groves had told her was true.

The guard at her side took her arm again and led her to the staircase on the west side of the temple which was still enveloped in darkness. She stared up at the top that was brightly illuminated by a bank of stadium lights in the distance.

Reluctantly, she climbed the first step, knowing that it began the journey to her death.

TEMPLE OF THE UNIVERSE
2012, ANCIENT CITY OF TEOTIHUACÁN

WITH HIS WHITE ROBE flowing behind, arms raised to the heavens, and chanting an ancient prayer, Javier Scarrow ascended one branch of the twin staircases that climbed up the center of the east wall of the Temple of the Universe. Bound by balustrades elaborately carved with a mosaic of geometric designs, the stairs rose 197 feet, the same as his Templo Mayor, to a flat platform at the top. Such sweetness Scarrow had never felt before as the eyes of the world followed him with millions of souls spellbound in awe. He was a living miracle, proof that his way was the blessed path for the universe. He was the new messiah, and the world was now convinced. With every step, a magnificent hallowed contentment welled up inside him. This was the crowning moment, and all the years, over so many lifetimes, all the work, all the determination and dedication brought to execution the greatest undertaking of all time. All that remained to fulfill his mission was now in the hands of his apostles who were back in their homelands ready to begin harvesting the Sweet Flowers for the garden of his gods. Spread before him were so many new converts who now believed as he did that the world, and how man treats it, must change forever. Combine that with the fact that the gods were about to be appeased with the blood drawn forth from the *xochimiqui* by his apostle—there had been no greater moment in the history of mankind.

The masses gathered below hushed, some falling to their knees, others silently weeping, but all fixing their eyes on their savior of the new world, the one who had just risen from the dead. He was within moments of the first sacrifice to the gods and in so doing, he would start the process of bringing the universe back into alignment and harmony—a new era of peace for all.

Scarrow took his last step before reaching the pinnacle. So sweet, he thought, standing on the platform. He smiled as he caught the first glimpse of his newest and final apostle, Hernán Cortés. The man emerged from the antechamber and came to flank the sacrificial altar hidden from those below by a stone wall. The sunlight glinted off the obsidian knife in Cortés's hand as if it were a mirror reflecting back its power to give life by taking life.

But this ritual would be performed out of view of the crowd. Scarrow had even negotiated in the media coverage contracts that there would be no aerial filming or photography.

Prepared to perform the sacrosanct ritual, Cortés's black painted body was partially obscured by a dark hooded cloak.

Hernán Cortés was the perfect example of the magic of dualities for which Scarrow's Aztec nation had always been fascinated.

Light and darkness, death and life, fire and water. Cortés had destroyed the once mighty nation. Now he was integral in the first step to bring it back to life. The irony caused a slight smile on Scarrow's lips. This was the end and the beginning. The very first sacrifice—Sweet Flower.

His senses flooded; the aroma of the incense, the sight of the altar and the apostle priest, the sound of people worshipping and praying below, the taste of victory electrifying the air, the pungent odor of smoke from the newly lit Eternal Flame, and the vision of the perfect sacrifice—his Sweet Flower, his Sweet *xochimiqui*.

Seneca stood near the fire clothed in a plain white tunic that would be removed before laying her down and arching her back over the altar stone. Her eyes were glassy from the narcotic, and strands of her hair fell across her face. She was guarded on both her right and left by two disciples.

"You are ready." Scarrow's words were not a question but a statement. "This morning, a new age begins with you."

Seneca sluggishly shook her head. "No. Don't do this."

Scarrow opened his robe, raised his face to the heavens, and welcomed the warmth of the sun on his copper skin that glowed in the early light as did his gilded breastplate and loincloth woven with golden threads.

Eyes closed, he spoke. "Most giving and resourceful *Quetzalcoatl*, I implore you, make it your will that your people enjoy the goods and riches you naturally give, that freely issue from you, that are pleasing and savory, and that delight and comfort. Let our sacrifices bring forgiveness and a return to universal accord."

He folded his robe about him once more and walked to a raised podium at the edge of the temple platform so he could address the crowd. When he came into view, the throng erupted into shouts and praises. It took several minutes for Scarrow to still them enough so that he could speak.

His voice was strong, and his words articulated with a charismatic command. "You have seen the spikes driven through my flesh, my blood spilled on the ground, my death, and finally you have witnessed the miracle of my resurrection. My sacrifice for you. Unequivocal proof to those who doubted. Hear my words, take my message into your hearts, become like the birds of the air. Shine like the stars in the—"

A noise diverted him, one that seemed to materialize out of the crisp morning air. It took a moment for Scarrow to recognize the sound. The whirring and *whop, whop, whop* of the long, flat blades and the predator scream of the jet turbines.

He squinted into the newly risen sun, but its brilliance blinded him. Switching his focus to the crowd below he saw people start looking to the sky, pointing, unsure. When it became apparent that the craft was hovering and intended to land, the masses scattered. The helicopter dropped, throwing up a cloud of dust and settling at the foot of the Temple of the Universe.

The hundreds of television cameras shifted from Scarrow's face to refocus on the sleek, bullet-shaped aircraft; its skin alien black, its knife-edged rotors slowing. The high-pitched shriek of the jets seemed to cut into Scarrow's brain.

His eyes flickered from one giant video projection screen to another, trying to identify the intruder. Who had violated his orders for no aerial coverage? Who dared insult the new savior of the world?

And then he saw the words—silver letters gleaming against the black metal. Two words that sliced deep into his heart with the same deadly force as an Aztec sacrificial knife.

Groves Consortium.

Security stood down as the side door opened and three men emerged.

One dressed as a cowboy.

CLIMB TO HEAVEN
2012, ANCIENT CITY OF TEOTIHUACÁN

Billy Groves reared back his head and directed his vision to the top of the Temple of the Universe. He saw Scarrow peering over the top, shading his eyes with his hand as if trying to get a better view through the glare of the sun and the dun-colored dust thrown up by Groves's chopper.

Matt put his foot on the first step of the pyramid's staircase to begin the ascent and take the silver chest to Seneca.

Groves snapped forward, gripped Matt's arm and pulled him back. "No."

Matt whipped around. "What are you doing?"

"Give it to me."

Al moved beside Matt and held up his hand. "Back away, Groves. Let him go. If there's a chance Seneca can stop all this madness as you said she promised, then we have to get the veil to her. Unless everything you've said has been a lie."

"It's not a lie. Your daughter and I had a deal. She wanted me to contact you, and I did. She wanted her father to come get her, and I've seen to that." Groves paused, and in a silent plea, first gazed at Al's eyes, then Matt's. "But let me take it from here. Just as I look at you, I want Scarrow to peer into my eyes and see into my soul—see the wretchedness that abides there day after endless day. The longing I have to finally be free. I want him to know my agony and understand that I'm ready for it all to end. Let me take it to her. I've earned that right."

Matt slowly settled the reliquary in Groves's hands. "I believe you have."

Handling the box as he would something so precious that he feared his clutch might damage it, Groves clasped the reliquary to his chest. "Thank you." His words were whispered as he turned and began his journey to the top.

He had come with no wig, no fake beard, no disguise. Just Billy Groves, the simple cowboy. He wanted to go out as the man he was before this nightmare began. The years of nutrition neglect and lack of physical activity had taken its toll, and every bending of his knees sent shocks of pain riveting all the way to his spine. His feet cramped in his boots, and his hips ached inside the denim jeans. After the first dozen steps he was winded and his heart beat like a frenzied bass drum beneath his ribcage. But he pressed on, now and again pausing to rest and look up at the sun-blinded, confused face of Javier Scarrow—the Emperor Montezuma II.

If Seneca could end Scarrow's horrific scheme and also extinguish his own misery—and he trusted that what she had told him about the angel's command to Veronica was true—it didn't matter how much he struggled for breath or how much pain his body suffered. After all, the physical pain wouldn't *kill* him. He would deliver her the veil and be ready to accept whatever happened next.

Long ago he had come to terms with God and repented for his sins. There was no fear of dying, only fear of living forever. He was climbing, not to the top of the pagan Aztec temple, but to eternal peace.

He was climbing to heaven.

ASHES TO ASHES
2012, ANCIENT CITY OF TEOTIHUACÁN

Seneca struggled to focus. She thought she detected bewilderment in Scarrow's body language. Instead of his projected confidence, his shoulders slumped and his jaw loosened as he backed away from the podium.

Her eyes went to one of the huge monitors. It showed a man slowly climbing the temple steps, his back to the camera as he neared the top. Whoever it was seemed to be having an unsettling effect on Scarrow. She concentrated, making a desperate effort to stay alert and trying to clear the blurriness of her sight. The heat from the Eternal Flame in front of her only added to the nausea and haziness. She glanced to her side and caught the glint of the obsidian knife in the hand of the black-cloaked priest standing ready to cut out her heart. The drugs made it appear as if she looked through a star filter on a camera lens, creating dramatic cross flares from points of light.

Oh, God, I don't want to die.

Visions sputtered through her mind of Daniel's last moments and the thrashing seizures of the man in Panama. Terrified, her panic soared.

Don't want to die.

Don't want to die!

Seneca lifted her head to glimpse the man climbing the temple steps. At first it was just the Stetson, but then the face.

Billy Groves.

As he crested the top, she saw the reliquary, and she let out a sob. When he had told her the tale of his encounter with the veil, she put his story together with Al's history of the relic and knew exactly what had to be done.

The angel's command to Veronica was in two parts; the first to wipe the face of the prophet. The second was to burn the veil, but *only after* Christ's ascension.

That was the key.

If Veronica had not touched Christ's face with her veil, He never would have been resurrected; He would have died like all other men. But she *did* wipe the blood and sweat from His face, and Christ rose from the dead. He didn't immediately ascend to Heaven. That came forty days later. If Veronica had destroyed the veil by fire during the forty days before the Ascension, Jesus would have died like any other mortal man. Seneca had been given the message to destroy the veil. She must finish what Veronica had failed to do. Obey the angel's command and this terror would end.

Groves stood at the top of the temple and held out the reliquary toward Scarrow. "You know what this is?" He hitched his head toward Seneca. "She tells me she can stop this madness. And I believe her. All she needs is what's inside here."

Scarrow moved farther from the edge of the temple, drawing both himself and Groves out of crowd and camera view. "No, William. You don't understand. If we do not return to the old ways, shed our blood to give back to the gods, the world will end as we know it. I am here to save us all. That is why I was given the gift of the veil."

"And I was given the same gift. But it was a mistake, and it's all got to stop. I don't know how to do it, but she does." Groves ambled past Scarrow to stand beside Seneca. He opened the reliquary.

Seneca's eyes settled on the veil and tears streamed down her cheeks.

The disciples guarding her backed away. Even her would-be executioner slinked into the shadows.

Groves delicately lifted the veil from the reliquary and offered it to her.

Before taking it, she painfully looked at Groves. "You know what this means?"

"I'm ready."

Scarrow rushed forward. "What are you doing?"

Seneca reached deep inside for the strength inherited from her mother, the strength she now had within every cell of her body. She dangled the veil above the Eternal Flame. "The angel commanded Veronica to burn the veil. I intend to finish what she started."

Scarrow's face paled. "Wait." Then his voice lowered to a consoling pitch, his charismatic intonations and inflections made the words seem to spool off his tongue like spun silk.

He came close. "Touch it to your face and live forever. You have witnessed up close what death looks like, felt the tremors of death in your arms, seen the convulsions as the body fights for one last breath. Your Daniel. My apostle. You know more than anyone. You would never have to go through that. A gentle touch to your face and you'll never suffer such a fate."

Seneca held the cloth close to her heart.

Never have to die.

Never.

Groves placed his hand on hers. "Is that what you want? Look at what it's done to me. Be brave, Seneca Hunt."

Scarrow gripped her wrist and lifted her hand and the veil close to her face. "Yes, be brave, give yourself this magnificent gift of immortality."

The next moment seemed to hang up somewhere in her mind, frozen in space, in silence.

"Nooooo," Scarrow wailed as she pulled away, her fingers uncurling, setting the cloth free.

Seneca watched it fall to the fire of the Eternal Flame. In slow motion it floated on the heat, winging as the updraft caught it, billowing and slipping downward.

Scarrow swatted at the cloth, attempting a rescue. But he was too late.

As the sacred relic touched the flames it fully opened revealing the image of Billy Groves. The edges curled, browned, and burst into flame.

The three stood motionless staring at the fire.

Seconds passed.

Nothing happened.

Groves's eyes emptied of hope.

Scarrow's expression shifted from horror to relief, to joy. He opened his arms and lifted them toward the sky, praising the gods. Finishing his prayer he looked at Seneca. "You were wrong and you have given up a gift you can never be offered again."

It was then that she saw a small trickle of blood drip from the sleeve of his robe and splatter on the ground, a tiny rose on the marble. She looked at his feet, the gold threads of his sandals suddenly stained red. The wounds from the spikes gaped open and blood poured out forming a crimson pool. Bright red splotches seeped through his robe—the dagger wounds from *La Noche Triste;* The Sad Night.

Seneca raised her gaze to meet his. Her reaction made him glance at his hands. Startled, his head jerked back up, and his eyes darted from her to Groves.

Billy Groves touched his chest where red stains bloomed across his shirt. Two old wounds.

Seneca placed her palm to Groves's cheek. "I'm sorry," she whispered.

Groves smiled. "I'm not."

ANOTHER DAY IN PARADISE

2012, FLORIDA KEYS

Seneca smelled the fresh scent of the ocean sweeping across Matt's second-story veranda. She stood by the railing and sipped a margarita, Matt beside her. She watched the ever-changing orange and red and purple as the sunset put on its final show of the day.

"Just another day in paradise." She held up her glass, and Matt touched the rim of his to it. "And I really like your new boat."

"The insurance payout was more than generous." Matt smiled proudly as he gazed in the direction of the brand new Boston Whaler moored at the end of his dock.

"Sariel II. Nice name."

"She's not only the main character in my books, she's the angel who pays my bills."

"You ready to get back to writing?"

Matt took a sip then nodded. "No choice. My deadline on the new thriller is looming large. You should see the emails from my agent and editor. In some courts they could be considered death threats."

"At least they're not from your radical readers who think you're a heretic."

"Oh, I get those, too. But after what you and I have been through, those wackos come off fairly mild." He turned to Seneca. "How about you? Ready to start the grind again?"

"Actually, yes. First, I've got to fly back to Mexico to testify in Carlos's trial. The courts have been on a fast track to get him convicted for planting the bomb that killed Daniel and the others."

"I hope you can feel some closure in seeing him punished."

She shrugged. "Some." Pausing for a moment, she thought of Daniel. The pale circle around her finger where the engagement ring had once been was a reminder of her loss. She had taken it off several days ago. It was time to move on. Closure meant healing. For the first time since the bombing, the pain didn't cut as deep. But it was still there.

"Yes, I'm ready to work. God knows there's plenty to follow-up on, starting with the Phoenix Apostles. Scarrow's *creations* are still among us, carrying on his mission, not because they believe so much in his message, but because they enjoy their task. Scary."

"Yeah, but tracking them down is nearly impossible. They're scattered across the globe."

"I don't think anyone really understands the whole conspiracy completely. I'm not sure I do. But the fact is, there are eleven potential mass murderers lurking out there in the shadows somewhere."

She turned her back to the ocean and rested her arms on the banister. "I'm also eager to investigate all the doctors and scientists who worked for Scarrow in the Bahamas. I know the Bahamian police have questioned them, but I want to get the real story of what went on in Azteca."

"What's going to happen to that place? And the Phoenix Ministry temple in Mexico?"

"Azteca is being turned into a tourist attraction. And apparently the new Groves Consortium board of directors is converting the Mexican temple into a nondenominational house of worship and charity outreach center. It's been renamed in honor of William Groves and his contributions to science and industry."

"I'm sure Groves would be proud, wherever he is." Matt seemed to grow serious. "Can I ask you a question?"

"Of course."

"The command to destroy the veil by fire, we saw it in the catacombs and again at the island penal colony. And yet, you said that when Al gave you back your camera, those photos were missing. The legend says that an angel gave that command to Veronica. Do you think the woman we saw in the catacombs …"

"Was an angel?" Seneca slowly shook her head as she looked into his eyes. "I don't know, Matt. What I do know is that my beliefs have shifted since this whole thing began. I used to think that everything should be scrutinized until proven true. Now I'm wondering if it's just the opposite. Maybe all things are possible until proven otherwise. And it's certainly made me look at death in a whole different light. There's a lot more to this life than we can possibly ever understand."

"You should read my novels. That's what Sariel says all the time."

She looked at Matt. "You know, in some bizarre incomprehensible way, I feel sorry for Scarrow—for Montezuma. In his mind he believed he was doing the right thing, nothing evil, nothing diabolical. He wanted to ensure the well-being of the world and the universe in the only way he knew how. I remember when I asked Daniel about Aztec human sacrifices, he said that we should try to understand the why as well as the what and the how. We have to understand the customs and the belief systems of other cultures, other civilizations."

"That's an interesting point of view." Matt motioned to the horizon. "Check it out."

Seneca turned to see a final unexpected burst of color as the sun set the sky on fire. "My God, that's lovely." She glanced over her shoulder. "Isn't that beautiful, Mom?"

Brenda Hunt sat in a lounge chair nearby, a light blanket wrapped around her legs. She wore a bright, flowered blouse, sunglasses, and a wide-brimmed straw hat. "Beautiful."

Al sat next to Brenda holding her hand. He leaned in and placed a kiss on her cheek. "Almost as beautiful as you, sweetheart."

As Seneca watched her mother and father together, she felt a surge of warmth rush to her cheeks. It was a sight she had never thought possible. Even if Brenda didn't know who Al was, there was a thread of love that wove its way through the convoluted labyrinth of her dementia and into the present.

The chime of her cell phone distracted her. Seneca pulled it from her pocket and read the display.

"Bad news or good?" Matt asked.

With a smile, she said, "It's a text message from my editor. He says he thinks I finally have enough for a story."

THE END

© Jerry Lang, University Studios, FL

Joe Moore (Florida) spent twenty-five years in the television post-production industry where he received two regional Emmy® awards for individual achievement in audio mixing. As a freelance writer, Joe reviewed fiction for *The Fort Lauderdale Sun-Sentinel, The Tampa Tribune*, and *The Jacksonville Florida Times Union*. He is a member of the International Thriller Writers, the Authors Guild, and Mystery Writers of America.

© Alexis Arce

Lynn Sholes (Florida) is a writing teacher on special assignment for Citrus County Schools. Writing as Lynn Armistead McKee, she wrote six historical novels before writing thrillers under the name Lynn Sholes. Lynn is a member of International Thriller Writers, the Authors Guild, and Mystery Writers of America.

Don't miss the other books in the Cotten Stone Mystery Series

THE
GRAIL
CONSPIRACY
A COTTEN STONE MYSTERY
LYNN SHOLES & JOE MOORE

THE GRAIL CONSPIRACY

A Cotten Stone Mystery

Lynn Sholes & Joe Moore

On assignment in the Middle East, television journalist Cotten Stone stumbles upon an archeological dig that uncovers the world's most-sought-after religious relic: the Holy Grail. With his last dying breath, Dr. Gabriel Archer gives it to Cotten, uttering "You are the only one" in a language she's heard from only one other person—her deceased twin sister.

What begins as a hot news story for the ambitious young reporter soon turns into a nightmare when the Holy Grail is stolen and strange "accidents" befall her dearest friends. Running for her life, she turns to John Tyler, a priest with firsthand knowledge of religious artifacts, for help. An anonymous source leads them to New Orleans during Mardi Gras, where an abominable experiment is underway that—unless destroyed—promises to unleash an ancient evil upon the Earth.

978-0-7387-0787-7, 360 pp., $5^{3}/_{16}$ x 8 **$14.95**

A COTTEN STONE MYSTERY
THE
LAST
SECRET
VENATORI
LYNN SHOLES & JOE MOORE

THE LAST SECRET

A Cotten Stone Mystery

Lynn Sholes & Joe Moore

In this riveting follow-up to *The Grail Conspiracy*, famed journalist Cotten Stone is at the top of her craft until one of her discoveries is proven to be a hoax. Without a steady job, credibility, or a shred of self-respect, the struggling reporter fades from the limelight. A year later at a famous Inca site, she unearths a crystal tablet that predicts the Great Flood and another final "cleansing"—yet to take place—to be led by the daughter of an angel. According to the Venatori—an ancient society of spiritual warriors—a series of these sacred tablets exist . . . and the last one holds the key to surviving Armegeddon. Racing to recover this last secret before the Fallen Ones, Cotten comes face to face with her terrifying destiny, a legacy to battle the Son of the Dawn until the End of Days.

978-0-7387-0931-4, 384 pp., $5^{3}/_{16}$ x 8 **$14.95**

THE
731
LEGACY
A COTTEN STONE MYSTERY
"A superb blend of science, myth, history, and imagination. The 731 Legacy is a labyrinth of mystery, crisply plotted and paced, with throat-grabbing twists. Enjoy."
—Steve Berry, New York Times bestselling author of The Templar Legacy
LYNN SHOLES & JOE MOORE